VELMA

STILL

COOKS IN

LEEWAY

VINITA HAMPTON WRIGHT

VELMA
STILL
COOKS IN
LEEWAY

BROADMAN
& HOLMAN
PUBLISHERS

NASHVILLE, TENNESSEE

0–8054–2128–9

Published by Broadman & Holman Publishers,
Nashville, Tennessee

Dewey Decimal Classification: 813
Subject Heading: FICTION

The two poems included in this book are by Lil Copan. German translation is by J. Dominik Harjung and Christina Klingler.

All the recipes in the book are creations of Vinita Hampton Wright.

Library of Congress Cataloging-in-Publication Data
Wright, Vinita Hampton, 1958–
    Velma still cooks in Leeway : a novel / Vinita Hampton Wright.
       p. cm.
  ISBN 0–8054–2128–9 (pb)
    1. Restauranteurs—Fiction. 2. Women cooks—Fiction. 3. Restaurants—Fiction. 4. Cookery—Fiction. I. Title.

PS3573.R548 V45 2000
813'.54—dc21

00–039751

1 2 3 4 5 04 03 02 01 00

To my mother Virginia,
who is never too surprised
when miracles happen.

Contents

In deinen stillen Stunden
richtest du
die Augen deiner Seele nach innen,
und
göttliche Kraft bemächtigt sich deiner;
verzehrt im Feuer die Ängste der Welt,
die dich allmählich umgarnten.

Und wie die Tür und ihre Angel,
so verbindet dieses göttliche Wirken
die Erde mit dem Himmel
durch menschliches Mysterium.

—Lenora Hamden

Translation:

In the silent hours
you lower your
soul's eyes
And
Divinity eats into you,
burns the tremours of the earth's
slow turning around you.

This Divinity, like a stable
door, fastens the earth
to the heavens
by a hinge of human mystery.

1

Fevers

The spirit lifted me up and bore me away; I went in bitterness in the heat of my spirit, the hand of the LORD being strong upon me.

—EZEKIEL 3:14

When I was a young girl, strange fevers would fall upon me. All of a sudden my temperature would rise and carry me away. Sometimes it lasted an hour or two; a few times it lasted more than a day.

Dr. Breem—who had treated my mother and her mother before her—couldn't determine the cause or cure. As I recall, he wasn't too patient with me. One day, about the third time Mama had taken me to see him, he peered down his ivory-white nose at me—I could stare right into his gray-haired nostrils—and told Mama I was the melancholy type and that I'd probably outgrow my dramatic flashes.

Mama nodded, her pocketbook tight against her tummy, and steered me out of the office with one finger pressing into my shoulder blade. We stopped at the drugstore for a chocolate sundae, then walked the nine blocks to home. Mama's humming that day was kind of aggravated, and I took care not to interrupt the fourteenth stanza of "Jesus Keep Me Near the Cross." Mama worked through a lot of her troubles by humming. It seemed to me that the harder she was thinking, the softer she hummed, sometimes leaving out several notes, as if the melody had disappeared into a tunnel and then blasted out at the other end without losing its place.

When we got home that day, Mama sat me down at the kitchen table to peel potatoes while she chopped celery and carrots for soup. After a bit she said, "Velma, it looks like we'll just have to turn these fevers over to the Lord. He's provided doctors for regular ailments, but when the doctors run out of ideas, then that's a sign. So don't you worry at all."

Mama talked about the Lord quite often, as if he were her closest friend and advisor. She could get away with that for some reason. I've known plenty of people who sprinkled their conversations with "the Lord," like in those E. F. Hutton commercials where a person mentioned Hutton and everybody stopped to pay attention. But I never did resent Mama's references to the Lord, maybe because I knew her to be a humble woman and a true, sweet Christian. In addition, Mama had the sort of strong presence that made a person hesitate to argue with her.

So when she told me not to worry about my fevers, I was inclined to obey. I don't remember being afraid, really. I'd just get hot and woozy and not care about my life. I remember thinking once, during a two-day hot spell, that probably just a nudge would put me into heaven, and I didn't think I'd mind. In some ways, my fevers were like a location that only I could go to, a place for being with just myself and thinking and dreaming without interruption.

My Aunt Trudy liked to sniff loudly and comment that I was "just like Mother," meaning my grandmother. She'd talk about how both Gran Lenny and I had sensitive temperaments and we got sick more than normal people did because we were so taken with our own dark thoughts. Back then, I thought that no one else in the family appreciated my grandmother, who was strange for that time in this little town. But I would have gone through a thousand bad fevers if I'd thought they would help me turn out just like Gran Lenny.

When I was in a fever, I would often dream a colorful, meandering dream and wake up to Mama or Gran Lenny sponging me off with alcohol mixed with water. Then I'd be gone again, and the dream would take up where it had left off. I would fly over the face of the world or find myself inside a huge tree that had rooms and furniture in it. Sometimes in the middle of the journey I would realize that I had company, someone I couldn't see but feel. I never talked about these dreams because they didn't fit the language of my everyday world.

As an adult, I've not had fevers like I did as a girl. But when they do come, they usually bring some unwelcome thing with them. When I was twenty, I went into a fever and dreamed about being underwater. When I awoke, I was losing my first baby. It was just a tiny gray sack with a tiny person in it who hadn't really formed yet. Albert and I buried it in a little jewel box in our garden and planted peonies on the spot. I stood there with the garden hose and sprinkled the fresh ground, and the water smelled like the water in my dream.

In 1979, I had a fever during the second week of August. I seemed to float for days and days, feeling everything I loved slipping over horizon after horizon. I lay on my back miles above the farmland, looking up at icy blue atmosphere, and I felt the chill. I woke up and put on my sweater, feeling death at the door. My mother lived with us at that time, and we knew she didn't have long in this world. Mama lingered just another week. I held her hand while she died and then long afterward as the heat left her body. I held her cool fingers, and they felt as fresh and blue as the sky from my fever dream.

These days, as much as I fear fever, it visits me once, maybe twice a year. It puts me in bed for two or three days, and that private location it takes me to is full of people from everywhere and every period of my life. I fly longer and higher, and the world I'm looking down on is wider, but darker and filled with more things I don't understand.

My name is Velma Brendle, and I live in Leeway, Kansas. That's in the southeast corner of the state, not far from Oklahoma or Missouri. You might know where Leeway is if you were related to someone here or if your car broke down here when you were headed somewhere else. Otherwise, you'll go the length of your life without ever paying us a visit. We don't mind that as much as you might think. A lot of people are meant to go into the bigger world, and they grow up in a place like Leeway and leave it when they're grown. We see them packing up, and we say that we'll miss them, and we will, but we know that this needs to happen.

But some of us belong in Leeway or some other such town. Our lives are full of loved ones and a landscape that's old and belongs to us. I sit under an oak tree in my backyard that my grandmother planted. Our family has cared for this tree through all kinds of seasons, splinting it after lightning struck and treating it for bagworms. I wouldn't say that I own the tree, but we do have a connection. It's important to me, as silly as that might sound to someone who has moved around a lot and lived in different places. Some of us just aren't meant to move. We're for staying and caring for things and keeping track and preserving the photographs and clippings that long-lost cousins or grandchildren will need in another thirty or forty years, coming back to Leeway to sell Mom's house or look for somebody's baptismal record. I'm proud to be one who stays. A lot of people in Leeway feel that way.

It's not a very big town—barely more than twelve hundred people. There's not a lot of money here. Portions of it are pure trailer park. But other parts are old and tree-lined and deep with color. My block is shaded almost completely by oaks and maples—sturdy, tall ones that also shaded the town's families three generations ago. Most months of the year, my backyard is cool and sun-dappled.

For thirteen years, I've operated Leeway's only real restaurant. It's six blocks from my house, down Pickins Street. On top of that, I janitor at Jerusalem Baptist Church, where I am also a member. The janitor job requires only a few hours a week, but it fills a need in my life. The sanctuary, with its high ceiling and tall, frosted windows, has always been a soothing place, especially during the afternoon when I'm the only one there. The cleaning doesn't feel like work, just something to keep my hands and eyes busy while my soul is doing other things. The windows let in light, but any objects or people outside are only shadows going by. I can't see them, and they can't see me. It's a good arrangement. Even during worship services, it's nice to have the light but not the distractions. Pickins is one of the main streets in town, and there's always some little drama going by. As it is, a good many Sunday mornings we can hear Maria Dalmazio calling for her cat, Theo. We can tell by the different pitches of her voice that she's walking up the street and calling, then turning around and walking the opposite direction and calling a little louder. As if she didn't know that silly cat would come home when it was good and ready. We just chuckle and go on worshiping. But if the windows were clear, don't you know we'd be craning our necks to see her go back and forth.

I have believed in Jesus nearly my whole life. That's not to say that I understand him much. I do trust him more than I used to. But it still bothers me that after all these years, Jesus hasn't offered an opinion or an explanation about my fevers and dreams. Some prayers you pray, and you really know the answer, but you just need some encouragement. Other prayers just take you toward questions and discomfort. I don't understand why this is so. But I've tried to build the habit of giving my fevers to the Lord. Some things you know you can't control anyway.

But these days I'm feeling at ordinary times the way I used to feel during fevers. Dizzy and slow and struggling to understand as scenes appear in front of me. Life itself has become a complicated dream, and I want more and more to slip out of it and find all the people who have drifted up into the chilly blue air.

I suppose I know why it seems that everything important has slipped out of my grasp. A lot of bad things have happened lately. In fact, the past two years have tried Leeway's people to the end of their resources. I've watched people lose important things, and it's made me shut my lips tight and fret against God. It's made me wonder what could be so important about pain that it should visit—so often and so freely—the people I love.

I may never understand, truly, the events that hurt all of us so. But I've decided that life has patterns and those patterns repeat themselves. They don't go the same way twice, but the same ten or twenty lessons keep working their way out. It seems that, over the past few years, lessons about death and loss just kept repeating, like the chorus of a bad hymn, the kind with a clunky rhythm and odd words. An unlovely melody that plays through your mind for days afterward.

If my husband, Albert, were here, he'd say that I'll make myself crazy, thinking over events again and again, wondering what else I could have done. "You don't rule life and death," he'd say. That's Albert for you. I think men just naturally rise up from their hurts and defeats and move on. I suppose I never was good at letting go. Partly it's my personality. But partly it's my faith. I grew up expecting a lot from God. And, truth be told, this past year or so I've felt that God didn't come through as he should have. What a thing to wrestle with. How does a person get over it?

I've never considered myself a fanatic, just a serious Christian. But sometimes you come to understand a thing in a way you never have before. And it doesn't make much sense, but you know it's absolutely true. You can't prove that it's true. You can't sit people down and explain it so that they're just as convinced as you are. But the thing is truer than your own name. And when that kind of knowledge comes to you, you're responsible to accept it and believe it. It's yours—you didn't ask for it, but it's yours—and Heaven's watching to see what you do with it.

Well, I feel a revelation coming on. I think the Lord is working out an extra big pattern here. I've never felt so strange for so many days at a time, with or without fever. And I can't help but believe that before long I'm going to wake up and something important will have taken place. For now, I just need to pay attention.

I haven't talked with my pastor about this. I know already that he wouldn't have much to say. Preachers tend not to talk about the private part of faith—the part that's separate from sermons or Scripture or traditions. What's in the center of another person's soul is something a pastor just doesn't know. And if he can't teach it with authority, then he'll stay clear away from it. Probably just as well.

I'm on my sunporch and the morning is quiet. The aroma of autumn has slipped into the breezes. It's rained recently, and my little town is so full and fertile that you would think it was early spring, the air green and yellow and reflecting off the late summer trees, which have not yet burst into fiery colors. The streets are so still that I can hear Don Bradley talking to his son from all the way down the block. They're deciding whether to chop down that big old cedar.

For just a second I imagined that I heard my old neighbors, Doris and her daughter, Shellye. So many times that kitchen window has been open and I could hear Doris buttering her toast, raking a knife across it again and again, usually after she'd been up half the night walking the streets, trying to smoke away another nervous spell.

I feel the peace around me this morning, and I try to reason with myself. I wonder why I can't let go of my sorrows. I don't know why events that are in the past can still have such a terrible hold on me.

But one evening last week I was dusting the bookshelves of the attic bedroom, the room that was my grandmother's, and I remembered a bit of advice she gave me once. Then I went to the drugstore and bought four "blank books," as they're called now. I took them home and sat at the kitchen table and wrote my name in each one.

Some of the old folks in church still use the expression "pray it through," which means that you pray until you know what to do next or until at least you have the peace to stop praying. I have to admit, though, that sometimes a thing won't pray through. Or it won't pray through in the ordinary way. Maybe some of us pray better with pen and paper. However you pray, it hurts just as much, or it lifts your spirit just as high. I know already that the prayers I'm about to write will probably hurt more than uplift.

When my son was small, he'd go through a little routine when I told him it was bedtime. He'd march around the house singing loudly, "I'm not sleepy and sleep is bad for me. Beds are for lazy old people, and Jesus doesn't want me to be." He wasn't much of a poet, but he believed in that little song and had to sing it every night, just to make his protest. Albert and I learned to let him sing it, usually about thirty times as he roamed upstairs and downstairs and around the furniture. We'd tell him it was bedtime awhile before it really was, because we knew he'd have to do his singing first. By then he'd be yawning and running his words together, and we'd put him to bed. We didn't even get mad about the song, or at Jimmy for singing it.

I've decided that Almighty God looks at my arguments in about the same way. Lets me sputter and make excuses, then about the time I wind down he gives me the same news as before, and by then I just take what comes.

I'm feeling like marching up and down and singing a little song of my own these days. It wasn't that long ago when I especially needed to hear God, and yet God always managed to be where I wasn't. So I finally accepted his absence and did the best I could. Now I'm sitting here in my empty house with these stiff, empty journals in front of me. And I suddenly find that God is sitting in the chair opposite me, like a teacher waiting for the student to get busy. Isn't that just like life— when you're ready to go off on your own without a care, the Lord shows up, bringing impossible requirements with him.

I had no formal schooling past high school, and I know that only writers write literature, because they're gifted to do it. But stories belong to us ordinary people. I'm not even that fond of my little set of stories, particularly some of the endings. But endings aren't up to me. The stories are mine, though, and they're outgrowing me, like starter plants begging to be divided and repotted. These stories are poking out of cracks and memories and even my daily thoughts.

The people in my stories—even the people who've done the greatest harm—are people I love dearly. When you see something in the paper or on the television about some awful crime, and they flash a picture of the person who did it, it's easy to hate that person, because he's just a face to you—and usually an ugly one at that. You see the photograph and you feel the anger rise inside you, and you feel all right about it, because it's worth getting angry about. And when you can stop at hate, things stay pretty simple. You pass a judgment and speak out of your righteous anger, and that's that.

But when you see the criminal in church every Sunday, hate becomes a complicated thing. Love is ten times as complicated as the hate. And forgiveness will tear you limb from limb.

In the meantime, while you're hurting and healing, you do whatever it is the Lord's given you to do. I cook. I look over a table full of good things the Lord's already made, and I turn them into my own sort of love. Sometimes I don't know what does people more good—my prayers or my recipes.

Last night I dreamed that I walked through the house and saw blood splattered everywhere. I got a rag from the pantry and turned on the faucet to clean things up, and blood came out of the faucet. I looked in the mirror and my face was streaked with it. Even the vegetables on my kitchen table looked cut up and wounded. Lord Jesus, deliver me from these awful places in my mind.

The worst memories seem to be the easiest to get to. But I can't start there. I'm not ready to write through the blood. First, I need to find words for the love.

Velma's Cabbage, Corn, and Green Onion Soup

4 to 6 cups chicken broth
2 cloves garlic, broken in two
$^1/_2$ teaspoon black peppercorns
I cup corn kernels, preferably fresh off the cob
I cup cabbage, white better than red, coarsely chopped
$^1/_2$ cup green onions, coarsely chopped
2 to 3 tablespoons butter or margarine
Salt to taste

Simmer broth, peppercorns, and garlic.

While broth is simmering, lightly brown corn kernels, onion, and cabbage in the butter.

Strain garlic and peppercorns from broth. Add vegetables to the broth and simmer until cabbage is tender.

Adjust seasonings and serve hot.

2

Shellye Pines

Ah, you shepherds . . . You have not strengthened the weak, you have not healed the sick, you have not bound up the injured, you have not brought back the strayed, you have not sought the lost, but with force and harshness you have ruled them.

—EZEKIEL 34:2, 4

In early spring of 1996, my neighbor, Shellye Pines, turned up pregnant. She was barely eighteen, a senior at the high school, and she'd been a member of our church since she was eleven or so. Everyone, including her mother, Doris, thought at first that they knew who the father was. Shellye was good friends with a boy in her drama club. They'd done little shows for the Lions Club and area churches. Sort of a dynamic pair. And in the way that people think husbands and wives on TV shows are somehow connected in real life, folks in Leeway just assumed that Shellye and Chris had a romance going.

But a few people closer to the situation knew that Chris had dated a girl from another school for a couple of years. He and Shellye were just good friends. I knew that because Shellye told me herself. She told me a lot of things, usually sitting at my kitchen table or relaxing with me on the front porch, which Albert screened in years ago. That sunporch is on the east side of the house, and it's shady and cool on summer afternoons. Shellye has visited me there regularly since she was six or so. I never knew if she found Albert and me all that interesting or if our property was as far as Doris would let her wander. Whatever the case, her busy self would land on one of my chairs two or three times a week. By that time, our own son was off to school, and Albert and I liked having the company. As Shellye grew up, she told me a lot of things she didn't tell other people. I think of it as the blessing of close proximity.

Other people liked to assume that they knew a lot about the Pines family. This happens in small towns, especially when a particular family is quiet and keeps to itself. I've known some very decent people who suffered just because they didn't talk enough to provide their own defense. A person can be on trial and not even know it, a jury of her peers hearing all sorts of things and making judgments, and suddenly she has a reputation she did nothing to earn.

Folks in Leeway thought they knew why Dave Pines took off when Shellye was five. Doris Pines was years recovering from that, and people could be pretty judgmental about it. They worried about Doris caring properly for her little girl. Now, I lived next door to them and knew that Shellye was doing as well as could be expected, given that her daddy had run off without a word. And Doris could appear crazy, but it was really just grief. She would keep to herself during the day and would walk around and around the block in the dead of night, smoking. She'd never smoked before her husband left. That one event seemed to change Doris's very personality. Her nervous habits were something of a legend. I know, not just because she was my neighbor, but because all of Leeway's legends begin at my café, where people get loaded on their favorite foods and then start talking as freely as if they'd drunk whiskey.

Doris would spend entire days on her back stoop, watching Shellye play, bringing their lunch and supper out and setting them up on a card table in the backyard. When another neighbor asked Doris why she was outdoors so much, Doris said she had trouble breathing when she was inside the house. Then again, she might watch movies for days at a time. Her favorite actor was Gregory Peck, and many's the gentle-weathered day when I've been in my own yard and heard that clear, deep voice talking from the dimness of Doris's living room. Doris also bought projects and started but didn't finish them, but if we institutionalized every person who had half-embroidered pillowcases tucked away in drawers, then they may as well slap big gray walls around the whole town. Doris had just about every kind of craft project invented, each one a third finished. During her worst spells, she would get out every one of them, arrange them around her living room, and cry and cry. She probably thought those silly things represented her real life. And when she got that way, she'd rave at herself for all her failures.

Given the absence of a father early on and a mother who existed in such a distracted state, no one was terribly surprised when it became known around town that Shellye was pregnant. I've seen the sad shake of the head over a cup of coffee more times than I can count. And during the week the news broke, I heard a lot of sympathy for Shellye as I worked the counter and poured coffee refills. I've got a couple of girls who wait the tables, but I feel out of touch if I don't work the floor a little myself a couple times a day. I hear enough out there to keep me up on the real news in town. It did me good to know that people weren't judging Shellye too harshly. But they did judge Doris, even if they pitied her. A woman who's been deserted by her husband is always left with unjust, invisible battles. She doesn't have the energy to speak up for herself, yet defend herself is what she must always do.

Dave Pines had been a well-respected man in Leeway before he walked out on his family. He was the type who wasn't particularly outgoing but always pleasant. He was on a community committee for beautifying Leeway's one, small park. He was usher at the Methodist church. When he took out without warning, he left big, ugly questions behind. And I know that, since nobody could imagine Dave being mean, most people figured that Doris had driven him away. Doris never said much to me about Dave, but I suspect that he was one of those people who make sure everything looks fine, even while his entire soul is in upheaval. So many easygoing people are like that. They don't fall apart for years, but when they do, it's practically permanent.

The Pineses moved to Leeway when Doris was pregnant with Shellye, bought the small tan ranch house next door to Albert and me. They painted the place a fern green, worked in the yard, and seemed to get along. He was the new manager at a chain restaurant in Helmsly, the county seat. They joined the Methodist church right away; why, I remember the church women throwing Doris a shower before Shellye was born. That was a happy time. They seemed like a nice, young family, just blooming.

Doris was real quiet, but she'd take part in things and was friendly enough. Mostly she seemed to like staying home with her husband and baby. She didn't socialize much or have a lot of close friends, which is probably why so many people misunderstood her later.

When I remember the two of them, I see Dave with his arm around Doris's shoulders in a protective, affectionate way. Doris seemed happy to be under his wing. Albert and I watched baby Shellye grow from a little blanketed blob in the carrier under the shade tree while Doris and Dave were doing yard work, to a five-year-old who liked to break out dancing whenever she heard any kind of music. I know for a fact that Albert used to turn the radio up in his shop, just so he could peek out the garage window and see Shellye start in with her tappy feet and swinging arms and swoony, little-girl hips. I'd hear him chuckling clear across the backyard.

One Sunday afternoon, Dave backed the Oldsmobile out of the driveway. He'd just taken out the garbage for Monday pickup. Albert said later that he thought it strange that Dave put a couple of those black garbage bags in the trunk of the car, but he thought they were clothes for the Salvation Army or some such. Dave pulled out then, drove down Pickins Street, and never came back. Later that evening, then again after dark, the living room light yellow and tired behind her, Doris stood in the front doorway and didn't say a word. Back then, her panic was the quiet kind.

The next days and weeks were a terror. There were police from the county and state both, eventually. The time just dragged by, filled with questions and tears and knots in everybody's stomach. We were sure Dave had been killed, the Olds carjacked when he'd had to stop for some reason along one of the empty stretches of highway that lay across the farmland in every direction.

After four months, Matt Johnson, a friend of Dave's at Leeway's Chamber of Commerce, received a letter. Dave was living with some friends in Harrisburg, Pennsylvania. He wasn't coming back. He wouldn't give details, even after Matt and Rev. Stevens, the Methodist pastor, called him up at the return address and tried to talk with him. He came to the phone only to let them hear his voice and know he was OK. They asked what was wrong. He said nothing was wrong. They asked if he'd run off with a woman. He wouldn't say. All he did was repeat what his letter had said, that he wanted a divorce and to give Doris everything and make arrangements with his lawyer for him to send child support, but through a third party. He would never come back to Leeway, he said. Rev. Stevens asked him how he could leave not only a wife who loved him but also a little girl who needed him, and Dave hung up. Rev. Stevens and Matt went together to tell Doris the news.

Well, maybe Dave off in Pennsylvania thought that he'd tied everything up, but most of us wished that he'd just let us think he was rotting in a drainage ditch somewhere. What a thing to do to a family, to a town that cared about you. The rumors and the speculations flew across the county as if they had their own radio frequency. A lot of people guessed that Dave had taken up with another woman, that he'd planned his escape for some time. No one had evidence of such a thing. But it was a story they could at least make sense of.

By then, Doris was out of her mind from the weeks of anxiety and grief, and it was impossible to tell where her tears of worry left off and her tears of anger and betrayal took up. We were sure this would finish her off. For a time, Doris's aunt from Springfield, Missouri, came to stay. She was the only family Doris had within a few hundred miles. And during that time it was Aunt Sal, not Doris, we'd exchange news with at the post office or Avery's grocery. Aunt Sal sort of stood in for Doris, even when it came to little Shellye, who grieved in a five-year-old way, knowing that she missed her daddy but not having many words for it. Aunt Sal told Rev. Stevens that Doris wanted to tell Shellye that her daddy was dead; that would be easier on the little thing than the awful truth. But the pastor convinced Doris that the truth would catch up with Shellye eventually, and it was probably best not to lie now. I suppose it's nearly always best to tell the truth, but I'd never want to make such a decision.

After a few weeks, Aunt Sal went back to Springfield. She'd helped Doris find a job as a receptionist for Dr. Saliman, Leeway's only dentist. So Doris made her way out into the town again, with less to say than ever. She did fine at the dentist's office, always very professional. But she was thin and gray-skinned and wouldn't look anybody in the eye. She managed to keep that job for three years, but then the nervous spells set in with a vengeance. Doris went to part-time and managed that all right. She went for a few visits with a psychiatrist, and it was probably some report from him that made it possible for Doris to get on partial disability. Dave was doing well in his new life, and he sent child support like clockwork. Aunt Sal once told me that Dave called Doris two times, once to say that it wasn't her fault and the other to work out something about their legal arrangements. Doris never spoke to anyone about it, at least not to me or to anyone I feed on a regular basis.

The sad part is that a lot of folks had never paid attention to Doris before, since she was so quiet and she blended in. And by the time the scandal hit and folks started going out of their way to notice her, she was in such bad shape that they assumed she'd always been disturbed and that her craziness was the reason Dave had left. The fact is, Doris never seemed off in any way to me, and I'd lived next door to her for more than five years. When I'd hear people talk about Doris's mental condition, I'd always be quick to jump in and say that she'd only been that way since the desertion. But people have to fill in the blanks. They'd rather have it wrong than leave it blank. They'd rather form opinions than live with questions. I came to Doris's defense when I could, but it never did much good.

Doris and I have had a sort of friendship over the years. When I'd been at Jerusalem Baptist for a while, I invited Doris and Shellye to go with me. Doris had dropped out of the Methodist community, just as she'd dropped out of other things. To my surprise, she accepted my invitation; she and Shellye went to church with me, and they went the next Sunday and the next. When Shellye was thirteen, right before our present pastor came to Leeway, she gave her heart to Jesus during church on a peaceful April morning.

But you never know what kind of impact a big loss will have on a child. Shellye had cried quite a bit the first few months her daddy was gone. Then she got quiet. Then she just seemed normal, a little girl becoming a teenager. And then, in the spring of '96, she got pregnant.

In Shellye's situation, just like in her mother's, people didn't have the whole story. They didn't know that, two months before word of the pregnancy got out, the girl had showed up at my back door, her eyes puffy from tears and with bruises on her wrists. They didn't know that Len Connor, and not Chris Baylor, was the boy who'd taken Shellye's virginity. And take is exactly what he'd done.

Len Connor was a senior on the honor roll. He was a member of Jerusalem Baptist, his parents and grandparents on both sides members there for years and years. A Christian boy who'd been sweet on Shellye for some time. Shellye had been too much in awe of him to actually go out with him. She told me this later, and that he'd asked her out after church one day, and she thought he was making fun of her. She never saw herself as beautiful in any way. That's why she liked drama so much, she said; she could become other people. I couldn't help but think that a daddy disappearing could have a lot to do with a little girl feeling beautiful or not. But then Len had asked her out again, and they drove over to Helmsly to see a show and then got pizza afterwards. On the drive between towns, on a back road, Len had stopped the car.

For a long time, none of us knew exactly what happened after Len parked the car. All I knew was the state Shellye was in when she got to my house, after running away from Len and hitching a ride from a farmer who nearly ran her over on the dark road. Whatever Pastor Thomas or the deacons or Len's family or anyone else said later, I saw what I saw.

Here was Len Connor, their golden boy in the youth group. He'd led his team to the state basketball tournament, and he'd been on Student Council, and he'd headed up a petition to get the school board to allow after-school prayer meetings on school grounds. The men in the church acted as if all of them were Len's daddy. They were proud of him, and rightly so. I could understand them not wanting anything to upset the boy's progress in life.

But Len was a young man, and, I suppose, like a lot of young men, full of ideas about himself and feelings he hadn't learned to control. And the night Shellye showed up at my back door, it was clear as day to me that she'd been forced upon. The fright on her face and the way her clothes looked told me that someone had raped her or tried to. Len hadn't beaten her or held a knife to her throat. But he made her do what she didn't want to do.

Shellye was always a sensible girl. Not the hysterical type at all, and quick to take responsibility for her actions. I'd never known her to be dishonest. And when I finally got her to talk, she said without a waver, "I yelled at him to stop, but it's like he didn't hear me."

I wanted to call Brennen Simms right then. Brennan's been Leeway's sheriff for ten years. He would have gone to Len's folks and dealt with it then and there. He would have talked to Shellye and her mom, and all of them together would have figured out the right thing to do.

But Shellye wouldn't go to Brennen. She was ashamed and afraid. "It's my word against Len's, and I know his parents don't think I'm good enough for him, or else he wouldn't have been so quiet about asking me out."

She didn't tell Doris either. I couldn't blame her. Doris did well those days to check people in and out of Dr. Saliman's examination room and pick up her own groceries. She could barely handle bad news when it was as trivial as Avery running out of a sales item by the time she got her shopping list together. Doris had enough burdens to bear.

Shellye said to me, about three weeks after it happened, "Maybe I'm pregnant, Velma." She was about a week late.

"Your mama needs to know."

"Not yet. Maybe I'm not. I'm not sick or anything."

"Not everybody gets sick."

"I'll wait—another week."

She waited two months, and, skinny as she was normally, she was beginning to show. It was spring, and cool enough that she could get away with wearing floppy sweaters or roomy jumpers.

"Shellye," I said, "You need to be under a doctor. You don't want anything to go wrong."

"Will you ask Mom to come over here so I can tell her?"

I brought home leftover chicken and homemade noodles. Doris didn't seem so distracted that evening. I almost wished Shellye would change her mind and not say anything. It was nice to see Doris calm and happy for a change.

When Shellye told her—before the apple strudel—Doris bowed her head and cried like a woman who was eternally tired. She didn't even lift her head when she asked, "Who's the father?"

"I can't tell."

"You have to tell. He needs to help."

"I can't tell you now."

The next day, Aunt Sal's Ford roared up the drive, and she and Doris took Shellye to a county health clinic.

Then Doris went straight to Pastor Thomas, because he was the one she told her troubles to. She told them so often that a weary look would come to Pastor's eyes when he saw her coming. Doris was too needy to notice that. The sun rose and set by Pastor Thomas.

I have to be frank and say that I'd never expected much from Pastor Thomas. He was always nice enough, and he preached a good sermon. It was hard to listen and not be moved, regardless of whatever else you knew.

I'd been a member of Jerusalem Baptist five years before Thomas came. We'd had mainly younger men, seminary students needing experience. That was all right, because you knew that whatever happened, the church wouldn't have long to endure it. For the most part these young preachers tried too hard and didn't listen enough. But most had good hearts. And our church felt that it was doing its part in God's kingdom by training young pastors to be better pastors.

When Thomas came, though, he intended to stay until he could retire. His wife had already had a breast removed. Clare was a sweetheart in spite of her trials. She was in her early forties, and he was nearly ten years older.

Jack Thomas knew how to talk with people and how to get things done. He won the vote with his sermons, which were entertaining to listen to and humorous in the right places.

He did so well that he'd be out of town, guest preaching at another church in the area at least one Sunday out of every month. And when Thomas got settled at our church, the men's attendance went up, that's a fact. There's not a Christian woman alive who would find fault with that. I've never been in a church that didn't have more women than men. Pastor Thomas came to town and got busy, and men who hadn't been in church for years got interested. In just a few months' time we saw the change.

But I didn't really like the man, and for a long time I couldn't put my finger on it. Then one Sunday, nearly a year and a half after he'd come to our church, I was standing near the door on my way out after morning worship. Three people were ahead of me in line to shake Pastor's hand, which is our custom. I could hear the emotion in Alice Sandline's voice when she shook Pastor's hand.

"You really spoke to my heart this morning. I've struggled so with understanding how to let the Lord fill the emptiness."

Alice had been a widow for about six months. My heart went out to her. Pastor Thomas smiled warmly and grasped Alice's hand in both of his. "Why thank you. God's Word is good, isn't it?"

"Oh yes. I've developed the habit lately of praying a psalm every morning—"

Just then, Frank Delbert, one of our deacons, came up from the side and said, "Jack, how many men are signed up for the retreat—who has the number, do you know?"

And Pastor let go of Alice's hand and started talking to Frank as if Frank were the only person in the room. I watched Alice's face wait, its smile fading over the next minute or so. Pastor didn't notice when she walked on out the door.

Alice was back next Sunday, and I don't imagine her faith suffered any serious setback from that incident. But I started noticing after that, how Pastor had the tendency to brush off the women in our congregation. He needed the men to like and respect him, and he went to a lot of trouble for that. The opinions that mattered to him were the men's opinions. In a Baptist church you expect the men to be the leaders, but most of the time they take note of the women's contributions. And a lot of the men in our church would bring heaven and earth together for their sisters in the faith.

But Pastor needed friends. He needed the deacons to like him and for other leaders in the community to respect him. Out here in the country, we still use the term "good ol' boy." Well, Pastor Thomas was one of those. The bad thing about good ol' boys is that they'll do about anything to keep from upsetting each other. Sometimes that means that they let things alone that they should stir up or challenge. And they hesitate to be tough with each other, even when being tough is called for.

Let's just say that there are times when a person should stand up and speak up, regardless of what others—even the good ol' boys—think. A lot of people in Leeway have always seen Pastor Thomas as a born leader. But there was a time when he was more likely to see where the line was already forming and hurry to stand at the front of it.

With Shellye Pines's situation, Pastor should have formed a whole new line. But he didn't. And I'll always fault him for that, even though I forgave him eventually. In fact, he and Clare are good friends of mine now. But I'm getting ahead of myself.

When Doris told Pastor about the pregnancy, he started asking too, "Who's the father?"

And Shellye asked me, "Could Pastor Thomas talk to me at your house?"

"I suppose."

"I feel better when I'm here."

That Wednesday night, after midweek service, Pastor Thomas came over for coffee and pecan pie, which I knew was one of his several favorites.

When Shellye told him Len Connor was the father, Pastor Thomas said the oddest thing:

"Why, Shellye, are you sure?"

"Sure I'm sure!"

"It couldn't be anybody else." He didn't ask it as a question, but that's what it was.

Shellye's neck and cheeks went red. "You think I'm sleeping around with all sorts of guys? You think I'm like that?"

"Honey, honey." Doris tried to settle Shellye, her eyes jumping between the girl and the pastor.

"I'm not saying anything of the kind, Shellye. We just need to be sure before we go pointing a finger at anybody. There's not somebody else you're protecting?"

"Why would I be protecting anybody?" Shellye pulled up her sweater to show her bulgy belly in the T-shirt underneath. "I'm sure not protected!"

"All right, all right. So you and Len got carried away. That happens sometimes."

"*He* got carried away."

Pastor shook his head. "Now, honey, it takes two to make a baby."

"But he forced me."

Doris's eyes were big as eyes could get. Pastor's mouth flapped shut. Finally, he said, "That's a very serious charge, Shellye, and you need to be very, very sure before you make that statement."

"I'm sure. I am totally sure. We were kissing and, well, he started feeling under my sweater, and I let him. I know I shouldn't have, but I let him do that. But then he started pulling at my leggings, pulling them down, and I didn't go along with that at all. I asked him to stop. I started pushing at him and yelling. But he—" She choked up suddenly, and her mouth jerked so that she couldn't talk.

Pastor Thomas leaned back in the easy chair, one hand in his lap and the other to the side of his face. He looked at Shellye hard, and I knew that he knew she was telling the truth. I saw it in his eyes. After a minute or so he said, "Well, I need to talk with Len and his parents."

"I don't want or need anything from him," Shellye said, heat in her voice.

"Shellye." Doris shot a hand out to rest on her daughter's arm. "He needs to help out. You don't have any idea what it costs to care for a child."

"That's right," said Pastor Thomas, getting up. Doris looked surprised that he'd be leaving so soon. "We'll get to the bottom of this, and Len will own up to his responsibilities."

I felt better, having seen the dead seriousness on his face and having heard him say that Len should own up to what he'd done.

But that's not where the line formed. Of course Len said it didn't happen the way Shellye said. Nothing like him forcing and her yelling. So Pastor Thomas decided that Shellye'd told the story because she was ashamed to have let things go so far.

In May, there was a meeting of the deacons, Pastor Thomas, Doris and Shellye, Len Connor, and his parents. I wasn't part of it, but I decided that evening to polish all the communion pieces and the altar candlesticks. The storage room was close enough to the conference room that I could hear most of what was said. It was a sad discussion.

Everyone had already decided that there had been no rape. Shellye spoke up twice and said loud and clear, "But he forced me. Why are you making this so hard on me, when Len is in the wrong?" Len protested immediately, getting madder the second time. Charlie Resnick told Shellye to stop being hysterical. Pastor Thomas was softer about it, saying that it's easy to remember something in a different light, especially if it was a bad memory.

Shellye said fine, she'd just go to the police. They said it was her word against Len's, and after all this time the police probably wouldn't investigate. She said they'd have to if she got a lawyer. They said Christians shouldn't take one another to court, and they quoted her the verse on it. That made her pause, and in the pause Doris said in a trembling voice that she just wanted to be at peace. Shellye didn't say more after that, at least nothing I could hear. The end of it was, it was decided that Len's family would help pay the hospital bill, but none of this would go to court. They stopped with that, because everyone was agitated and tearful.

Just two days later, Shellye came to my restaurant in tears. It was mid-afternoon, a slow time, and I saw the look on her face and motioned back toward the kitchen. We'd hardly let the door swing shut when she said, "They want me to give up my baby!" She put her hands on her tummy. "Pastor Thomas says there's a Christian agency that helps girls in trouble by giving their babies to Christian couples who can't have their own. It's *my* baby!" She sat at the chopping block and wiped tears off her cheeks. "It's part of me! I didn't plan it, but it's happened, and it's in *my* body!"

I heard customers come in. I peeked out the kitchen door and saw that Sheri was handling them. I turned back to Shellye. "I don't think they look at it as taking something away from you, honey. They're trying to do what's best for everybody. It's still your decision."

"It doesn't sound like it to me. Everybody's against me. Why would they let me make a decision? They didn't even believe me. I did the right thing and told the truth, but that didn't matter to any of them." She blew her nose into a paper towel.

"It matters to me."

Shellye sat on the stool and watched me grill hamburgers. "I don't want to turn my baby loose and then wonder her whole life if she's all right. I couldn't do that."

I turned the burgers over and laid a slice of cheese on each. At that time in my spiritual life, I wasn't hearing the Lord's voice too much. But I imagined that if I could, he'd be telling me to just cook and not talk. I couldn't find any words that seemed right. It was an impossible situation, and no matter what happened, someone would be hurt, and someone else would be mad.

Shellye stopped coming to church after that. I think that what hurt her most was not being believed. And then not being trusted to be a decent mother. She didn't understand, as I did, that the adoption business had to do with the Connor family's reputation and with keeping peace in the church. To Shellye, it all felt personal. I tried to explain, but she couldn't hear me. I wish I'd understood her mind better then. I was always pretty pragmatic about things. You figure out what needs to be done and do it. You learn what the truth is and accept it. My mother brought me up to deal with hard times that way.

Shellye just wasn't able to see life as it was. The first thing she saw, I think, was that her daddy hadn't loved her enough to stay in her life, and that her own love hadn't been strong enough to help her mother get over her emotional problems. And Len would rather have people think badly of her than tell the truth about himself, and the important people in our church didn't care enough about her to believe the truth about her and protect her reputation. All those things formed their own pictures in Shellye's mind, and those pictures got in the way of anything else she needed to see. I didn't even see it then; I was just trying to help Shellye get through a hard situation.

I can remember Shellye helping me snap beans when she was about twelve years old. Not many kids would bother snapping beans with the woman next door. The girl has always just given herself away to people, always so free and ready to smile. She could come into my kitchen and make me feel welcome in my own home. She could look wise as an old angel, too. I used to imagine that she was an angel, lent to us for a little while.

Shellye's Green and Red Eggs

The red part (best if you do this first):
Mix all these ingredients together and set aside.

> 1 ripe tomato, finely chopped
> ¼ cup fresh cilantro, finely chopped
> 2 tablespoons radish, finely chopped
> 2 tablespoons plain yogurt, you can also use sour cream
> 1 teaspoon mustard
> 1 teaspoon sugar
> 1 tablespoon balsamic vinegar
> Salt and pepper to taste

The green part:

> ¼ cup onion, finely chopped
> 1 clove garlic, minced
> ¼ cup green bell pepper, finely chopped
> 1 tablespoon vegetable or olive oil
> 1 teaspoon oregano
> 2 cups of greens that cook quickly, such as Swiss chard or spinach,
>   washed and chopped
> 4 eggs
> ¼ cup milk
> ½ teaspoon curry powder
> Salt and pepper to taste
> ½ cup Parmesan or Swiss cheese, grated

In a large, nonstick skillet, saute onion, garlic, and green pepper in the oil. Add oregano and stir.

After the onion has softened, add the greens. Stir ingredients, cover, and cook on low heat for 5 to 7 minutes until greens are tender.

Stir together eggs and milk. Add curry, salt, and pepper and whisk well. Pour that mixture into the skillet and stir until all ingredients are evenly distributed over the bottom of the skillet. Cover and continue to cook on low for a few minutes.

When the eggs are firm, sprinkle the cheese evenly over the eggs. Cover and remove from heat for 5 minutes to let the cheese melt. Divide into 4 servings.

Serve warm with 2 to 3 tablespoons of tomato relish per serving.

3

VELMA'S PLACE

The Lord called to the man clothed in linen, who had the writing case at his side; and said to him, "Go through the city, through Jerusalem, and put a mark on the foreheads of those who sigh and groan over all the abominations that are committed in it.

—EZEKIEL 9:3–4

M y life has revolved around three places mainly. My house, which has a story all its own, in the family for three generations now. My restaurant, which has gone through some changes lately but has nearly always been my second home. And my church. I've been its janitor going on eight years. Three places that make me who I am, and they're all within ten blocks of each other. That tells you a lot right there. I've been to a few places—out East, to visit my Aunt Trudy's family, and to the Southwest, when Jimmy was in junior high and couldn't soak up enough about Indian ruins. He and Albert and I drove all over New Mexico and Arizona for two weeks one autumn. It was such a beautiful trip that I regretted later being so worried about being away. I suppose that no matter where I might travel, I'll still be right here in Leeway.

When I was a girl, I wrote little stories that took me where I wanted to go. And they generally didn't need to take me out of Leeway, just deeper into it. My stories usually had to do with Cherokee Indian princesses or strange little people who lived underground. I would find places in this town, places that seemed magical or beautiful or scary, and I'd think of things that might happen in those places. I made up a story once about a sinkhole just a half mile from our house. The place was on the edge of a field, barely into the woods, and a couple of cottonwoods leaned over it. There was a sorry fence around it and a sign warning us kids to stay away. According to the grown-ups, why, children, dogs, cats, and entire cows had disappeared down there. But where the woods began there was a slight rise that gave you a nice view of the sinkhole. One day—I must have been eight or nine—I decided that people probably lived down there. They would have to be very small people, and they would also have to be mute, or else they would have been discovered by now. I decided that they had their own sign language. In case they didn't, I invented one for them. I worked so hard on those imaginings that eventually I met Cecil, the mayor of their underground village. Cecil and I had a number of conversations, and in all of them he was amazed at how smart I was. But then the shadows of the cottonwoods would get wider and deeper, and I'd scamper home.

I blame this wild imagination on my grandmother, who was an actual writer. In my grammar school years, when I'd try to write something and I wasn't happy with it, she'd say, "Write *to* someone. It will have more purpose then." My grandmother was the only person I knew to write to, since by the time I was old enough to write much of anything, Cecil the mayor was long gone from the picture. But Gran Lenny was not a person you could cuddle up to and share your secrets with just any time. And once you did dare to show her anything on paper, she was tougher than any English teacher. There were a few, very few, times when she'd look at my work and say, "What lovely thoughts you have, Vellie. And how sharp you are to recognize things." Once she actually used the word "beautiful" to describe something I'd written. I still call that praise to mind when I need help through a trying day.

Now that I've decided to write about recent events—about Shellye and Doris and the rest of us—there's no Gran Lenny to write it to. I'll have to make up someone, a stranger passing through town who wouldn't know anything about me or about those I love. He's stopped in for a hot meal. I don't know even know his name. But I have him placed at the corner booth, facing the post office. I'll story him over coffee and my best pie.

A real story doesn't require a special, make-believe place. Our lives get lived out in the open, with people walking in and out of them as they please. And the people who walk through your days and nights are helping write your story. There's not a thing you can do about it.

In 1982, the Masons and Eastern Star both gave up the space they shared in the corner of one of Leeway's older buildings. It was just a big cavern of a room, with tall windows all along the two street sides. The family who at one time had owned most of the buildings on that block was moving back to its roots in West Virginia, and they weren't interested in collecting rent on that one remaining building. Avery Lemons, whose grocery was right next to the empty space, was the only other renter. He was in his fifties and going strong, and his middle son, Thad, was going to take over the grocery when Avery retired. So it didn't surprise anyone that Avery bought the building. We thought he might expand the grocery. But the place sat for a full year. Rumor had it that Avery was looking for someone to rent the space from him, another business of some kind. But in Leeway, which had been shrinking since the 1950s, new businesses didn't just appear.

To city people, empty buildings are part of life. People come and go—businesses too. But in Leeway, Avery's grocery, the bank, the post office, the beauty salon, and this former large corner space, which had been a dance hall way back when—these places made up the heart of what had been a nice little town earlier in the century. A lot of towns in the country used to be bigger and busier and brighter. Leeway was never huge, but it provided the basics to a fairly large farming community. And probably half of the families who lived here were third generation. In such a town, people take it personally when buildings get empty and run-down. So there were a number of conversations about what to put in the vacant spot that would restore to the town some of its old charm.

At this particular time, there was a Lutheran church in Leeway, and I had belonged to it since childhood. Except for Mama, our entire family belonged to the Lutheran congregation. At some point further back than I could remember, Mama had succumbed to the more emotional (and, frankly, more friendly) Nazarene church in the east part of town. Our whole family on both sides was Lutheran, and I believe that Mama shifting over to "that sect," as my aunt called it, caused a rift at home. But Mama had that ability to do as she pleased without looking like a liberal or a troublemaker. Sometimes I went with her to the Nazarene church, and it always felt good to be there. But I didn't feel comfortable leaving the Lutheran circle, which held all the other people in my life.

We Lutherans had a once-a-month Sunday lunch fellowship. At one time it had been a potluck. But by the time most of my people were dead or gone, I had became the Lutherans' main cook. I'm not sure how that happened. A few of the other women usually brought desserts, but I'd cook half the meal at home and the rest on the dilapidated stove in the church kitchen. The floor slanted, and you couldn't bake anything in the oven without it going lopsided in some way.

So when that building space downtown came up empty, Betty Webb, wife of my old friend Bailey, had the bright idea that I may as well cook all the time and get paid for it. Betty didn't do much but try new dessert recipes and scour the country for sales most weeks, but she managed to have a plan for everybody—who should marry whom, whose kids should enter what profession, what color so-and-so should paint his house. The Webbs were Baptists through and through, but Betty had shown up at a few of our Lutheran lunches. The woman had connections all over town, and any event requiring chitchat or buffet sampling usually had her on the guest list.

Since Betty was such a chatterbox, and since her suggestions went unheeded so often, it surprised me that, when she mentioned "Velma" and "restaurant," a lot of people looked up from their newspapers and thought it was a great idea. But turning the space into a restaurant meant putting in stoves and cabinets and more sinks and bringing the place up to code.

I still don't know how my husband managed it all. Albert had a circle of buddies who worked out a lot of the town's dilemmas while they sipped Pepsis in the late afternoons on the shady benches that faced the junior high softball field. I told Albert that if he got the place turned into a restaurant, I'd go there every day and cook. If I'd known what that would mean to my life, I would have had the sense to be frightened about it. But I was feeling pretty invincible in those days. My boy, Jimmy, was nineteen, away at college and doing well. All I had to do was take care of Albert and myself and go to church. I was forty-one and healthy. With no child at home, I felt that I had energy to spare.

Albert had only limited tolerance for Betty, although Bailey was a good friend of his. But Albert knew a resource when he had one. He went to Betty and told her to find as many secondhand dining tables and chairs as she could. He gave her a price range and turned her loose. I've never seen Betty so stimulated before or since that month or two when she was upending half the state and parts of three others looking for tables and chairs to furnish our little restaurant. I'll give Betty this much: she recognizes quality. She had Bailey out in the garage stripping down pieces, taking them apart and gluing them back together, putting on coats of varnish. She had two women at the Baptist church making seat cushions of several styles to go on the chairs. They made matching tablecloths, and then we bought clear plastic covers for them.

There weren't many fixtures in the place, but one cantankerous toilet in a closet and, of all things, a huge chandelier that hung from the center of the room. Albert & Company found some restaurant owners from the area and got them to come over and give advice. They managed to situate the stoves and ovens so that they could be vented out the old chimney. They built a partial wall that divided the kitchen from the dining area. The old maple counter, sturdy as ever, was stripped of its original varnish. The space under and behind the counter transformed easily into shelves for glasses and plates and silverware. They expanded the closet and turned it into two working bathrooms. And, after days of staring up at that mountain of a chandelier, Albert hired some dependable boys to climb ladders and clean it. It was a few weeks before we could find an electrician to rewire it and fit it for new bulbs. The walls were replastered and painted a clean off-white. Betty found decorations and knickknacks of all sorts to stick on wall space. The church ladies kept their sewing machines humming, and before we knew it, there were light, lacy curtains in the windows.

On the outside, under the restored shingle awning, Albert hung a pretty little sign: VELMA'S PLACE. He hung the thing three different times, taking it down to touch up the paint job or to make it hang straighter. I'd stayed away during all the construction, but I sat on the bench outside the new café and watched him and listened to him grumble for nearly an hour, messing with that stupid sign. After that was done to his satisfaction, he wanted to carry me over the threshold, but I'd gained a few pounds since our wedding more than twenty years before. Plus Albert's back was bothering him, so we held hands and walked into my place together. Bailey and Betty and a half dozen others stood there with us and sighed and gave half-nervous laughs. We were either out of our minds or at the beginning of a good thing.

The sign indicates, in smaller letters, that I serve breakfast, lunch, and dinner, but that's never been accurate. Even as I gathered help for the cooking and waitressing, it was clear that I'd go to an early grave if I kept the place open for all three meals. We decided that most folks would be more likely to come up for breakfast and coffee than be frequent supper clients. So for all these years, I've served breakfast and lunch Mondays, Tuesdays, Fridays, and Saturdays, and opened for brunch through supper on Thursdays. It's been my policy not to work on the Sabbath, and taking Wednesdays off gives me the rest I need.

Leeway folds up pretty early in the evenings, and if folks want to really "eat out," then they'll go to one of the many restaurants at the county seat, which is just a few miles away. There's usually a good-sized group that's ready for a home-cooked meal Thursday evenings at my place. It's gotten to where it feels like a big family dinner.

There are a couple of fast-food places at the edge of town, close to the highway. Eddie Marantino has a sorry, run-down little place on the other side of town where he serves burgers and hot dogs and ice cream and not much else. A lot of the kids eat there, because it's not filled with old folks the way my place is. I consider my restaurant more of a diner than a dining experience. But important things happen when you eat even simple food. VELMA'S has its place.

Most of my customers are middle-aged if not ancient. Quite a few of my regulars are people I went to school with, years and years ago. The café is our way of keeping in touch. And there are a lot of older people in this town who have lost spouses. It's a depressing thing to cook for yourself, looking across the table at the bank calendar on the opposite wall. A hard thing, being alone, and eating alone is harder still.

One of my favorite aspects of the restaurant is that long, old counter, from the saloon and dance hall days. Bailey found some photos at city hall, of the people out on the dance floor looking formal, and of buggies and carriages parked all down the street. He got copies made and had them framed, and they're hanging on the east wall near the counter. A lot of widowers eat at that eternally long counter, and I can visit with them while I cook, just the little serving window/partition between us.

Some of the youngsters eat at the counter, too. There seem to be two groups of kids in Leeway, the ones who eat at Eddie's and the ones who eat at my place. Eddie's crowd has a roughness to it, and that's probably why most of the younger kids and church kids end up at my counter. I like to think they feel safe, sort of like at Grandma's.

Not long after the restaurant opened, my son, Jimmy, came home on spring break. Albert and I had convinced him to spend it with us rather than working himself to death before school started again. Jimmy came to the café every day to visit with people and eat more than his share of my lemon meringue pie.

"Mom, you were made for this place."

"You think so?" Now that my son was getting older and more handsome by the week, I felt shy around him sometimes. I'd look in the mirror and wonder what he thought of belonging to such a lumpy, middle-aged woman. He looked like the kind of young man who would have another kind of mother.

"Sure. This is the happening place! Classy, too. Maybe I should quit school and learn to be a short-order cook."

"Of course. That's exactly why we sent you to college."

"You should install one of those frozen yogurt machines. Eddie has one, you know."

"So you've been to Eddie's?"

"Have to make the rounds. He still doesn't clean the grill more than once a week, from the smell of the place."

"Tell me you didn't eat anything."

"I had a hot dog. All he had to do was pull it out of boiling water."

"I'll bet this sandwich that the water never reached a boil. I can make you a hot dog, you know."

"Yeah, but it wouldn't have that Eddie's ambiance."

"Stay out of my pie then." It was so good to have my baby home. So nice to be teased the way only a son can tease you.

I was glad to see Jimmy growing up and feeling his way into the world without us. But as he walked out of my daily life, half my job was disappearing. Now Jimmy and I talked, but I couldn't do much more for him. I made sure he was well dressed—took him shopping even when he protested—and I made sure he ate well when he was home, even sent food with him when he'd go back to college. But the day-to-day mother time was all spent—the looking after and fixing up and just being around the house.

Albert and I had fallen into a comfortable pattern of taking care of each other, so comfortable that it hardly felt like effort anymore. We got our own breakfasts. He worked at the plant, took care of the car, played at his woodworking in the garage, and did the yard work. I took care of the house and put a hot meal on the table every evening except Thursday, when Albert would join the group of us for dinner at VELMA'S. I'd rub his back and shoulders with liniment most evenings, and he'd sit on the couch with me and massage my feet after I'd been on them all day at the restaurant.

Every now and then Albert would show up for lunch on a Saturday and shoot the breeze with Bailey and John and a few others. But Albert was even quieter than I was; we used to joke that it was a wonder Jimmy learned to talk at all. Albert would let people all around him do the talking, and with Bailey for a friend, there tended to be no silent moments. But every now and then Albert could offer a comment that would hit the air like a shock of electricity. It could be a humorous remark or some serious statement, but Albert's few words were always potent. The other men had a lot of regard for my husband. He was quiet, but they knew he was always paying attention. That's a skill I learned from him.

So starting a restaurant career at age forty-one sort of allowed me to stay involved with life now that my baby was out of the house. I'd never done anything else to distinguish myself in Leeway, except when I married Albert, whom everybody thought was a good catch. Lord only knows how I accomplished getting Albert interested in me. Everybody knew that Sissy Fenders had been after Albert all through high school, and Sissy was full of energy and had flippy, shiny hair and talked non-stop, so maybe in Albert's mind I was a welcome relief. Maybe I should have been grateful to Sissy for making me look so attractive. For certain, my marrying Albert represented a big victory in a lifetime of contests between Sissy and me. But that's another story.

VELMA'S has never made much money, I'll admit. Many of my customers are on fixed incomes, so I keep my prices low. I've usually served what I considered to be plain home cooking with an occasional flair. My life tends to be pretty calm, and I go on adventures by changing ingredients and seasoning from time to time.

We decorate for all the major holidays, with paper pumpkins or valentines or candy canes stuck to the windows. One year the second-grade class asked if they could display their Thanksgiving art, and I said yes, and my windows have been Leeway Elementary's exhibit space ever since. We had so many fliers and ads taped to the one wall that I finally bought the largest corkboard I could find, and that's now the community bulletin board. I know, this sounds pretty quaint and out of touch in a day when everybody does everything by computer and little portable phones. But that bulletin board is always full, and we don't leave anything on there for long. There's always a new grandchild's picture to show off or another car or camper top for sale or some event coming up at one of the churches or clubs. We post articles from the newspapers about happenings at the school, birth announcements or obituaries about friends and families. We even have our favorite comic strips.

After the restaurant opened in 1984, there were a lot more people walking through my life, writing my story. Overall, I enjoyed the work. Jimmy graduated with honors and got himself a nice position in an international software company, and he finally got married three years ago, but we never see him. His work has him going all over the world. And his wife's parents have a lot of medical problems. I think poor Jimmy spends most of his vacation time trying to help them out. That makes me proud of him. But how I miss that boy. I hint appropriately about grandchildren. From his voice over the phone, I can't tell if they're not trying or if they're trying and having trouble.

Then, when I'd been running the restaurant for three years or so—that would make it about 1987, one afternoon Maryann Holt and two other women from church came in and actually sat at the counter instead of their usual table by the window. Their faces were full of anxiety.

"Reverend Griffin is leaving," said Maryann.

We just looked at one another. We had seen this coming. Rev. Griffin was past retirement age, and his grandchildren were multiplying down in Texas. No one would blame him for getting down there and enjoying them.

At that time, there were only about fifteen people attending the Lutheran church. We'd talked of closing the doors a number of times, but Rev. Griffin was willing to stay on, and we were willing to have him. But we knew that the day he retired we'd be hard put to find someone else. There was a larger Lutheran congregation not fifteen miles away in Helmsly. It would make perfect sense for the few of us in Leeway to go over there.

Within two months, our church was closed. I'd walk by the empty building of an evening, taking a slight detour after closing the restaurant, and look at the dark stained glass and the lilac bushes along one side of the building, and just cry. I even cried for those miserable hot summer Sundays when I had slaved over the broken-down stove, cooking the fellowship dinner. I cried for the stove and the kitchen, for the sweet old sanctuary, kind of a dark, cool place that always felt immediately quiet.

Worse than the closing was the demolition of the building that happened just three months after that. Matt Wellsburg, who owned one of the nicer homes in town, bought the church lot and built an even bigger home. Some of us were mad at him for a while, but eventually we realized that the church was never going to reopen. It would be easier to see a family living there than the ghost of a congregation haunting an overgrown churchyard.

The church furniture was auctioned off, from hymnals to the walnut pulpit. The small pipe organ was bought by a Methodist church in the next county. The pulpit was bought by the small museum at the county seat. The pews, all of them walnut, too, and beautiful as the day some craftsman had made them, were bought for a decent price by the Jerusalem Baptist church, just a few blocks south and east of my own house. I forced myself to go to the auction, and I watched the pastor and other men from Jerusalem Baptist load the pews in fours and fives onto someone's flatbed truck. I saw them gently lift the pew I'd sat on for years and place it on the truck bed and tie it down tight and wrap old blankets and quilts around it so it wouldn't get scratched. I saw the little rack my hymnal had always rested in. The pew looked lost, all covered up, the carved end of it shining a golden brown in the late morning sunlight.

At that moment, I made another decision that changed my life more than I could have imagined. I decided to just follow my pew. The next Sunday, I was sitting in Jerusalem Baptist as a visitor, and a month later I was baptized into the fellowship. Go fifteen miles away to worship in someone else's community? I couldn't do it. The Baptists and Lutherans had behaved together for years and didn't have much out of common besides a few hymns and habits of worship. I've been a member of Jerusalem Baptist ever since.

The people in my life are either from VELMA'S or from the church, and a lot of the time that's the same group. Pastors and their staffs have informal meetings at VELMA'S. Or they bring people in just to talk.

At VELMA'S, it seems that all our lives and stories come together. When people come in, for even just a glass of iced tea or a cup of soup, they bring everything with them—their anxieties and their jokes, letters from relatives and whatever gossip they picked up walking over here.

I've been fairly religious my whole life, but I never really prayed until I started coming up here every day, dealing with the public. Every table I set has prayer requests sitting there, spoken or not. I can't get away from people's troubles here. Makes me wish I could pray better myself.

So much of the time praying feels like throwing words at wall-paper. You address them to God and hope they make an impression. The preachers talk about being a prayer warrior. But I'm more like a prayer short-order cook. See a need, cook up a prayer. It's the best I can do. I pray as much as I do because I'm not very good at it. If I knew what I was doing, a little would go a long way. All I can do is keep sending them up. Jodie Hayes comes in at noon with that look, and I know his boss is piling too much work on him. Toni Perotti stops for coffee near closing time and I can tell she hates the thought of going home to Donny, mean as he is. I know that when Jack Rader comes in of a late afternoon for coffee, he's keeping away from the bar down the street by having coffee and pie at my place. But then weeks go by when I never see Jack, and I know he's fallen off the wagon again.

I see the boys and girls flirt with each other over burgers and fries and play nervously in their ice cream when they're trying to say the right thing or to find the right love. Sometimes the hardest thing is hearing the kids talk. Some of them seem so old to be only kids. They talk as if they don't hope for much in life, and that's not healthy in young people. When you're young, you're supposed to set your hopes high, and by the time you've grown up a bit, you're able to accept the reality that's somewhat lower than those first hopes. I hate seeing youngsters so cynical.

All these things concern me, and how can I not pray? Most days I just let the names and faces fall through my mind and trust the good Lord to catch them.

You'd think that in a town as ordinary as Leeway, truly bad things would never happen. On the whole, people here are decent. But as I write through all this about my town and my restaurant, my husband and son, my friends, I feel a heaviness at the back of my mind. It's almost like a person standing in a corner of the room, ready to step up and point out all the parts I've left out.

The strange thing is, once I had the restaurant, life got a lot sharper, because every day I learned a little more about people and their struggles. While the restaurant fit me so well, it pushed me into a harder existence. I've had more sleepless nights. And I've begun to believe there's such a thing as evil. I should have believed it all along, because it's in the Bible. But you hate to give attention to something so bad; you want to give your time and strength to good things—feeding people, for instance.

One evil that befell us happened hardly a year after the Lutheran church closed. Betty fell down her basement steps and badly injured her head. For days, we thought she would die. She didn't, and then we almost wished she had. Her mind was never the same after that. She could talk some, but she'd mix up the order of her words. A lot of the time her eyes looked completely blank, just flat glassy color in her eye sockets. Most days she knew enough to take care of herself, but there were nights, during the period before Bailey took her to the rest home, when she'd get agitated and take off her clothes and try to visit people in the middle of the night. Bailey had to put locks on all the doors, locks that Betty couldn't reach or find keys for.

Bailey tried to care for her at home, and he did, bless his heart, for three years. But Betty gradually got worse and couldn't care for anything about herself. She lasted nearly two more years in the nursing home. After she went there, Bailey ate at my place every day—he still does.

We left Betty's obituary up on our bulletin board for nearly a year, along with a copy of the memorial service. We collected other things relating to Betty's life and put them up there, too. There was a particularly funny letter she'd written to Grace Burns when Betty and some other church women had gone to a conference in Kansas City and absolutely everything had gone wrong. They'd had a flat tire, with all of them dressed up and none of them strong enough to loosen the lug nuts; and the hotel had lost the reservation so four of them had ended up in one room; and the food they ate at an all-night place had given all of them diarrhea; and they'd gone to the wrong place for the meetings and then lost the car in the huge parking garage. Then someone had lost her purse, and they'd spent half an afternoon trying to find the cleaning lady who spoke Philippine or some such. The letter went for six pages, all in Betty's exaggerated way, and she'd ended it with, "What a wonderful conference—the Lord has done great things. I'll never forget this trip." We also put up a picture of her and her two little granddaughters, Emily and Laurie. In that picture, Betty looks like a young woman, full of life. That's what we try to remember. Betty was the type of person you always imagined being around to help manage things, to be a friend no matter what.

My grandmother gave me my first journal when I was nine. It's still in the attic bedroom, full of things that were important to a nine-year-old in 1952. Gran Lenny wrote every day, in the morning and again in late afternoon. I asked her why one time, and she said, "To sort out my thoughts and to remember my dreams. To keep a bookmark in my important chapters." An ordinary person talking like that would sound snooty. But those words were natural to Gran Lenny. She said that most writing is for the writer's sake and needs no reader at all. Gran Lenny was not a warm person. The war had taken many things from her, and a few people in our family considered her halfway to loony. But she was the first person after my parents whom I truly loved. And she taught me how to treasure my life. She taught me how to write down my days. And I've found that, as hard as it can be to write painful things, it often helps.

I've tried writing about Betty, to put big bookmarks in those important chapters, but I'm always disappointed in my descriptions. If I describe what Betty actually looked like, people who didn't know her already wouldn't be interested. Just a grandmother who ate too many desserts and liked to talk to every human being she met. I try to write down my thoughts of her, and I just end up telling stories from her life. Although I don't see myself as a storyteller, I've been listening to other people's stories for years. I could give a detailed history of half the families in this town. I could write stories until I turned one hundred, and still have stories to spare. Of course, the most important stories are the ones no one wants to remember, much less hear. We've learned some hard lessons lately—more like afflictions of knowledge. I try to mention these stories and people look at me as if they're in a hurry to go somewhere else. I feel so frustrated by that.

I think I took the janitorial job at Jerusalem Baptist partly because my life was so heavy with other people's stories. I took the job just a couple of years after I started the café. The teenage girls they'd get to clean the church did a good enough job, but no one ever deep-cleaned the place. No one looked after the woodwork properly. By then, I was in my mid-forties, feeling more tired from running VELMA'S, and some folks, including Albert, thought I shouldn't add a cleaning job to that.

But I was finding the need for a quiet place, a room with no people and no noise. When I'm cleaning the sanctuary, which is often late Saturday night or early Wednesday morning, I'm the only person there.

It makes me calmer somehow to be in the Lord's house, polishing those walnut pews, putting fresh flowers on the altar, wiping cobwebs out of corners. Sometimes I hum the songs Mama used to hum when she was working out problems. Sometimes I quote poems my grand-mother wrote when I was just a girl. Sometimes I just cry and clean.

I think about my friends and family when I'm in the sanctuary. I think about them in a calmer, more direct way than at any other time. Sometimes, all I do is replay memories. I remember Betty and all those tables and chairs. I remember Bailey's face and the way his walk changed after he'd taken Betty to the nursing home. If I'm lucky, the good Lord will accept those memories as prayers.

I think of my dear husband, Albert, so much with me and yet so absent too. In all my storytelling, our relationship is the most impos-sible to give words to. In fact, I can review entire, long memories with-out my husband in them at all. Maybe someday I'll write Albert's and my story. Now is not the time.

In honor of Betty, my friend, I've kept a recipe—one of several dozen she offered over the years—for a cake-pudding dessert. Most of the desserts she clipped out of magazines were much too complicated for restaurant use. But this one worked, and it always pleased her to find servings of it in the counter display case.

Betty's Banana-Chocolate Pudding Cake

1 cup flour
2/3 cup sugar
4 tablespoons unsweetened cocoa powder
2 teaspoons baking powder
1/2 teaspoon salt
2/3 cup chopped walnuts
1 banana, halved lengthwise and sliced
1 tablespoon vegetable oil
1/2 cup milk

1/2 cup sweetened condensed milk
1/2 cup milk
2 tablespoons unsweetened cocoa powder
1/2 teaspoon vanilla extract
1/2 teaspoon almond extract

Heat oven to 350°. In a large mixing bowl, combine the flour, sugar, 4 tablespoons cocoa, baking powder, and salt. Add the walnuts, banana, oil, and 1/2 cup milk. Spread this batter (it will be fairly stiff and very sticky) into a lightly greased 8 x 8 baking pan.

In a small saucepan over low heat, combine the sweetened condensed milk, 1/2 cup milk, 2 tablespoons cocoa, and the extracts. When the cocoa has dissolved and the mixture is hot, pour it over the batter in the pan.

Bake 35 to 45 minutes, or until the liquid has set. Do not overbake. Serve warm with whipped cream or vanilla ice cream.

4

Gran Lenny

To them you are like a singer of love songs, one who has a beautiful voice and plays well on an instrument; they hear what you say, but they will not do it. When this comes—and come it will!—then they shall know that a prophet has been among them.

—EZEKIEL 33:32–33

Bailey Webb used to eat at my café three times a week; I set my calendar by him. Monday for a late breakfast—ham and eggs, biscuits and gravy. Tuesday lunch—split pea and ham soup with saltines, chased down with rice pudding. And Friday lunch. My special on Fridays was always meatloaf (or baked fish, for the Catholics), and Bailey liked two servings with brown gravy. From time to time, when his daughter, Leanne, was getting onto him about his weight, he'd have a little sliver of meatloaf, half as many mashed potatoes, and ladle brown gravy over white bread, which was his idea of cutting calories.

Bailey and I had attended the grammar school together, and he'd always been a head and a half taller than all the other kids. I never thought of him as fat, only solid. A more loyal man I've never known, excluding my own husband. And Bailey, even at his bulkiest, could outwork any man born in the same decade. Bailey labored over other

people's automobiles and was known for being honest. If you didn't
need a new part, he didn't try to sell you one. If he could find what you
did need in one of the three junkyards within twenty miles, he'd go
scavenge it. Considering all those fine points, it was hard to be critical
of his extra pounds. He had a weakness for good food. And no cook I
ever knew could get upset about that kind of weakness.

He also had a weakness for gossip, and that did irritate me. Feeding people all day long, I can't help overhearing their lives. I hear lots
of gossip I have no control over. But hearing it so many different ways
and from so many different sources makes me more hesitant than ever
to trust it, no matter where it comes from. Since Bailey and I go back
so far, I've never felt I was out of place calling him down when his
tongue got wagging.

One Tuesday in late May, he was sitting at the counter, finishing up
his soup. He tapped his spoon against the dish a certain way when he
was winding up to throw information my way.

"So how much money did Sissy Fenders come into, anyway?" he
asked.

"What money?"

"That old Mr. Fenders left her—last month. I heard it was near
fifty thousand."

"Don't you start."

"What, start? It's the gospel truth."

"There are only four Gospels."

"Well it's true as them."

"I've not heard a word about Sissy coming into money. And I hear
everything around here."

"Maybe people are just being considerate, knowin' that you and
Sissy aren't best friends." He took an extra long swallow of coffee. I
didn't answer him.

Sissy and I went way back, too. She'd loved tormenting me when
our families were neighbors. Every day I breathed, Sissy was at our
backyard gate, challenging me to some kind of contest. Who could do
her multiplication tables fastest, or who could read this book without
making any mistakes. Or who was tallest or had the nicest shoes.
Sissy's family sure didn't have money then, but they had more money
than mine did. I didn't like contests of any kind, but somehow Sissy
was able to pull me into one on any given day. I didn't lose that much
of the time, but it made me feel bad to have to stand there in my own
backyard and prove myself.

As we grew into our teens, Sissy continued to point out to me how she excelled. Our sophomore year, she got a date to a school dance with the boy I liked, and wouldn't she just have to take the garbage out to their backyard compost, in view of our supper table—in her dance dress. I'd never seen her take out garbage ever before, and here she was, parading down the garden path in bright blue, carrying coffee grounds and potato peelings like a queen.

Sissy went after Albert, too, and that was one time I was mad enough to stand up for myself. But I took my mother's advice for once and did the exact opposite of what I felt like doing, which was to have a catfight with Sissy at school in front of everybody. But catfights weren't really in my nature, and Mama said that I should show Albert what an absolute lady I could be, which would contrast with Sissy's flirting and badmouthing. Gran Lenny, who rarely got involved in family conversations, did join that one, and she told me Mama was right. So I didn't fight fire with fire. The more attention Sissy demanded, the calmer I got. It worked. Albert keyed into me and me into him as if we'd been designed that way all along. Sissy became like a pesky mosquito, and Albert just swatted her away.

Ever since then, Sissy hadn't had much to do with me. We were too old for backyard contests. Sissy's family moved to Tulsa for a number of years. Her older brother stayed in Leeway, already married and employed. Sissy would visit town to see him about once a year. She had married a man, had two children, and divorced him about ten years later. Then, just a few years ago, she had married a wealthy widower named Leland Scott. This suited Sissy, because Leland was wealthy and prestigious, traits that Sissy had always imagined should be hers. We never heard much from her, back in plain old Leeway.

To hear that Sissy Fenders Scott (no one could remember the first husband's name anymore) had come into even more money didn't really ruin my day. I suspected that Bailey had told me so I could get used to the idea before I overheard it at some other time. He wanted me to be able to say, "Oh, I knew that. Lucky, huh?" as if it didn't bother me at all. And actually, it didn't. I'd ended up with the right man after all, and a son I loved and good people in my life. Sissy's latest husband was a real estate developer, and we'd heard all about their huge house in one of Tulsa's up-and-coming areas. But people thought of Sissy mainly as a wealthy woman. They thought of me as the person who offered them hot meals and friendship. So what Sissy had in dollars, I had in smiles and small talk.

Bailey's voice broke into my memories. "She's wanting to set up her niece here in the antique business. I heard she's sniffing around Avery's to see if he might like to retire soon and close the store. Got her eye on that space."

"Now *that* I just don't believe. Avery wouldn't know what to do with himself if he didn't have the store. And Thad's going to take over before long."

"Some say Thad may be changing his mind."

"Nobody's said it here." I made a little grunt, then, as I wiped the counter down for the third time. Then I had to stand still, because I recognized that grunt. I'd just made the sound my grandmother used to make when company had stayed too long. It drove Mama and Papa nuts, wondering how long it would take Lenora to start getting discourteous when people were over to visit. At least she only grunted and then rose like a judge from her chair and went upstairs to her room. She'd never say anything mean to people, just that little grunt that told everybody she was bored. When I was a little girl, I followed Mama's example and got embarrassed about it. But as I got a bit older and learned to know my grandmother better, I always felt a little proud that she spoke her own mind.

"Oh well, Velma, even if Sissy's niece ends up with her little store next door, it wouldn't be the same as Sissy herself being here. I think she's in Tulsa for good. Need to get that Thomas jalopy going." Bailey slid off the stool, one cheek at a time. I gave a little laugh. Pastor Thomas had more car trouble than any man of God I'd ever known.

"Take care, Velma."

I watched Bailey step into the shade of the awning and then into the bright sun on the street. He crossed it to walk down the shady side, where our little park was, to get to his garage two blocks down. I saw him pass two older gentlemen who sat on a bench under the mimosa tree. It looked like Mike, our retired postmaster, and his buddy Tom, who had moved to Leeway when he retired from the railroad. They nodded to Bailey as he walked by. Tom's hand was resting on a cane, and for an instant he looked just like Mr. Barnhof, who'd been dead nearly twenty years. Thinking of him made my mind circle around again to my grandmother.

Lenora was always Gran Lenny to me. My favorite photograph of her is one I took myself with the new Brownie I'd received for my tenth birthday. Gran Lenny was sitting on the bench in front of Barnhof's Pharmacy with Mr. Barnhof and the tailor, Mr. Grimes. She tended to talk more with the men in town—was never one to wander the neighborhood chattering with other women. She liked to smoke occasionally, and that day she was puffing away with the gentlemen as they talked politics or books or the weather. Gran Lenny was in her late sixties then, and she wore trousers like a man. Trousers and a shirt and an olive-green cardigan. She wore a touch of rouge and lipstick, a locket of German silver, and her waist-length hair, with dramatic white streaks in it, bundled up at the back of her head. Usually her black-rimmed half glasses hung below her collar by a chain. Gran Lenny's feet were deformed from arthritis, and I can't remember a time when she wasn't wearing sneakers, white and clean as if she never wore them out on the sidewalks and streets of Leeway.

There she sat, feet glowing white in the shade of the awning, Mr. Barnhof on one side and Mr. Grimes on the other. I aimed the camera and told them to smile. The two men obliged me, but Gran Lenny dipped her chin and shot a black, unblinking gaze through my lens. I knew better than to ask twice, so I sighed and snapped. But just before I hit the button, Gran Lenny's mouth opened, and she flashed the most wonderful smile I'd ever seen. Her eyes seemed to have happy secrets behind them.

I've often regretted that I didn't find the courage during those years to ask my grandmother important questions. But when you're a child, you don't know what those questions are. Some questions don't present themselves until the people who might have answered them are already dead. But I can't help but think that I could have paid better attention, even back then.

Lenora was full-blooded German, tight-lipped and a mystery to most people. She immigrated to Philadelphia near the close of World War I, her soldier husband dead and her two daughters with her. The older one, Gertrude, my Aunt Trudy, was twelve, and my mother, Greta, was five. They lived with cousins who had been in Pennsylvania for a generation already. Then, five years later, Gertrude married another immigrant, a house builder who had dreams of being a wheat farmer in the American Midwest. A short span of years and a series of moves later, they landed in the eastern part of Kansas. They brought Lenora and teenaged Greta with them.

Gran Lenny was one person who would have been happy never to see Leeway. Back in Germany, when she was a young woman, everyone had called her Lenora. She had studied literature at the University of Munich and was known as a poet. She had kept some of her literature books and poetry collections, but they disappeared sometime during my early childhood.

Gran Lenny could be stormy and silent all at once. She preferred to stay to herself up in the large attic bedroom. That small domain was hers alone, and Mama was the only adult who ever ventured up that final flight of stairs; for some reason she could be in Gran Lenny's presence when others couldn't. Aunt Trudy was the older of the two daughters, but she and Gran Lenny did well to exist in the same house. Aunt Trudy would chop vegetables loudly in the pantry so no one could hear her muttering about her mother.

A few people close to the family knew that Gran Lenny wrote poetry, but she didn't let anyone read her work. Mama told me once that that hadn't been the case in Gran Lenny's younger years. She and other writers would meet at each others' homes and read to one another. And when Lenora was particularly pleased with something she'd written, and when it had gone over well among her peers, sometimes she would recite it at the dinner table at home. Trudy and Mama were little girls then. In fact, Aunt Trudy really remembered more about those years, but she hardly ever spoke of them.

Mama said that Gran Lenny's poetry took a sad turn once she came to the States. It was the war and all the death the war had brought that changed Lenora's words. But when I was a girl and Gran Lenny allowed me to read some of her poems, they weren't about the war at all, or about moving to Philadelphia and then ending up in Leeway. They were about things a person might not notice in the course of the day—the way sunlight drifted over the petunia bed or how music changed into something else when you listened to it from a distance. She did frequently use heavy words, but in a lovely way. When I read them, I felt as though I'd lifted the lid of a box and found strange, beautiful things inside, objects that gleamed in odd, new colors—both dark and light. They were objects I didn't recognize, but it made me feel rich just to have the lid up, looking at them.

I didn't think about any of these things when Gran Lenny was actually alive. She was just Gran Lenny to me. She lived in the family house and had what people called a dark temperament. But now that I'm moving toward the age she was then, I wish I had known the right questions to ask her. I want to know what it was like to leave her house in Munich and her circle of artist friends and her reputation and her books. I want to know if coming to America made it hard to write her poetry again. Or if she wrote letters to the other writers back in Germany. I helped her burn nearly all of her keepsakes just before she died, and the only letters with German postmarks on them were from an aunt long gone and a cousin from the other side of the family. No Munich addresses at all.

Mama used to say that Gran Lenny was always better off than she seemed, that she enjoyed being alone and spending hours just thinking. Mama said that a person didn't change personalities simply because she changed locations. But I've since wondered how much of what Mama said was designed to protect me from the truth.

What's strange is that I was the one person in our family who got close to Gran Lenny. I was small and quiet, and by the time I was eight or nine, Gran Lenny was letting slip to me bits and pieces of her life. She was her most generous when she decided, very occasionally, to feed us. When she cooked, she would serve up helpings too large even for the biggest man among us. With her own life, though, she seemed stingy, and asking her personal questions usually dampened her mood. But I was just a child, and she seemed to like me most of the time, and I learned how to ask questions without really asking. Come to think of it, I do the same thing now, when I talk to people and want to know how they are but feel uncomfortable asking directly. People open up to me as if I was Dear Abby, and I guess I have that moody old woman to thank.

Gran Lenny talked most easily and happily about words, about their shades of meaning and the best order to put them in. She talked about words as if each and every one of them were a person. "This word is too weak. It cannot convey what it needs to mean. Always look for a word that is stronger and more articulate." "When you put the word at this place in the sentence, it just sits there. You want every word to *move*, even if just a very little movement. If like that it sits, people will think it died." "Do you mean a yellow that is happy, or a yellow that is sick in its organs?" I learned most of what I know about people from the way Gran Lenny talked about words. When I would dare to bring her one of my English assignments from school, she would act annoyed, but in a few minutes she was chattering like an old gossip.

Gran Lenny kept journals. She liked to sit in the kitchen while she read or wrote in one of her many notebooks. She said that the light through the south window was just right. Sometimes she'd not write for a long time, just sit and study the grain of that maple tabletop.

I liked being around my grandmother, but she didn't like people bothering her while she read or thought or wrote. And it was hard to know for certain that she wasn't doing any of those things. But kitchen noises didn't seem to disturb her, so the summer I was nine I began to find chores to do in the kitchen while she was writing. At first, I'd gather forks and cups and plates (some of them from underneath potted plants) to put in the kitchen sink, would wait until the water had filled it up to the top, pouring in the soap, my hand swishing suds, glancing over at Gran Lenny at the kitchen table. I'd wash everything in sight, then clean cabinets and about every surface I could find.

Then one day I glanced toward the table and Gran Lenny was staring at me. Her eyes were black as ripe olives. "Vellie, I'm hungry. Find something, would you?" The eyes shifted back to her notebook.

I felt a panic but found a few things I wouldn't have to cook, since Mama didn't allow me near the stove. In a few minutes I set a plate in front of Gran Lenny. She saw what I'd done and put down her pen. "Well."

I'd spread peanut butter over saltine crackers—then swirled just a dab of dark Karo syrup on each. A shiny apple sat next to the crackers. Next to the apple was a dill pickle.

"Vellie, you have an interesting mind," Gran Lenny turned the plate slowly so she could see it from every angle. "Why the pickle?"

"If your tongue gets tired of the sweet, then you can have sour."

"And the apple?"

"Because it's good for you. I'd slice it and make it pretty, but Mama won't let me use knives."

Gran Lenny stepped over to the knife block and pulled out the paring knife. She sat down and began slicing the apple. "May I share with you?" Her heavy eyebrows were sharp against her pale forehead. She held up an apple slice.

I said yes. Gran Lenny kept nodding and said again, "You have an interesting mind."

When we finished, she wiped her mouth and said, "Stop with all the cleaning. You're too young to have dishwater hands."

I felt scolded, but then she said, "Every day at ten you come in here and fix a snack for us. I need to take a break by then, and a bit of food helps me think more clearly."

Before long, Gran Lenny got tired of my limited menu. She'd get up from the table and make our snack. Right away she caught me sneaking looks at her writing. The first time, it was a poem. She said, "Go ahead and read it."

After I stared at it a few seconds, she said, "Read it out loud. A writer must hear her work if she wants to find all its flaws."

I was suddenly scared, staring at the journal page. These were Gran Lenny's private words. It didn't help that they were in German.

"Bring the chair here next to me. I can help you with words you don't know."

That's how I learned to read both poetry and German.

So some days I made our mid-morning snack. Other days Gran Lenny made it. When she got up from the table, she would always turn her notebook to a page she didn't mind my reading. It was nearly always a poem. I would never have thought to turn the pages myself. I stayed right on the page she left for me.

By the time I was ten, Gran Lenny was cooking lunch for us and teaching me her favorite dishes. And I was reading well, even had the courage to offer my opinion sometimes. A time or two, I substituted a word as I read. She caught that in a flash, but said go ahead, she could always consider an improvement. Sometimes she would explain why her word was better. Only twice that I can remember did she agree that I had found the perfect word and directed me to mark through hers and put mine in. I wouldn't have glowed more if you'd named me First Lady.

When I was twelve, I began creating my own recipes while Gran Lenny worked. Lunchtime would come, and I'd set a plate in front of her. After we had eaten, she would either tell me, "Write this one down, Vellie" or "This needs some adjusting." To her, words and cooking required the same kind of skill and care. There was a difference between marjoram and rosemary, and that difference could mean success or not. There was a difference between "blueness streaming down the sky" and "bluish streaks in the clouds," and because that difference was important to Gran Lenny, it became important to me.

I never became gifted with words, as Gran Lenny was. But when I was fourteen and had prepared dinner for Aunt Trudy and Cousin Elizabeth and others who had traveled to have Easter dinner at our table, Gran Lenny announced, "Velma is a chef, and the rest of us merely cooks." For a long, glorious, fearful moment, all eyes turned to me, little Vellie who wasn't much to look at and who was generally shy, and they smiled. And my father raised his hands and applauded.

The others followed him, smiling brightly. I giggled, and then I started to cry and left the table. I heard Papa say with a chuckle, "Lenora, you've embarrassed her."

"She'll live through it." Gran Lenny had returned to her pretense of being annoyed with all of us. But after that, and ever since, I've cooked as though I were a chef. A person's words have the power to create, not only on paper, but in another human being. Gran Lenny helped God that day to create me. I was born again in a way different from being born again at the altar of the church. Gran Lenny had rebirthed me. That's what it felt like at least. I do believe that I'm still living as the person I became that evening.

I've really let my mind run on about Gran Lenny. I actually go a long time without thinking of her much, all these years after her death. But any grief brings her back to me. The grief I feel these days makes me long again for my grandmother.

One memory stands out—of a day (I was probably ten) I read aloud a poem she had finished. It was about a flower that bloomed during the night and about a little girl who came to sing her own little song when the flower opened. When dawn came, the flower closed and the little girl went home. Her home was so ugly that she wouldn't speak all day, but save all her words for her night flower.

I finished reading. Gran Lenny asked, "Why are you looking like that at me?"

"Your poem hurts me."

"How does it hurt you?"

"It's gray and sad. A lot of your poems are like that."

Gran Lenny, her back straight as always, gave a sniff and turned back to the kitchen counter. She was cutting up meat for stew.

"It's about night and death," I said. "I don't like reading about those things."

"Then stop reading!" She turned just enough for her eyes to glitter at me over her half glasses. "I don't ask you to read them."

She turned her back to me again. I really wanted to read Gran Lenny's poems, but at the moment I didn't know why. And with her back to me, I felt as if I'd just lost a good friend. The only thing to do was cry.

So I sniffled as quietly as I could, looking away from Gran Lenny and into the living room. I heard her stop with the knife and put it down. I felt her stare at the eye-level cupboard in front of her. Then I felt her turn around slowly and walk the three steps to the table and sit down. She always smelled of lavender.

"A writer is not a short-order cook. Hamburger for this person. Potatoes and pork for that one." Her voice was sharp, but I could tell she was trying to be humorous. "We develop tastes from our experiences. Many of my experiences are gray and sad." She slapped the tabletop lightly with the palm of her hand. "And this is what I write. Sometime maybe I can write happy just for you, OK?"

"OK." My little tears dried up. "But why can't the girl at least bring her friends at night to see the flower? Does she have to be so lonely?"

Gran Lenny tightened her lips, not in anger, but in thought. Then she shrugged. "I don't know. I didn't think about her having friends to bring. The poem was about her."

"Are you the little girl?"

We stared at each other. Her eyes opened a little wider, from surprise I suppose, and mine opened wider, too, because I'd frightened myself by being so direct.

"Well." Gran Lenny stared at me a bit longer. "I suppose I could be, yes. What do you think of that?"

"I don't want you to be by yourself in the dark." I felt tiny pinpoints in my eyes.

"Oh child." She closed her eyes and sighed. "You think too much. But since you can't help yourself, think about this: *you* are my night flower." Her eyes got wide a last time, and she tapped my arm with a long, strong finger. "Hmm?" Then she got up from the table and went back to the meat on the counter. "Enough poetry for you. Be outdoors for a while." She muttered something else in German and laughed a little bit to herself.

Now I watched Bailey make his way, bearlike, down the street, and I stared at Mike and Tom and tried to see Mr. Barnhof and Mr. Grimes and Gran Lenny. But the picture wouldn't come. I turned back to my counter and my kitchen and the near-empty restaurant. There were just four other customers, all sitting near the windows, finishing their lunch. I wondered, as I've often wondered, if Gran Lenny had ever expected me to be a real chef in some big city. I wondered if it would disappoint her to see me still in Leeway after all this time. And if she'd ever thought I would write more than English papers, maybe go to college, maybe write about times and places outside of my own town.

It did bother me to know that Sissy Fenders Scott might make her way back to Leeway again. I'd always prided myself on not collecting enemies. But some enemies you don't collect; they just show up and decide to stay. Gran Lenny managed not to have enemies. For one thing, she made a point of pretending her English was not so good, although she had better command of English than most people. She made a point, too, of keeping people at a distance. She said one time that most enemies are friends who went sour. I suppose that staying up in her room kept away the people who might have turned sour on her. I knew she'd had some good friends back home, the Grettingers. My mother Greta was named after them. Gran Lenny had some books in which they'd written greetings. She had letters, too, from years and years before. I do believe that Gran Lenny's dearest friends were books and the words that filled them.

I wish Gran Lenny were with me now. Now that words are rushing at me too fast to count and memories are suddenly around every corner. My grandmother was haunted by memories, some I didn't know about until long after she was gone. Then I understood that a lot of what she wrote was just to get her through those memories. Even her poems, sad as they were, were a kind of salvation to her.

I hope that the writing and remembering I'm doing now will save me too. I find that not only am I haunted by my own memories but by those that belonged to my mother and to her mother before her. What an odd legacy, and what do you do with it? Keep passing it on? I think some things are better not remembered, and though they are inheritances, they are not good gifts.

Gran Lenny's Pear & Beet Salad

2 pears (not over-ripe) julienned
2 medium beets, cooked whole, cooled, peeled, and julienned
1 tablespoon butter
1/4 cup red onion, finely chopped
1/8 cup orange rind, finely chopped
1/4 cup golden raisins
1/4 teaspoon allspice
1/4 teaspoon ground cloves
1 tablespoon brown sugar; dark is best
1 tablespoon cider vinegar
1 tablespoon water or orange juice
Salt and pepper to taste

Combine beets and pears. In a small skillet or saucepan, melt the butter. Saute onions with the orange peel.

Add raisins, spices, brown sugar, vinegar, and water or orange juice to the onions and orange peel.

Cook the sauce on medium-low heat not more than 10 minutes. If the sauce thickens too much, add a little water or orange juice.

While sauce is still warm, pour it over the beets and pears. Stir well and refrigerate. Serve cold.

5

Cousin Howard

Mortal, your kinsfolk . . . your fellow exiles . . . are those of whom the inhabitants of Jerusalem have said, "They have gone far from the Lord" . . . Though I scattered them among the countries, yet I have been a sanctuary to them for a little while in the countries where they have gone.

—Ezekiel 11:15–16

When Albert's cousin, Howard, called in late May of '96, he asked if he could come to Leeway and live with us while he died. We'd not heard from him or anyone from that branch of the family for about six years. All Howard would say was that he had cancer and he didn't expect to last but a few months, or a year at most. He didn't go into detail, and of course I didn't ask for details.

Howard had been laid off from his job before the diagnosis, so that once he needed treatments, there was no health insurance. That's the short version. There was a lot about Howard's health I didn't know for a lot of the time he stayed with us, some of it not until right before he left us.

When he called that May, Howard was about to lose his apartment because he'd had to quit the new job he'd had for only a few months,

He'd been sick about a year. He said to me on the phone, his voice clear but tired, "I just don't have the strength right now to find another job. I don't want to work the last months of my life. And I want to be with family when I die."

He didn't have to make a case for us; we decided the moment we heard his voice that we'd be happy to have him with us. Howard said he could be on a bus in four days, if somebody could pick him up in Parsons. We told him to tell us the time and place.

It happened that Bailey Webb and John Mason were going to Parsons to an estate auction on the same day Howard was arriving, so he rode back to Leeway with them. I knew both of them would talk his ears off, but if anybody could make him feel welcomed into Leeway, it was those two.

The last we'd seen Howard was when he was twenty-six and had just got his master's degree in business. Howard's dad, Harvey, had decided to bring his new wife to his high school reunion in Leeway, on their way to a vacation in New Orleans. Howard had come along because they were going to drop him off at a friend's in Springfield. Howard was quiet and polite, but it was clear he wasn't too interested in Leeway or any of us relatives. Albert and I had figured out by the end of the visit that Howard and Harvey had barely said a word to each other the whole time. And Howard and Pearle never spoke to or looked at one another at all. He was a thin young man with dark hair and light freckles. And he was angry.

I wondered how much angrier Howard would be now that he was thirty-eight and dying. I was a little afraid of that—would he never talk to us, or would he sit up in his bedroom and make unreasonable demands? It wasn't lost on me that he was asking to stay with us instead of with Pearle, Harvey's widow, who lived in Parsons. It would have been natural for him to at least visit Pearle before he came on to Leeway. But Bailey told me later that Howard had been sitting at the bus station half the day as if he had no family in town. He was pleasant with Bailey and John, and he seemed to enjoy hanging around the auction. But he never mentioned his stepmother. Bailey said how sorry he'd been to hear of Harvey's passing, and Howard just looked at him, sort of blank. My, you never know what's going on in a family. I would curl up and die if my own son never wanted to talk to me. I don't see Jimmy more than once a year some years, but once we get together, we jabber like old ladies in the post office lobby.

So the day Howard came up our front walk, carrying one suitcase with Bailey carrying another one behind him, I prepared myself to make conversation. I was remembering that afternoon's visit back when he and Harvey and Pearle had stopped by. I didn't expect a warm, older man to smile at me as if he'd waited years to give me a hug. He said, "Cousin Velma, it's so good to see you." Then he put down his suitcase and grabbed me and held on for a long time. "Thank you for letting me come stay a little while," he said in a shaky voice close to my ear.

"You're always welcome here, Howard. Wish you hadn't waited so long to call."

I sent him and Bailey upstairs to the east bedroom with Howard's luggage. I made coffee. Howard asked if I made the pie, and Bailey informed him that I made three or four pies every morning and that I had my own restaurant.

Sitting across the dining room table from Howard, I could see that the faint freckles were still there, scattered across his nose. But the color of his skin was more pale than fair. On the surface, his eyes looked fine, but if you looked right into them for long, you felt yourself touched by pain. For a second, Howard's eyes reminded me of Gran Lenny. His fingernails were bitten and sore looking, and the veins stood out along almost hairless arms. He was wearing a dark green pullover, with the sleeves pushed up nearly to his elbows. His lips were chapped. The jeans he wore stuck out on him, almost a size too big. He'd let his hair grow down to his collar and combed it back away from his face. Nice teeth. The only thing that looked unhealthy about him was the whole picture of him. If you saw just his eyes or his legs or the way his shirt fit him, you wouldn't think he was dying. But back up a step and take in the whole man, pressing himself into the back of the dining room chair, sitting not quite straight, something seemed small and weak about him. He let his arms rest on the table while we talked, and it occurred to me that he seemed to be propping himself up. Something about the way he sat gave his body a tired, uncomfortable look.

After a while, Bailey left. I took Howard on a tour of the house, showed him where the food and dishes, linens and towels were, how to work the coffeemaker and the washer and dryer. We ended up in his bedroom. This room, the largest of the two bedrooms on the second floor, had been my room when I was a girl, then Mama's room when she was a widow and Albert and I had taken her and Papa's room downstairs. We'd offered to let her keep the first-floor bedroom, but she wanted a different room that didn't remind her so much of Papa. Now, with Howard sitting on the bed, I felt that I was in a different house altogether. So much of what makes a room familiar has to do with the people in it. Howard sat on Mama's pinwheel quilt, and I noticed the darker patches more than the lighter ones. I'd always thought there was a lot of lavender in the design, but Howard's dark clothes and hair brought out the small strips of black and brown. It didn't look like an old woman's bedspread anymore. That little transformation seemed strange to me.

"Thank you again for taking me in," said Howard, looking nervous for the first time, maybe because he was alone with someone, no one else around to carry conversation. He pushed the hair back from his face for about the eleventh time that evening. "To help me out like this on such short notice."

"I just hope you'll make yourself at home. I'm a little concerned that you're so far from your doctor. Will you see somebody around here?"

"Uh, yes, I'll be looking into that in a couple of days." He cleared his throat. "I've got enough prescriptions to get me through the month, but I suppose whoever I go to will want to do all his own tests." He looked up at me. "Then again, I don't think any of the medicine's doing much good. I may go faster and easier if I don't fool with any of that."

"So they don't give you any hope at all?"

"Not really." Howard cleared his throat again. "I mean, they'll treat symptoms for as long as I last, because that's what they're supposed to do. But symptoms are just symptoms." He pushed back his hair again. "I'm feeling pretty tired."

"I hope you sleep well. Just poke around in the bathroom until you find whatever you need. We hardly use the one on this floor, but there should be toothpaste and shampoo and the like."

"I'll be fine." Howard was up and pulling back the quilt and the sheet underneath. He looked so eager to be asleep that I thought he might crawl in with his clothes on. I shut the door behind me.

The next morning was Thursday, when I open the café later and serve evening dinner. By eight o'clock, I had pancakes and hash browns for us to eat at home. Howard came down the stairs in sweatpants and a T-shirt.

"I didn't know if you'd be up this early or not," I said, pouring him coffee.

"Hard to sleep with all these aromas coming up the stairs. Is that the newspaper?" He sat at the kitchen table and reached for the paper. I noticed how bony his arm was. His hair was combed, but his eyes were still trying to open up.

"What do you plan to do with your time?" I asked. Then I regretted it right away. What a thing to ask a dying man. But Howard looked up and seemed to be searching for an answer. He crunched on a slice of bacon.

"Well. I need to write some letters. Let people know the situation. Not a lot of people—I never had a lot of friends. But there are several people I've known a long time who would want to know."

"That sounds like a good thing to do."

"And I thought I'd try to take walks every day. Just quiet walks in the country to clear my mind."

"You've come to the right place. Go eight or ten blocks in any direction and you're in the country around here."

"I like to read, and I've never had time to read a lot of the books I've heard about."

"I know what you mean. So many good books to read, but I fall asleep by the second page, no matter what it is. Once I'm home and off my feet, the energy just drains out of me."

"That's been the worst thing about being sick. I'll be in the middle of something and then suddenly get so tired I want to die." Howard didn't look at me when he said this. He didn't appear to be talking to me at all. His eyes were focused somewhere out the window.

We didn't have much to say after that. I went up to the café and thought about Howard and his plans. Something didn't add up right. I liked Howard—had liked him the minute he came up my walk. But I found it hard to believe what he said. Oh, I believed he was dying, but his plans didn't sound too convincing. He reminded me of my son Jimmy, when he was little. How he would tell me stories, and I would know he was making up every last word, but I also knew he believed every word, too. Those times, I wouldn't get after him for lying. At some level, he was being truthful, so I just let him be.

I decided that, at some level, Howard was being truthful. But I wondered how much of the truth Howard had hold of. He was doing the right things, preparing himself for death, as much as a person can.

But there didn't seem to be much feeling in it. His feelings weren't living even in the same house as Howard. That made me worry.

On Sunday, I got ready for church as usual. I don't cook breakfast on Sundays. Just put cereal and fruit on the table. And I leave early to open the church and make sure no one's messed up the sanctuary or Sunday school rooms since Wednesday night prayer meeting. I was halfway out the back door when I heard Howard's voice calling from the dining room.

"You going to church?"

I turned around. Howard looked sleepy, but he was dressed.

"Yes. I have to open up the building."

"Oh." He looked at me, that blank look again. Then, out of the blankness, his mouth formed words. "Can I come?"

"Of course! You want to walk up with me now? Or come later, in time for Sunday school or church?"

"I'll go now, if that's all right."

We walked together through the breezy morning. I like the way May can be cool but not chilly. The sun was up, and the colors outdoors were fresh, just grown out of winter. Buds and leaves everywhere. Smell of grass and water hoses. Howard perked up a little, keeping a healthy pace with me.

We went inside the church, and I cracked open about half the windows in the sanctuary to let the fresh air move through and chase out the smell of closed-up winter spaces. Lonnie Myers came in a half hour later to practice the piano. That twenty minutes or so has always been a pleasant time for me, when the church is empty except for me straightening the altar flowers and Lonnie playing through hymns. Lonnie plays as if she were taking a stroll, as people trickle in, in all their various states of mind. Older folks generally just find their pew and sit quietly or visit with one another. The young people burst in and add movement to the room. And the families—well, anyone who's ever gotten a carload of kids ready for church and moved a husband out the door in clothes that match knows that peace of mind does not occur on Sunday mornings. The mothers arrive with their faces tight, trying to work bits of hairdo back in place while herding little ones to their respective spots. Dads either aren't awake yet or are in a bad mood because they are fully awake and don't want to be. Teenagers don't want to have anything to do with moms or dads, and the little ones think the morning and the sanctuary and everything in them were placed on earth especially for them.

It's quite a wonder, watching people come in the doors before worship. It's even more wonderful to watch them be transformed after a bit of prayer and singing. Their faces relax, and Pastor Thomas gets them to chuckle a bit, and the little ones snuggle into their parents' sides, and at that moment when Mom and Dad look down at those little heads, they have peace on their faces and gentleness in their eyes.

I didn't have time to watch folks this morning, because Howard stood close beside me, and I introduced him to just about every person who walked in. I'd tell them who Howard was, and their faces would light up, and they'd reach out to shake hands. Howard was eager to receive their fellowship. I watched him talk with people, and he looked hungry to be welcomed. There was a moment when Tanya Reddings stood, a child on either side of her, talking with Howard as if they were old friends, and I had a funny sense about Howard. That maybe if he weren't standing there in Jerusalem Baptist this morning, he would be in some horrible trouble. A chill ran through me, and I asked Jesus to make sure I knew what to do with Howard. On the one hand, he'd been real straightforward with us about his situation, and I trusted him. But on the other hand, I suspected there were secrets, I hoped not ugly ones.

We had a sweet time of worship that first Sunday Howard was here. Sometimes the weather and the angels conspire to give us an especially nice time. The breeze made everyone feel calm, and it seemed that all the hymns were favorites. And, in spite of my struggle to make peace with how Pastor Thomas and the deacons had dealt with Shellye Pines and Len Connor, I was able to listen with humility when Pastor preached. And some of what he said rang true to me.

I'd noticed that Shellye wasn't there. It had been only three weeks since that awful meeting with the deacons and two families. And Shellye hadn't been back to church since. As I looked around at the good spirit that morning, and as Howard sang along beside me through every hymn, I wanted to have Shellye there, too. She was going to have a baby, and she needed good people around her. Except that, in her mind, no one at the church wanted anything to do with her. I tried to figure out what I could do to fix that.

"That's a really nice church, Velma," Howard said as we made our leisurely way home after the service. "Thanks for taking me."

"I'm glad you came. You can come all the time. We'd all like that."

"It's been a long time since I've been to church. I quit in my teens, you know, like a lot of kids."

"Most people come back sooner or later. Especially when they start having babies."

"Or when they have a crisis." Howard kicked a small stone so that it skidded ahead of us. "Hard times make you see things differently. Shoot, when you're a kid, you feel like, one way or another, you'll beat every trouble that pops up. Maybe that's for the best. Otherwise, young people would never leave home or try anything." He laughed a little, but he sounded tired.

I thought a moment before I spoke again. "You know, Howard, I've known John Mason for years—the deacon you met? He can be a good one to talk to when a person has a lot on his mind."

Howard was quiet so long that I feared I had offended him. Then I heard him sigh. "Not much to talk about, Velma. I've made some big mistakes in my life. And now my life's about to be over. I don't know whether to be mad or repentant. I don't know if praying or talking to a deacon or preacher is what I want to do."

"I can understand that. Just know that, if you want to talk, there are people around."

The next evening, Howard was so weak, his hands shook while he ate. I tried not to look alarmed from across the table. I'd brought us home leftover chicken and noodles, Monday's special. He'd take a few bites, then rest his head in his hands.

"Is there anything I can do?" I asked. I felt Albert's breathing next to me. I could feel how worried he was, too, about Howard.

"Oh, no, I don't think so." He took a deep breath, only it didn't seem to fill his lungs at all. "This damn thing has just got hold of me." His voice trembled. "One day I think I'm feeling better; the next I'm afraid that if I go to sleep, I won't wake up."

"Oh Howard." I could see that the man was trying not to cry. "Are you sure we shouldn't take you to the hospital? Are you having trouble breathing?"

"Yeah, but the breathing part's panic—you know, anxiety attacks. They come as a result of everything else." He'd recovered for the moment, and he looked at us, his eyes still a bit moist. "If I went to the emergency room, they'd run all the same tests on me every other doctor has run when I got like this. And they wouldn't know any more afterwards than I knew going in. I've been going through this for nearly a year now. I'm paying off bills from my second and third trips to the emergency room. I'm not paying any more."

He took a moment to recover from making such a long speech, then picked up his fork and ate another bite of chicken. Albert and I watched him and, although Albert didn't say anything, I knew he was angry. Angry that a young man should be so sick and have no hope of recovering. Angry that we couldn't do anything. I looked at the chicken and noodles and creamed peas and wondered if there was anything else I could cook, maybe a calf liver or a big steak, something that had strength in it.

Howard stayed in bed the next three days. He had a bloody nose that was hard to stop, but it did eventually. He got up to have early breakfast with me, but he didn't walk with me to the café. As far as I knew, he spent the day upstairs sleeping, and then he'd bring himself downstairs to have supper with us. By the third evening, he looked a little better, almost had regular color in his cheeks. Friday morning, he walked me up to the café. He stayed there most of the day, sitting at the counter and introducing himself or getting introduced by me to the regulars who came in.

On Saturday, Howard left me at the café and walked two blocks over to Leeway's two-room library. No sooner had he disappeared from my doorway than Bailey walked in. I heard the jingle bell on the door as it opened, but it didn't jingle the second time, the way it does when the door closes behind a customer. I peeked out of the kitchen and saw Bailey half in, half out of the doorway, looking in the direction Howard had just gone.

"What are you looking at?" I called.

"That cousin of Albert's." Bailey walked up to the counter and took his perch. "How old did you say he is?"

"Thirty-eight."

"Lord, he looks older than that. What's wrong with him?"

"Cancer."

"What kind?"

"I don't know. He didn't say, at least not yet."

"He taking treatments?"

"No. I guess the treatments did all they could. He came here to die."

Bailey slurped his coffee. "You think he's telling the truth?"

"Why wouldn't he?"

Bailey shrugged. "Got something to hide?"

"I've not got that impression."

"Maybe he's got AIDS. It's incurable, and it affects just about everything. Some people get sick one way, others in other ways. It can look like a lot of different diseases. Is he married?"

"Not that I know of." That last question made me think. How could such a nice young man not have a family of his own? After all, he'd only been sick for a year or so.

"You think he's homosexual?"

I stopped wiping the counter and looked at Bailey. "Why in the world would you even think that? Even if he has AIDS, everybody knows a lot of people get it who aren't homosexual. Where do you get these ideas? For heaven's sake, don't repeat them anywhere."

"Oh, I wouldn't do that. I just don't want you taken advantage of."

"I won't be. And I think he'd say if he had AIDS."

"Why?"

"Don't know. But I think he'd say."

Leave it to Bailey to put thoughts in my head. I found myself watching Howard extra careful during the next couple of weeks. Even on his good days, he looked so gray and weightless, I didn't expect him to last a month.

The next Sunday afternoon, Pastor Thomas knocked on my front door. As I walked over to open it, I thought through every possible thing I could have forgotten to do at the church. Was the women's Bible study tomorrow? But that was usually the third Monday.

"Hi, Velma. How are you this afternoon?" Somehow, the man always sounded too formal when he talked to me. I'd known him for years but still felt a bit of discomfort around him.

"Fine. And you?"

"All right." He stepped into the living room. It was a warm day, but he wore his suit jacket, which usually meant that the visit was official. "Howard asked me to come by. Is he here?"

"Oh, have a seat, Pastor. I'll get him." Pastor Thomas sat on the sofa, and I went up to the second floor and found Howard in the small, overstuffed chair near the window.

"Pastor Thomas is here."

Howard didn't say a word, just got up and followed me downstairs. He went into the living room and greeted Pastor Thomas, and I headed for the kitchen to put on water for tea. Pastor had cut back on his caffeine and had stopped drinking coffee past noon.

One feature I've always enjoyed about our house is that there are no doors shutting off the kitchen from the dining room or the dining room from the living room. That part of the house is like a continuous room, with large, arched doorways making a tunnel from one end of the house to the other. And sound carries through the tunnel real well. So, as long as I didn't clatter around too much, I could hear Howard and Pastor's conversation. I didn't catch every word, but I was able to make sense of most of it.

Howard: "Velma may not have told you, but I have a terminal condition."

Pastor: "No, she didn't tell me. I suppose she thought it best if you tell me yourself. I'm so sorry to hear that."

Howard: "I could last a few months or a year or more. The condition gets worse and better on its own, it seems. For a while, the chemo worked, but then it didn't. I'm off the treatments right now."

Pastor: "How can we help you, son?"

Howard: "I'm not sure. I'm not sure I believe in Jesus or in anything much. Never been one to pray. I feel like I should be preparing myself somehow. But I'm pretty ignorant when it comes to spiritual things."

Pastor: "Well, most of us are ignorant, but God takes us right where we are. And when we cry out to God, he helps us believe."

Howard: "That's good to know."

Pastor: "We can start by praying a prayer right out of the New Testament: Lord, I believe. Help my unbelief."

Howard: "Yeah, I think I could pray that. . . . I need help with things like making a will, uh, taking care of things . . . some days I don't concentrate well enough to remember my name. I may need to live in a home or something . . . I don't know what to do . . . Velma's been generous to welcome me here, but I can't be a burden . . ."

By then, Howard was weeping. I could hear what sounded like short sighs—they could have been someone laughing quietly. But they were a sick man's sobs. The tea was ready, but I stood with the tray at the kitchen counter, knowing I couldn't walk in just then.

Pastor: "Howard, we'll do one thing at a time. And God will give you enough time to do whatever you need to do. Let's keep that in mind, all right?"

Howard: "I don't want to take up too much of your time. I know you look after a lot of people—"

Pastor: "God will give me the time I need, too. Now, let's pray a bit, shall we?"

Then Pastor started to pray, and I knew it would be at least five minutes before he finished. I put a cozy around the teapot and sat at the table and tried to pray, myself. Now that Pastor was praying, his voice was low and soft, and I couldn't understand him. But the sound he made floated through the rooms of my house. The sun was drenching the dining room right then, specks of dust sparkling in two or three paths from the window to the old buffet against the wall. Through the sparkles I could barely see Pastor Thomas and Howard in the living room beyond the archway. I sat at the table and listened to the tick of the clock on the buffet and listened to the sound of Pastor's voice. There was nothing to do but sit and be still.

Well, Howard was on the church's prayer chain quick as a wink. He had people praying for him every day. Pastor saw to that. And in the next couple of weeks, as Howard rested in the living room most of the day while I worked at the café, folks would come by to sit and talk. When I'd come home of an evening, Howard would tell me who had come and what their news was. Sometimes he'd tell me what they'd prayed for him.

I began to see that Howard liked the attention. I got the impression that he had spent most of his life keeping to himself. The way he carried on when company came, telling little stories from his life, I could tell this was a pleasure to him, having someone to tell things to. But mostly he told stories from his childhood and school years—nothing from recent time.

One evening after supper, Howard turned to me just before going upstairs to his room. "You know, Velma, I was never involved with a church up in Wichita. Too busy. And God isn't someone my mind turns to naturally. I've never been a spiritual person. But I'm seeing now what I missed." He didn't give me time to say anything, just turned and went upstairs.

I hurt for him, being isolated all that time when he was so sick. He told me that back in Wichita he'd been too sick some days to even get out of bed, but there had been nobody close by who knew him. He'd moved from one apartment complex to a cheaper one when he lost his first job, and he never got acquainted with his new neighbors.

We liked Howard's company—nice to have a younger person in the house, at least younger than Albert and me. Howard represented a branch of the family—Albert's father's brother's family—that had never stayed in good touch with the rest of us. Albert had told me once that his uncle Harvey had had harsh words with Grandfather early on, and that had put a wall up in the family. I couldn't help feeling that in caring for Howard we were making up for some of the years of silence. With family, you don't always have the opportunities to help. People don't write or call. They get ashamed when the troubles come. Or they get resentful about one thing or another.

Howard did some light work around the house, and some days he walked me up to the café and had a bit of breakfast before coming home. Some days he was real weak, and there were plenty of us to wait on him. The attention didn't seem to spoil him. The journey toward his death opened up a small season for him, and he bloomed and even enjoyed himself in some ways.

I knew that Albert didn't mind Howard being there, whatever Albert thought of his Uncle Harvey. But I knew better than to try to make Albert's and Howard's paths cross much. Albert has always been a private person. We gave Howard the east bedroom, with a little half bath. Often the light would show under his door until three or four in the morning. He'd get restless and watch his little TV or read or work jigsaw puzzles—we had a closet shelf full of them, and we set a little card table up in Howard's room. Albert said that some people get a lot of energy just before they die. I could see the truth of that in Howard.

One evening as I was headed up the walk toward the house, my feet crying out from their day at the café, Doris Pines yoo-hooed at me from her yard. Only, with Doris, "yoo-hoo" came out as a strange sort of melodic whisper. Doris couldn't deal with volume of any kind, particularly her own.

"Oh Velma! I need to ask you something."

I crossed my yard to where only a slim flower bed of marigolds separated Doris and me. "How are you, Doris? Nice day to be out, isn't it?"

"Does . . . does that Howard need anyone to look after him during the day?"

"We have a number of people stopping in."

"—because I'd be happy to help. Since I'm just next door." Doris's left hand grabbed her right wrist, both forearms pressed against her stomach. This was her semi-relaxed pose. Relaxed was both hands, clenched into fists, in her pockets. Her upper teeth worked away at the dry skin on her lower lip.

"Well, call Clare and see where there's an opening for visitors in the afternoon. She's keeping track of all that." Clare was Pastor's wife, a woman who got things done. While the men who made the decisions argued and discussed and appointed committees, Clare got on the phone or behind the wheel of her red Ford Fiesta and brought heaven and earth together.

Doris nodded in comprehension. "I'll do that. It's so good of you to take him in. Do they know how long he has?"

"No. They don't think it's long, is all I know. And I don't question Howard about it."

"I can understand that." Doris unclenched her arm long enough to pat mine. "I so appreciate you, Velma."

"How's Shellye?" I asked, knowing that I might get any one of a range of reactions.

Doris's eyes flitted away from me to explore the flowers to the right and left of us. "She doesn't say much. I hear her crying in her room. She doesn't argue or fuss with me, goes to the doctor when she's supposed to." Her words were cut off by an involuntary taking in of breath. After a second, she let it out and forced out a few words with it. "It's hard to talk to her. I've told her what I think is best, but you know children. They make up their own minds."

"Has she decided? About adoption?"

"I don't know. The woman from the agency has called three times, but the conversation is always short. Shellye doesn't want to make a decision yet."

"Well, she has time."

"Not a lot."

"No, but some. And it's an important decision."

Doris took another sudden breath, and I knew our conversation was over. She was squeezing her arm again and chewing on her lip.

I reached over and patted her shoulder. "Tell her hi for me. Tell her to come over and visit." Doris nodded and turned back toward her house, and I turned toward mine. My heart was beating hard. Sometimes being around Doris made me feel so helpless.

In no time at all, Howard had been with us a month. We had a routine, and the only thing that was unpredictable was how Howard would feel from one day to the next. He went to the Sunday and Wednesday night services with me, and during the week, three or four visitors would come by. Doris had begun to come over on Thursdays. Howard didn't say much about her, except that she was "an odd one, isn't she?" Odd or not, she arrived like clockwork and found interesting things to bring him—books and magazines, two new jigsaw puzzles. Since the weather was so nice, they set the card table up on the sunporch, and there was always a puzzle-in-progress on it.

One Friday evening, Howard and I were out there having coffee and lemon meringue pie. I saw Doris come out to her back step to shake out a throw rug. I called to her.

"Doris! You and Shellye come over for pie. We've got plenty—slow day at the café."

Doris stood straight up and looked over at us. Then she called back, "Shellye's inside. We'll be right over."

Then it was the four of us watching from the patio as the evening slipped in and brought out a few goose bumps. Shellye looked as if she'd gained some weight. Her belly was showing a bit more. She didn't try to hide it anymore, now that everyone knew.

"So when will your baby be born?" Howard asked. It didn't seem like a rude question at all, coming from him. He was sort of huddled into his chair, the way he always gathered his body into one place, as though he could start losing limbs any minute. But his face was easy and open, and he looked at Shellye expectantly. I'd not told Howard about Shellye's situation, but I suspected that he'd heard about it from some of the church people. He looked at her now without judgment.

"Sometime in November." Shellye looked at her pie, then glanced up at Howard. She saw that he was smiling at her, and she smiled back. "Sometimes it seems like a long time, and other times I get in a panic."

"That's why you need to decide what to do." Doris said this quietly but very clearly and immediately took a sip of coffee, not looking at anybody.

"As soon as I know, I'll decide, Mom." I could tell from the little edge in her voice that Shellye had been fending off Doris as well as a lot of other well-intentioned people. And I could tell by a certain tilt to Doris's look that she was as angry about the situation as she was worried. I had the sinking feeling that they weren't getting along well at all.

"I'm sure that whatever you decide will be just the right thing." Howard made a point to look at Shellye until she looked back.

At about the time Shellye looked up at him, so did Doris, and there was a look in her eyes that seemed suddenly unkind. She said then, sounding a bit breathless, "So, Howard, I can't believe that an eligible young man like you doesn't have a girlfriend or wife tucked away somewhere."

You could have sliced through the silence with a thread. Shellye's eyes got wider. Howard's color went to red, then white. He swallowed and seemed to weigh his words.

"Some time ago, there was someone. Not now. Not with me in this condition."

I could see that Doris was working on another question, and I broke in.

"We don't mean to get so personal, Howard. We're just looking out for you. Are you good for another slice?" I picked up the pie plate and waved it in his direction. I threw a look over to Doris and saw that she had gone back to her piece of pie, piercing off little ridges of lemon with the tines of her fork. For a moment, all we heard was the clicking against her plate. I looked at Shellye, who was glaring at her mother. My little dessert party wasn't going too well.

Howard shook his head, as if he'd just come out of a daydream. "No, Velma, I'm done for the day. You folks'll have to excuse me." He took his plate into the kitchen, and I watched him fade back into the dining room.

"We need to go too, Velma. Thanks for the pie." Doris placed her empty plate with its fork on the little serving table, rose from the chair, and brushed the crumbs from her shirt and slacks. She wore a lot of pantsuits, the one-color kind, light blues and yellows and sage greens. She was slim as a model and kept everything wrinkle free.

"I'll stay a few minutes and help clean up," said Shellye. Doris glanced back but didn't say anything. She walked quickly back to her yard and house. Shellye and I carried dishes and cups into the kitchen. There was still a feeling of tenseness in the air, but I was happy to have Shellye back in my house. I told her so, and that I'd missed her visits lately.

"I've been awful, I know," she said. "Haven't talked to anybody much lately. I feel so trapped—wish I could leave this town for a while."

"Do you have someplace to go?"

"No. Mom's Aunt Sal in Springfield. But staying with her would be worse than staying here. At least Mom gets into one of her spells and just stops talking. I can have peace and quiet sometimes."

"You can come over here whenever you want, if you need some peace and quiet."

"I don't feel comfortable coming over while Howard's here. He needs the quiet worse than I do."

"But most of the time he stays to himself. You wouldn't bother anyone."

She stayed long enough to wash the dishes and sit in the family room with me to catch the evening news. But Shellye didn't have much to say anymore. It seemed to me that all that had happened had stolen her words, her energy too. She was too tired for a girl her age, even if she was pregnant.

I went upstairs to knock on Howard's door before going to bed. "Howard? I'm going to bed now. You need anything?"

The door opened. Howard was in his pajamas. I could tell he'd just washed his face, because his hair was damp at the fringes. "I'm fine. Sorry if I spoiled the party."

"Oh, it was already winding down. Doris doesn't mean to be nosy."

"There are some things I can't talk about right now. I don't mean to be rude." More and more, I saw sadness in those eyes that brought Gran Lenny back to me full force.

"Oh." He remembered something suddenly. "John Mason and his wife are looking into hospice care for me. Can you believe how helpful everybody is?"

"Yes, I can. I should have thought of that by now—the hospice."

Howard waved as if it were nothing. "Pastor Thomas suggested it, and he and John talked with me about it this morning on the phone. As things get worse, I don't want you to be overburdened."

"Oh, Howard, don't think in those terms."

"Anyway, we'll get something worked out. I wanted you to know."

I walked toward the door, turning back to say, "Hope you sleep well."

But Howard didn't sleep well most nights. We'd hear him up at all hours. And I knew he was in considerable pain some days. At times I massaged his neck and shoulders. A couple of times he cried while I did that. I asked if it hurt, and he said, no, it didn't. But it was such a comfort to be touched, he said, to have people who cared for him.

But some days, he was stronger. Most mornings, he accompanied me to the café. We'd hardly say a word, just be still in the soft air, while the sky was light pink. Howard put on the first pot of coffee, washed and drained the salad lettuce. I fixed eggs and cheese for us both, while the rolls were rising, and we watched the town start coming out of its doors. About the time the breakfast people had come in, Howard was tired and ready to head home and sleep some more.

One morning as we sat at the counter having our eggs, Howard said out of the blue, "Velma, I've spent so much of my life trying to find out who I am and what I want. Now all of a sudden I don't have much time, and finding myself just isn't important. I just want to enjoy each moment, enjoy people."

"Have you written any of those letters you talked about?" I asked. "You were going to try to get in touch with people."

He looked down at his coffee cup. "I try, but haven't been able to finish a single letter. The words just don't come."

I was sorry I'd asked. I didn't know how to help Howard. And Jesus wasn't giving me much help. I'd prayed a lot for Howard since he'd come to stay. But I couldn't see any kind of movement anywhere, except that Howard kept having bad days.

When I'd close the café and walk home through the shady streets, I knew Howard would be waiting for me, in the family room with the newspaper. I never had time for the paper in the mornings or any other time of the day. But late evening I'd sit with my feet in hot water while Howard read—or I should say, summarized—the news. He would have already been through the paper, as well as three local newscasts, but he'd be ready to share all of it with me.

Once, he stopped mid-sentence and said, "Words are wonderful, aren't they?" I thought of Gran Lenny and said, "Yes, wonderful, and you can do so much with them." I was too worn out to tell Howard about my grandmother. I wasn't sure it would be that meaningful to him. And, seeing Howard on his way to death, I didn't know that I could bring myself to remember in detail other people I'd lost, some of them many years ago.

Howard's Midnight Sandwich

1 ½ tablespoons capers*
1 teaspoon sweet hot mustard, but not the very hot
    Chinese mustard
1 cup Cheddar or other cheese, coarsely grated
1 or 2 teaspoons olive oil
¼ cup onion, finely chopped
1 clove garlic, minced
2 English muffins
1 to 2 tablespoons olive oil or butter

*I've also used pickled jalapeños or pepperoncini, finely chopped.

Mix the capers and mustard into the grated cheese.

Saute onion in the oil in a small skillet. After a few minutes, add garlic and cook another minute.

Add the warm onions and garlic to the cheese mixture and stir; the heat of the onions will melt the cheese a bit so that it holds together.

Pull apart the English muffins and spoon cheese mixture onto one half of each muffin. Cover with the other half.

Heat a bit of olive oil in the same skillet the onion and garlic were cooked in. Put the cheese sandwich in the skillet and cook until the muffin is somewhat brown on the bottom, then flip and brown the other side.

You can use almost any kind of semisoft cheese. You can also saute mushrooms, bell pepper, or other vegetables with the onion, and you can add whatever spices you like. Howard always liked a bit of cayenne pepper in his. Sometimes we used curry and green olives instead of the pickles and mustard.

6

Our House

I will make them and the region around my hill a blessing; and I will send down the showers in their season; they shall be showers of blessing. The trees of the field shall yield their fruit, and the earth shall yield its increase.

—EZEKIEL 34:26–27

In 1988, George and Susie McCallum's liquor store and tavern burned to the ground. Back then, they were across the street from VELMA'S. It was a Monday, one of my busiest days. And a couple of junior-high boys sitting at the window facing McCallum's saw the smoke first. It rose up in a straight gray stream from the back of the building, George's storage area. Someone ran over to tell George, and George got as far as the storeroom door and could feel the heat before he even touched it. He called our volunteer fire department. Avery the grocer, who's a volunteer, ran across the street to help, his butcher's apron still on. But the fire had already gotten into the walls and the wiring, and before we knew what had happened, the whole building was in flames. George and Susie stood on the walk in front of VELMA'S, along with all my customers and a number of other people who had gathered. We were helpless as could be. I brought out my most comfortable chair, and Susie sat there and watched her business burn.

We all knew it was more than a business. Susie's father, Alex Harper, had moved to Leeway forty years before and started the tavern in one of our old storefronts. The Harper family lived in the small apartment above the tavern. Eventually they added space for the liquor store. Then little Susie grew up and married George, and George went into the business with Susie's dad, who had no sons. The tavern and the store prospered, and George and Susie bought a house big enough for Susie's parents to live with them. So the Harpers finally moved out of that little apartment. Then Susie's father died, and Susie ran the store while George ran the tavern. For years it had been called Harper's because Alex never gave the place a name. Twenty years after Alex passed, folks began to call the two businesses McCallum's. Except that some of the older folks went to their graves calling it Harper's. But to Susie it had always been the same. It was home. It was more home to her than VELMA'S was to me. Susie and George knew the town by heart and probably knew deeper secrets than I did, because folks often talk about things when they drink that they'd never talk about otherwise. In spite of all the hard stories Susie had heard, she was the calmest, most levelheaded soul I ever knew. Not only did she run the liquor store but she gave George four sons and a daughter. They ran in and out of the tavern and store like flies on a summer day, but not a one of them grew up rotten. The McCallums never made excuses for the nature of their business. The whole family attended the Catholic church every Sunday for years and years. And George and Susie put every one of those kids through college.

Susie was silent while their building burned. She sat on the chair on my sidewalk and held a cup of coffee until it was cold and just stared at the flames and clouds of smoke, watched the men run here and there, shouting, asking each other questions. When all was done that could be done, everybody stood still, smudged and quiet. We didn't try to comfort. We didn't speculate about what had caused the fire. Avery's apron was completely black, as were his arms up past his elbows. They'd managed to save the cash registers and a few pieces of furniture. The safe was too hot to touch, buried as it was into the flaming walls, but it was fireproof and they would go back to it when it had cooled down. George stood in the middle of the street and uttered a few curses, but they sounded more like words of awe than of anger. George also crossed himself, which I've always seen as the Catholic's quick prayer without words. Such a huge, uncontrollable thing, a fire that swallowed up a family's livelihood. What could be said? And you could shake your fist at the sky only so much.

At one point Susie said, "Glad there's no wind anyway." A little later she called to George that he should call their kids who lived in Neosho, let them know he and Susie wouldn't be coming this weekend. Then, as the fire calmed under the fire hoses, she put a finger to her lip and said, "Oh, you know, I never did get that trunk of Daddy's clothes out of the apartment. All those old suits. He was so particular about the way he looked. And—oh, he had photos and newspaper clippings too. My, I should have moved all that stuff out of there last year. I cleaned all of it out except for that trunk. Couldn't move it by myself, so thought I'd wait until George or one of the kids could help. Daddy was so careful about his things." She said all this while she watched the flames back down under the fat streams of water. Fire trucks from three different towns were in the street, their hoses lying in giant tangles like lazy snakes. "Oh, Daddy, I'm so sorry," Susie said then, and we could see she was crying. They were soft, quiet tears, just like Susie herself. I stood behind her and patted her back. I thought how unbearable it must be to lose such a part of your own history.

Sometimes my own house is noisy with memories. The air in the rooms and the stairwells and closets won't settle down. I notice when I'm here by myself. I'll be reading in the quiet and suddenly feel the need to listen. I'm never sure what I expect to hear. And I don't know whether to be hopeful or afraid. It's a peculiar thing to get old. You're being pulled at from all directions, past, present, and future. You find yourself answering to more than one group of people, because you get messages from folks that have come and gone from the different stages of your life. One day I'm serving a young woman and her husband chicken tenders and salad, and who I'll really be seeing is someone I was in high school with. Or the mailman will holler through the screen door on a Saturday, and I'll expect to see Mr. Henry, who delivered milk when I was a girl. I believe more and more that time has its limits, that there won't always be partitions between past and present. There are words in the Bible to that effect. But I see the evidence, too, in how clearly I can see and hear people who aren't part of my present. Oh, I don't mean like seeing ghosts. I'm talking about memory. Feelings. Certainties that have no rhyme or reason to them.

Some rooms of this old house have always seemed older and darker to me than others. A few folks have claimed for years that a couple of the older homes in town are haunted. I don't believe that people's spirits stay around after they've passed. Not from being unsettled or from wanting to talk with loved ones. If that were the case, nobody would stay in the graveyard. Who ever dies settled? And a lot of loving people die when they'd rather stay to be with their children or parents or husbands or wives. There would be ghostly whispers everywhere. Nobody—especially the living—could be at peace.

Now that I'm old enough to look back on the seasons and see pieces of our lives that were missing, I think the noise in this house is really my own. It's my heart trying to tease out the unspoken things in this family that should have been spoken. Or maybe the sounds I think I hear are all the desires of my people that were left longing. Until I married Albert and made my home here with him, I didn't know a person could be happy in the present moment. Before that, the people who lived here were hurting after the past or working themselves senseless toward tomorrow.

I took a break from writing this morning, to tend to the laundry. I've washed curtains all day. Amazing how much dirt settles in them and how gradually. When I took them down, they were stiff in my hands and blacker than dirt. Sneezed the morning away. I actually put the living room set through the washer twice.

At least the basement is cool. I caught a whiff of old cider while I was wrangling curtains into the washer. Can't imagine where that smell came from. We've not had cider down there for years. The sharp smell of it, hitting me suddenly like that, made me remember so many things at once. It was probably similar to when a person's life flashes before her, when she thinks she's about to die. Only I smell the past and feel that I'm about to live it once again. I saw glimpses of Daddy and Sam, cleaning a pile of dead rabbits in January. My, the sausage we made. In the dead of winter, the smell and sizzle of it would fill the house.

I saw Mama and Aunt Trudy in the opposite end of the basement, bent over bushel baskets of apples. Fresh picked from the Aimses' place just outside of town. The fruit was bumpy-round, mottled green and red, darker where it had been bruised. They'd roll across the floor and rest under the basement steps, because the basement floor always tilted ever so slightly there. And I couldn't see the apples without seeing Mama's pies, lined up on the counter, the crusts in a rippled crisscross pattern and fine sugar across the tops twinkling in the sunshine.

Gran Lenny liked her cider warmed, spices and lemon wedge soaking in it. When autumn winds got sharp at evening, Aunt Trudy took care to fix Gran Lenny's cider. Sometimes she'd send me up the two flights of stairs, a stein full, its cinnamon stick bobbing. The air around my legs would get warmer when I reached the stairs to the attic room, because heat from the kitchen went straight up the stairwell. For a while, late in the day, Gran Lenny left her bedroom door open to let in enough warmth so that she could read comfortably in the rocker next to the window while she sipped her cider. She liked to watch the trees get dark against the cold, white sky.

Albert and I have lived here in Leeway all our married years, and I was born in this house. At the time, Aunt Trudy and Uncle Sam lived here—he'd built the place himself—and Gran Lenny lived in the large attic room. Mama and Papa lived down the street, in a much smaller house. The story is that when Mama went into labor at four in the morning, Papa filled his garden wheelbarrow with blankets, put Mama in it (Uncle Sam owned the only car in the family), and wheeled her the three blocks down the alley and up to Aunt Trudy's back door. Papa could just have easily have run down there and brought Aunt Trudy and Gran Lenny to our house, but in our family, which wasn't very big at that time, all important events happened in Aunt Trudy's house. It was roomy and had two bathrooms. Its kitchen was large and was the center for all family business. And the east bedroom upstairs was designated "the guest room," where all sorts of people had their babies or recovered from illness—or retreated for a while to grieve their losses. It would be easier for Mama to give birth in that house, where Aunt Trudy and Gran Lenny already were and where all the cooking and discussing happened, than for them to bring all their midwife business down to our house.

When I was a girl, I used to stand in the bedroom on the second floor where I was born and try to imagine how it happened. Tried to see Mama in such a condition and Aunt Trudy and Gran Lenny working side by side for once. Pictured Papa and Uncle Sam downstairs drinking coffee at the kitchen table. I was born in March, when the winds were their worst. Every March is still blustery here in Leeway. The winds make noise all day and night, whipping against the side of the house and moaning around corners and rattling through the trees. My little infant cry must have sounded pitiful in the midst of all that. I wonder if the sounds of violence outside made Mama hug me tighter. Just a week after my birth, a tornado took out a block of Leeway's modest business district. Took the roof off the two-room library and left Lemons' Bakery in pieces. Aunt Trudy liked to say that my stormy temperament only made sense, given the month I came into the world.

This house is kind of a fortress, though. Stocky square and resting on a full basement with foundation walls a foot and a half thick. March comes around and all it can do is whistle through a tiny crack here and there. The same with the ice storms in January. They put a glaze on the brick that just seems to make it sharper and sturdier.

After Uncle Sam passed of a heart attack, Aunt Trudy and their daughter went back east. Gran Lenny was still alive, and as a matter of family unity, my parents moved into the big house, with her still occupying the third floor. Payments were worked out, modest ones over the next twenty years, but my parents got the deal of a lifetime. Any house built by my Uncle Sam was made to stand for at least a century.

Now the house is Albert's and mine. It is dark brick and solid as houses come. Uncle Sam was a mason who'd built a number of brick and stone houses in New England, where he'd worked with his brother. Sam had spent his life in crowded places, tripping over people and pavement, and he got it in his mind to be a wheat farmer and brought his family to the Midwest. That was just a year or two before the stock market crash of '29. That and the drought years of the Great Depression prevented Sam from ever getting set up with a farm of his own. He ended up building houses for farmers and for townspeople who lived in farm country. It turned out that he liked his work more out here in the open than he had in the cities. He was a buddy to every farmer around, but he made his living still, building things. The irony of it was that, when they first moved to Leeway, Sam had such a fever to own land and plant wheat that he built his own house in a hurry. At that time, this street was the north edge of town.

The house was well built to be sure, but Sam's creativity was sort of in a lull, and the place has never had much character, except for what it soaked up from the people who lived in it. It's two and a half stories with a full basement, all of it just stacked on top of itself. Sam didn't even build a porch until they'd lived here three or four years. And he always regretted that he'd not put a fireplace in one of the upstairs bedrooms, above the fireplace in the living room. Sam only lived to be fifty, so he never had the chance to build another house the way he could truly build one. Trudy hankered to be back in Philadelphia; she practically gave the house to my mother and toted a truckload of her most prized possessions back to where her heart was. They had one daughter, Elizabeth, who was happy to move with her mother out of farm country and back east. Within a year, Elizabeth found a husband, so I suppose it was all in a plan somewhere. Some lives appear to have a plan, and Trudy was the type that pretty much presented her life outline to the Lord and his angels and tapped her foot until they got with it. She got away with that, maybe because God admires spunk.

So the house was built by Sam, sold to Mama and Papa, and passed on to Albert and me. It holds all our memories in its little nicks and paint shades and hinged doors and custom-built shelves, closets, and cabinets. They used decent wood back then, and the women in our family were always enthusiastic about polished woodwork. This place is filled with it, most of it a deep, cherry grain, and there are certain places—in doorjambs and on the stair banister particularly—where the imprints of our hands still dip slightly. Sam, Papa, and Albert all liked to stand in the kitchen doorway and brace themselves while talking, as if that were the place the man of the house should always be when important subjects were in the air. Cup of strong coffee in one hand, the heel of the other palm on the doorjamb. All the gesturing happened with the hand that held the coffee cup, meaning there was always some wife or sister-in-law dabbing up coffee spots from the floor right there, where the black stuff had sloshed out in a moment of feverish conversation.

There was a time when the memory marks in my house bothered me, as if the place wasn't really mine. But now that I'm staring back on more than half my life, I can see that you never live your life alone, anyway. You *are* your family and all their experiences. They *are* with you, no matter how many coats of paint you slap onto the woodwork (not that I would have ever committed a crime like that, even in the fifties and sixties, when it was the popular thing to do). My family in this house comforts me now. Their conversations still wander the rooms and hang near the ceilings, some days more than others.

In my dining room is a large, heavy buffet; it practically fills one end of the room. It's so old the finish has gone dark to where you can hardly tell what sort of wood is there. It was my mother's buffet, given to her by her Aunt LaVonne. It doesn't match anything else in my house—not the table and chairs or the hutch where I keep my good dishes. I keep it because it was Mama's. And I keep it because it would take six strong men to get it out of my house. And there are a lot of things in it I'm not sure what I'd do with. Family things—receipts and photos and old books and odds and ends. I know they're in the buffet because they were important to someone once. It would seem arrogant of me to throw anyone's precious memories into a big trash bag. Even though most of my family's gone now, I still have cousins scattered around the country. I think that, sure as I throw away something, some cousin's granddaughter or nephew will show up, needing that very photograph or book. So I leave all of it. Every four or five years I take it out and look at it, dust it off and put it back inside and close the doors snug. I can't lock the buffet because they don't make keys like that anymore, and the original was lost when Mama was still alive.

Most days I don't think about all the bits and pieces tucked away in the darkness. Just as I don't think of all the memories that hang like cobwebs in this old house. I'm the third generation to live here.

One Wednesday not long after Howard came to stay, Shellye came over. I think she and Doris had been arguing. Howard was at the library, something to get him out of the house but that didn't take a lot of energy. Shellye noticed Mama's rose-covered china vase on the buffet. I told her its history, which included my mother's life and her mother's and a war and changes of location. It's amazing what memories one little vase can stir up. Shellye was so fascinated, for reasons I can't imagine. She's never known any of my family except for Albert. But she drank in the information like soda pop on a hot day. We studied Gran Lenny's sugar and creamer, her wedding gift from when she was a newlywed in Munich. We went through Aunt LaVonne's silver and all of Mama's tea sets and Daddy's collection of salt and pepper shakers. Then to all my little ceramic roosters and hens. Those made Shellye giggle. It kind of broke my heart, because later I realized that what I did with Shellye I wish I could have done with my own daughter. Sometimes I'm jealous of Doris, Lord forgive me. Shellye and her mom are so different, but Shellye and I have understood each other since she was just a little thing.

Since I never had a daughter and my son doesn't care much for *things*, as he puts it, I decided that day that I would leave a lot of my family dishes to Shellye. She would care for them and remember their stories.

After the business with Len Connor was out in the open, Shellye found excuses to be in our house. Mostly she sat at my kitchen table while I worked, or sat on the sunporch with me and we did crosswords together.

I asked her one evening if she and her mom had talked much about the pregnancy.

"I tried to talk with her one time, but she started talking about what we should have for dinner and whose turn it was to clean the bathroom. I don't think Mom has any more room in her life for bad things."

"You may be right, sweetie."

After that one uncomfortable evening on the sunporch with Doris and Howard and Shellye, I determined to get Shellye in my house more often, never mind Howard living here and never mind Doris feeling nervous about Howard's past or Shellye's future. I decided to hit spring cleaning in early summer, and I asked Shellye to come help me. Little by little, every evening, we cleaned out each and every kitchen cupboard and drawer. Actually, I'd sit at the table with my feet soaking, and she'd put every item on the table so I could make a judgment about it. It gave her someplace to be during the long, humid evenings. Doris came over a couple of times, but the clutter and clatter must have bothered her, because she made excuses to go home after a few minutes.

Howard got in on the fun. I watched him and Shellye unloading and cleaning and reloading cabinet space, and I could see that they were good for each other. Oh, I knew nothing permanent could come of it. Howard didn't even make plans anymore, and Shellye needed to make important ones. But they were more relaxed with each other than with anyone else.

"I don't know if it's such a good idea for Shellye to be at your house so much, Velma," Doris said through my screen door early one morning. I hadn't even got out of the house. She was in slacks and shirt, but had house slippers on. "I think it upsets her to be with Howard."

"What do you mean? They're good friends for each other." I'd never noticed myself sounding irritated with Doris before. But her nervousness seemed more like meddling these days.

"She's very vulnerable right now, that's all."

"Howard would never do a thing to hurt her—or anybody else, for that matter. She's a woman now, Doris. You need to let her be."

I couldn't see clearly how Doris looked at me then. The sun was shining at an angle on the screen door. I thought it was probably best that I didn't see her clearly. In that instant, I thought how good it would be if Shellye just moved in with us. Then I scolded myself for being so resentful. For thinking I knew better than the girl's own mother.

Doris didn't say any more after that. She began to show up with Shellye. She'd sit in my living room near the open front door and smoke, no television on or anything. She'd just sit, making sure, I guess, that she heard everything we said. After a while, we didn't notice her. We went from the kitchen to the pantry, and from there to the dining room and the big buffet.

As we went through all the family heirlooms, Doris moved to a straight-backed chair next to the arched doorway. I'd have Shellye take out some piece and pass it around. Doris asked questions about this and that family member. Howard was quiet while we went through those things. He was quiet the way people are when they don't want to miss anything. I took the opportunity to tell him about family he'd never known. At those times, Doris got quiet too, as if she might be comforted by being surrounded by someone else's memories. The two or three evenings we spent in the dining room, I felt that I'd been given gifts that others could only look at. The family portraits, lined up, the stories that came with every dish or memento. Here was Howard, cut off from nearly all his family, at a time when a person should be surrounded by loved ones. And here were Doris and Shellye, alone in a town small enough to make being alone a significant thing. They were all three sitting in my dining room, feasting on my family. I felt generous. I felt sad.

But after we'd spring-cleaned the dining room, after we'd gone through all the objects and their stories, I felt Doris fall into an easier state. I sensed that she and Howard would not be enemies, no matter what Howard's past was. It was the strangest thing, to have that little rift healed in that way.

I tried to talk to Albert about it later. About Doris not being so tense and about Howard listening so intently when I told him about his family. But I ended up talking about other things—about Albert and me and all our years in this house. I talked through all sorts of memories that evening and into the night. The bedroom window was open, and the light felt eternal and full of comfort, and Albert felt so close to me. I talked and talked about so many things we'd done together. Then I'd remember the longing in Howard's eyes—longing to belong somewhere and have people around him—and I just kept remembering. Finally, I wound down, and Albert's voice was very gentle, but his words hurt me.

"Vellie, all your stories won't keep the boy alive. When it's his time . . ."

"Don't say such things! You of all people shouldn't be so harsh about death." I turned over and looked out the window at the night sky, that white-gray color that never really gets dark in the summer time. The clouds were blurry, because there were tears in my eyes.

"This is my home, Albert. I have the right to welcome the world in. To give them comfort for a while."

"Just for a while. Don't be so afraid of losing people, Vellie."

My husband can seem harsh sometimes. I don't think he resented my having Shellye over so much or going on about my memories. Albert just always knew when I was trying to avoid something painful. Like the time he practically dragged me to the doctor because of my stomach pains. We both knew it was serious, but I was afraid to know how serious. I didn't want to be in the hospital. Sure enough, I had to have my gall bladder removed. And I did spend some time in the hospital. Albert never said, "See, what if I hadn't made you go?" He sat quietly in the corner while Jimmy gave me what-for for neglecting myself.

Maybe the reason I didn't want to go to the hospital was that I thought I could never feel better outside my own house. That wasn't long after Mama passed, and I was clinging hard to the memories then. Even if I was going to be sick, I wanted to be in my house, with Mama and Gran Lenny. I needed them.

Now Shellye is in this house, too. In the same way my family's story is mine, hers is mine. We never plan whose stories will get mixed up with ours. Maybe that's just as well. But we don't have as much control over our lives as we think. A little girl without a daddy walks into my kitchen because she smells *stollen* baking, and there you have it. She's caught up in the fragrance of the bread and the sound of Albert's whistling down in the basement. Her stories get caught like bits of dust on the ceiling beams. Her face plants itself in the kitchen curtains.

One Tuesday evening, Shellye was having supper with us—Doris was down with a headache—and Pastor Thomas knocked on the back door. He was on his way home from the church and needed to pick up my spare set of church keys for a young men's group that was meeting tomorrow afternoon. It was warm, and his jacket was off. He stepped into the kitchen and greeted each of us, his eyes resting on Shellye.

"Shellye, good to see you. How are you feeling?"

Shellye glanced at him, then looked back at her food. "All right."

A bad silence followed. Shellye wouldn't be rude to the pastor, but she didn't want to talk to him either. I think Pastor Thomas really cared for her welfare, but he had to have known that he'd done wrong by her. Me, I didn't know what to say to anybody.

Howard spoke up. "Rev. Thomas, I can't thank you enough for the way your folks have kept me company." This, thank goodness, took the conversation in a comfortable direction. I didn't know if Howard knew what he was doing or not. As he and Pastor talked, Shellye got up from the table and took her plate to the sink.

"Stay for apple spice cake?" I asked.

She shook her head and smiled. "I'll take some of this casserole over to Mom, though, in case she's able to eat later."

We wrapped up a plate for Doris. I noticed that Pastor and Howard had come to a lull in their conversation. When I said, "Bye, Shellye," it sounded too loud.

"Hey, see you later," Howard called after her. She was on her way down the back walk. She didn't turn, but called back, "See you later."

Pastor was watching Shellye, and he looked as if he wanted to say something. Instead, he clapped Howard on the shoulder and said good-bye to us. He walked out the same back door, but took the turn in the walk that led to the front yard.

"It's a shame that Shellye's dropped out of church," I said softly. I could still see Shellye and Pastor, as they both walked to different edges of my vision.

"She's been hurt," Howard said.

"Yes, she has. And I know she's still getting pressure to give up the baby."

"Do you think that's a good idea?"

"It always seems like a bad idea, separating a child from its mother. People have good arguments for it, though." I sat back down at the table. No one said anything. The daylight was getting soft and faint. It entered the house and lay across floors and furniture, across our arms and faces, the same way light filtered through the frosted glass at church and lay across the pews. Some times of day seem sacred, as if the Lord created light to act a certain way and make people reflective.

For just a little while—through about half the month of June— Albert's and my house was filled with people. Howard and the church folks who came to visit. Shellye and Doris. The place was never quiet— there was always someone moving around. Even a person sleeping has a certain sound.

Doris's Potatoes and Green Beans in Rosemary Sauce

2 cups potato, diced or sliced
1 cup frozen green beans
1 cup vegetable or chicken stock; for white sauce use milk
2 tablespoons butter
$1/4$ cup white or yellow onion, very finely chopped
1 to 2 teaspoons fresh rosemary, finely chopped
2 tablespoons flour
2 to 4 tablespoons cream cheese, optional
Black pepper, freshly ground is best
Salt to taste

Cook cut-up potatoes until tender. Cook frozen green beans according to directions. Drain potatoes and beans and combine. Cover to keep warm.

In medium saucepan, saute onion in the butter. Add flour and mix. Add the liquid and fresh rosemary and stir, cooking on medium heat until the sauce thickens. If using cream cheese for extra richness, add it after the sauce begins to thicken and stir until the cheese melts. Add vegetables, salt, and pepper. Serve warm.

7

A Good Night

All the trees of the field shall know
that I am the Lord.
I bring low the high tree,
I make high the low tree.
I dry up the green tree
and make the dry tree flourish.
I the Lord have spoken;
I will accomplish it.
                    —Ezekiel 17:24

The third Saturday evening in June, I was dusting in the sanctuary. Once a month I polish all the pews and the woodwork with lemon oil. I never do that the same weekend that I sprinkle deodorizer on the carpets before vacuuming, because the floral and citrus scents would fight each other. I do love it when God's house smells of lemon. Makes me wonder what incense in the tabernacle smelled like, back in Old Testament days. Was probably something spicy and Middle Eastern, like cloves.

In the midst of the oil and the fragrance, a stranger came in through the double glass doors that separate the sanctuary from the foyer. He was mid-thirties, tall and straight, black hair with some gray at the temples. He wore gray slacks and a short-sleeved, dark blue pullover. The man walked right in and took in the room with his eyes. At first he didn't see me.

"May I help you?" I called, trying not to startle him. He looked at me and smiled, and I liked him right away. He walked over to me quickly, putting out his hand. He had a warm, friendly grip.

"I'm Jacob Morgan. I'll be the evangelist for the revival this week. Just stopped in to see where I'll be speaking."

"Oh, I should have known. I'm Velma."

"Good to meet you, Velma. You're working hard for so late at night."

"Have you found the pastor? He would be home now, but we could call him."

"Just came from there. On my way home, but drove by here and saw the lights on."

"Where's home?"

"Bender Springs."

"Oh yes, I've visited over there a couple times. We're so glad to have you, Rev. Morgan."

That was the extent of our conversation. Rev. Morgan wandered around the sanctuary a few minutes, stopped in the center of the room, facing the altar, and seemed to meditate. Then he headed back down the aisle and toward the double doors, waving at me. "I'll see you this week?"

"Yes. I'll be here every night."

Howard was asleep on the back porch when I got home. The old glider is loaded with cushions, and it makes a nice napping place. I've slept out there in the heat of summer; the screens around the porch keep most of the bugs out. It was feeling chilly, so I covered Howard with an afghan Mama had knitted way back when. I decided not to wake him to eat leftovers. He looked worn out.

When Jerusalem Baptist goes into revival season, I nearly wear myself out. I shouldn't say "season," because generally our revivals last only a week, but life changes in a lot of ways during that time. There are services every night, which means that the church needs to be straightened if not cleaned every night, late, after everyone has done their crying and praying and left. After being at the café all day and then attending the service, I have to put on my patience cap, as Mama used to call it, to wait for the sanctuary to clear out so I can do what needs to be done. I can't just sleep later and let the café go. My customers would be put out with me, and it would make them feel bad about the church, for causing the inconvenience.

With Howard at home, my nights were getting later. He often had the need to talk past ten o'clock. He hadn't filled me in on his life to his satisfaction. Just like when you're getting acquainted with any person, becoming friends, there are those first dozen or so discussions where you tell the stories you want that person to know about you. You fill him in on the bad things you think might affect his opinion of you if he hears them somewhere else. Your favorite opinions get aired. It's a natural process, but I was unnaturally tired that week, and I listened as best I could to Howard's life. Worst of all, Howard wasn't sleeping much in those days. He was having night sweats, and he would've kept us both up until three in the morning if I hadn't been willing to say, around midnight, "Well, Howard, I've got to be at the restaurant at five." He'd make a quick shift then and apologize for talking so much.

He was looking forward to the revival, which didn't surprise me. He'd been real receptive toward church from the beginning, and he was there whenever the doors were open and he was feeling up to it. The first night of the revival, I had to go straight from the café to the service, and I called Doris and asked if she could walk with Howard to the church. When I got there, the two of them were sitting together, and Doris was talking and nodding to him. She was dressed up in a light blue dress and sandals. And her smile seemed so calm. I wondered if Howard was having a good effect on her. The three of us walked home together in the cool of the evening, after I'd taken fifteen minutes to straighten things up when the service was over. Shellye hadn't come— she hadn't been to church at all—and I didn't mention it to Doris.

The third night of the revival, Howard was sleeping hard in his room, so I left without him. Since it was Wednesday night, a church night normally, the crowd filled most of the pews. Rev. Morgan's preaching was getting a good reception. He didn't walk up and down and yell, which was a nice change of pace for revival time. I found myself enjoying his words and the way he used them.

I always sit in the very back, north side, in case I need to adjust the thermostat or close a door or point a visitor to the rest rooms. About two minutes before the service started, I sensed someone at the other end of my pew. I looked in time to see Shellye sitting down. She didn't see me, so I got her attention, and she smiled and scooted toward me. The child looked scared, only deep in her face; a stranger wouldn't have seen it. I could only imagine all the emotions she was going through. A number of church people saw her and gave her a second look. One or two sent a little wave of greeting, and a few of them poked whoever was sitting beside them and leaned to whisper. You'd think they'd not been brought up to have manners. I could see that Shellye was aware of all this. I asked how she was feeling, and she said that she was hungry all the time. I patted her leg and told her that's a good sign.

I felt such relief to see the girl there, given all she'd been through with people at church. So many of them were tight with the Connors. Tim and Melanie, Len's parents, and his younger sister Leslie were there tonight, sitting four rows from the front on the other side of the aisle. Shellye glanced at them, but they didn't know she was there. Len was away visiting cousins in Nevada, Missouri, at least that's what Melanie told me. It's awful, but after what Len had done to Shellye, I kept imagining what other sorts of meanness he was up to. My opinion of him was forever changed, even though I hardly knew him. The Connors were hoping he could get a scholarship to Kansas State in Manhattan. The boy had always done well in basketball, in science too. Of course he was just going ahead with his life, never mind the situation Shellye was in.

It takes a certain kind of religion to put on a revival. First of all, you have to believe that people are capable of change, and that's hard to do when you live with them and know how often they fall into the same bad habits. You also have to believe that it means something to say to others that you're sorry and that you'll try harder. It takes a certain kind of person to say that in the first place, but it takes a bunch of other people to believe it and to be there and hear the person when he says that he's sorry. It's almost as if, if you don't have someone to confess and speak your intentions to, you can't do what you're trying to do. In some ways, it's a haphazard mess, as Gran Lenny liked to comment, concerning church. You live your life with these people, and none of you does very well at your promises, but you just keep living as if the promises will come true anyway.

I've sat in my back pew for years now, and I've watched the same people make the same speeches more times than I can count. But you know, I never mind when they walk toward the altar to pray and make their commitments and confess their sins. I'm always happy to see it. It's not the type of thing I could be happy about if I didn't believe that there's more happening than those speeches. Sometimes I think that in heaven all our promises are being kept, and we're doing everything right; it's just here in this old world that we can't succeed. I don't pretend to understand. And I never expect as much from revival time as some people do. A walk down the aisle never changed anybody's life that I could see. That little walk is just a few steps that don't count until they're added to a lot more steps out in regular life. But a few steps in church somehow make it easier to walk right once we're outside. I go to church every Sunday and Wednesday. I need reminding of heaven at least that often. I'm not ashamed to get reminded.

That night, Rev. Morgan's words had a particular power and gentleness:

"Sometimes I look at a person who's going through really hard times, and I say to myself, *I could never go through that. I wouldn't hold up.* But you know what? If I were in that situation, I *would* be able to go through it, because God would supply the grace. He gives grace when we need it, usually not before. That's how we go through life, moment by moment, counting on the grace and the strength to be there when it's time.

"If there's something you know you're called to do, and it scares you and you're hesitating to go through with it, please remember that God's grace will be there. If you're walking God's way, you'll be given whatever you need to make the journey. Maybe you need to straighten out a relationship. All you can think is, *What if I'm always alone?*

"Maybe you need to quit your job or some hobby because it's keeping you from living like a Christian. A man in our congregation had to do that very thing. He was working for a company that was doing immoral things, misrepresenting itself to the public, taking advantage of people. First he protested from inside. He had a fairly high position, too. He did all he could to make things change. But too many others wouldn't change. So he walked out. Five years from retirement. He thought, *How can I just quit? What if I can't find another job? What if, what if . . . ?* And he didn't get another job right away. That was a hard time for this man and his family. He had a higher calling, and God gave him the grace to stick with it.

"We don't need to be the people of *what if,* because we're already the people of what *is.* And what is, is God's love, grace, peace, power, mercy, strength."

Rev. Morgan's words felt good to my spirit. Money was scarce—the café had never turned much of a profit. And I didn't know yet what medical costs were in store for us, given Howard's condition. He'd stopped chemotherapy before coming to Leeway. It had stopped doing any good and just made him sick. He was on a waiting list, he said, for a donor for a bone marrow transplant. But when he stopped treatments, he'd faced the fact that his days were numbered. I hoped he would still get medical attention as he needed it, and you never knew what Medicaid would pay and what it wouldn't. That's all the insurance he'd had for some time.

I knew all this when I told Howard to come live with us. It wasn't just money, but time and energy caring for a man who may soon not be able to do much for himself. As Rev. Morgan spoke about grace, I realized how little sleep I'd gotten lately, and that most days, when my mind wandered, it ended up in a place of worry and fear.

But Rev. Morgan was right as rain. I bowed my head and told the Lord I'd stop stewing and just wait for him to come through. I must confess that I cried just a little. Sometimes it can be a relief to recognize your own lack of faith, to just say, "Lord, I need help."

About the moment I dug into my purse for a tissue, I felt the pew shake. There was Shellye, holding her stomach, head bent to where her chin touched her blouse. There were tears running everywhere, and she was sobbing without making a sound.

"Shellye, what's wrong? Are you in pain?" I kept my voice low enough that the people in the next pew couldn't hear. Shellye shook her head. She got up and headed for the bathroom. I decided not to follow her. By the time she came back, her face was dry, though her eyes were pink and puffy. She smiled at me, just a small smile, and she listened peacefully to the rest of the sermon, which was almost over.

Morgan was a young man, for a revival preacher. So many of them are older, and they've preached so long that their voices are always hoarse, making them sound as if they've been drinking and puffing for twenty years. Morgan sounded younger and smoother, but he didn't mince words, and at the end of the evening he gave an old-fashioned "invitation"—the opportunity for people to walk up to the altar to pray with him or with Pastor Thomas. While he invited, the rest of us just sang. We were on the second verse of "Just As I Am" when Shellye stood up quickly and headed down the aisle.

I knew that Shellye had been a born-again Christian since she was thirteen, so I was interested to know what moved her toward Rev. Morgan. They knelt at the front pew and prayed while the music and the singing kept going through verses three and four. I saw Shellye put a tissue to her eyes as she sat on that same pew when they were finished. Meanwhile, two other people had walked up to pray. When the song was through, the praying wasn't, so Lonnie continued to play softly until Rev. Morgan and Pastor Thomas were finished.

At our church, we've always given people an opportunity to say to the congregation why they came forward to pray. It's not something they have to do, but most of the time they're more than willing to share with us what has happened to them. The first person to speak was a high school boy who had decided to give his heart to Jesus. The next was Clarice Tyler, who everybody knew was having all kinds of trouble with her daughter. When Jacob Morgan put his hand lightly on Shellye's shoulder, we all got very quiet. I wondered if she'd come to confess to the church that she was pregnant out of wedlock, although everybody in town knew it by now. Shellye started to cry just a little, and Brother Morgan waited patiently. When the girl spoke, her voice sounded loud and sharp over the hot silence in that room.

"Most of you know I'm going to have a baby. I'm not proud of how this happened, but God has made me so certain of his love, that I have the courage to do the right thing."

I saw Pastor Thomas smile. His shoulders seemed to sag with relief.

"I've thought about how hard it is to be a single mom, and I knew I couldn't do it. I've been so depressed lately, trying to figure out what to do." She had to stop and let out a couple of tears. "But I know now that God will give me the grace to raise my child with his love. And I just wanted to stand here in front of all of you and say that I'm dedicating my life to being the best . . ." Poor Shellye couldn't finish. I heard a sniffle or two from the congregation. I also saw Pastor Thomas's shoulders stiffen.

Rev. Morgan was getting teary himself, a smile lighting his face. He squeezed Shellye's shoulders and addressed the rest of us.

"What courage it takes to step into an uncertain future. Yet Shellye has made the choice the Lord has led her to. Shellye—" He turned to look into her eyes. "You need to understand that God never meant for us to make our journey alone. That's why we have the church, the body of Christ." He looked out at all of us. "I would like, right now, to see who will stand with Shellye as she seeks to be the kind of mother God wants her to be. Who will stand with her and her child to support and encourage them?"

The church was more quiet than I'd ever heard. A few seconds went by that could have passed for half a day. I looked at the backs of the heads of people I'd known most of my life. I could tell they were looking away from Shellye. They'd been put on the spot. Rev. Morgan couldn't know what he was asking; he couldn't know the circumstances that had led to this moment. To him it was just a beautiful decision made by a pregnant girl. From where I sat I could see Melanie Connor cross her arms. Tim Connor cleared his throat and stared hard at the candles and the collection plates.

A long moment went by. Rev. Morgan stood there, his gaze taking on something besides joy and gentleness. Pastor Thomas didn't move off the pew. He seemed to be holding his breath. Whoever stood up now would be agreeing that Shellye was doing the right thing, and all the deacons and Pastor Thomas didn't think it was the right thing. Most of the people in the room knew what the prevailing opinion was.

I could see that Rev. Morgan was measuring what he should say next. Shellye's gaze went just above all the heads, not making eye contact with a soul, not even me. She was being judged, and she knew it. But her chin was tilted just so, and I knew she would follow through with her choice no matter what happened in the rest of the world. I got up from my seat and walked down the center aisle. My feet are small, but they made a joyful noise, wood planks creaking loudly under the new blue carpet. Shellye saw me, and she smiled bravely. I came closer and saw Rev. Morgan smiling too, his eyes swimming. He shook my hand as I came up to them. I gave Shelley a quick hug and kiss and stood beside her. I heard Rev. Morgan say, "Praise the Lord" softly. Then Shellye and I looked out over heads together. I could feel my legs shaking in their bones. I've never been one to stand up in front of a crowd. I just serve crowds and then clean up after them. I wanted to close my eyes and wait for this event to be over. But I grasped Shellye's hand, which was shaking in rhythm with mine.

I focused my gaze on the big clock above the wall heater in the back of the room. Then I caught movement at the edge of my vision. Just to the right and several pews up, I sensed a person rising. It was Annie Smith. Her blue-gray hair moved up the aisle, and I smelled her perfume as she passed in front of me and stood on Shellye's other side. By then, two or three other people were moving. Janice Long, the Sunday school director. Bruce Barnes, one of our farmers, who had three grown children and seven grandchildren. His wife Cynthia was right on his heals. Then came Barbara Milson, Sam Cook, Judith Blessant, Carl Renfro, Sue Baines. Half the church was rising out of its pews. By now I was looking at faces, some I knew well. They were beaming, and their eyes were spilling over. They looked at me but mostly at Shellye.

I watched her eyes meet their eyes. I thought the power around us would melt us all. I felt for a few moments as if I would start flying around the sanctuary, the way I had often flown in my fever dreams.

Two or three minutes must have passed. All you could hear were feet moving and sobs escaping. And there were now more people standing at the front with Shellye and me than there were people in the pews. Tim and Melanie Connor and their daughter Leslie were still seated, looking like a desperate island in the middle of a fast stream. Then Leslie, no more than fifteen, shot up and away from her parents. She practically ran down the aisle and just hugged Shellye and cried. I looked to see her parents' reactions, but Tim was gone. Then I saw that he wasn't gone, but on his way to us as well. The look on his face could have washed the whole town clean. I looked back at Melanie in time to see her walk out the back door.

Well, it was a time I wouldn't have wanted a stranger to come in, because we were all laughing and crying, making a racket, and hugging Shellye. Rev. Morgan had given up trying to hold back his tears. He looked as if this was what he got into the ministry for. Pastor Thomas had stood. He smiled warmly, knowing he was beat. Whether or not he felt it was God who had beaten him was hard to say. But he moved into the crowd to stand near Shellye. I was close enough to hear him say, "Shellye, I think you can see how many people love you." Shellye nodded and gave him a hug. Pastor wasn't expecting that. He hadn't shed a tear until then, and he turned away to grab hold of his composure.

I sang out loud while I straightened up the sanctuary that night. Then I went home and listened to Howard as if his every word was a gift. I went to bed at 3:30 and didn't sleep at all. I just kept playing over and over how the people in my church had stood up for this desperate, sweet child. I cried and told the Lord that it was nice to see something go well after the hard things we'd gone through. That may seem like backhanded praise, but I guess I get my directness from Gran Lenny, who, the one time she was compelled to say grace before dinner, had said in a loud, unprayerful voice in front of guests: "God, you see us here about to eat. We're glad to have a good meal in front of us. Help us forget the times we've been hungry. Help us eat in peace and talk without arguing. These are miracles, I know, but you're God. You can do anything. We're just asking that you do something. Amen."

Jacob Morgan's Good-Ending Pudding

Pudding:

1/2 cup pitted dates, chopped
1/2 cup golden raisins
1/2 cup toasted hazelnuts, chopped
4 cups stale bread, torn into pieces
1/2 cup cold coffee
3 cups milk
4 eggs
3/4 cup sugar
1 teaspoon cinnamon
1 teaspoon grated lemon rind
1/4 teaspoon nutmeg
1/4 teaspoon cloves
1/2 teaspoon salt

In one bowl, mix together the dates, raisins, hazelnuts, and bread. Mix the remaining ingredients in a second bowl, then pour that mixture over the bread, fruit, and nuts. Pour all of this into a well-buttered, 2-quart baking dish, preferably a glass one.

Bake at 350° for 60 to 75 minutes, or until set. Cool about ten minutes before serving warm with sauce ladled over it.

Honey-orange sauce:

1/2 cup honey
1/4 cup butter
1 cup orange juice
1/2 teaspoon cinnamon
dash of salt

Melt the butter and honey together in a small saucepan. Add the orange juice, cinnamon, and salt. Let the mixture simmer on low heat for about 10 minutes. Then spoon the sauce over the pudding.

8

Grady Lewis

He said to me: Mortal, all my words that I shall speak to you receive
in your heart and hear with your ears; then go to the exiles, to your
people, and speak to them.

—Ezekiel 3:10–11a

You never know how God's going to answer a prayer or who he'll
use in the process. After watching that process for years now, I've
decided that the Lord has a sense of humor, but that sometimes his
answers haven't fully arrived when we think they have. In fact, sometimes, looking back on it, you don't know if God answered your prayer
or merely gave you what you asked for.

I've always been impatient with prayer, like with everything else. I
used to plant bulbs of an early morning and be back that evening to
check their progress. "You'll stare them back into the ground," Albert
would say.

After Shellye walked forward that night at the church, she started
attending regularly again. It seemed that the Rev. Morgan's affirmation
of her decision had pretty much stamped a "hands off" on Shellye's
life. Although a few people still murmured about what a bad decision
it was—her keeping the baby—no one openly spoke to her about it.
Pastor Thomas made a point of welcoming her when she walked in the
door the next Sunday morning, after the revival was over.

By her second Sunday back, Shellye found herself the object of attention of two young men in the church. It was the strangest thing. One was a boy she'd actually dated a couple of times, Steve Blocker. A good kid, but a year younger than Shellye. Steve lived with his mother and no one else, a quiet boy everybody liked but nobody expected to amount to much.

"So, what's Steve up to these days?" Howard asked that Tuesday evening as we drank iced tea on the patio and watched fireflies float over the lawn. I was surprised that he would be so direct, but he'd gotten to be that way with Shellye, and she didn't seem to mind, although Doris would still twitch where she sat, not sure of what was going on. It was clear, though, that Howard was out to protect Shellye, as if she were his daughter or little sister.

"Oh, Steve's nice. He wants us to date. But we've never had much to say to each other. And he's young, you know." Shellye's honey hair shone blond in the bit of moonlight that had filtered through the maple's branches right above us. It seemed odd for this mere girl to talk about someone else being young. But we knew what she meant. She wasn't going to be young much longer, with a child on the way. And Steve might try to be a husband and a father in the same year, but that was a lot to ask.

"You don't need to rush," said Howard. His voice was relaxed and happy, as if he, himself, had all the time in the world.

"A baby's a big responsibility to handle by yourself," said Doris. She was trying to make her voice relaxed, too, but it wasn't. I heard Shellye sigh loudly. I was glad it was too dark for us to see each other's faces well.

The other man who began to talk to Shellye was Grady Lewis. In the minds of a number of people, Grady was a true find. Twenty-six years of age and the graduate of a Bible college somewhere in Oklahoma. He was working on more ministry schooling through correspondence courses from that same school. He had a business degree, and he was assistant manager for an auto supply store. But Grady liked to say that auto parts was just his occupation. His "vocation," as he put it, was making disciples.

Grady was tall and wiry, black-eyed and black-haired. Sometimes he led mid-week prayer meeting. He'd look across all of us intently, seeming to make a challenge of some sort. His voice sounded as if it came from another part of the room—deep and full of its own echoes. It was a true Scripture reading kind of voice. And sometimes, as he read Scriptures aloud, it looked to me as if Grady were listening to his own voice the way he'd listen to another person. I suppose it would be accurate to say that Grady Lewis took himself quite seriously—just one of the reasons I found it difficult to.

Grady met with some of the young men for prayer and Bible study and for what he termed "one-on-one" time. I got to see Grady two or three times a week. He'd bring a disciple into the café for breakfast or lunch or just coffee, and that Scripture voice would rumble around the room.

Grady began to call on Shellye at home. Howard was first to observe this, and he wasn't happy about it. I didn't know whether to be happy or not. There was no tangible reason not to like Grady. He just didn't have a personality that was easy to warm up to, unless a person wanted to be taught.

Shellye came over to visit with us about every evening after I got back from the café. I could tell after a couple weeks of Grady which days he'd been over to see her. Shellye would have the look of a child about to jump off the high board for the first time. My boy Jimmy had that look when he took swimming lessons over at Helmsly. For reasons unknown to Albert and me, our boy had been afraid of water since his first bath. Jimmy was so sensitive around any water that Albert decided to have a professional teacher have a crack at the boy's fears. So I took Jimmy to the Y once a week for most of a summer. Jimmy was small and looked like a bunch of sticks walking, but he was a good boy and went to his lessons like a little soldier. And eventually he did learn to swim—well enough not to drown in deep water anyway. And every week he wore the same expression—of a person doing his duty because what was asked of him was reasonable and the request of people who cared about him.

Shellye had that very same look on the days Grady had been by. She was bravely considering that she should "do the best for everyone involved." Grady's interpretation of that was that she marry him so that the baby she carried would have two godly parents and Shellye would have the support she needed.

In some ways, it was a fine idea. Grady was the stable sort, had had his job for five years and owned his own place, kept it up nice. He was respected in the community because he didn't womanize or drink or smoke or any of the like. I know for a fact that certain single women in the church over the years had set their sights on him. He was a good man and spiritual, too, a combination often hard to come by.

I saw Grady stop at the Pines's home a couple of evenings, dressed nicely but not fancy, his thick hair combed back and his face looking twice shaved. One time he brought flowers, another time something in a covered dish, from his mother, I guessed. Each time he stayed about an hour. One time Shellye left with him about dinnertime and arrived home at dark.

Howard, Albert, and I discussed this business. We decided that if Shellye would love Grady, then this could be a good solution, an answer to prayer even. Shellye was shy to talk about this little courtship, and we honored her silence. But from across our properties, we couldn't tell whether or not she was growing to like Grady.

Doris, on the other hand, could hardly contain herself. She stood in the middle of her yard one afternoon and fairly shouted over to me what a fine man Grady was. "Such a godly man. So polite and knowledgeable about the Bible. And he works so hard at the church and is so helpful. And handsome, don't you think?"

I shrugged a little. "Nice looking enough."

"—he just adores Shellye. I think he'd do anything for her. And you see how he takes care of his mother—always looking in on her and helping her out. That's hard to find these days."

I told Doris I had a pot boiling on the stove. For some reason it irritated me to hear about Grady's attributes. I felt bad about that. I know I've always been too critical of people. But with Grady, I had to think of Shellye too. And Shellye had said precious little to me about this whole business.

Pastor Thomas and a couple of the deacons were rooting for Grady. To most people at church it was an awful shame that Grady hadn't yet found a suitable wife. Often, they'd bring up that Grady'd been engaged to a young woman at the Bible college, but she'd broken it off and had married another student, and they'd gone off to be missionaries somewhere in Southeast Asia. At twenty-six, poor Grady already had a tragic past. In Leeway, there has always been an abundance of marriageable women and a shortage of decent men. So the feeling I perceived in a number of people was that Shellye had better grab Grady while she could.

I was concerned that Shellye find someone who truly suited her. But I began to see her face soften when Grady was around. And I reminded myself that a lot of men entered marriage pretty rough and immature and then became fine men. And Grady not having a stunning personality wouldn't mean so much in the long haul. Some of the best husbands aren't that fascinating on the surface, but they're good as gold underneath.

"His voice is comforting," Shellye said one day, helping me pick flowers for the church altar bouquet. My day lilies were ablaze in three different colors. Orange and yellow and pink reflected off Shellye's face. She was smiling.

"Well, it's a deep voice—a good reading voice," I said.

"I love the way he tells me how much the Lord is concerned for me and my baby. When he tells it, I'm able to believe it more."

"That's good."

After that, I watched my thoughts about Grady. I told my critical self to just hush up.

Summers go by faster every year. One day you're pulling the lawn mower out of the shed to see if it will start; the next you're taking it for its weekly stroll around the yard, just to keep up with the weeds. Over the past few years, we've hired a boy down the block to do it, and I'm always anxious that first week the grass is needing cut, hoping he won't wait too long. Then I'm paying him every time I turn around.

It was mid-July, and Howard was still hanging on. He had good days and bad days, sometimes several in a row. He'd gotten hooked up to a Doctor Henderson over at Helmsly. Howard had seen him the first time during June, and they'd gotten all of Howard's medical records sent from Wichita. Since Howard was on state assistance and not a real insurance plan, Dr. Henderson had to finagle a bit to get Howard what he needed. Standard drug treatments were covered, but anything new wasn't. Henderson said that Howard's type of illness was unpredictable and that it couldn't hurt to try new combinations of treatments, that just because chemo hadn't worked before didn't mean it might not make a difference at another time. Whatever the case, Dr. Henderson was committed to helping Howard stay as comfortable as possible. I asked Howard what that meant exactly, but he wasn't too forthcoming. He'd chatter about anything else, but his own medical situation was another matter.

One Friday, Bailey brought Howard back from an appointment, dropping him off at the café. Howard sat at the far end of the counter and dumped out a paper bag. There was a whole pile of medicine samples.

"He loaded you up this time, didn't he?" I asked.

"These are mostly for pain and nausea. Just symptoms, but they're treatable anyway."

I poured Howard some coffee, and he held the cup in both hands, as if it were January outside instead of July. "He's wanting me to see a specialist in Joplin. Maybe start the chemo again."

"Well, Howard, it couldn't hurt to try more treatments if there's some hope."

Howard didn't look at me. I could tell he was ready to head for home and sleep the rest of the afternoon. "Hope's almost worse than no hope. If you hope, the letdown's a lot harder. And, boy the treatments before made me sick. I'd rather be dead, I think."

"I've never suffered anything like that. And I'd never tell you what to do. Just tell us how we can help."

That evening, Shellye, Doris, and Grady showed up on my patio. Grady came up the back walk, a cold watermelon on his shoulder. I decided I could get used to the man.

"Well, Grady, how are things?" Howard asked.

"God is good. God is good."

"Is he good in any way in particular?" This was Howard's type of humor, and I confess that being around me had contributed to it. Sometimes we talked about Pastor's sermons, and, well, I just speak my mind. If a stranger were to walk in on our discussions, he might think that we're sacrilegious.

"Well, no one else knows this yet, but," Grady couldn't hold back a smile. "Pastor Thomas has asked me to do a series of Bible studies on Sunday evenings during September. And I'm pleased with how the Lord has led my preparations."

"They'll be five Sunday evenings, an hour and a half each," said Shellye. She gave Grady a proud little smile, and he seemed to gain an inch in height. It touched me to see that little exchange.

"What's the topic?" Doris asked, leaning toward Grady with great interest.

"The Book of Romans. You can't get more basic when it comes to the fundamentals of our faith."

"You'll go just straight through the book?" asked Howard.

"Yes. With five weeks, we'll have to hit the highlights, but I think its message is especially relevant today, and people need to hear the truth—to counteract all they hear in the media and in society at large."

"Hmmm." Howard slurped loudly on a bit of watermelon. "It's true we hear a lot of different opinions, isn't it?"

"Well, the Bible is more than just an opinion."

"Oh yeah, you're right about that."

"The thing I appreciate so much about Romans, is it's so straightforward. Says in clear language how sin is sin and the wages of sin is death. Who is saying that anymore?" Grady's voice was loud for such a soft, breezy evening.

"Pastor's never minced words about sin," I said. Howard was picking seeds out of his wedge of watermelon with his fork, looking intent on sending every last one of them to the grass at the edge of the patio.

"That's true. That's what I like about this church. I went to a church a few years ago that had all but lost its grip on the Word of God. Everything was 'This is how I *feel* about this issue.'"

"It's good that people can be honest about the way they feel," Shellye said quietly.

"But we aren't to be led by our feelings. That's what I'm getting at. You have to be led by the Word and only the Word. Nothing else is reliable." Grady's tone was gentle, but I saw a tiny, hurt flicker in Shellye's eyes.

Grady put his plate down and reached into his shirt pocket. He pulled out a New Testament and thumbed his way to a certain spot. "It's right here. . . ." While Grady read and then explained the passage, I didn't listen, just watched Shellye's face. She settled back in her lawn chair, one hand on her growing tummy, and watched Grady, full admiration in her eyes.

Howard didn't seem to listen either. His eyes were focused somewhere out in the yard, where the fireflies and breeze kept up their dance.

After a while, Grady walked Shellye and Doris over to their house. He went inside with them.

"He'll make a good preacher, that's for sure," Howard said, but I didn't hear the admiration in his voice that I'd heard in Shellye's or in Doris's.

"That he will," I said, gathering up dishes and napkins. Then I felt the need to say, "And he'll settle down in a few years. Preachers just naturally are full of fire."

Howard laughed. "Grady'll burn down the whole county if he's not careful." I noticed then that he was breathing with some difficulty. He'd had intermittent breathless spells almost since the first week he'd moved in.

"Do you need to sit down? I'll get the dishes."

"Oh, maybe." Howard was back in the chair already. His whole arm shook as he returned the dishes to the patio table. I picked them up and went inside. The sink was half full of water when I heard Howard call my name, sounding scared. I went out and sat in the chair next to him. We never knew when one of these anxiety attacks would come over him.

He was white and sweaty and breathing fast. "Sorry, Velma. It was such a good evening." He raised a thin arm and wiped sweat from around his eyes and nose. He hung onto the chair for dear life. He just kept breathing faster.

"What can I do?" I asked, trying to sound calm. Howard was look-ing worse. After a few horrible moments, he said, voice trembling, "Velma, maybe I should go to the emergency room. This feels different from other times."

I heard Grady's car door slam. He started the car, and I headed across the lawn to stop him. "Grady, Howard's having a bad spell. We need to get him to the hospital." I hadn't even finished speaking, and Grady was out and hurrying toward Howard. We helped him into the car. By then, Doris had looked out her window and seen the commo-tion, and she and Shellye both came out and watched us drive away. They said they'd be praying. I clasped Howard's arm. He looked at me, and his eyes were all lit up with too much energy, as if all his alert sys-tems had been turned on at once.

Grady drove faster than I imagined he would; I knew he was the type that believes in driving the speed limit. But he drove fast and prayed out loud, and I was glad his voice boomed so. It had the ring of authority, and it sounded strong enough to keep evil away.

The nurse in the emergency room took one look at us and paged the doctor who was on call. There was a flurry of people and machinery, and Howard was swept away from us. We waited more than an hour to know anything. Grady called Pastor Thomas, but he wasn't home; Clare took the message and promised she'd tell him the minute he walked in. Then Grady called several of the young men he'd been dis-cipling, and they prayed over the phone.

I didn't have any words for the Lord. I just sat and waited to know what the Lord would allow us this night. I've been in a number of rooms in which people died. It only takes one experience like that to teach you that when the Lord decides to take a person home, prayers don't make any difference. Not in the outcome anyway. All prayers seem to do at that time is help you face the God who's about to do whatever he's about to do. You feel helpless but, in a strange way, cared for too.

It turned out that Howard had reacted to one of the new medica-tions. The doctor on call got in touch with Dr. Henderson, and they figured out what to do. About midnight, they decided that Howard was back to normal enough to go home.

The ride home was quiet, except for Grady saying, every few miles, "Praise the Lord, Howard. He upheld you." Howard didn't answer. He got as comfortable as he could in the backseat and was sleeping by the time Grady pulled into my drive. Grady helped Howard up the stairs and was gracious when I thanked him several times for helping us. All he would say was, "The Lord knew what you needed, Velma. He's always watching over us."

I let Grady let himself out. I stayed in the chair by the bed to watch over Howard. He slept calmly, but I still felt the need to stay close. Even though I couldn't pray, it seemed that being in the room was a prayer of its own.

By the end of July, Grady and Shellye had set a date. They would be married in early September.

The morning after Grady had asked Shellye to marry him, Shellye came by the café and showed me the ring. It was a nice ring, and it looked as if it belonged on Shellye's finger. I gave her a hug.

"Well, miss, you're about to have a family of your own!"

"I'm ready, Velma, I really am." She smiled. "I want to ask you something, though."

"What's that?"

"Could I work part-time here at the café?"

"Well, hon, sure. I can always use some more help. Nothing full-time for now."

"I don't really want to work full-time. And once the baby's born, Grady doesn't want me to work outside the home. But we'll have a lot of expenses coming up with the baby, and there's some work he wants to do on the house. He says certain things never bothered him so much when he was there by himself, but he wants to fix it up really nice for us."

July was also the month that Pastor Thomas started having back trouble—severe pain in his lower back. He had Dan Mallory, one of the deacons, fill in for him two Sundays in that month. Days when I'd be cleaning the church and Pastor would be in the church office, I'd walk by the door to say hello, and he would look up, his face pinched. Anyone could see he was suffering. But I thought I saw other problems in his face, too.

I said something to Clare a time or two, but she didn't supply much information. I worried then that it was family trouble. Pastors will keep family troubles a secret until something big happens, like a divorce or a resignation. When Pastor and Clare went away a couple of weekends, they said it was to go to a clinic in Kansas City to get treatment for his back. I hoped that was all it was.

Welcome to VELMA'S PLACE

Grady's Favorite Skillet Supper

1 cup of the large-link smoked turkey sausage (1 sausage),
   sliced into bite-sized pieces
1 tablespoon vegetable oil, if needed
1/2 cup red onion, coarsely chopped
2 cups of potatoes, cubed
3 cloves of garlic, minced
4 cups of fresh kale, washed and coarsely chopped
1/2 to 1 cup chicken or vegetable stock
2 to 4 tablespoons brown sugar
1 to 3 tablespoons hot-pepper vinegar*
1 to 2 teaspoons fresh rosemary or sage

Brown the sausage in a large skillet. Adding oil if necessary, add the onion and potatoes. After both have browned somewhat, add the garlic and greens. Stir and cook for a minute or two, then add enough stock to half cover the contents of the pan, cover with a lid, and cook until greens and potatoes are tender, 15 to 20 minutes. (Be careful not to overcook.)

Add brown sugar, hot-pepper vinegar, salt, pepper, and herbs to taste. Serve hot.

*Make your own hot-pepper vinegar by slicing the ends off a few jalapeños or chili peppers and putting them in a jar of white distilled vinegar. After a day or two, the vinegar will be hot. Taste to see how hot the vinegar is before adding it to a dish. You might use a tablespoon of hot vinegar and then add regular vinegar if more is called for.

9

Sissy Fenders

They even sent for men to come from far away. . . . For them you bathed yourself, painted your eyes, and decked yourself with ornaments.

—Ezekiel 23:40

The first Thursday noon of August, Bailey parked himself at the counter and asked for a small serving of biscuits and gravy. John Mason, Bailey's buddy, cut straight to the cherry pie. I'm so used to the two of them gabbing about anything and everything that I hardly ever listen closely. Their noise is often more like background sound than it is information. But that afternoon they drew me in.

"So I guess there's gonna be a big wedding huh? Between Shellye and that Grady?" John's bushy eyebrows went halfway up his forehead. John's a kind soul, always finding the good in people and in situations. He's a good balance for Bailey, who missed his calling as a private eye—you know, one of those aging, bumbling fellows you see on television who end up catching the criminal in spite of their arthritis and poor hearing. I could picture big ol' Bailey in a trench coat, the belt all tangled up, moseying along my counter from one customer to the next until he found something wrong with somebody.

"Yes," I said to John. "Those two act like puppies around each other. I guess it'll be OK."

"Why wouldn't it be OK?" Bailey asked.

"Grady's a good guy," John said, swirling a bit of pie crust in the puddle of ice cream on his plate. "Well, I don't know him really, but I hear good about him. He's always been real active at church. I hear that he'll probably get elected to the board of deacons once he's been married a while."

I could tell from the way Bailey was playing in the gravy that he was working on some theory or that he wasn't feeling peaceful. "Tom Banks saw Doris walking the street in front of his place," he said, "at three in the morning yesterday."

"Yes," I said. "She still takes her walks. But she's happy as can be about Shellye and Grady."

"It'll be nice to see something work out for that family for a change." Bailey paused hardly a second, then asked, "How's Howard doing?"

"It changes from one day to the next. Mostly he's wrung out."

"That's cancer for you."

"That boy has a rash on his chest that looks like a map," John commented.

"A rash?" Bailey asked over his coffee cup.

"Yep. I drove through Velma's alley yesterday morning—chasing down that cockeyed dog of mine—and Howard was taking out the trash. Looked half asleep, and his shirt was open. Dark red patches. Wonder if they itch."

Bailey looked at me, eyes sharp. "He ever mention that, Velma?"

"Why would he? He's got all kinds of symptoms. I don't ask questions—not my place to."

"Tell him to try calamine lotion," said John. "It's been around forever, but it does the job on a lot of things. He may as well try it."

"I'll tell him if it comes up." I left them and walked back to the kitchen. I didn't feel like talking about Howard's symptoms. I wished John hadn't seen any rash. It just seemed that I should protect a guest in my house from others' scrutiny. But that was going to be hard to do.

That evening, the bunch of us regulars gathered for dinner. I'd fixed a huge pot roast with carrots, potatoes, and onions. There were thirteen of us, including Grady and Shellye. They enjoyed getting congratulated and teased about their upcoming marriage.

Midway through, the conversation took a cold turn.

"Well, it was the oddest thing this afternoon," said Sarah Blanchet, our postmistress. "Tom Fenders walked in to pick up his mail, and he told me his brother-in-law had died. Killed in a car wreck yesterday morning. Tom's driving to Tulsa for the service tomorrow."

The dead man was Sissy Fenders' husband, Leland Scott. Murmurs rose around the table. What a shame; you just never knew when your time was up. As a group, we wondered how Sissy was doing. As I've already said, Sissy was not my favorite person. But you don't wish the death of a loved one on anyone, unless you're just evil. I'm acquainted enough with grief to shed tears on the spot when someone else has a loss like that.

Normally, if Sissy Fenders Scott's name came up, there would be at least one person with a critical remark. She'd always put on such airs around most of us. But that evening, we said what a shame it was, and then we ate quietly for a while before changing the subject.

Just a week later, we learned that Sissy was coming to Leeway to stay for a while with Tom and his family. And, sure enough, a few days after that she showed up in town. I saw her in Avery's on Monday afternoon, when I ran over to pick up more onions and milk. She was talking with Avery pretty intently, and I didn't interrupt them. Sissy still looked picture perfect, even at our age. But her face made me think of a bare lightbulb, you know, with the shade removed, blank but burning. I knew that look; it was her grief. Nothing exposes a person more. Sissy didn't see me, and I decided to wait until another time to offer my condolences.

I never expected Sissy to show up at Jerusalem Baptist, but the next Sunday she did. I was sitting in my usual place in the back, and she brushed by and sat in the pew directly in front of me. Hair all done up perfectly and a little summer hat on. I had to give my thoughts to the Lord, because, even with Sissy's recent grief, I couldn't feel charitable toward her now that she was sitting close enough to touch. I tried to follow Pastor Thomas's sermon, but he was taking more than adequate time to walk us through 2 Timothy 2, verse by verse, and I didn't feel much of it applying to me. Plus, he'd preached these same verses many times before; there must have been something in them none of us got, as he was so reluctant to let them go. So I sat and stared at Sissy's magazine hair and the tiny yellow silk roses on her hat, and I began remembering each and every time she'd tried to make me look bad, all the little contests, her shameless behavior toward Albert when we were just girls. I sat there and asked the Lord why he'd never seen fit to move her to apologize to me for being so deliberately hurtful. As was usual at that particular time in my life, the Lord offered me a big silence. So then I just felt disgruntled at everybody.

After the closing prayer, I tried to get away, but Sissy turned around to me directly and said, "Velma, so good to see you."

"Yes. I'm so sorry about your husband. We all hated to hear."

"That's very kind of you." Her smile was deceptively genuine. "I couldn't bear to be in that big old house by myself, and both my girls have their kids and their own lives. Decided to come back here for a while."

"I hope it's a good stay for you."

"The folks at this church are so nice, I think I'll make my church home here for now."

I'd never known Sissy to think seriously about religion before, let alone refer to church as any kind of home. She walked ahead of me out of the sanctuary, and I watched her greet others and others greet her, and I knew that she would move in here and establish her own little kingdom. Sometimes it seems that the Lord favors the people who need affirmation the least. And he doesn't have time to hear the prayers of the rest of us. This was my thought as I watched Sissy make her rounds of Jerusalem Baptist. Then my thoughts were brought up short, and I was ashamed of myself. Sissy had just lost her husband. Who needed affirmation more than a woman fresh from her husband's graveside? That kind of a loss should be hard enough to pay Sissy back for every hurt she'd caused others over the years. But of course, that's not how we pay for our sins. We don't even pay for them ourselves. That's what Jesus did. I guess he knew that the bad and good would never add up evenly or cancel each other out. There's no system in this life to really take care of the good or the bad. It's a mystery.

Seeing Sissy again and feeling those old resentful feelings made me wonder if I'd grown in my soul at all over the years. Every year that passes shows me even more how much I depend on the Lord to get me over being myself.

A day or two after that, I was shopping early in the morning, picking up my day's produce at Avery's, and he walked up beside me.

"Hey Velma, I'm about to be under new management."

I just stared at him. He owned the whole building, including the part with VELMA'S in it. "What do you mean?"

"I'm selling the building to Sissy Scott. She offered a better price than I thought I'd ever get around here. We're getting papers drawn up."

I kept staring at Avery. I thought my heart would blow through my ribs.

"What . . . how will that affect the café?"

"You'll just pay rent to her instead of me, I guess. Probably won't affect you at all." He continued down the aisle, stopping to put the pears in a more stable configuration. "Goodness, I may retire sooner than I'd planned. The last few years have taken a lot out of me. It's awful getting old, isn't it?"

I couldn't answer him. My ears were ringing. I thought I'd come down with a fever. Of all the turns of events—Sissy Fenders being my landlord. Why, once she owned the building, she'd have all kinds of say about my café. She could just waltz in and start making demands, changing things, or charging higher rent. Of course she'd raise the rent.

I paid for the produce, and Avery rolled the full cart over to the café for me.

When I told Howard about Sissy that evening, he couldn't believe it either. But he had no way of knowing all the meanings of Sissy Fenders owning VELMA'S.

He got more of an idea the next day. He was having breakfast with me at the café, and I'd served a couple of the early risers their eggs and sausage. Then the jingle bells on the door sounded, and there was Sissy, coming straight for us. She walked up to Howard and me. I had enough presence of mind to introduce them. I offered her coffee, and she asked if I had hot tea. I drew hot water from the coffee machine and gave her a tea bag and lemon wedge. She sat at the counter next to Howard and dipped the tea bag over and over again. Even at seven in the morning, she was dressed up and looking professional.

"How's the café business, Velma?" she asked.

"About the same as always. We're doing OK."

"Doing more than OK," Howard chimed in. Of course we *weren't* doing more than OK; Howard knew that I didn't make much off the place.

"It's so hard to make a good profit in the restaurant business," Sissy remarked. She squeezed the tea bag against her spoon and set it on the saucer, then made a shield around the lemon wedge with one hand while squeezing it with the other.

"We make enough. Only so many people around here to come in and eat," I said.

"Still, it's a shame it's not easier to turn over a bigger profit." I wondered then if she'd managed to get her hands on my records. I wondered if a landlord had the legal right to get financial records of businesses that rented from her.

Then Sissy changed the subject, asking about folks around town. So we talked politely about this old schoolmate and that friend's granddaughter and another person's business or health problems or funeral. After a short while, Sissy had finished her tea, leaving a lavenderish lipstick print on the white mug. She left a nice tip and waved good-bye as if she and I were old friends. For all I know, we *were* friends in her mind. Maybe the only friends she'd ever had were people who let her walk all over them.

"Wow," Howard said, watching her cross the street. Even through the glass door, we could hear her heels clipping against the pavement. "She comes in like a whirlwind, doesn't she?"

"Always did." I put the cup with its grinning lips into the sink.

"What do you think she's up to, asking about your profits and so forth?"

"I think she's probably got other ideas for this space and is just waiting to prove to me how unsuccessful VELMA'S is so she can close me down."

"Oh, you think? You're the only restaurant in town."

"It would be just like her to bring in a whole other business—some glitzy restaurant from out of town. I'll bet she's already making plans."

"We won't let that happen, Velma." Howard's voice had that not-a-care-in-the-world quality to it. I didn't know how he managed to be so optimistic, with one foot in the grave.

"And how can we do that?"

"Increase our profit margin."

I laughed so loud that Hank over in the corner booth looked up from his crossword puzzle. "You're a wonder, Howard, you really are."

"You think I'm crazy, I know, but I'll start making some plans myself, how's that?"

I waved a dishrag at him.

I thought Doris wouldn't survive Shellye's engagement. Every glitch in her personality stayed glitched full-time. I don't think the woman slept during the entire month of August. One Wednesday afternoon I saw Grady's mother, Thelma, come out the back door of Doris's house. They were working on the wedding plans together. From the expression on Thelma's face, you'd have thought they had just finished negotiating an arms treaty. Thelma was so glassy-eyed and out of breath that she didn't even see me sitting on the patio with my iced tea and a magazine.

Shellye started working for me in the middle of the month. She was showing quite a bit, but that only made her sweeter, and the customers were completely charmed. I made sure she wasn't on her feet too long at a time, giving her sit-down work when I could. She could manage the grill while sitting on a tall step stool, and I didn't mind waiting the tables more.

Grady had lunch with us every day, and he and Shellye were king and queen of Thursday evening dinner. More and more, our conversation was about the wedding. It would be at the church on the second Sunday afternoon in September. A pastor friend of Grady's from Oklahoma would do the ceremony along with Pastor Thomas. The vows would be traditional, only with additional Scripture readings. A good florist in Helmsly would handle the flowers. Shellye was still shopping for her gown.

It upset me, though, that the gown would be beige and not white. It took most of an afternoon for me to get Shellye to tell me that Grady had made this decision. Since it would be so obvious to everyone that she wasn't a virgin but seven months pregnant, Grady thought a white gown would be not only hypocritical but an affront to Christian chastity. Shellye didn't seem to mind, but I simmered most of the week over that one. In my mind, Shellye was still a virgin. She'd not given anything up of her own will. I'd go home in the evenings and fume at Howard and Albert both. They didn't say much, although I could tell they weren't happy. I supposed they were so quiet because I was making so much noise.

One afternoon, Shellye came in to work her half shift, and she was smiling so that I couldn't imagine what was up.

"Velma, I have a favor to ask you. Sit down."

I sat at one of Betty's tables, my favorite one with the little knobby feet. It's a terror to clean but has character. Shellye sat down across from me.

"We want to have a reception, a nice reception for all the wedding guests. We're figuring on about fifty-five people, including Grady's college friends and people at church."

"That sounds like a nice idea.

"An early evening supper a little while after the ceremony." She paused.

"That would be nice," I said.

"We'd . . ." Shellye looked at me shyly. "We'd really like it if you cooked the meal and if we could have the reception here at VELMA'S."

Her eyes shone at me, and I was overcome. I've always imagined that the baby I lost was the daughter I would never see grow up. But I looked across the table and knew that the good Lord had given me a daughter anyway. I finally said, "It will be the most wonderful honor of my life, Shellye, to cook your wedding dinner."

For the next few days, I slept even less than Doris did. In fact, one morning at 3 A.M., I was in the kitchen going through all of Mama's and Gran Lenny's recipes and all of my own, and there was a tap at the door. Doris stood there in her pink jogging suit.

"For heaven's sake, Doris, come on in."

"What in the world are you doing up at this hour?" She had a cigarette. I pushed a dirty coffee cup toward her to use for an ashtray. When Doris tapped ash off her cigarette, she looked in touch with life. She even looked as if she controlled a lot of her own circumstances.

"Oh, trying to come up with the wedding menu. I can't settle my mind down, though. I cook every day for a crowd, and this thing is unnerving me."

"If it will be too much, Velma, you don't have to do it. I told Shellye it was a lot to ask."

"It's not a lot to ask! I want to do it. I'm just too giddy to make a decent plan."

"Well, what do you have in mind so far?" Doris squinted a bit and looked at me through smoke.

"I figured a soup and a salad, a meat, a starch, vegetables, bread, dessert. Pretty standard."

"What do you decide on first?"

"Usually, you plan the meal around the meat. Certain things go better with pork or chicken or beef. Once you're settled on the meat, other things can fall into place."

"Chicken's pretty foolproof."

"Yes, most people like it. And most people eat it all the time. I'd rather serve something they're not as accustomed to."

"They eat beef a lot too."

We sat there a moment. I was leafing through recipes in Mama's old binder, smaller than a normal notebook, its cover a slate-blue cloth.

"I hardly ever eat pork," Doris said. She took another draw on her cigarette.

"Yes, that's more of a specialty, isn't it?"

"And it's hard to find pork dishes that are really that good, you know? So much of the time they just remind you of beef or chicken dishes you'd rather be eating."

I looked at Doris, and she at me.

"Doris, are you sleeping at *all*?"

"Oh, I don't know. Most days asleep and awake feel like the same thing. I wish I could be a real person for a change, especially now that Shellye's approaching the most wonderful day of her life."

I kept staring at Doris, wondering how she could be making so much sense and talking so calmly, all the while thinking herself crazy. I thought that maybe we should have more of these early morning talks. Maybe when she got this exhausted she was just too tired to put up her defenses and worry about what she said. Maybe fatigue was what helped her be with her true self.

"Mama used to make the most wonderful pork cutlet with apples and prunes and walnuts." I paged quickly to that section of Mama's book. "And, yes, here's the tart brown sauce she'd serve with it."

"Prunes, huh?" Doris was squinting at me again.

"Well, I could leave out the prunes, if you think they would put people off."

"It sounds very good, except for the prunes."

"All right. I'll adjust." I showed Doris the facing pages with the recipes carefully written on them. We looked over the recipes together, and by the time we'd read through them, we were certain that we'd found the main dish. I didn't mention that it had been a winter meal. Mama would use dried fruit and the apple butter she made and preserved every autumn. We'd take a bite of the fruit and the sauce and feel those clear, bright days again, tingling on our tongues.

Doris sat with me at the table until nearly 5:30, and by then the sky was getting light, and we'd put together the entire wedding menu.

Wouldn't you know, on the day I'm running on hardly any sleep at all—the last day of August—Sissy Fenders Scott walks into my café.

"Velma, I'm buying out Avery. You and I will need to talk a little, once the transaction's complete. Could I have some hot tea?"

I couldn't think of what to say. I set the tea in front of her. "I hope it can wait until after the eighth. I'm doing a big dinner; don't have time for much else."

"Oh, of course. That's Shellye Pines's wedding, isn't it? She and that Grady make a handsome pair." Sissy was being entirely too friendly. I gave a Gran Lenny grunt, in spite of my best manners.

"I'll just get in touch with you after that. The sale of the building won't be finalized until then anyway. Then we can chat. Could you put this in a paper cup to go?"

I gave her the cup, with a lid. She walked out as stylish as ever. I was too tired to be very upset. I just worked through the afternoon, thinking what a nice thing it would be if the last meal I cooked at VELMA'S was a wedding feast.

Baked, Fruited Pork Cutlets with Tart Brown Sauce

4 slices of boneless lean pork, can be cutlets or slices from a small roast
1/4 cup red onion, slivered
1/4 cup carrot, sliced thin
1/4 cup chopped walnuts
4 tablespoons butter
2 tablespoons brown sugar
allspice
cloves
1/2 cup tart apple, sliced thin
1/4 cup pitted, dried prunes, chopped coarsely
1 orange, sliced (optional)

Tart brown sauce:
1 package brown gravy mix
3/4 cup apple butter

With a meat mallet, pound pork slices until they are 1/4 inch thick. In a skillet, saute onions, carrots, and walnuts in half the butter. Add the brown sugar and a dash or two of allspice and cloves.

Preheat oven to 350°. Melt the rest of the butter in a baking dish to grease the bottom.

Arrange a few apple slices and prunes on one half of each of the pork slices. Add 1 or 2 tablespoons of the onion/walnut mixture. (Don't use too much onion mixture; what's left over can be added to the tart brown sauce.)

Fold each pork slice over and hold in place with one or two toothpicks. Place each stuffed slice into the baking dish. You might brush some butter over the top of the meat to help it brown as it bakes. You can also put a fresh orange slice on top of each cutlet.

Bake for 30 to 45 minutes until meat is tender.

Tart brown sauce:
Make gravy according to directions on the packet. As the gravy thickens, add the apple butter. Add any leftover onion/walnut mixture. Let the sauce simmer 10 to 15 minutes. Serve warm over the stuffed pork pieces.

10

Doris Pines

Mortal, you are living in the midst of a rebellious house, who have eyes to see but do not see, who have ears to hear but do not hear . . . Therefore, mortal, prepare for yourself an exile's baggage, and go into exile by day in their sight . . . Perhaps they will understand, though they are a rebellious house. You shall bring out your baggage by day in their sight, as baggage for exile; and you shall go out yourself at evening in their sight as those do who go into exile.

—EZEKIEL 12:2–4

Sometimes I thought I had Doris Pines figured out, but most of the time I knew she was beyond me. There was something very unsettled about her, unfinished business, I guess, that went back to the desertion, but maybe even further back than that. Some conflict took root in her life, and it managed to stay and grow and establish its own life inside her. After all that time, Doris acted and talked the life of that thing and not her own life. She couldn't sit still for more than half an hour. Usually about ten minutes into the sermon, she left to walk around the block. She made it back in time for the closing hymn, and then she often cried. She was busy with half a dozen projects at one time—that, or she got fatigued and took to her bed.

Just about anything stopped Doris's progress. The TV schedule changing made a shift in her week, and someone's offhand comment would set her reeling for days. She needed her routine. This had been a problem sometimes when Shellye was in school, trying to take part in drama and volleyball. Most of the time she could hand Doris a schedule of rehearsals and practices, and Doris was OK with that. But if anything came up that wasn't on the schedule, Shellye would have to look elsewhere for transportation. Doris worked mornings for Dr. Saliman, always arriving and leaving right on time. She picked up the mail at a certain time and started dinner at a certain time. She even straightened the living room at a certain time. Shellye usually managed to get rides with friends, but once or twice she came over here, eyes big with panic. Albert, bless his soul, loaded her and her things into the pickup and took her where she needed to go.

We got to know Shellye quite a bit when she was in school. She was younger then, and Doris's spells bothered her more. Shellye came to the back door one evening, asking if she could see what time our clocks said, because their electricity had blinked and she needed to reset their clocks. But I didn't figure she'd be close to tears about that. She stood in our kitchen and stared at the clock above the sink and asked, "Can you tell if somebody's dying?" She said that her mom had a fluttery heart. Shellye was only eleven then.

I've done my best not to blame Doris for the stress in her daughter's life. Blame is a hard thing. It goes naturally with justice, and we seem to have the need to blame someone when a bad thing happens. But the closer you look at who you're blaming, the more you see how she has a load of her own, and she meant no harm. I see it all the time with the people at church. Because I'm the janitor, in sort of a service role, and because I cook for everybody, they talk to me more than they probably should. Some falling out will happen between two or three people, and I'll end up hearing all sides. I've learned to stay off all sides.

I confess that I'd never thought Doris was an adequate mama for Shellye, especially considering the special emotional needs the girl had after her daddy left. But if Doris did anything, she tried. She tried all day long, and every minute was its own little exercise in trying. She tried so much that she couldn't let herself rest. So I had to be merciful in my heart toward Doris. She was my neighbor, and she'd never done a spiteful thing to me or to Albert in all the years we'd lived next to each other. She wasn't mean to Shellye as far as I knew. Her main failing with

Shellye was that she was sort of absent. She was absorbed in her own hurts, and Shellye had suffered the neglect.

I'll never know exactly how Doris coped with getting ready for Shellye's wedding. I was busy enough, preparing for the reception. Whatever state Doris and the rest of us were in, the wedding happened on a most beautiful day, and the ceremony went without a hitch. The church was full. I panicked a bit, because I was only prepared to feed sixty people—well, sixty-five if I had to, you always have extra just in case—but we'd required RSVP, and I told myself to concentrate on the wedding ceremony and go into my cooking frenzy when it was appropriate, an hour or so later.

Shellye and Grady were married a few days after the atmosphere became autumn crisp. There's a certain aroma that slips into the breeze then. It's hard to describe, but one day it's not there and the next day it is, as if the air has just arrived from another country. And its presence makes you stop on your way to wherever you're going and breathe in deeply. On that day every year, I take a gulp of that air, and suddenly I'm breathing in all the autumns of my childhood, of my early marriage, of the years when my boy was little. When the sky and trees get that sharp and spicy quality, you know there's such a thing as eternity, because suddenly you're so close to your past and your future too. Why, I feel as if I could take a step in any direction and be age seven or seventeen or a hundred and two.

And during the first few days of autumn, people get a little giddy. The café crowd is louder and happier and has more energy than during the summer months. There's a brightness that sort of hangs around people, makes them more interested in each other and in life. So the crowd that sat respectfully in Jerusalem Baptist Church that Sunday afternoon was, underneath its quiet demeanor, nearly drunk with the very air.

Shellye was seven months pregnant, glowing and breathless and entirely beautiful. Lana, of Lana's Salon four blocks from the café, had outdone herself. Shellye looked like royalty, her hair swept up and tiny cream-colored roses set naturally in a little crown on top. Shellye had chosen a pearly beige dress with a bodice that easily slipped around her growing breasts and with pretty layers of rayon falling waistless to the floor. She carried a bouquet of pink and cream roses.

Grady wore a sharp, black suit that made him look even thinner than he was. If the rest of us were drunk on the atmosphere, then I would say Grady was close to passing out. The way he looked at

Shellye made my heart do dances. I scolded myself for doubting the goodness of this union. The man was so in love he could hardly see straight. So was Shellye. The only thing that made her more sensible than the rest of us was the baby inside her. There were moments when we could almost forget her condition, but she told me afterwards that the little thing had moved all during the ceremony.

"Right when I was supposed to say, 'I, Shellye Pines, take you, Grady Lewis,' she pressed on my bladder so hard I thought I'd have to say, 'Excuse me' instead and run for the bathroom!" Shellye said this to me as I stood in the receiving line and hugged her. I'd never seen her look so happy. I could also see that Grady wasn't pleased with her sharing that with the world, but Grady would just have to loosen up. Marriage tends to have that effect.

I stayed only long enough to congratulate the two of them and compliment Pastor Thomas and Grady's friend for the fine service. Then I hopped over to the café. Howard went with me, along with several of the women from Jerusalem Baptist. Once I had announced during Sunday school that I was looking for volunteers to help serve the meal, I'd had no problem getting help. I put people at their stations. The tables were arranged and set. We'd used the set of nice china that someone had long ago left to the church—that was for the wedding party. Everyone else got "Velma Ware." But we'd bought nice napkins and had candles and flower arrangements everywhere they'd fit.

I hate to sound boastful, but Shellye's wedding feast went flawlessly. It was all in all a blessed day. My only disappointment was that, in the end, I didn't get to bake the wedding cake. We decided to have a professional baker handle that. I'm a cook but not really a decorater, and I told Shellye that she needed something extra pretty for this occasion. Given how busy I was with the rest of the meal, giving up the cake was the sane thing to do.

And Doris, bless her, didn't have to go out walking a single time. Not through the ceremony, not afterwards while people made their slow way through the receiving line in the church foyer. Not during the meal, which went on for a couple of hours, and not through the cutting of the cake. I kept my eye on Doris, off and on, but she was just fine. She may have gone walking that night, but I was so exhausted from putting on the wedding feast that I slept and didn't know a thing.

Doris kept coming over to visit us in the evenings. Before Shellye moved into her own home, I'd always figured that it was Shellye who came to visit and Doris who just came along. But Doris was making regular visits on Tuesday and Friday evenings. She did that through the end of September and into October. Sometimes she and Howard would be visiting when I came home from work.

It can take me awhile to see what's right in front of my face, and we were nearly into October before it occurred to me that Doris came to visit Howard, not me. And she wasn't making church visits. She wasn't as flighty, either, around Howard, the way she had been in the beginning.

Howard clearly liked the company on the one hand; on the other, he seemed uneasy with it. It had to do with him dying, I'm sure, not wanting to be involved in a romantic way with anyone. But he didn't say a word to me about it, and he didn't discourage Doris. He didn't flinch or act uncomfortable when she'd step over to pat his shoulder or smooth his hair before she left to walk across the yard to her own house.

I didn't know what to make of this, but decided that it was best if I didn't make anything of it. In matters of romance, I've never claimed to have any expertise. I married young and never needed to look anywhere else, because Albert and I always got along. He wasn't necessarily a flowers and candy man, but we had our own romantic expressions.

Did Howard and Doris have little expressions going on? I tried not to find out, but at the same time I did. I didn't even know what I should think. But then, not two weeks after the wedding, a ruckus hit Jerusalem Baptist, and Howard's relationship to Doris seemed unimportant in comparison.

John Mason never meant to harm Howard; John's not that kind of man. All he did was ask Howard, after church on Sunday, in front of two other people, how Howard's rash was. At least this is what Doris told me later. I was somewhere else at the time, talking to Lonnie I think. She'd done an exceptionally nice piano piece for the offertory that morning. All I knew was that when I went to the back of the church to join up with Howard and walk home, he looked ill and angry and afraid, and everyone around him was quiet.

I got there in time to hear Bud Hanks ask, with a nervous little laugh, "You don't have anything you can pass to the rest of us now, do you?"

Howard couldn't seem to find words. He coughed and tried not to look at anybody. He said to the floor, "I'd not be standing here if that were the case."

Then everybody sort of broke up and Howard and Doris and I walked toward our houses. Just a few yards away from the church-yard, Doris sputtered.

"What business does he have asking you a question like that?"

"It's OK, Doris."

"No it's not!"

"I must have missed something," I said.

"You didn't miss anything." Howard's pace had picked up, almost as if he wanted to be away from Doris and me.

By evening, I knew what the fuss was about. I went to the evening service. Howard didn't, was too fatigued and had a queasy stomach. Doris didn't either, but she usually didn't.

Carol Wennedka stopped me as I headed for my place in the back pew. "Velma, there's some concern about Howard's illness." She pulled me into the parlor, behind the sanctuary, and looked as if she was try-ing to pry my mind open with her eyes. "Has he ever said what kind of cancer he has?"

"No. Does it matter? The man doesn't expect to finish out the year." I didn't mean to sound so irritated, but I know what gossip looks and sounds like. I've seen it often enough among my customers, and, sorry to say, in my own church parlor.

"Is there a possibility that he's hiding the truth from you?"

"Carol, for heaven's sakes, what is this about? What was that busi-ness this morning about, people asking him if he is contagious? It's no one's business!"

"It is if he's putting anyone in danger."

"How would he do that?"

Then I felt someone slip up from behind. Charlie Resnick, one of our deacons. He touched my shoulder gently. "Howard's symptoms look a lot like AIDS." He didn't say more, just looked at me.

"People have all sorts of symptoms when they're this far along with cancer. You, Charlie, of all people, should know that." Charlie had lost his mother to breast cancer, not three years before.

"I know, I know. But people would feel a lot more at ease if Howard would provide a little more information. That's all we're saying."

"What if he did have AIDS? We'd kick him out?" My, sometimes I sound like Gran Lenny—her tone of voice, even the choice of words.

"Of course not. But we'd know better how to counsel him. And . . . we could take whatever precautions were necessary. There are children here in the church, impressionable young people. We have to think of everybody."

I couldn't see straight or listen during the entire service that evening. Grady was into his second week of the Book of Romans, and the main points he kept bringing out had to do with sin. I'm no theologian, but I know there are plenty of love verses in the Book of Romans. It seemed to me that Grady looked at me several times while he was going on about sin, but that was probably my imagination.

Anger kept me stirred up the whole walk home. Howard was asleep in his room. I wanted to talk to Albert—he's always been so level-headed—but I didn't feel very close to him that evening.

And as I drifted off to sleep, finally, I realized that part of what had me so stirred up was fear. For all I knew, Howard had come to us with full-blown AIDS. Maybe that was why, after all these years of no contact, he chose to come live with us. Of course we'd know nothing about him, his past, his illness. No one could blame him for keeping quiet about it. Leeway's not a very sophisticated place, and people can panic easily over something they don't understand. Right then, I felt pretty panicked myself.

I was distracted all the next day at the café. Shellye worked that morning, and I think I hurt her feelings by not being more talkative. I couldn't tear my mind away from Howard and what looked like an explosion ready to happen at church. Shellye almost had to grab my shoulders to get my attention about 10:30.

"Oh, Velma, a man called while you were at Avery's. A Henry Carpenter. He wants you to call him back. I left the number by the phone."

I frowned at her while my mind got hold of the name.

"Do you know him? He didn't sound like a salesman, but I didn't promise you'd call, just that I'd give you the message."

"I know him. Did he say what he wanted exactly?"

"Just that he wants you to call him. He wanted to know how you were. Who is he?"

"We share some history I'm trying to forget. I've no reason to call him." I headed back toward the kitchen, and Shellye seemed to ask the next question with care.

"If he calls again, do you want me to tell him not to call anymore?"

"I don't know. You shouldn't be rude, I suppose. He probably won't call again."

Mama always said that troubles come in bunches. Shellye was happily married now, but this new mess with Howard, and now a call from Carpenter, the last man on earth I wanted to deal with. I didn't have a bit of room for any of my past troubles right now. I kept waiting for Sissy Fenders Scott to come sashaying in the door to announce her plans for my life and my business. And during a fine autumn Avery wasn't getting very good apples. I couldn't imagine how that would happen. I had all kinds of plans for apple dishes, and yet I was disappointed half the time with the produce I got. If Avery didn't find better sources, I'd have to shop out of town and pay more and possibly cause hard feelings with Avery, something I couldn't afford to do, with the building changing hands. He and Sissy seemed to be pretty friendly, and I had to be careful. Just thinking about all the possibilities for bad news in my life made me want to take to my bed and pray for a fever.

It's not a good thing to think bad of a person. I thought about this as Howard and I walked to the café on Tuesday morning. Once you have bad thoughts of a person, he gets on a different track in your mind. You're subject to your own bias then, and in order to think anything good about that person ever again, you have to backtrack in your own head and heart. Most of us are too lazy to do that.

But I knew that, even as we walked through the pleasant, chilly air, breath frosty white in front of us, Howard was getting shifted around in the minds of some people, possibly a number of people all over town. I'd have to listen close to the gossip that drifted around the tables.

Howard wasn't the only person my mind worried over that morning. I was fighting myself to think good of Grady Lewis. He was now Shellye's husband, and I owed it to her to think well of him. Anyone could see that Shellye thought the world of Grady. But he had been at the edges of that little group in the church parlor Sunday morning. He hadn't said anything, but I'd seen something in his face that still upset me, deep down. I had the feeling that Grady would be one of the first people to hammer Howard with questions if he was afforded the opportunity. I knew this because Grady had a drive to always be dividing the right from the wrong, the moral from the immoral. That was clear from the talks he was giving Sunday nights on the Book of Romans. By the verses he chose to emphasize, I could tell that judgment was important to him. It was in his nature, and that seemed like a big flaw to me.

But Shellye, my dear girl, looked up to Grady so, and she went about decorating their house and getting ready for the baby. I saw them at the Furniture Warehouse shopping for curtains and a coffee table. His hand was around her waist, and she leaned into him in that comfortable, snuggly way, as much as she could as pregnant as she was. Shellye had a cute waddle and looked like one of those M&Ms on the commercial, all fat candy body and a big smile and skinny arms and legs just sticking out. Grady was lanky and tall and made me think of Abe Lincoln, had Lincoln toted a Bible. I could see even from a distance that Grady would tramp to hell and back to be a good husband and father. I guess what worried me was that he had the look of someone who'd been marching a long while already, and the baby wasn't even born yet.

Doris's Summer Salad

Fresh leaf lettuce
12 young asparagus tips
4 green onions, trimmed and cut in half
1 young zucchini or yellow squash
1 cucumber
¼ pound Swiss cheese
8 cherry tomatoes

Dressing:

9 tablespoons salad oil
3 tablespoons honey
6 tablespoons lemon juice
3 teaspoons prepared horseradish, the creamier the better
3 tablespoons fresh basil, minced
½ teaspoon salt
freshly ground black pepper

Tear lettuce into bite-sized pieces and arrange on four salad plates.

Wash asparagus tips and trim off any tough parts. Wash and trim green onions. Arrange 3 asparagus tips and 2 onion pieces on top of each plate of lettuce.

Slice squash and cucumber into narrow strips 2 to 3 inches long. Arrange 3 of each on top of each salad.

For each salad plate, quarter and arrange 2 cherry tomatoes.

Slice the cheese into narrow strips 2 to 3 inches long and arrange 6 on each salad plate.

Combine dressing ingredients in a small jar and shake. Drizzle the dressing over each salad. Finish with some freshly ground black pepper.

11

Mama

Your mother was like a vine in a vineyard
transplanted by the water,
fruitful and full of branches
from abundant water.

—EZEKIEL 19:10

Albert and I moved into this house with Mama after Papa died in a
car crash when he was just sixty-five. Mama was sixty-two. That's
not so very old, but Mama had had a bad heart her whole life. Some
days it seemed she was sixty-two going on eighty. I knew that tiredness
for days at a time meant that her heart was struggling.

On days when she was especially weary, I'd feel little spikes of
panic along my arms. Mama would sleep in the rocker in her bedroom,
her head a little to one side, and her mouth open just enough to show
the edges of her lower dentures. She snored softly, the sound making
its way through rooms to find me wherever I was. That whisper would
reach me as I cooked dinner or folded laundry. I'd hear it and have to
go to Mama's bedroom door just long enough to watch her and be sure
she was breathing freely. I'd see her resting so still in that rocker, her
hair fuzzy around her head with the light from the window behind her.

I had more energy when Mama lived with us than at any other time in my life. Her stillness gave me the need to keep moving. Guess I just decided never to be weary. Fatigue scared me back then. Now it's just an old friend, and we have an understanding. When fatigue comes to visit, I oblige by sleeping through our conversation. I don't worry about dying now as much as I did while I was waiting for Mama to die. We were with her five years before that happened.

What I didn't expect was for Mama's death to hurt me so. She was ready to go, was right with God and was plagued more by weariness than by pain. We knew and she knew that it was all right. Her last days were sweet, all sorts of people dropping by for Mama to grasp their hands and say encouraging words. They'd dissolve into tears, and she'd just smile, sunken deep in her chair full of cushions and comforters. Her hands looked like marble, almost like elegant sculptures you'd buy to set on a favorite table. But her skin felt soft and tender as fresh dough for sweet rolls. I cooked and cooked there at home, for all her guests. We shared meals and told stories.

Then she slipped away during the night, and I felt my anchor to the world tear loose. My whole life got ripped up as Mama's spirit eased itself out of our house. You just feel that your mama will always be close by, to help you on your hard days and remind you of the truth when your mind and soul are confused. But Mama was gone, and I couldn't believe the Lord would do such a damaging thing. I was thirty-six; my son Jimmy was fourteen.

I had cared for Mama at home all that time. That was a few years before I started the café. Then, after Mama died, Albert and Jimmy and I rattled around in rooms that sounded hollow as drums. For a time, we spoke in whispers and tiptoed. But eventually you get over that sensation that a house isn't really yours. Over the years since then, we've made it our own place.

But houses do have a certain character to them. Maybe from all the interactions between people who live inside the rooms. The attic room still holds Gran Lenny's poetry—and her various moods. The basement was full of the family's men—it was where they kept their guns and played cards, where they put together toys on Christmas Eve.

Like a lot of old women in old houses, I keep pictures of loved ones all around me. Most of my favorite photographs are on Mama's buffet. My history's lined up along Gran Lenny's lace runner from Brussels.

I used to explain to visitors who all the people were in those pictures. I don't do that anymore. It's hard for people outside the circle to connect with or care about people inside the circle. I have devoted about half a journal to little summaries about every person whose photograph sits on my buffet. Sometimes, when I'm having tea at the dining room table early in the morning, I sit there and sip and study the faces of my family.

Not long after Shellye and Grady married, news of trouble in the Connor house started making the rounds. We could hardly believe it. Melanie had been having an affair with Jason Jones, a farmer who lived just outside town. Jason had been divorced for a while, his two small children coming for weekend visits mainly. You'd have thought that Melanie Connor would find somebody high and mighty to commit adultery with. But evidently they'd been carrying on for at least a year. Tim Connor had happened to take the back road home from work one afternoon, because his brakes were acting up; he drove by Jason's place and saw Melanie's Mercury tucked under the shade tree beside the garage. As the story went, he didn't stop, just drove home and waited. When he asked Melanie about it, she told him straight out that she wanted a divorce.

I thought of how Melanie had sat like a statue that night at the revival when Shellye made her decision to keep her baby. Tim had stood with the rest of us, but his wife just looked at us, almost as if she didn't understand what was happening. I'd sympathized with her, because standing with Shellye could have looked like she was standing against her own son.

I sipped coffee with Bailey one day in late September, and we discussed the Connors' situation. When Bailey left, I kept thinking about Melanie Connor and what made it possible for her to ruin her family like that—without saying anything to Tim about being unhappy, without any warning at all. An unexpected thought of Mama came to me just then.

My mother had died at peace, but I could never be completely at peace about her, partly because I knew how unhappy some of her life had been. She'd married James Hannover mainly because she was moving into her late twenties and Trudy and Sam were ready for her to be out of their home. Trudy and Mama just had different personalities. They never fought outright, but there was always some tension in the air between them.

I didn't know until I cared for Mama in her final months that she'd never had much feeling for my father. He'd been a good husband and provider, a good father to me, and Mama had had no complaints about married life in general. But she confessed to me that it had been something of a relief to her heart when Papa died. She'd spent all their married life acting as if her heart was content. After all, James never knew that she wasn't really in love; he'd been honest in his love all along. It would have crushed him to know. So I suppose that Mama had done the right thing. She'd married a good man to stop being a burden to her family. And she'd been a faithful wife. She'd actually fallen in love with another man in town—she didn't tell me this until just weeks before her death, and when she did, she couldn't speak louder than a whisper. This other man had moved to town with his brother after Mama and Papa had been married about three years. Mama talked with him at Lemons Bakery one day and felt that he really was the one who should have been for her.

On the Saturday evening after Bailey and I had talked about the Connors, I was cleaning the Sunday school rooms in the church annex when Clare Thomas came in. She had boxes of supplies she'd saved up for the little ones when they did their crafts. Clare hardly threw anything away; I supposed this came from being a pastor's wife. When you live on the salary of a small-town pastor, why you're tempted to put used plastic wrap through the dishwasher. Clare put her boxes of egg cartons and empty toilet paper rolls in a cabinet of the first/second-grade classroom.

"What are you doing here on a Saturday night?" I asked, swiping the dust rag along the bookshelves in the hallway.

"Cleaning house."

"Pastor cleaning it with you?"

"No. He's out at Tim Connor's place." Clare sighed. "What a mess." I was pretty sure she was referring to the Connors and not her house. She looked at me. "You're working up a sweat. Let's steal some Cokes." We traveled the corridor that took us into the church kitchen, the dining hall just beyond. Clare reached into the refrigerator and pulled two Cokes out of their plastic rings. I could see the little sign that warned everyone that this was the youth group's pop.

We sat on two stools near the island that had kept who knows how many potluck dishes warm while prayer meetings had run long.

"It's scary to me how a person can act like everything is just fine and then—boom! walk out," Clare said. "I can't believe that Jack could be going out on me without my picking up on it. Why, we're tuned in so close to one another. I can't imagine a marriage being any other way, but I suppose a lot of them are."

Since I'd had Mama on my mind, I found myself talking about all the years she'd pretended to be happy but wasn't. I nearly got teary when I talked about the young man Mama should have married.

"It bothers me how some hurts in her life were never healed," I said.

"Oh, I know what you mean. I hate unfinished business."

"You'd like to think that the Lord would help you resolve problems in your life before taking you home. I feel uneasy when a person dies so un-healed."

Clare took a swig of Coke. "Do you think God requires us to be completely healed—before we enter Heaven, I mean?"

I couldn't tell if she'd just asked me a question she knew the answer to or not.

"Well, I suppose not, since so many faithful people die full of hurts."

"I don't think that not being healed is considered a sin," Clare said. "And how did your mama know that other man was the one for her? Sometimes the ones we're the hottest for are the worst ones for us."

"You sound as if you're speaking from experience." I could see a story lurking in the eyes of Pastor's wife.

"I suppose I am. Did I ever tell you I was engaged three times before Jack asked me?"

"Why no." I couldn't help but wonder how Pastor Thomas had been the best choice out of four men. Lord forgive me, but that's what I thought.

"I always had this gift for dazzling the most handsome, conceited, and worthless men in the county. Back then, I looked all right myself. I still don't recognize this thing that I see in the mirror these days. But first there was Larry Larrimore—what a name, huh? Looked like some movie star who'd just flown in from the beach. Blond and blue-eyed. Knew he was cute, too. Guess he decided that he deserved a cute girl, so he acquired me. I swear, the boy had not a serious thought in his head. Everything revolved around his car. I came home one summer evening, flashing this tiny diamond chip, and said to my parents, 'Guess what? I'm engaged.' And Daddy said, 'No you're not.'" Clare let out a throaty laugh. "He just bellowed, 'You take that thing off your finger. You're too young, and you hardly know him.' So, you know, back then a girl did what her daddy told her—I took it off and made a scene and wailed for a week, which was about how long it took for Larry to find another gal. Then there was, let's see, Ralph Newly. Dark, smoldering eyes, and serious thoughts going on all the time. But he just came unwound if someone, especially a girl, disagreed with him or proved him wrong. I couldn't even have a decent argument with him. And, when I was working in Coffeyville, this clever guy in our accounting department—Don."

Clare drifted away on that last name. Don must have been the hardest blow on her young-girl heart. "A good soul, but not a Christian. And he had too many family problems to count." She smiled a little and looked at me. "To think I almost abandoned my faith just to make a life with him. But my older sister, bless her heart, sat me down and told me what was what. Made me so mad at the time, but the more I thought about it, the more I knew she was right. It happened that the boy Julia had been dating had seen Don around town up to no good—nothing criminal, just not a real wholesome guy, which was what he looked like. Julia never said so, but I think she was trying to avoid telling me that Don had been seen with more than one other girl. I'd suspected but wouldn't allow myself to consider it."

"Maybe Tim Connor suspected too, but didn't want to face it," I said, and Clare nodded.

"Then Jack came along, interim pastor at the church I was attending there in Coffeyville. There weren't the kind of fireworks I'd come to expect, but I knew from the beginning we would be good for each other. And we have been."

Clare seemed to realize the time suddenly. "Well, I've bent your ear around backwards, haven't I? What were we talking about, anyway?"

"Oh, Mama and her love life." I laughed. "As if it makes any difference now, with her in Heaven."

"Velma, I think that sometimes people imagine that something could have been different, but the life they got really was their life. Maybe your mama didn't have the romance she'd always wanted, but maybe that wasn't as important as other things. A lot of people have had to give up dreams."

Clare was nearly out of the kitchen when I worked up the nerve to mention Howard. "Are a lot of people really thinking Howard has AIDS?"

Clare's happy, nostalgic look disappeared. "Rumors are floating around. Jack's planning to talk with Howard soon."

"I've never felt right, prying into the details. All he wants is a peaceful place to die."

"I know, Velma. That's what we want for him. But he may have to be more forthcoming for some people to settle down."

For old times' sake, I got out Mama's blue book and cooked up some old family recipes that evening. Hot potato salad with wine vinegar and bacon. Sausages. Even opened a can of sauerkraut. I hadn't made it from scratch for years, since Albert never cared for the smell of it all over the house for days afterward.

Howard snarfed down every bite almost as fast as I could put more helpings on his plate. Some days his appetite would speed up, and I couldn't find the bottom of his stomach.

"Why don't you serve this at the café?" he asked.

"Huh! I'd never hear the end of it."

"It's good!"

"It's German, and it's different, and nobody would like it."

"What are you talking about, Vellie? It's ethnic. Ethnic's *in*."

"Where?" I sent him a look and put a hand on my hip. "Where is ethnic in? Not around here."

"It's probably best if you didn't speak German around the kids at school," Mama whispered to me in the kitchen as she helped me into my coat. "It's all right to practice here at home, but not in town."

"Why?"

"It upsets some people. This country just got finished with an awful war, and German people aren't too popular right now."

"But everybody knows us."

"They do, but I think that at the moment they'd prefer we weren't German."

"What does Gran Lenny think?"

"She thinks what she will, but you need to listen to me and not cause trouble."

"She says I have a gift for language."

"You do, sweetheart, but let's keep our language to ourselves for now."

"If you want to give Sissy a real reason to close me down, then you just convince me to put on a German menu."

Howard must have seen both my look and my hand on the hip. He didn't say anymore that evening. But the next day after church, when Shellye and Doris came over for fresh apple pie (Grady was in a meeting at the church), Howard threw the whole subject open without my permission.

"Don't you think people would come from miles around to eat at an authentic German restaurant?" he asked Shellye point-blank. He turned to include Doris, who was already paying close attention to his every word.

"Oh, yeah. I don't know of one anywhere around here. You have to go quite a ways up north or go over to Missouri to find German food."

"See, Vellie. Your café would fill a real need around here."

"It already fills a need. It gives older folks a few decent meals every week."

"But you're not making enough. If you want to give Sissy a reason to keep you open, then you need to generate more clientele—fast."

Shellye looked up in surprise. "Sissy Scott? She doesn't want you to stay open?"

I waved off her panic. "She's never said as much. But I don't feel secure the way things are now."

"Well, I think Howard has a great idea."

"Have you eaten any of the German dishes she makes?" Howard asked. Both Shellye and Doris shook their heads, and both raised eyebrows at me.

"Oh, and we could redecorate, give the place a whole new look," said Shellye.

"What would we name it?" Howard asked.

"I'd hate for it not to say VELMA'S," said Shellye.

"I agree. That's got to stay," said Doris.

It got real quiet while everybody but me tried to think. When I looked at Howard next, he seemed to be hyperventilating. "VELMA'S LITTLE GERMANY."

Shellye squealed, and Doris made a pleased sound, nodding and looking with shining eyes at Howard.

"Oh my," I said. "Nothing subtle about that, is there?"

"Subtle is not what you need. Not anymore, Vellie." Howard was quite pleased with himself. I cleared the pie dishes off the table and tried to ignore Shellye and Howard and Doris. But even from the kitchen I could hear them in the dining room, making plans for my life. "God loves you and has a wonderful plan for your life" as the saying goes. But I don't think it's God who has all the plans. I think people plan what they want and then look for evidence that God's behind it.

Even after all these years, I didn't feel comfortable flying a German flag. There were a few discourteous incidents at school when I was just a child. Other than that, I couldn't recall being mistreated in Leeway, but we'd always done our best to be good citizens and to blend in with the rest of the community. There was no German neighborhood, as there was back east where Aunt Trudy and Elizabeth lived. I generally had never felt different for having the heritage I did. I felt different mainly for having an eccentric grandmother living in our attic, but that had never seemed to have much to do with being German immigrants.

After our company left, Howard sat at the dining room table, scribbling ideas into a notebook—for the café's redecoration, he said. He looked so happy that I decided to just let him concoct his scheme for now.

But then the phone rang, and in a few seconds, Howard's happy tone was gone. I saw his face change, and I came to stand in the doorway, in case he would need me in some way. I didn't hear anything but these words:

"Well, Pastor, what I have is called Chronic Myelogenous Leukemia. Its symptoms look a lot like AIDS. Rashes and fatigue and all the rest are common with a blood disorder. The rashes aren't contagious either. It's like my blood is seeping up to my skin sometimes and then it goes away. Anyway, I'd appreciate it if you'd pass this information along. I'd hoped to have peace and quiet when I moved here. But some people think they're entitled to know everything about me, I guess."

Howard was quiet while he listened to whatever Pastor was saying. Then he said, an edge of hurt in his voice, "I think I'll stay home from church for a week or two. I'm just too weary to answer any questions. I don't even want to look at people right now. Thank you for telling them what they need to know."

Howard hung up the phone and then sensed me standing there. When he looked at me, I just shook my head sadly.

"I'm so sorry, Howard, that people jump to conclusions so fast and talk so much. Please don't give up on God or on church because of this."

"I'm not giving up. I'm just very tired. There's a difference."

He got up from the kitchen table and kissed my forehead as he passed me on his way upstairs to bed.

Welcome to VELMA'S PLACE

Mama's Beef Patties

1 pound lean ground beef
¼ cup red onion, finely chopped
¼ cup dill pickles, chopped
1 egg
⅓ cup bread crumbs
1 teaspoon sage
½ teaspoon salt
¼ teaspoon pepper

Mix ingredients well and form into patties. In a skillet, brown on both sides until done.

Sauce:
1 small can tomato sauce
1 cup cola-flavored soda pop
2 tablespoons vinegar
1 to 2 tablespoons cornstarch

In a small saucepan, combine tomato sauce, soda pop, and vinegar and simmer about 15 minutes. Combine cornstarch with 2 tablespoons cold water and stir into sauce to thicken. Pour sauce over cooked meat patties.

12

Len Connor

Because you have brought your guilt to remembrance, in that your transgressions are uncovered, so that in all your deeds your sins appear—because you have come to remembrance, you shall be taken in hand.

—EZEKIEL 21:24

This will sound strange to some people. But there are days when you wake up and feel the power upon you. You just know Someone's beside you. It's as if God himself is laughing at your jokes. And the weather lays itself gentle at your feet. On such a day, I see people and want to walk up and put my hands upon them and ask God's blessing. I think I could say a word and make the world treat them a little better.

The third Thursday in October was like that. I woke up later than usual and felt rested. Something inside me took a slow, easy pace, and I had my toast and oatmeal at the dining room table. The cherry wood shone, and yellow leaves tumbled through the grass outside.

That morning it seemed as if there was time enough in the world for everything and that I had the strength to do whatever I really needed to do.

At about 9:30, Len Connor appeared at my front door. That was a surprise to me, but his eyes were pretty wide open too, as though he were shocked, himself, to be there on my step.

"Hello, Len." I said this politely, but didn't open the door for him to come in. This boy—and he did look like a boy, not a man—had wronged our Shellye and let a church full of people look on her with shame.

"Hi. Uh," he said, scratching his cheek, "is Shellye here?"

"No, she isn't. And I don't think it's a good thing for you to be looking for her." That seemed to knock the wind out of him, and suddenly I felt I'd been cruel. "Come in?" I opened the door, and he followed me into the living room. We sat down.

"I, uh, just wondered how she was doing. I saw her at the pharmacy a couple days ago. She's not having trouble with the baby, is she?"

"No, the pregnancy is fine. She's due in about four weeks. Did you know that?"

He shook his head, looking sad. "We haven't talked or anything. My folks said I'm not to be involved."

I studied him while he rubbed his shoe into my carpet. A nice looking boy, muscular from all his sports, brown hair cut short. He looked a lot like his mother, Melanie. Thinking of her and the way she'd broken up her family, I decided to go the extra step and be kind to her son.

"But I—I mean—there's not much I can do, I guess," Len said. His eyes had a bit of hope in them, maybe that I would come up with something.

"If you could, what would you want to do?"

"Stay her friend. See the baby sometimes."

I found myself believing that he cared about Shellye and the baby. But I couldn't put out of my mind the condition Shellye had been in when she'd run away from him that night in the spring. I sat there and asked Jesus for wisdom. None seemed to be forthcoming, so I just said the first thing that came to mind.

"There are some hurts that need to be cleared up before you can be friends—don't you think?"

Len looked at his feet. "Yes." Then he looked at me. "But my folks told me to stay away, and Shellye won't even look at me. I'm stuck."

"You need to respect your folks, but they may not always be right."

"I wish I could be sure what was right."

I was ready to give him chapter and verse on what was right, beginning with not bullying Shellye in the first place, not putting her in the predicament he had. Sure, she was married now, and it looked as if things would work out, but my sense of justice hadn't been satisfied. I thought of all sorts of suggestions for Len Connor, but usually those strongest urges are the wrong ones. Plus, I was seeing more by the minute that Len wasn't so much some maniac rapist as he was a gifted young man who'd been told his good points far too often. He needed a strong hand on his life reminding him that the world was not created for his personal satisfaction.

So I stood up and said, "I guess you've got some praying to do then." It sounded more stern than I meant it.

Len sighed as if I'd just asked him to win the lottery. I showed him to the door and watched him walk away. Then I felt guilty for having been so short with him. I usually pray while I'm cleaning the church. And I pray for my customers while I serve them at the café. But after Len left, I made myself a cup of tea. Then I sat at the dining room table, the same place where I'd had such a promising start to my day.

"Lord, if there's a way for these two kids to make up and heal some of this awful business, then you need to do something. Or tell me what to do." Then I talked through some ideas and waited for the Spirit to nudge me on the right one. There were no nudges, but I've learned that you can't plan a nudge from the Spirit. That kind of nudge can come anytime, so you have to be paying attention all the time. I think God decided to work this way to keep us from getting lazy.

Some people think it takes a simpleminded person to sit down and talk with the Lord over tea. For a lot of my younger years, probably because Gran Lenny had seemed so cynical about religion, I'd thought such devotion was crazy too. Mama being so devoted was a problem for my unbelief, because I couldn't help but respect her. You rely on your mama for so much. And once you imagine she might be crazy, even in just one part of her life, all of your own life feels less secure.

As it turned out, Mama had little to do with my belief in God. I was married but not a mother yet when the real belief happened. The day I met God in a personal way, it was as if someone had walked into the room. I remember being shocked completely, but warm, too, as if someone held me.

I'd already lost one baby. And when I realized I was pregnant again, a fear took me over. I couldn't even bring myself to tell Albert. All of a sudden my life was in front of me, only it wasn't a life of good events and people I loved, but an eternity of wondering which things would turn out all right and which things would hurt me. I wasn't sure I could handle all the mysteries of life and death, even the one mystery I might be carrying in my body at that moment.

One morning I sat on the bed after Albert went to work, and I wasn't sure I could stand up and walk into the next room. I was completely paralyzed. Would I have this baby? Or would it die inside me, too? Would it grow up only to get hurt again and again?

Then Somebody walked into the room. There was no face or body, just a presence, and I knew without thinking Who it was. I didn't know from any other time I could remember. From before I was born maybe, or from my dreams—those ones that always ring true but are from no real place or time you know of. God was standing there, enjoying my surprise. God was telling me that life would go on and that my worrying about it wouldn't make any difference, and why didn't I just try trusting him for a change?

I'd spent my earlier years proving to myself that all the church business was so much nothing, that love could never last and sin couldn't be solved. But with the Lord suddenly standing there, I knew that the church business was just scratching at the surface of the real business. That all my little proofs were nothing but the tantrums of a person desperate to do as she pleased. The Lord enjoyed my surprise at just how clear the truth could be. And that presence just stared through my soul to the wall on the other side and then said with a little smile, "Well?"

I've been a Christian ever since, through all kinds of good and bad times. I've not needed to fret and question so much since that day. I read the Bible and listen to others teach it. Sometimes the words make sense, and sometimes they don't, really. But it's the Author who breathes close to my days, who watches my life with everlasting patience and calm. When you trust the author, you don't get so nervous about the hard parts of the Book. You figure that for the one who wrote the Book, seeing us think and search is half the point.

Wouldn't you know that Shellye stopped by the very evening after Len had talked with me. She usually didn't visit in the evenings, and she hardly ever did these days without Grady. But she knocked on the door well past seven, all by herself.

We sat on the porch and had ginger-sage tea. It's good for the stomach, and mine was nervous. Shellye looked like a little mother already, plump belly and round cheeks. She seemed fairly content. We talked about what she might need for the baby. They had a crib and a little washtub, were going to pick up a car seat this week. She and Grady had prepared their smaller bedroom to be the nursery. I knew that the women at church were planning a baby shower for her, but so far that was a secret.

When she got up to leave, I said, my heart speeding up, "You won't believe who came by to see me today."

"Who?" She looked so calm, I hated to bring up Len.

"Len Connor. Came by asking how you were. I don't imagine he'd ever ask you directly himself."

Shellye's face paled a little. "No, we've not talked at all since that meeting at the church. His dad called a couple times, after that night at the revival. To assure me that they'd help out financially, with the baby. With being married to Grady now, I told them it wasn't necessary."

There was a hardness to Shellye's jaw.

"I think Len's feeling the guilt now," I said.

"About time."

"Maybe the two of you should talk."

She looked as if I'd betrayed her. "Why?"

"I have the feeling he might actually apologize if you give him the chance."

"He'd better be ready to stand in front of the church and tell them the truth. Then I'll be willing to talk to him." Shellye headed for the door. She was mad, and I was sorry I'd brought up the subject. As I watched her walk away from the house, her shoulders had that wounded set to them, and I realized just how deep the wound was. Shellye came to church regularly now, taking her place as a decent woman and the wife of a church leader. But that didn't completely make up for the damage done by the Connors and other church people, just a few months ago.

Len Connor stopped in at the café two days later, the first time since all the business with Shellye. Shellye was working that day. Len sat at the counter. Shellye was waiting tables and pretended not to see him. I walked over and asked what he wanted, and he ordered a chocolate sundae. I gave him a sharp look but got the ice cream. I felt him watching me and wanting to talk.

"Do you think Shellye would talk to me if I said I wanted to apologize?" He glanced around to be sure no one was close enough to hear us. Shellye was on the other side of the room.

"I don't know. This probably isn't the place to ask her."

"Would you ask her?" The boy looked determined.

I shook my head, not in answer to his request, but to show him how little I thought of how he was going about this—putting Shellye on the spot. I managed to be in the kitchen when Shellye came back there. She slapped open the door and then sat on a stool near the canned goods, looking angry and scared.

"What's he doing in here?"

"He wants to apologize to you, is what he told me." I felt a bit breathless, in the middle of this drama.

"*Here?* What's he thinking about?"

"We can meet him together at my house after we close up here."

Shellye held her abdomen. The baby must have been awake and moving around. "I don't know. Why can't he just leave me alone?"

"It would be good for the two of you to settle things."

"There's nothing to settle. He lied, and I'm the one who's suffered."

"But if he apologized for that, would it help at all?"

"I've got to pee." Shellye slid off the stool and went through the kitchen door to the women's bathroom at the far end of the café. I quickly checked to be sure the customers out in the dining room were happy, then went back to the kitchen to wait for Shellye. When she came back, she was calmer. "OK. You tell him that I'll meet him at your place tonight at eight o'clock. Grady's got one of his guys coming over for prayer time then. He won't even miss me." I picked up a sad little note in her voice.

I went out to the counter to tell Len, who was so nervous he'd eaten the sundae in record time. I told him to be at my house at eight. He left a big tip and beat it out the door.

"Whatever you do," Shellye said, as we were closing up awhile later, "don't say a word about this to Grady. He's real protective. He'd want to be there, and I can't handle that."

"He doesn't need to be there. I'll be close by, in case it doesn't go well."

I got home and immediately made my best scones, with walnuts and orange rind. Howard came downstairs, from a late afternoon nap.

His appetite wasn't much lately, but the smell of scones baking seemed to make him happy.

"Howard, Len Connor's coming over in a while. He and Shellye are going to have a talk. Just so you know."

"Huh." Howard followed my movements around the kitchen. I threw together chicken salad sandwiches for us.

"Is it a good thing that they're going to talk?"

"He's coming to make an apology. It should be a good thing."

"Is it all right for me to be here?"

"Of course. I'll be here too. We just need to let them alone."

It was too chilly to put anyone on the sunporch, even with plastic over the screens. I closed the curtains to the living room and turned on the reading lamp between the sofa and the easy chair.

Shellye was there right at eight, and Len showed up two minutes later, looking pale. I put them in the living room with the scones and some hot chocolate.

I ended up in Howard's room. He was propped up in bed, watching a murder mystery. I did my best to concentrate, but after ten minutes had to go downstairs and wander near the living room, just to be sure that things were all right. From the stairwell I could hear conversation, which sounded calm enough. I couldn't make out words. I went back up to Howard's room.

"Seems all right so far," I reported.

Howard tried to distract me from worrying over Len and Shellye. "Have you ever read Agatha Christie? I can't remember if the book went like this or not. Have you read *Death on the Nile?*"

"A long time ago. That's what this is?"

"Yep. Pretty good movie, actually."

By the time the second character in the movie had turned up dead, Shellye appeared in the doorway. She was smiling.

"Come on in, sugar," said Howard, patting the bed. She sat on the foot of it, and Howard muted the TV.

"How did it go?" I asked.

"It was good," she said. "He said that he should have been honest with Pastor Thomas and everyone. That when I said 'rape,' he got scared and just convinced himself that things had happened in a different way. That he just couldn't think of himself as a criminal." Shellye said this while looking at the silent TV. "I said that I'd been scared too, especially when I found out I was pregnant. And that when he treated me the way he had that night, it made me think I didn't mean anything to him, that he was just using me."

I could tell from her red nose and the puffiness around her eyes that she'd shed some tears. Her voice wobbled some.

"Was he just using you?" Howard asked, very softly.

"No, I don't think so. He says he's not sure why he forced me, and he's scared to know why. And now that his mom's run out on his dad, he thinks that maybe he'll turn out like that, ruining people's lives. So he wanted to tell me how sorry he was and that he knew I never was a tramp or a liar. He's going to tell his dad the truth as soon as he works up the nerve. But with all his dad's gone through lately, Len hates to add more to it."

Shellye was still looking at the TV. "Anyway, I believe he really is sorry, and he's happy that I'm married now and that things will be OK."

"What about the baby?" Howard leaned closer to Shellye. "Will you ever tell her?"

Shellye shook her head slowly. "I don't think it's right for the baby to grow up having Grady as her dad but then being told he's not her real dad. But so many people around here know already that Len's the dad. It's real complicated, and I don't know what to do. Len wants to be able to see the baby, but I told him it's not that simple. He understands, but we're not settled on how to handle everything yet. I'm going to use your bathroom, Velma." She hoisted herself, belly first, off the bed.

Howard and I waited in silence, not knowing what to say to each other or to Shellye. When Shellye came back in, she said good-bye. "See you at church Velma. Hope you have a good day tomorrow, Howard." This last line had become standard around our house, because none of us took good days for granted where Howard was concerned.

That Thursday, a rough-looking old man came to the café and sat down in the far west booth. I'd never seen him before. His running shoes were falling apart, as if he'd dug them out of someone's trash barrel. The suit jacket had been a nice tweed once but now looked stained and slick with wear. Pants two or three inches too long, the backs of the cuffs ragged from trailing on the ground behind him. Scroungy beard and a complexion ruddy not from health but from being out in the weather too much. I could remember the hobos wandering through town when I was a girl. They'd jump off the freight trains that ran through the west part of town several times a day. They were of every race, age, and ethnic origin, but they all had the same broken shoes and the same texture to their skin. Smoothed down but hard. White men looked redder in the face, and black men looked grayer. Zeke was white, probably in his mid-fifties. Sheri, the girl working the tables that day, looked a bit scared, so I walked over to take his order. I expected to smell him before I got to the table, but he had the odor of someone who'd been working outdoors all day, not someone who never bathed.

"What'll you have?" I tried to see his eyes better, but his hair fell over them.

"How much is a cup of coffee?"

"Eighty cents."

He seemed to consider that.

"Refills are free," I added.

"Is it any good?" I saw one eye glinting behind strands of gray hair.

"What, the coffee?"

"Yeah. Has it been settin' in the pot all day? Does it taste like a tin can?"

Of all the nerve. I looked down at him and was glad his hair kept him from seeing me purse my lips. "Coffee never has the opportunity to get stale around here. That's my third pot today. And I've never heard any complaints."

"Guess I'll have some—in a real cup, no Styrofoam."

"Anything else?"

"You serve leftovers at a discount?"

"No. I generally don't have leftovers, and if they're not worth the full price I wouldn't put them on the table." I was surprised at how defensive I sounded. He was just an old man, maybe homeless. But I didn't like his manners.

"How much is the toast?"

"A dollar."

"That include jelly?"

"Yes."

"You got real butter? I don't like the fake stuff."

It would have been a humorous conversation, except that the man fairly growled the words at me. I started to growl back, but I suppose my upbringing or the years of listening to sermons stopped me.

"Tell you what. I'll throw in the toast with the coffee."

"Now that's more like it. I'll have wheat toast will real butter and jelly, and don't burn it, or the char will upset my stomach."

I didn't answer, just went back and rolled my eyes at Sheri.

A few minutes later, I took him a plate with three slices of wheat toast and a little dish of grape jelly. I remembered the go-the-second-mile part of Jesus' famous sermon and put on some hash browns too. I set it and a fresh cup of coffee in front of the man. He didn't look up or mention the hash browns.

"Never seen you in here before," I said.

"Never been here before."

"You got family around here?"

"No. My family was all up around Salina."

"I'm Velma."

"Like the sign says," he grunted. He put four heaping spoonfuls of sugar into his coffee and stirred it, the spoon clanking against the cup for a long moment. "I'm Zeke," he said suddenly, but with no more friendliness than before.

"Well, Zeke, hope you like the toast." I walked away, but heard him say behind me:

"I might have some bacon if I come in here again."

I shook my head and wondered how many restaurants in the area had provided him with free meals lately.

Brennen Simms came in for lunch, and I described Zeke, who'd left right after he finished, leaving not eighty cents but fifty.

"I know him. Most of the time he lives just outside Bender Springs. Camps out in the old Johnson farmhouse. Doesn't cause any trouble, so they let him be. Think he worked for a mineral company over the Oklahoma line."

"He didn't seem dangerous. Mean-spirited though."

Brennen chuckled. "If he gives you any trouble, just let me know. He shows up at the truck stop over at Bender Springs sometimes. Audrey feeds him lunch for taking out garbage, except that he usually develops a back or knee problem about the time they get to the garbage part."

"Brennen, how do you keep up with all this information? You must know every person and every farm in four or five counties."

"I just know people who know. Sheriff at Bender Springs talks my ears off every time I run into him. The highway patrol guys fill me in." He leaned back on the stool, pretending to look important. "It's that law enforcement network, you know."

Zeke showed up a few days later. He sat in the same booth, looking cagier than ever.

"Coffee still fifty cents?"

"It's still eighty cents."

"Does it still come with toast and potatoes?"

"It never came with toast and potatoes. I was just generous last time."

"Not feeling generous today, huh? Figures. Just give me the coffee." He made a grunt, and I wanted to smack him in the head. But darned if I didn't stick a slice of toast and potatoes on his plate. My Bible teachings dug in a little harder, and I threw in two slices of bacon. For once I wished Howard were there to click his tongue at my low prices and generosity.

Not only did Len Connor talk to his dad later that week, but he also spoke to Pastor Thomas. I wouldn't have known except that Saturday evening I was straightening up the sanctuary a bit and happened to walk by Pastor's office to turn off the hall lights. I heard Grady's voice.

"If he admits that he forced her, then he should be prosecuted!"

"Now Grady," Pastor said quietly, "if Shellye and Len have resolved things, and if Shellye has no intention of going further with it, then the best thing is to leave it be."

"He should suffer the consequences, instead of getting off scot-free. Since he's gotten away with it once, how many more girls will he hurt?"

"Judging from what Len said to me, I don't think we need to worry about that. This has scared him enough that he's going into counseling."

"These therapists are all secular humanists. They never call a sin a sin."

"I've referred him to a Christian counselor, someone I know personally."

"I don't want that boy anywhere near my Shellye or my child."

"He has no intention of interfering with Shellye's life now. I made sure we were clear on that."

"Unless he confesses before this entire church, I don't want to see him walk in the door."

By then, I was clear up to the door, which was cracked open an inch. I stood to one side and shamelessly stuck my ear near the opening.

"I think that a confession to the entire church would cause more trouble. He's asked Shellye's forgiveness, and he's confessed to me and asked me to tell the deacons. We don't need to involve anyone else."

"So he just gets away with it?"

"No one 'gets away' with it. We pay in one way or the other for our actions. After all, Len won't ever know this child as his—I think that's a pretty strong punishment, don't you? And he appears to be genuinely regretful and repentant, so as far as I'm concerned, this business is closed."

"He'd better not come near my family."

"I don't think you need to worry about that. You concentrate on your family—that will give you enough to worry about for many years to come."

"And she'd better not have anything to do with him, I don't care if they forgave one another. She's my wife now."

"Of course she is. No one would say otherwise."

"I just don't want him to sweet-talk her into thinking he's anything he's not."

"Let's just be glad they've found some resolution. It's an incredible thing they've done, coming to terms this way, and we should thank the Lord for his mercy."

I could tell the conversation was winding down, so I crept away quickly, and left by the back door.

Welcome to VELMA'S PLACE

Scones for Friends

2 cups flour
½ teaspoon cinnamon
¼ teaspoon nutmeg
2 tablespoons sugar
2 teaspoons baking powder
½ teaspoon baking soda
½ teaspoon salt
1 teaspoon grated lemon rind or orange rind*
¼ cup pecans or walnuts, chopped
8-ounce container lemon or orange yogurt; can be low- or nonfat
⅛ cup oil
¼ cup milk

*When using lemon yogurt, I use lemon rind and pecans. When using orange yogurt, I use orange rind and walnuts.

Mix all the dry ingredients, including the lemon or orange rind and the nuts.

Add the yogurt and oil and mix. Add milk a little at a time, just enough for the dough to be sticky (may not need the entire amount, or may need a little more).

Turn out dough on a well-floured surface. Knead dough just until it's not sticky, adding flour as necessary. Pat out in a large circle about ½-inch thick. Cut the circle into eight wedges like a pie. Put the wedges, an inch apart, on an ungreased cookie sheet. Brush with some melted butter or a little milk and sprinkle tops with sugar. Bake at 400° for 8 to 10 minutes or until golden brown.

13

The Birth

But I the Lord will speak the word that I speak, and it will be fulfilled.
It will no longer be delayed; but in your days, O rebellious house, I
will speak the word and fulfill it, says the Lord God.

—EZEKIEL 12:25

What I love most about babies is how fresh they are. It doesn't
matter how they were conceived—in a loving embrace between
husband and wife or in a sinful heat between drunks. The baby comes
out steaming like a perfect pudding, and all you can do is clap your
hands and feel your whole self open up. Eyes, ears, mouth, arms,
heart—everything just springs wide. You're ready to accept the child
and all the future you don't even know yet. A baby brings into this
world her own portion of hope. You can't resist wild, wonderful day-
dreams when a newborn is in the room, making its little sounds.

Shellye's baby entered the life of Leeway at six in the morning on a Sunday. During the ten o'clock morning worship, Grady bounded in, causing Pastor Thomas to stop in the middle of the Scripture reading.

"We have a little girl!"

We applauded and got misty while Grady stood among us and beamed from east to west. After the applause had died down, Pastor asked, "Well, are you going to tell us the name, or what?" Grady got embarrassed, and we chuckled at him.

"Lisa Layne. Lisa Layne Lewis. Eight pounds, three ounces, nineteen inches long and—" Grady struggled to put the words together. The man looked entirely addled. "—and very, very pretty!" We laughed again. Then Pastor Thomas offered a prayer. Grady stayed long enough to sing a hymn with us. He was on his way back to the hospital when I stopped him at the door.

"Did it go all right? How's Shellye?"

"It went fine, Velma, the Lord blessed us!"

"Shellye's OK?"

"Yes, real tired. And they had to take some stitches, but the baby's real healthy. I never saw her so happy."

"Good. You give her my love." I patted his back as he went out the door.

When they came home two days later, it pleased me to see Doris pack a little bag and go stay with them. She had the look that said, "I'm going to be a good grandma, even if I'm scared to death" as she got into the car with Grady. I knew that once upon a time, not that many years ago, Doris had been a good little mama to Shellye, so it seemed almost like old times, the times before Doris's nervous spells.

I visited them the next day, on Wednesday after I cleaned the church. It was just Doris and me there with Shellye, and Shellye was nursing Lisa Layne. The two of them seemed like one person, the way mothers and newborns often look. Shellye was already getting her color back and not looking so tired. Doris and I hardly let her leave her chair for anything, and the minute the baby needed a diaper change, Grandma or Aunt Velma was snatching her up. It had been a while since I'd held someone so new. A baby's practically weightless in the beginning. And the funny thing is that a brand new baby doesn't do anything but eat, sleep, and get rid of what it eats. But still you can't tear your eyes away.

Bailey Webb once remarked that he couldn't get interested in his grandbabies until they were a few months old. "Before that, they don't *do* anything," he'd said, a bit disappointed. I'd told him that they didn't have to do anything. But maybe a man doesn't tune into a baby in the beginning. I can watch a baby *be* for hours and hours. Every little expression or hint of sound is like a new language you're dying to understand—or a very old one you're trying to remember. It's almost like waiting for God to speak audibly after you've prayed a prayer that turned you inside out. A little baby moves her hand or quirks her eyebrow, and you know there's importance in it. Or maybe just mamas and grandmas and aunts know it.

The next Sunday afternoon, Shellye and Doris, Grady, Grady's mother Thelma and his sister Nora, came over for dessert crepes and hazelnut coffee. They rang my front doorbell, and I pulled back the curtains to see the lot of them smiling and shining in the pale sunlight. Shellye's cheeks were a healthy pink, to match the baby's. We sat in the living room and I held Lisa Layne, who of course was sleeping, just making little faces and sounds. I always have the feeling, when I hold a newborn, that she's from another world, sent for a visit. I sit there and wait for those new eyes to open and look at me, and I hope that when that happens I pass the grade. The little one smells and feels so new, and I suddenly know how old and worn out I am.

Doris stayed awhile after Shellye and the others had left. She and Howard sat in the living room quietly, her on the love seat and him in the reading chair near the built-in bookcases.

"What a darling little granddaughter you have," I said, as I refilled Doris's coffee cup.

"I'm not ready to be a grandmother, Velma."

"Oh, sure you are. You already look like a natural."

"Don't tell me that! Do I really look that old?"

"That's not what I meant! I meant that it looked like being a grandma would come naturally to you."

"Doris, you look way too young to be a grandma," said Howard, holding out his cup for me. "Being a grandma doesn't mean you're old."

Suddenly, Doris sniffled. She set down her coffee and rested her face in one hand, trying to hide from us.

Howard got up from his chair and sat next to Doris on the love seat. He was making comforting sounds. "Hey, hey . . . no need to be sad." His voice was hoarse, the way it got sometimes when his blood count was low. Doris leaned into him a little, and he put an arm around her shoulders, letting her nestle into him.

"I'm alone now! Shellye's got her own life, and I'll just rattle around in that house forever."

"Does this seem alone to you?" Howard said softly. "You're not alone as long as you have friends. And you've got Vellie and me and Amy and Diane and other people." Amy and Diane often visited with Doris in the church foyer after morning worship. They'd even gone shopping together. It amazed me that Howard would think of something like that. Men usually let those kinds of details slip away.

"I thought I was all alone not that long ago," Howard was saying. "But in just a few months, here I am with a church family and my own family and neighbors." His voice shook a little. I went back to the kitchen to do dishes. It seemed to be a private moment. I hadn't realized how close Howard and Doris were becoming. I wondered what Doris would do when Howard finally left us.

When I finished the dishes, I ventured near the doorway to the living room—in time to see Howard tip Doris's head back just slightly and kiss her right on the lips. I should have retreated, but it was so odd to see them actually kissing that I stood there stupidly. Her arm came up around his neck. After a moment or two, they came up for air. I backed out of the doorway.

Shortly after that, Doris went back to her house, and Howard went to bed. He didn't say a word, and neither did I. I didn't know whether to be uncomfortable or happy or what.

That evening I took out my journal and tried to describe Lisa Layne. I wanted to remember every moment I'd held her. I wanted to capture how happy Shellye was and how peaceful Doris was, gazing at her granddaughter. I knew there must be a way to write it, but when I tried, the words kept dodging me, like handfuls of butterflies.

I once asked Gran Lenny if she wrote about family events in her journals. She said yes, but not in a way that made for storytelling.

And she'd made me burn her journals right before she died. It was one of the worst days of my life. My fifteenth birthday. A black, black day, because we all knew that Gran Lenny was dying. She knew it before we did but chose to tell us a week after New Years. My birthday is January 14. By then, Doc Breem was buzzing in and out of the house on practically a daily basis. Gran Lenny was developing fluid around her heart, and he said she wouldn't live long. The day of my birthday she was too ill to eat any of my birthday cake. I made her special chicken and rice soup, with a lot of sage in the broth, but she couldn't bear to have it near her. Her face and arms were as white as the streaks in her long black hair. And her eyes were as dark and moist as a puppy's. She sat up in her bed, a cool green bed jacket gathered around her. I sat in the chair next to the bed while she sipped some weak tea. As I watched her, I fingered her silver locket, which now hung at my own throat—Gran Lenny's birthday present to me. Inside the locket were pictures of Gran Lenny and the Grandfather Henri I'd never known. She was twenty-two and he was thirty-one.

"Vellie, I need your help," she said, her lips just above the china cup. Steam made a thin line from her nose to her right eyebrow.

"Whatever you need." My voice sounded as though it belonged to someone older and stronger.

"I need you to do something with my journals."

"What do you want me to do?"

"I want you to burn them."

She sipped the tea again, and I could hear my own heartbeat in my ears.

"I don't understand. You've spent so much time writing them. Why would you burn them?"

"I don't want anyone else reading them." Her eyes turned sharp, and I felt wounded. She didn't even want me to read them. She'd stored up treasures from her own life, and yet I would never own a single one.

"Some of the poetry we'll save," she said. "I've marked those pages for us to cut out. Those are yours to do with as you wish."

"OK."

"But everything else—with my own eyes I must see it burn."

"Yes ma'am."

"You don't approve."

"I just don't see why. What difference would it make for someone to read your words when you're gone?"

"Those journals belong to God and to me. They are a record of a relationship. And it is a very private thing."

"Other people might not learn from it?"

"I don't think so." Gran Lenny laughed, making a squeaky sound in her windpipe. "It has not been an ideal relationship. Long ago, after the Great War, I made an agreement with Almighty Got." Her accent was always more pronounced when she was ill or tired. "He could have my soul, but I would keep my mind, see?" Her eyes seemed to ask for some kind of response. I nodded, not understanding.

"The soul can bear things the mind can't bear. Forever the soul lives, and so further it sees. But the mind sees the war, the loss, the bodies with their names erased, the betrayals. The mind can see only this. It remembers this, and it is *angry*." Gran Lenny's whole body trembled with that word. "I said to Got, 'You do what you wish with my soul, but my mind, my words, will say what they will. No other way can I live on this earth.'"

"How can you divide up like that, your soul with God and your mind with you?"

"Nothing is divided. It is a way of seeing life. I could not forget my griefs, even if I wished to. You take away the grief, you take away parts of Lenora. In heaven, God can take the griefs I carry there with me. While I am here, my words to God, many, many days, are ugly with pain. As I write, I make my pain speak articulately. God can listen. People cannot understand this. You will burn my books, and I will rest in God, and my pain will be silent. If I did not put my anger on the pages, it would have hurt so many people, even you."

"Do you not go to church with us because you are angry?"

She simply pointed at me. "I am angry at the church most of all."

"The people have always been nice to you. The pastor has come to visit so often."

"I speak of another church in another place. That is all the church I know. Maybe this is wrong, to think this way. But I cannot help that."

"The church back in *München*?"

Gran Lenny looked past me. "When I was young, it was a good place. Its people were good then. But later . . . when you are older, you will read about these things. By then, there will be many books about them." Her head was crooked back as though she were already dead. She breathed deeply as she could for a few seconds, then said, "Please get my books."

She directed me to her shelf of journals, and we went through them together, cutting out poems—not all of them, maybe half of all she'd written. I noticed that no page that had poetry on it also had journal writing on it. She'd known all along that the journal part was not for keeping. Then Gran Lenny asked me to open the large trunk against the wall, the one that contained comforters and keepsakes. I handed her letters, books, and other items. She looked briefly at each thing, then handed it to me to put in the box. She did this quickly, so I didn't have the chance to look at anything myself, and she didn't tell me about anything, except that she pointed out a couple of names on envelopes and told me which distant relatives they were. Even the Grettingers' books and letters were tossed on the pile with no reverence at all.

"Help me sit near the east window. I want to watch you," she said. The east window overlooked the backyard and alley, where the burning barrel was. I scooted the small stuffed chair and footstool to the window and pulled back the curtains. The sky was still gray-white, treetops growing sharp and black against it. I helped Gran Lenny to the chair. She felt almost weightless. I helped her settle into the blanket and pillow I had put in the chair, and I lifted her legs to the footstool and covered them with another blanket.

"Open the window."

"It's so cold!"

"I don't care. I like the sound of a fire at evening's quiet." I opened the window, then carried the journals down the back stairwell, stopped in the pantry for the matches, and hauled the box outside.

I couldn't bring myself to dump the box over the side of the barrel. I set down the box and threw in the letters first. Then I picked up the journals, one by one, and stacked them in the barrel. I tore a few pages out of the top one to get the fire started. I'd placed the older journals, which were drier and more brittle, on the top, knowing they'd catch sooner. They did. In just a few moments, the whole pile was blazing, Gran Lenny's words singing and snapping and hissing, their smoke smelling dusty and inky. Only then did I look up at the third-story window. Gran Lenny's pale face shone out of the dark room behind her. She leaned out of the window just enough to have the crisp evening air around her face. Her striped hair hung down from either side—there was no breeze at all.

Gran Lenny didn't speak. She smiled, but just barely; it looked thin and brave, not showing any teeth. She seemed to grip the scene with her lips, which had been untouched by lipstick for several days now. Her eyes looked wider and brighter than usual. She rested folded arms on the windowsill.

"Makes a musty smell, doesn't it?" she commented.

"Yes. A lot of noise, too."

"That doesn't surprise me. You think God is relieved, not having to listen to those pages anymore?"

I turned back toward the barrel, because I was crying. The smoke stung me, and Gran Lenny's face and voice stroked across my heart with such sweetness that I wished I could die with her. No one would ever understand me again. No one would love my cooking the way she did. No one would hold my life in place. Gran Lenny had held me steady just by being in the house, up in her room or at the kitchen table. Quiet and somber as she was, difficult to understand, antisocial much of the time, she had held me just the same. And it had been a great comfort to me, knowing that through all the events in our lives, all the great and small and happy and painful things, Gran Lenny was tending to all of us, her pen moving patiently across page after page, writing our lives, keeping bookmarks in the important parts. I watched all of our days slither into the gray air, smelling of age and decay.

Remembering that day put a pall on my attempt to write about Lisa Layne's birth. It irked me that that memory would come to visit on such a good day. I wrote two or three paragraphs about Shellye and Doris and Lisa Layne visiting me. I recorded that Lisa Layne had opened her eyes twice the whole time, and she'd looked at me like someone ancient and good.

But then I wrote about how I hoped Shellye and Lisa Layne would have a happy life with Grady. God bless him, I still didn't like the man very much. He always seemed to have something to say and to say it too loudly. But everyone could see how much he tried, how hard he worked. I just hoped that he would love Shellye and their daughter, and that the love wouldn't feel like work to him. I hoped he would learn to sit and do nothing sometimes. Do nothing but enjoy his wife and little girl.

I started to write about Howard and Doris, but it was too raw and secretive a thing to mention even in my journal. Maybe what I'd seen was nothing, or meant nothing. I was still too rattled to put my thoughts around it. I tried to put the image of each of them—Doris and Howard—into my mind to offer to God as prayer, but wouldn't you know the only image that would come was them locked onto each other at the mouth. So I gave up trying to pray and went to bed myself. Poor Albert had to listen to me mutter my confusion as I drifted off to sleep.

The very next morning, Sissy Fenders Scott showed up outside my café. She had two men with her, nicely dressed, with legal pads in their hands. She was pointing at my eaves and the windows in front. They were in earnest discussion about something. After ten minutes, I went out to see if they needed anything.

"Oh, don't bother yourself, Velma. These gentlemen are refurbishing our building. I'm going to replace these old awnings and redo the front. How are these windows? Letting in too many drafts in the winter?"

"They're fine, thank you."

"Well, I'm going to replace them with new storm windows, the double-glass kind that are better insulated. It will save on heating bills."

I almost asked if this meant my rent was going to double, but I chose not to in front of the two men.

Sissy's fast if she's anything. The next week a work crew came in and set up chaos on my front walk. The first thing they did was take down my sign. I didn't see where they put it. That was a Tuesday, one of my busiest days, and I couldn't tear myself away long enough to inspect what these men were doing or ask any questions. Around lunchtime, Sissy came in with a sheet of paper. On it was a schedule of what the crew would be doing and roughly when. They would install the windows first, meaning that I may have to close down for a day or two.

"How else does this affect the café?" I asked.

"It may keep a few customers away, because of the noise. Other than that, it will only affect the café by making it look nicer!" Sissy had that sparkle in her eyes that I had often found so irritating.

"How will this affect my rent?"

"The rent?" She appeared to have to think about that, as if she hadn't planned some while ago exactly how much she was going to raise the rent and exactly when. "I don't foresee any changes that way, although, the way tax laws change every year, I can never say for sure. But these outside improvements are on me." She smiled, satisfied with herself. "Any indoor improvements, though, please ask me about. If you ever want to change anything, I'll need to be in on that decision, naturally."

"Of course." I left Sissy abruptly to check the dozen or so tables that had customers at them. When I turned back to Sissy, she was gone.

Howard wasn't nearly as concerned about all this as I was. "Hey, it should help business, and that's what we want, isn't it?"

I sighed without answering and went up to bed.

In the dark, I tried to talk with Albert. This was the type of thing he'd always been good for, helping me see things in a logical way. But as many times as I'd try to bring up Sissy and the pain she was causing me, I couldn't bear to mention her name in his presence. Even now, with both Sissy and me in our mid-fifties, she was the pretty one. When she moved out of Leeway, I never thought about it much. But now here she was, shining as she always had. I think Albert has always been fairly happy with me. But deep inside me, Sissy still brought out the fears that had plagued me when I was a girl.

Sunday Dinner Rice

I cup uncooked rice
I tablespoon olive oil
I red bell pepper, diced
¾ cup slivered almonds, toasted*
salt and pepper to taste

* Toast almonds by tossing gently in a dry skillet or baking in a medium oven. Be sure to watch them, because once they begin to brown, they can burn easily.

Cook the rice according to instructions.

While the rice is cooking, saute the red bell pepper for 5 to 7 minutes.

In a large serving dish, toss together the pepper, almonds, and rice. Add the seasoning of your choice. Serve warm.

14

Thanksgiving

On the inside, around each of the four courts was a row of masonry,
with hearths made at the bottom of the rows all around. Then he said
to me, "These are the kitchens where those who serve at the temple
shall boil the sacrifices of the people."

—Ezekiel 46:23–24

In this part of the state, the first month or two of winter is usually
mild. We hardly ever have snow before January. But by Thanksgiving, Leeway had been gray, gusty, and sharp cold for a couple of weeks.
It wore a person out to walk in that wind; it was almost like a being
that followed you or jumped from around a corner to catch you off
guard. And the sky was white, so white the buildings in town looked
dirty against it—dirty, square, and shut down. All down Pickins Street
I could see leaves and paper and twigs scattering, all faded into gray and
making a dry racket as they flew and collided with walls and pave-
ments. Those days, full of chill and noise and sudden movement, put a
panic deep inside me. It was dark by six o'clock, but the wind hardly
settled down. We were all shut up so tight in our houses that one family could forget the others existed. It didn't help that, during the week

before Thanksgiving, there was a persistent drizzle. The wind slung the drops around so that it didn't seem like a drizzle at all, more like a thin rain driving hard into our faces and down our necks and through any gaps in our clothing. During that week I was happy to work at Velma's late into the evenings. I did my cooking for customers, plus my own holiday cooking.

I decided that, even with Howard as a guest in our home, we could do without having Thanksgiving dinner at the house. Shellye had invited us to spend the day with her and Grady and Lisa Layne and Doris. That was the first week of November. Well, I knew that with a newborn it was useless to try to plan anything, let alone entertain people. Before I could get back to Shellye and say that we appreciated it but would decline, she got back to me, by phone, and said in a small voice that Grady was taking them to his mother's and Shellye had to cancel her plans. I told her that was fine, and it was a good year for her not to be entertaining. She seemed to force out a friendly laugh and said that, yes, she still wasn't getting much sleep. The laugh bothered me. So did the thin sound of her voice. But I figured it was fatigue and nothing more.

I saw Shellye less often than ever before, and when I did see her, Grady was along. He played the proud papa well enough. But he liked to guide Shellye around, suggesting where she should sit and what else she might do. The overprotective type. He'd read all the baby books and had something to say about everything they did with Lisa Layne. Grady explained about her feeding schedule and why Shellye would nurse her until she was at least nine months old. Shellye was busy cuddling Lisa Layne during these two or three visits. She didn't take her eyes off the child.

Anyway, I decided to have the café open on Thanksgiving. For the first time since I'd owned the place, I would open on the holiday. It just seemed the right thing to do. A number of my customers were alone this year or they or someone in the family was sick, making it a hardship to put on a dinner. I decided to prepare a Thanksgiving lunch and dinner, cooking only foods that fit in with that.

A week before Thanksgiving—on the Thursday before, in fact—a stranger showed up at the café and lingered most of the afternoon. She was mid-thirties I guessed, attractive enough and slim but not skinny. Full, dark brown hair and a friendly face. She wore nice blue jeans and a fuzzy pullover, dark purple. Her glasses fit her face exactly, looked like she was born with them. She came in about two o'clock, looking like a college student, hauling a bagful of books and notebooks. She had a full lunch but ate it slowly, gazing out the window between bites. There was a book open in front of her, but she didn't turn the pages very often.

I thought right away that maybe she was a writer. She had that intelligent, thoughtful look about her, and once she finished lunch, she ordered pumpkin pie and coffee and took her time while she wrote in one of the notebooks. She accepted two or three refills on the coffee, didn't appear to be in a hurry to finish.

At about four o'clock, I decided to be friendly and ask where she was from. She looked up at me in mild surprise. I warmed up her coffee and waited politely for her answer.

"From Wichita. I teach literature courses at a community college there."

"Oh, I should have known, with the books and notebooks."

She was smiling pleasantly.

"What brings you all the way to Leeway?"

Her smile twitched a little, and I could tell she was considering her answer.

"Oh, I used to know someone who lives here now, at least that's what I've heard—that he lives here."

"Really? What's his name? I meet nearly everybody, sooner or later."

"Um." She wiped her mouth thoroughly with the napkin, leaving no lipstick at all. "Howard Brendle. I'm not positive he lives here, but a friend of a friend told me, and I was, um, traveling this direction anyway, and thought I'd stop by, but then—" She laughed at herself. "—I got to town and realized I didn't even have an address. That's thinking for you, isn't it?"

I set the coffeepot on the table and sat down opposite her, feeling a bit lightheaded. "Why, yes, Howard's my husband's cousin. He's been here in Leeway for about six months." I almost mentioned that he lived with me, but realized I didn't know a thing about this woman, and then I wondered if I should have found out more before saying what I'd already said. "How do you know Howard?"

For the first time, she looked uneasy. She stared at me as if she didn't quite understand what I'd said. "Howard really lives here, huh?" She paused. "How's he doing?"

"Oh . . . all right."

We looked at each other in a measuring sort of way. She rubbed her thumb against the edge of the pie plate.

"I only ask because . . . I know he's been pretty ill. I—actually, I made the trip down to find him and see how he's doing. You say he's all right?"

"All right considering how sick he is."

Her face clouded, and I had the feeling that she and Howard were more than passing acquaintances.

"Mind if I ask your name?" I asked. I made a point to smile, to put her at ease.

"Deborah Beckers."

"I'm Velma Brendle. Nice to meet you." We shook hands over the table.

"I know that Howard left Wichita pretty quickly," I said. "I suppose he didn't have time to let all his friends know."

"Oh, I knew he was going. I just didn't know where."

"You went to school with him?"

She smiled shyly. "He was a student of mine nearly three years ago. I teach some continuing education courses, you know, for people wanting to grab a course here and there, not full-time students. Howard was in one of my evening classes."

"Well, Deborah, I'm sure he'd be happy to see an old friend. Why don't you stay for supper? Howard always comes on Thursdays. It's a pretty set crew of us that eats here this evening."

"Oh." Deborah looked at her watch. "I'm not sure that would be a good idea. And he's not expecting me."

"Howard's always ready for company."

"He lives near here?"

"He lives at my place." I saw her surprised look and added, "He came here because he wanted to be with family. . . . Did you know he's got a terminal condition?"

Deborah's eyes got misty. "Yes, I know. But he's doing all right?"

I shrugged. "As well as you'd expect. We have good days and bad days." I leaned toward her. "Please stay. He's hungry to be connected to people these days."

Deborah drew back suddenly. She picked up the book bag and started jamming books and notebooks into it.

"It would be a shame for you to come all this way and not see him," I said as gently as I could. I saw her swipe at her eyes. She squared her shoulders, and I sensed that she'd done that a lot in her life. Her eyes told sad stories, but none I could interpret just then.

"I don't know how much to tell you," she said, looking directly at me. "I'm glad that Howard is welcoming company, but that kind of hurts me, too. Howard and I were engaged. He broke our engagement a week before he came here."

"My word, I had no idea."

"I didn't figure he would tell anyone about me." She sniffled and rose from the booth, slinging her backpack onto a shoulder. She pulled a twenty-dollar bill out of her jeans pocket and handed it to me. "Thank you, Velma, for telling me how he is. I just needed some little bit of information." Her voice faltered, but she recovered with the next breath. "Please promise you won't tell him I was here."

"Are you sure this is the right thing to do?"

"I haven't been sure of things for a very long time. Although I was sure that I loved Howard. I still love Howard. But he's made his own choices, and I won't intrude. If he wants to talk to me or see me, he knows exactly where to find me."

"Why did he break your engagement?" I had no right to ask such a question, but at the moment I was grabbing for anything that would keep Deborah in my café a little longer. Of all times for Howard not to stop by to visit with me as I got Thursday supper ready.

"He said he was no longer sure that he loved me enough to marry me." Deborah stood near the door, half turned in that direction and half turned toward me. "But he came to that conclusion all of a sudden. I thought maybe he'd met someone else."

"There's no one else that I know of. He's just here with us."

There were no tears in her eyes now. She started out the door.

"Shall I call you from time to time, let you know how he is?" I asked. "Would that help?"

Deborah seemed to consider that for a moment. Then she unzipped a side pocket of the backpack and took out a little notebook. "Maybe it wouldn't be a bad idea for you to have my number." She wrote a phone number on a sheet and tore it out. "But you don't need to call on a regular basis or anything like that. Just in case of emergency." She handed the paper to me, and I put it in my apron pocket. "Thanks so much, Velma. It's nice that I happened into Howard's family. I can tell he has a lot of love and support here."

"We do care for him a lot. I never really knew him well before, but it's been a blessing to get acquainted with him."

"Please." Deborah leaned toward me for emphasis. "Please don't tell him I was here."

I shook my head. "I'm not sure it's right, but you have my word."

She walked out into the glare of the cold sky, got into her Toyota, and was gone in a breath.

As it turned out, Howard didn't come to supper. I got home later and found him sleeping in front of the television. I looked at his face and saw a different person, a man with real love in his life, a man who'd walked out on a good woman. Oh, I didn't know Deborah at all, after such a short meeting, but I could tell she was a good woman, the kind that would be a friend forever and make sacrifices and hold a person's hand to the very end. I sat in the easy chair across from the sofa Howard slept on, and I felt anger at him, possibly for the first time since he'd come to stay. Anger at how unfair he'd been to Deborah. Angry, too, that he'd never mentioned her to me. He'd discussed every topic imaginable with me, late at night or over our breakfasts together. But not a word about something so important. Why, it made me so angry I almost woke him up to give him a talking to. But I'd promised Deborah.

And then there was the Doris problem. After the kiss she and Howard had shared a couple of weeks ago, it had become clear that Doris wanted it to lead to more. It was just as clear that Howard was ambivalent. I'd thought it was mainly because his days were numbered. Or maybe it was because he didn't really feel much for Doris in a romantic way. But now. Lord help us, what a mess life was becoming.

On the day before Thanksgiving, Leeway's white sky turned a steel gray-blue. The clouds were so dense they looked painted on, several coats deep. The wind didn't let up all day. And by evening, the sleet had begun. I heard it hitting the windows of the café like so many plastic BBs. The wind would whip and a million BBs would hit the front windows at once. I kept stuffing turkeys and peeling my sweet potatoes. At midnight, there were dishes full of food from one end of the kitchen to the other, casseroles full of dressing, pots of gravy bubbling, green beans and sweet corn simmering in their spices. Cranberry sauce cooking, bread baking. The cook in me was happy as could be, but the rest of me listened to the onslaught outside. I switched the radio from the classical station to the local weather. The ice storm had hit a four-county area. A number of roads were already closed. In many places, the power lines were weighed down with ice, and some folks were without power.

The newswoman hadn't even finished her report when the lights of the café went out. At first there was nothing but darkness, but then my

eyes picked out the blue flames of my gas burners. I stood still, a vegetable knife and celery stalk in my hands, until I could see clearly
enough to move somewhere and do something. I got to the phone.
Howard answered.

"Vellie, just stay where you are. Power's out everywhere, and the
sidewalks and streets are sheets of ice. I knew I should have driven
down to get you two hours ago."

"No power at the house either?"

"No. It's a wonder the phone's working."

"I've got tomorrow's dinner on the stoves. What a mess."

"Keep the burners on, because the heat's already shut off."

"Oh. You're right." I thought then about our house, that big
house. It was heated by a gas furnace, but the thermostat was electric.
I mentioned something about it, and Howard said he'd already taken
care of it. I thought of Albert suddenly, but Albert was always fine in
tense situations. He was the type who'd be off somewhere, reading the
paper by candlelight. I always knew that at least one person in my
home would be good in an emergency. As it turned out, Howard wasn't
doing badly himself.

"Well, I guess I'll keep cooking," I said, peering out the east windows and seeing no street lights on.

Howard laughed. "Why not? It'll give you something to do. But
you can't be around fire and hot food in the dark. You'll scald yourself."

"I've got candles. If I can find them is the question."

"You want me to come down?"

"No. You'd fall and break something."

I found the candles and set them all along the counter and in several spots in the kitchen. I popped the turkeys in the ovens, took the
cranberry sauce off the heat and set it near the windows to cool, not
wanting to heat up the dead refrigerators. I just kept working on
Thanksgiving dinner. Since the radio was dead, I tried to sing. I never
did have much of a voice, but it sounded even smaller and shakier there
in the dim, quiet kitchen.

At two-thirty, somebody knocked on the front door. Bailey and
Sheriff Brennen Simms stood on the dark sidewalk, glistening like ice
monsters.

"Vellie, are you out of your mind?" With the wind so loud and
both men wrapped up to their cheeks in scarves, I didn't know which
one had asked the question. I told them to come in out of the weather.

"Have some pumpkin pie. You guys look frozen. I took it out of the oven awhile ago. I made six of 'em. Who knows who's going to eat them all." I guided them back through all the candles. They stopped grumping right away about me being crazy and started commenting on all the food smells that were hitting them.

"Turkey done, too?" I knew that was Bailey's voice.

"No, it's got several hours yet. There's dressing cooling. Gravy's probably too cool by now." They both decided to have gravy on their dressing anyway. I watched them eat, not being a bit hungry myself, just tired from being up so long. As Bailey and Brennen scarfed down my food, they filled me in on damage all over town. Three big trees were down. Everybody was without power. Half the phones were dead. And six cars were in ditches, waiting to be pulled out. Bailey and Brennen had had a hard night of it and couldn't stay long.

"Maybe I should just keep all the burners on and keep the food warm? It may be one of the few places with a hot dinner tomorrow, huh?" I looked from one face to the other. Brennen considered this.

"You got gas heat at home, right?"

"Yes."

"Then let me take you there. Leave the ovens on for your turkeys. You can light the burners with matches tomorrow if you need to. You honestly going to be open tomorrow?"

"That's what I planned."

"Well, better wait and see if anybody can get out. The streets are real bad; I'm tellin' everybody to get where they can be warm and stay there."

I put all the food where it needed to be for safekeeping, basted the turkeys one last time, and left the ovens on low. Bailey took one arm and Brennen took the other, and they fairly slid me down the walk to Bailey's four-wheel drive, which was the sheriff's vehicle for the time being. Then they slid me down my own walk and through the door. The house was warm, and I went straight to the couch near the living room register and stretched out. The next thing I knew the sun was striking through the sheer curtains, and it was morning. I raised up to look out the window and was blinded by millions of ice sparkles.

I saw Shellye at my kitchen table. Howard was sitting across from her. They weren't saying a word. I got up and walked in to see them, and I saw that they were eating oatmeal.

For just a second it seemed completely natural for Shellye to be sitting at my table. But in the next second I felt my stomach knot up.

"Where's little Puddin?" That was my name for Lisa Layne. Shellye smiled when I said it.

"At Thelma's." Her voice made a big echo there in the bright kitchen, with the brighter ice world gleaming outside all three windows.

"Somebody sick?" I didn't know what to ask, but neither person was giving me much help.

"A little. Lisa Layne's been a little congested. Grady's doing a new correspondence course, and he couldn't concentrate for all her fussing. Lisa Layne and I went to Thelma's, and Thelma said I should be with Grady but leave the baby with her. She's real good with Lisa Layne. I never worry." Everything Shellye said made sense, but she said it too fast. I looked at Howard, who didn't seem to know what was going on either.

"So how did you get over here in all the ice?"

"Walked. It's not that bad on the grass."

"So Grady's studying at home?" Howard asked, his voice hardly there. Some days the fatigue practically erased it.

"Yeah. When he's studying or praying, he doesn't know if we're there or not. Just thought I'd stop by."

"Well, we're glad you're here. Boy am I glad we run nearly everything off gas," I said. "Anyone want coffee the old-fashioned way, cooked in a percolator on the stove?" I tried to sound cheerful. It was shiny as Christmas outside. The kitchen was toasty warm, because the furnace was fine and the sun was coming full into the east window near the table. We could hear wind whistling around the corner of the house and through the oak tree's bare branches. It was a fine day to be in a warm kitchen with good friends. But both my friends looked too sad to speak. I could tell that Howard was sitting there to be polite, that he really wanted to be in his bed and away from people. The only times he was standoffish was when he was tired or weak, or when his bones hurt.

"No power yet?" I asked.

"No," Shellye said. "But it's warming up, and the ice should be melting with the sun out like this."

"I wonder if I should try to put on dinner."

"So many of your customers are up in years and have no business trying to walk out there," Howard said softly.

"You're right about that. I guess it wasn't a very good plan."

Shellye took her oatmeal bowl to the sink and rinsed it. "How would you know the weather was going to do this? When has this ever happened at Thanksgiving?"

"That's true. Oh well, the food will keep."

"Could I go by the café and pick up some pie to take to Thelma's? I was going to make the pie, but our stove's electric."

"Of course. Let me get dressed and we'll walk down there."

"Oh, you know what?" Shellye looked at me and then at Howard. "Thelma's got an electric stove too." She giggled. "Pie may be all we have, except for some salads she made ahead."

I can be pretty slow sometimes, but between the three of us, it took about five minutes to come up with a whole new plan for the day. I called Bailey and asked how he would feel about being Meals on Wheels. There was no point in putting on a dinner no one could get to. But who knew how many people couldn't even cook their Thanksgiving dinner? Bailey helped us make a list of the older folks who had no family around. We'd feed them first, then check on our regular customers to see who was without dinner. We set the price at a few dollars per plate, just enough to pay for the groceries I'd bought. Howard sighed during that conversation, said no wonder I never made any money. But Bailey and Shellye and I hardly heard him.

We dropped Shellye back at Thelma's, because she was nursing and unable to be away from Lisa Layne for very long. But she made phone calls from there and then called Bailey and me at the café with lists of people who needed dinners. Howard couldn't do much more than help me heat the food and assemble dinners in the carryout cartons. Bailey fetched Ed Turnbull, and they drove all over town making deliveries.

It certainly wasn't the holiday I'd planned. All my tables were decorated and ready for a crowd, but they stayed pretty and empty the whole day. A couple of widowers stopped by and ate their dinners at the counter. The whole while, the sun blazed over the streets, and by afternoon, you could hear thousands of drips everywhere and the town smelled of ice thawing.

Bailey took Howard home around three. His look worried me. I was used to seeing him tired, but a light inside him had gone out this day. On Thanksgiving, of all days, I watched a darkness creep into Howard's face, and it made me afraid.

I got home early evening, and Howard never came out of his room. I knocked on the door around eight o'clock.

"Howard, can I get you anything?"

"No. I just need to rest."

I let him be. And, sure enough, the next morning, he came down for breakfast. His face was puffy, and he wouldn't look at me.

"How did you sleep?" I asked.

"Not much."

"Your legs aching?"

"It's hard to tell where the aches begin and end."

"I'm so sorry."

"Maybe I can sleep some today."

"Tell me if I can do anything."

"No, Velma, there's nothing you can do." Then Howard put his face in his hands and started to cry. It was a tired, hopeless kind of crying, the kind I've witnessed so many times with friends who've lost a husband or wife or child. It was that alone-in-the-world crying. All I could do was sit there.

"I don't want to die." Howard barely got it out before sobs grabbed his words away. I got up and stood behind him, squeezing his shoulders. By then I was crying too.

As that week wore on, it seemed that Howard's emotions had finally come home to roost. He'd weep, and then he'd sit like a stone and talk and talk. He talked mostly about the things that had never turned out in his life. He talked about his failures, the big ones and the little ones. He talked staring at the wall or out the window, and tears would dribble onto his shirt. Even through all the talking, he never mentioned Deborah.

I called Pastor Thomas, and he made sure a couple of deacons came by during the days while I was at work. Pastor himself came over several times. One evening he was still there when I got home.

"How is he today?" I asked.

"It's been a bad afternoon." Pastor sat at the kitchen table. I put on the teapot. In that moment we felt like friends, although I still sensed a lot of things between us that were uncomfortable.

"He's afraid to die," Pastor said, staring at the sugar and creamer.

"I don't think he's been afraid before."

"Well, he is now. He believes that the Lord is with him, I think, but it doesn't really register. It's like an irrational fear."

"Do a lot of people go through that?"

"I think so. Most people are more afraid than they think. They talk about their faith up until a certain time, and then they finally face what's happening, and the fear comes. But most of the time the fear leaves and the peace arrives, toward the end."

"So you think the peace will come back to Howard?" I sat down across from Pastor Thomas while the teakettle made sounds of firing up.

"We have to trust the Lord to give us the faith we need." Pastor looked straight at me. "And sometimes there's a matter the person hasn't really settled yet, and once that's done, they can be at peace."

I came so close to telling Pastor about Deborah. I'd thought of nothing but her for the past couple of days. When I thought that Howard was about to die, I'd actually planned to call her. But then we could see that he probably wasn't dying just yet, that he was going through a spiritual crisis. And I wasn't sure that was the best time to call the woman Howard had not yet mentioned to any of us.

So during the next few nights, Howard didn't sleep, and neither did I. We sat in front of the television, propped up like dead people. He stayed awake because he was afraid that he might not wake up again if he did sleep. I stayed awake trying to come up with ways to get him to tell me about Deborah.

That's how the rest of November and the beginning of December went. Full of tears and fears and darkness. To make matters worse, Shellye and Lisa Layne both got bad colds, so except for a couple of times when I took soup over to Grady's, I never saw my darling girls. Doris spent some time over there, caring for Lisa Layne as much as she could. But one evening she came to my back door and said that Grady made her nervous. I asked her in, even though it was ten at night, but she said no, and later when I was nearly asleep in bed, I heard the familiar soft pad of her walking shoes on the pavement of Pickins Street. She was wandering and smoking again. That night I talked Albert's ear off, about all the people in my life who were suffering. Albert's a good listener, but it seemed that he was helping me less and less. So much of the time I forgot about him altogether, our connection was so slight. So I had another grief to add to my life—losing my husband and a good friend. In some ways, of course, I'd already lost him. Well, I'm getting to a topic now that I can't write about.

The first two weeks of December were mild, so mild we walked around in shirtsleeves part of the time. And the sun peeked out of gray, swollen clouds most days for a little while. But the life inside all of us was barely a glimmer, peeking out of big silences and sadnesses and dreads.

And just when I thought we were getting a bit of energy back, just when Howard was not crying so often, all hell broke loose. And it was my fault. Me, just trying to help.

Len Connor called me and said he wanted to see the baby. He just wanted to see her and Shellye for a little while. He hadn't attended church in a while. Even though he and Shellye had made up, I think he felt embarrassed to be there, now that the pastor and deacons knew what to really think of him. So he wanted to meet Shellye and Lisa Layne privately. He wouldn't cause trouble, he said. Well, I mentioned this to Shellye, and she got a worried look on her face.

"Oh, Grady would never stand for that."

"What harm could it do?"

"I don't think it could do any harm at all. But Grady sees Len as a threat or something. He as much as told me that even if I fell in love with Len, I couldn't leave the marriage. Like I'm going to fall in love with Len!"

"I can see where he might worry about that. You and Len were sweet on each other in the beginning."

"But I'm married to Grady, and I love Grady, and the last thing I want to do is spoil that. Len's definitely in the 'just friends' category now."

"So you don't want to meet Len, over here, just the two of you and Howard and me?"

She thought a moment longer. "That should be all right. You set it up. Tuesday evenings, Grady meets with these men for discipleship training. That would be a good time."

So I set it up, and the next Tuesday my living room shades were drawn, and Shellye and Len sat on the love seat together while Len cuddled Lisa Layne. It broke my heart. I've often wondered if their beginning had been different, if Shellye and Len could have made something together. Len didn't try to elicit any pity, but I could tell that as he held his daughter he was thinking of the future he'd never have with her.

But Len was entirely proper. Shellye picked up Lisa Layne at one point, turned her toward Len, and said, "Lisa Layne, there's your Uncle Len! Give him a smile now—show him how gorgeous you are!"

I stayed nearby the entire time (Howard was upstairs watching TV or sleeping), and it looked as if this meeting had been a good idea. After a half hour or so, Len stood. He put a hand on Shellye's shoulder.

"Thanks, Shel, for letting me see her. She's beautiful, and I know she'll grow up in a loving home." His voice was strong, not hesitant at all. He wasn't asking Shellye to consider him again. He wasn't asking for anything. Shellye smiled up at him, and it was clear that the forgiveness between them was true.

Len was headed through my kitchen and to the back door, when a knock sounded on it suddenly.

"Velma, I need to come in." It was Grady. Len and I stared at each other. Then Len stepped back and nodded toward the door. I opened it, and Grady was through it in a split second. He saw Len, and his face turned white.

"I knew it!"

"Len just came by, Grady," I said quickly, "while Shellye and the baby were here. He's leaving now. Did you know that he's going to college in Manhattan—starting in January?"

Grady fairly pushed me aside as he reached for Len's arm. Len backed away, but not fast enough. Grady caught him in a grip.

"Hey, Grady, what's wrong?" Len tried, unsuccessfully, to sound calm.

"I'm protecting my family from you." Grady's face was inches from Len's. "Don't you ever, ever come near them again."

By now, Shellye had come into the kitchen, looking scared and clutching the baby. "Grady, what's wrong? He just came by to see Lisa Layne. He hadn't seen her yet."

"He has no right to see her. He has no rights at all. I'm only sorry he's not in prison."

"Grady, let's go home. We sat in Velma's living room for about twenty minutes, and he was leaving now. So let him go."

"What's going on?" Howard, sleepy eyed but waking up quickly, appeared behind Shellye in the kitchen doorway. "There a problem?"

"No, there's no problem," I said, moving toward Grady. I placed a hand on the arm that was clenching Len's arm. "Len's leaving, and Grady will take Shellye and the baby home now."

Grady's arm didn't budge. His glare was locked onto Len, who was beginning to look truly scared. Len was younger and more athletic, but Grady was larger.

"Grady, let him go. Let him go home now." Howard took a few steps toward Grady, Len, and me. As he was about to reach us, Grady shoved Len against the refrigerator. We could hear Len's head conk against it. He nearly lost his balance.

"Grady Lewis, what are you doing?" Shellye shrieked.

"Don't you ever—" Grady pointed a shaking finger at Len. "—ever come near my family again. Do you understand me?"

"Yes, I understand. I didn't come to upset anybody or hurt anybody." Len rubbed the back of his head.

"There's no cause to get violent here," Howard said, putting himself between Grady and Len. He looked shrunken and gray beside both of them. "We're civilized people, we can talk things out."

"He's *not* civilized," Grady said tightly, spit escaping toward Howard's face. "He doesn't deserve to lay eyes on that baby. Or my wife."

"She's not your baby!" Len had recovered now, and he was red faced. He pushed past Howard and stood nose to nose with Grady. "She's yours only because you married Shellye. But she has none of your blood, thank God. Don't you ever lay hands on me again, you—"

Then Lisa Layne broke into a full cry, and I never understood what it was Len called Grady, which was just as well. He stormed past Grady and out the door. Grady started after Len, but Howard caught Grady by the jacket. The force of Grady moving away fairly flung Howard into the kitchen table. For the first time, I stopped being shocked and got mad.

"Now just stop it! Look what you've done!"

Grady turned back in time to keep Howard from hitting the floor.

"You just settle yourself down and take your wife and baby home," I said, feeling my jaws tighten and my face heat up. "No more of this ridiculous fighting in my house."

By now, Shellye was at Howard's side, and she was crying, and Lisa Layne was crying. Grady just huffed and mopped his face with his hand.

"I'm sorry, Velma. I lost my temper. I'm just trying to protect my family. That's all I'm doing."

"Well, they didn't need any protecting until you walked in. Just go home." I gave Shellye a long, firm hug and kissed the baby's tear-wet face. Howard was seated at the table, holding his head and panting.

"I'm sorry, Howard," Grady said, laying a hand on Howard's shoulder. Howard was too weak or too shaken to lean away or say anything in return.

Shellye bent to give Howard a hug good-bye. Then she hugged me again. She walked past Grady without looking at him. She was holding her baby tightly. Grady sighed heavily and followed her, stood by looking lanky and helpless while she strapped the baby into the carrier and then got in the car. She let him shut her door. He'd walked over, since that was their only car. He got in it and pulled out of the drive, backing up and not looking toward my house.

Just two days later, Shellye called me to say that she needed to be home with the baby more and help Grady study. She wouldn't be visiting for a while.

"I'm so sorry I encouraged you to let Len come over," I said.

"It's not that, Velma. It's just taking me a while to get used to being a wife and mom. I've been letting things slip and need to spend more time in my own house."

She was lying pretty well, but I knew that I had made a mess of things. I didn't see Shellye again until Christmas that year. I called a couple of times, asking if I could bring some leftovers by, but she always had a reason not to let me come over. I wondered then what other thing I'd done to make her angry at me or not willing to trust me. I searched my memories until my mind was worn out.

But I knew that my hands would be full now with Howard. We took him to the emergency room two weeks before Christmas, and his doctor insisted that he get a blood transfusion. Howard agreed but without much emotion. I remember feeling chilled to the bone when he said, while we waited outside the treatment room, "If I died right now, it wouldn't matter at all." I think I may have said it wasn't true, that it would matter. But Howard didn't hear me. He seemed resigned to death, but not ready to die. I didn't feel that he had come from fear to peace just yet.

Bailey's Healthy Pasta Sauce

1 28-ounce can of crushed tomatoes or 4 to 6 garden-ripe tomatoes
2 tablespoons olive oil
1 small onion, minced
5 cloves of garlic, minced
¼ cup fresh parsley, chopped
1 tablespoon oregano
1 teaspoon salt
2 cups fresh spinach, washed and coarsely chopped
1 tablespoon sugar
2 tablespoons balsamic vinegar

If using garden tomatoes, put them whole into boiling water for about a minute. Take out of water and let cool; the skins should peel off easily. Discard skins and stems. Chop tomatoes.

In a large, heavy skillet, saute onion in olive oil. After about 5 minutes, add the garlic and cook a minute more.

Add the tomatoes to the skillet. Add parsley, oregano, and salt. Cook on low-medium heat for 20 minutes.

Add the chopped spinach, sugar, and balsamic vinegar. If sauce is getting too thick, add a bit of water or vegetable stock. Simmer for another 20 minutes. Remove from heat.

If you have a hand blender, carefully puree the sauce right in the skillet. If you don't have a hand blender, put the sauce in a blender or food processor and puree. Doing this will give the sauce a richer flavor.

15

Christmas

As a pleasing odor I will accept you, when I bring you out from the peoples, and gather you out of the countries where you have been scattered; and I will manifest my holiness among you in the sight of the nations.

—Ezekiel 20:41

Albert fell silent shortly after Thanksgiving. He'd been doing that more and more, and the direction of things worried me. I couldn't get excited about the holidays. Jimmy, off doing business in New Zealand of all places, wouldn't be home at all until well into spring or summer. He had his wife's parents to think about, too.

When a person falls silent, it never helps for other people to get noisier. I decided to just get through this new spell. Albert broke my heart, but he wasn't meaning to. He was running out of things to say, and my only worry was that he would never want to talk again.

In early December, Howard decided to take a part-time job at Leeway's little public library, which was exactly two square rooms filled with books, most of them without their original covers. He said that he liked the quiet and he found a lot of interesting things to read. But I knew that he told a friendly lie. He didn't want to be around customers at the café anymore. His illness shone out of him like a sickening light. He was thin and hollow faced, and his hair was dull, and his skin was the color of asbestos. Sometimes he wore a mask to protect him from other people's colds. He knew that people gazed at him when his head was turned. He knew how sick he looked and how discouraging it was for my regulars to have to see him like that every day. I know that's why he stopped coming down in the evening to walk me home. I never closed at closing time, because my late afternoon regulars couldn't unpark their bottoms until the last drop of coffee was gone. I didn't mind too much. A lot of times I'd cleaned up, was ready to go, and had the luxury of visiting without doing four other things at once. This was when Howard used to stop in. But he didn't do that anymore. Took the afternoon shift at the library and then went directly home.

I think he decided to do a little work, too, so that he wouldn't be alone with his grief so much of the time. He still had crying spells, some he thought we didn't hear. And he would sit for the longest time, looking sadder than death. Filing things in alphabetical order and sorting books didn't require a lot of thought but filled his mind with something besides the end of his life.

One Tuesday evening, while we sat in the living room having coffee, Howard turned to me, his eyes very clear.

"Tell me about Albert. I hardly know anything about him."

"Hard worker, faithful husband, good laugher, no nonsense. Cooks the best trout I ever had."

Howard looked as though he were studying me. I didn't feel like being questioned more about my husband. But I could see that Howard thought I should say more.

"I love him like my own soul, and he loves me the same," I finished.

Howard gave me a warm smile and nodded. "I understand. If you ever want to tell me more, I'd be happy to listen."

Albert seemed even quieter, after that little talk I had with Howard.

So December, for me that year, was pretty empty, even though I was busier than ever. Or at least I was tireder than ever. I opened and closed the café the same times and days, but by the end of each day my energy was gone. Howard made himself scarce, and Shellye was avoiding me, and Albert had gone silent.

In winter, Leeway gets cold and white—not from snow, or much of it, but from all the color draining out of things—the grass, the sky, even the buildings. It's a pale place to be in winter. People go outside mainly to take out garbage or bring in firewood. Everything active is shut up inside, muffled.

That closed-upness made my loneliness harder to bear, and those December days drained themselves of more than color. The everyday life of them—the voices laughing and eyes meeting and people hugging—seemed to slide out of the town's cold, quiet edges.

I thought and thought about whether to put up a Christmas tree. I hated to be an old humbug, with Howard living there and feeling bad so much of the time. He was so depressed he didn't even mention the holidays coming up. But I was able to talk him into helping me decorate VELMA'S. The third Saturday of the month, the two of us put a real tree in the northeast corner, where the windows meet. As much as Howard could throw himself into any activity, he threw himself into that. It was amazing to watch that poor, sick man work so hard to make so few people happy. But it got me off the holiday hook. I didn't buy a tree for the house.

I did help Doris pick one and put it up in her sitting room, which faced my backyard. That way, she said, we could both enjoy the lights at night. Flighty as she was, Doris was a dear.

"How's Shellye and the baby?" I asked as we strung the lights.

"Oh . . ." After a moment, it seemed that Doris had forgotten the question. I heard the rattle of her arms reaching through pine branches near my head. Then a voice came out. "I don't see her much. I think she's losing weight."

"What? She's already thin as a rail."

"Then again, maybe it's just the clothes she wears. She used to look so nice, even right after Lisa Layne was born. But she's started wearing baggier things now."

"You don't think she's pregnant again, do you?"

My question caused Doris's head to pop out of the greenery. "Oh, Velma, don't even think it. It's too soon."

"Is she mad at me?" I asked.

"Mad! I can't imagine about what. Where did you get that idea?"

"She doesn't seem to want to talk to me anymore. I thought it was because of what happened with Len."

"She's not said anything like that. Why don't you call her?"

"I've called a couple of times, but Grady has answered, and she can't come to the phone."

"Grady needs to relax a little. He's gotten to be so particular. She cleans that entire house once a week—I mean, scrubs the whole place. What woman in her right mind does that? She's too tired."

"Is she all right otherwise?" We were both on the same side of the tree now. Doris had plugged in the lights, and the tree twinkled at us shyly in the daylit room.

"I think so. Just worn out too much of the time. But I guess that goes with the territory. Lisa Layne is going to keep her in shape for years to come. I can tell already. Such an active baby. Curious as can be."

"Shellye was like that. I remember her escaping out your back door a couple of times, once naked as a jaybird."

We laughed at that memory. Doris just shook her head. She didn't jump into the story or add any other stories. Those memories belonged to the Dave years, and she'd never said a word to me about him since he left.

Our family had always celebrated Christmas on Christmas Eve. It was one time of the year (the other being Easter) when Gran Lenny allowed herself to be in a true mood of celebration. The women would cook sweets and marinate meats the week before and then cook all that day. Gran Lenny and my aunt and mother would be elbow to elbow in the kitchen, chattering and fussing, and the house would fill with ripe, spicy smells.

Albert and I had carried the tradition along with our son. But this year Jimmy wouldn't be here. Albert didn't offer a word about the holiday.

"Not sure how we'll do Christmas this year," I said to Howard, a few days after we'd decorated VELMA'S.

"I've been wanting to talk with you about that, Vellie." The circles under Howard's eyes were a lavender shade. He looked more concerned than I'd seen him in a while.

"What's that?"

"I, uh, need to be away for Christmas."

"Oh?"

"It's . . ." He sat down at the kitchen table and put his head in a palm. "I need to go see my stepmother, Pearle. You remember her?"

"Oh yes." Pearle was the third and final wife of Howard's dad. I hadn't even thought about her. To my knowledge, Howard had had no contact with her since coming to Leeway. He never spoke of her. Since he had been grown by the time of the marriage, it seemed unnatural to think of her as a stepmother.

I noticed that Howard was looking at me for some kind of reaction. "See, Pearle and I have had some fallings out. Since we were never close, it didn't seem that important. Mainly, I didn't like the way she insisted that Pop travel all over the place with her. He was feeling pretty bad the last few years of his life, and she had him doing tours of everything—the British Isles, New England in the autumn, Santa Fe at Christmastime. She'd never had much money, I think, and so Pop was her chance to do all the things she couldn't do before. And he would have done anything for her. But she shouldn't have demanded so much, especially during that last year. I really let her have it then, and . . ." Howard shook his head. "After he died, I said some pretty mean things. I don't know what got into me. Probably felt guilty myself, for not having a better relationship with the old guy."

I didn't know what to say.

"I said some things to Pearle that she probably didn't deserve. I'm feeling the need to make amends. She'll probably spend Christmas alone, anyway. She never had children, you know."

"That sounds like a good thing to do."

"I'd rather be here. But I should go. And Christmas is a good time to make amends and be with your family. She's family in a loose way."

"Mind if I come along?" I couldn't believe I'd invited myself. Howard seemed surprised too.

"Really? You'd like to come?"

"I'm just not up to celebrating this year. Things around here . . ." I didn't really want to go into my problems with Albert.

"I understand. Vellie, it would be great to have you along. Let's just do the trip together."

That's how we handled Christmas. I figured we would go and sit in this old woman's house, and Howard would say his piece, and we'd all go out for turkey dinner at a local cafeteria, and that would be that.

On Christmas Eve, Howard slept away the afternoon and evening. I let him be, since he had to save energy for the next day. I fell asleep in front of a live Christmas Eve show on the television. No house full of aromas or happy people. It didn't feel like a holiday at all.

On Christmas day, I left Albert in his quiet corner of the house. I said good-bye but didn't wait for him to say anything back. Deep inside I was so sad, but part of me was set on getting through this empty time. I could be strong partly because I knew my husband's silence had no anger in it. Albert was changing, and it seemed to be something that just needed to happen. But I missed him so. He wasn't punishing me; he was just going someplace else for a while. What hurt me most was that I couldn't help him at all. I could hold his face in my mind, hold it up to the Lord Jesus, but I could not be in that dark quiet with him. The Lord knew that, and I had to be satisfied that somewhere, out at the edges of our wondering, were God's big arms, holding both of us tight.

Christmas day was full of sun, and the countryside was hard cold, too cold to even be frosty. That's unusual for my neck of the woods. December is often mild. Many's a Christmas Day when I've been outdoors in barely a jacket, taking a walk in the town's holiday quiet. But the weather this day clamped down like an old man's frown, and nothing moved. No breeze at all, but the air was sharp and had a weight to it. The old Plymouth huffed along, its heater making too much noise for Howard and me to talk much.

Howard looked as pale and blank as the winter sky. Dark scoops of cloud hung where his eyes should have been. He was as sober looking as I'd ever seen him. For a while we had the sun coming straight into the car on us, and I turned the heater down a notch.

"Have you planned what you're going to say to Pearle?" I asked.

"Somewhat. Depends on how talkative she is. I worry that she'll irritate me right off the bat. She's good at that."

"Hmmm. Maybe she'll behave since it's Christmas—and since I'm along."

Pearle lived in the kind of house wealthy people built at the turn of the century. It was lemon yellow with dark green trim, two stories and a half, a chimney and three gables, and a porch halfway around one side. The porch sat several feet from the ground, with neat latticework beneath it that matched the trellis at the far end where dormant rose vines stuck, brown and twisted. I guessed it to be an eight- or nine-room house, as Howard and I stood on the brick walk in front. Years ago, a lot of towns had those brick walks, with the company's name stamped in each brick. The house in front of us looked steady and graceful, tall maples on the north and east, bending a bit like old people watching over the place. Stick bundles of bare bushes marked off the edges of the wide, brown yard. Everything was neat, put away, swept off.

I could go on about my impressions. I've always noticed the details of houses and yards. Sometimes I think I can understand the people who live in a place if I study the place enough. I wanted to stand on the walk and soak up more impressions, but the wind had kicked up, and I could tell that Howard was feeling tired and worried and wanted to get the day over with. We walked up to the steps of the front porch.

The dark green rail was sturdy. I could see a large wreath of fake ever-green fastened to the front door, gold bells and multicolored ribbon arranged on it in a way that made me think it was new and expensive.

Howard pushed the doorbell, a small round button the color of yellowed ivory. In just a few seconds we saw the heavy inside door swing back. Even with the storm door between us, we could feel heat from inside the house press against the glass.

I saw Pearle's hand before I saw her face. It was a small hand with dainty beautiful rings on the forefinger and ring finger. One ring had a bright blue stone. The other was a wedding band with diamonds across the top. The blue stone on the forefinger brought out a large vein that ran along the back of her hand. Looking at the hand made me feel that the visit would go all right. Sensitive and jeweled but not flashy or tense. A soft, fine hand.

Pearle's face was like her hand, calm and with color in the right places. Blue eyes and fair, soft skin that gathered into wrinkles where laughter leaves its marks on a face. Pearle's face was narrow and set off by silver-white hair. A gray knit dress, belted at the waist, gave her a soft look. Her sixty-some-year-old cheeks and lips were brightened with a bit of pinkish plum color. She smiled at us immediately, pushing the latch on the storm door to let us in. Those blue eyes had a nervous brightness to them.

"Pearle, this is Velma," Howard said when we'd barely stepped inside.

"I'm glad you could come, Velma." Pearle reached for my hand. Hers was warm as fresh bread, and soft.

"Dinner will be ready in another twenty minutes," Pearle said. "I just put the rolls in the oven."

I'd smelled the yeast the minute we came through the door. Well, I knew then that I liked Pearle. She made her own dinner rolls and had the good sense to bake them so they'd be eaten fresh. Her dining room table was already set with good china, salads, and relishes.

She led us into the adjoining sitting room. It was a rich looking place, cushioned and curtained in dark roses and greens, smelling like freshly laundered sheets. Howard sat in an easy chair. Pearle and I shared the couch, our knees angled toward each other.

"This is a beautiful room," I said. Pearle's face relaxed a little more. She smiled at me, looking hopeful.

"You like it? I just redecorated last year. After Harvey died, I needed to keep busy, and the room had been beige and brown for twenty years." She laughed a little, and I did too, the way you laugh, not because anything's funny, but because you want everyone to feel at ease.

I glanced at Howard, who wasn't laughing. He looked like a junior high boy who was wearing a nice suit for the first time. I could see that it was a good thing I'd come along.

"It's so hospitable of you to have us here on Christmas Day," I said.

"I'm very glad you've come." There was a tiny tremble way back in Pearle's voice. She sat perfectly straight, a graceful woman, but I noticed that her hands were not folded but clenched together on her lap.

"Yes, thank you," Howard said, his voice raspy like it often was when he was tired. "You've gone to a lot of trouble."

"It's not trouble. It's good to see you." Pearle's eyes locked onto Howard's face. I could see her reading all the illness in his features. "I hope the trip wasn't too hard on you," she added softly.

"No harder than anything else right now." Then Howard made his own put-at-ease laugh. He shifted in his chair, and a crack of light from the window blinds appeared across his forehead. I could see little drops of sweat from where I sat.

"Deborah called me a couple weeks ago. She asked about you." Pearle leaned back in her chair, looking tired for the first time since we'd arrived. "Do you ever call her?"

"I haven't in quite a while. She still working at the college?"

"Yes. Teaching almost a full load of classes, I heard. I think she bought a house recently."

"That's nice. I'm glad she's doing well for herself." Howard looked at me, his eyes blank as the winter sky.

"Is she a friend?" I asked.

"Yes, a good friend," Howard said quickly. I glanced over at Pearle and saw her looking at Howard, waiting for him to finish. But of course that's all he said, and she decided not to take the subject further. She must have known that they were engaged, if she was still keeping up with news of Deborah off in Wichita. I grabbed in the air for a follow-up question that would get either Pearle or Howard to release more information, but couldn't think of anything. It was probably the look on Howard's face that stumped me. He wasn't about to say more. And Pearle wasn't going to push him.

So we passed the time with talk of our towns and churches. Pearle was a Methodist. She invited us to their Christmas service later that evening.

The oven timer dinged. I could see Howard slump a little when Pearle left the room to take out the rolls.

"I'll help her set dinner on the table," I said, walking past Howard. I reached down to give his knee a pat.

If I got started describing the wonderful meal Pearle set before us, I wouldn't get to the real story. The three of us sat at the holiday table, Howard and me facing each other and Pearle at the head. She'd lit a charming little set of candles at the fourth place where no one sat.

"May I ask the blessing?" asked Pearle.

"Why of course," I said, and Howard nodded.

Some people have the gift of praying out loud. I don't, but Pearle definitely had the gift. I closed my eyes and settled in, feeling God's love gathering us. A strong, present peace. In between Pearle's spoken words I slipped little silent prayers of my own. *God, help Howard. Give him words. Make this all work out.*

Pearle finished and arranged the serving fork on the plate of turkey so that the handle faced Howard. "Howard, why don't you get us started."

Howard reached for the fork, even lifted it a few inches, but instead of stabbing some turkey, he put the fork down on his empty plate. As he did this, a sigh came out of him that seemed to fill the room. Pearle and I looked at him.

"I'm sorry, Pearle, but—" another, smaller sigh—"I need to get some things said before we go any further."

I didn't look at Pearle but could feel her tense up.

Howard's eyes flashed my direction, but then they settled on Pearle. When he spoke, his voice was suddenly strong.

"You and I have had some harsh words between us, and I think it was mainly my fault. I don't even remember how everything happened now, but it doesn't matter."

Pearle swallowed but said nothing. I had the feeling she'd known something like this was coming. She sat there, straight as ever, determined, it seemed to me, to be a lady regardless of what came out of her stepson's mouth.

"I've spent the last couple of months taking stock and putting right what I can. I just wish I had the time to come around to better feelings about you and Pop. A lot of hurt happened before you came into the picture. But Pop's already gone, with nothing settled between him and me."

"He had no hard feelings concerning you, I can assure you that," said Pearle. "He talked about some things before he died. He wanted you to know that he had no hard feelings."

"Well, I wish he'd have told me himself."

"I know. I wish he had too. But I hope you can believe what I'm telling you. I wouldn't lie about something so serious."

"I'm not saying that you lie. I'm just saying that it would have been nice to be with him more, to hear some things straight from him."

Pearle slumped back a bit in her chair, and I could see then what a stressful day this was for her, and how tired she'd been for a long time, grieving a dead husband and worrying over a dying stepson who wouldn't come to see her. She straightened up again, though, after a few seconds.

"Your dad could be contrary. I know that as well as anybody. I don't know that you could have done much more to patch things up with him, Howard. I couldn't say such a thing then. I couldn't say anything that didn't support him. But he did bring some things on himself. I know I blamed you more than I should have. I'm real sorry about that."

The way she said "real" brought out a country accent I hadn't picked up before.

"I'm sorry, too, for making things hard. I'm not sure how I could have handled anything differently, to be honest. More and more, I just feel trapped in myself." Howard's voice broke. The air got tense for a moment or two, while he struggled and choked with hardly a sound, and Pearle and I waited and wondered if we needed to do something. But Howard cleared his throat and took a big breath. "I'm trapped in my own faults and shortcomings. It's a desperate way to be. But dying has brought out all those things, and I still don't know how to fix them." He sniffled, dabbed at his nose with the napkin. "I just want you to know that I'm sorry for making things so hard during a time when you needed help. I wasn't the stepson I should have been. I feel helpless to be anybody else, but I know I should have been better."

With that, Howard picked up the fork and drove it into two large slices of turkey breast. He shook the meat off the fork and onto his plate, then held out the fork to Pearle.

Pearle didn't take the fork. She took Howard's hand, just for a second or two, grasped his skinny, gray wrist and squeezed. I looked at her face and saw a tear like a tiny pearl slipping down and making a little streak in her plum-colored cheek. "It's all right, honey," she said very softly, then slid her hand from Howard's wrist to take the fork. She served herself, and Howard passed the dressing in my direction. We commenced with our meal, quiet, relieved. The sun was so bright on the dead lawn outside that it almost looked as if snow had fallen. I heard a sudden scratching sound. Pearle saw me look up and around the room.

"That's my cardinals. They've built a nest in the trellis outside the south window of the living room. Built it while my curtains were drawn, didn't know there was anything human here, I guess. I opened the curtains last week, and there he was, perched on the edge of a nest. She wasn't around, and he started and flew off when I drew back the curtain. So I closed it to leave them in peace. But if I'm careful I can peek out the side and see them fluffed up and snuggled in. That trellis is so thick with dead honeysuckle that you'd never see the nest from the other side."

We talked more about birds. About flowers and gardens. Pearle and I talked about ice skating on ponds out in the country when we were girls. We visited like old friends, and Howard ate in peace, asking us questions that would set us off onto new sets of stories. Around us, the house was completely quiet except for the soft scuffing sounds of the Cardinals outside the window and the furnace cutting on and off, regulating heat to the large, quiet rooms.

We stayed until four, then headed back to Leeway, thanking Pearle for the invitation to Christmas services. Both Howard and I needed to be back home, me to be with Albert and Howard to be with himself in a chair nearby. Howard loved people, but he required more and more time to himself these days. He read a lot, and he napped a couple times a day. Mainly he sat and stared without seeing. I guessed he was staring into his own soul, doing what he needed to do to ready himself. It was a strange thing to live with someone who was walking without a doubt toward death. I could be cooking and cleaning and chattering about daily business, yet know that Howard was, in the midst of my ordinary day, dealing with eternal business as he sat in my easy chair a few yards away.

When Howard and I got home that evening, it was nine o'clock and dark and cold enough to tickle the insides of our noses. The kitchen light near the back was shining a weak bluish tint onto the side yard. We opened the back door and there was Shellye sitting at the kitchen table. The baby carrier was on the table near Shellye's elbow, a corner of pale green blanket draped over the side.

Shellye turned when we came in the door. "Hey, Velma, Howard. D'you have a nice Christmas?"

Howard was about to drop, but he paused to squeeze Shellye's shoulder. "It was a good day," he said.

"Things went OK with Pearle? Mom told me you were going."

"Yes they did. More than I expected."

"Not more than *I* expected." I said.

Howard made a little smile at me. "I know. For you, today was just one more prayer you could tick off your list."

"I brought you some homemade caramels and cherry chocolates. Grady's sister makes them." Shellye nudged a small cardboard box covered with red cellophane.

"That was nice of her." I pulled the blanket back enough to soak in the sight of that little angel face in the carrier. Sound asleep, making baby snores.

"She was real good today. I'm glad. Crying makes Grady's mother nervous."

I thought it a bit sad that after a few months of knowing the Lewises Shellye still called the woman "Grady's mother." Her actual name was Thelma.

"Where's Grady?" I asked.

"Home. Got a new CD player and is getting it all set up. I should go." Shellye got out of the chair slowly, probably stiff from having a leg curled up under her. "I mainly wanted to wish you a Merry Christmas."

"Why, I'm glad you're here. Are you cold?" The girl was trembling.

"Think I'm coming down with something."

"You don't look good."

"Just need more sleep." She grabbed her jacket, which was slung over another chair. When she raised up her arms to slip into the jacket sleeves, her sweater sleeve slid up, and I saw that the underside of her forearm was purple.

"What in the world did you do to your arm?" I grabbed the sweater and slid it up further. Sure enough, a big ugly bruise.

"I don't know, exactly. I slipped the other day, you know, when it was so icy? Slipped and fell against the car. I must have done it then. But you know how your whole body aches when you've fallen like that, because all your muscles tense up. I didn't notice my arm hurting more than any of the rest of me." Shellye gave a laugh and finished putting on her jacket.

"Can you manage the baby carrier? Does it hurt to lift things?"

"I'm fine. Just a little ache. It hurts mainly when something bumps it. I'll be OK." She pecked me on the cheek. I wouldn't settle for that; I held her in a hug and felt her squeeze me back. We didn't say anything. Then she stood back from me and looked into the living room, where Howard had settled for the moment in front of the TV news. "Bye, Howard. Merry Christmas. I'm glad it went all right."

"Bye, sugar. You need any help?"

"No, I'm fine." Shellye picked up the sleeping baby in the carrier, acting like it didn't hurt at all. She'd lost every bit of weight she'd gained during the pregnancy. She was as thin and wiry as ever. I figured she bruised so easily because she had no meat or fat for padding.

My heart felt little stabs as I watched Shellye strap the baby into the car and get in and back out of the drive. After such a nice Christmas day, all I wanted to do was cry. I stood there and watched the car head down the street, watched the taillights shrink away. I asked myself what was wrong with me, so weepy and sad from seeing the girl who'd become a daughter to me. She didn't seem mad at me after all. Here she was with a family of her own, a sweet baby she loved and was such a good mother to. Shellye's life had fallen into place, and she was doing so well. Was I just a selfish old woman who didn't want to share the girl? I missed her being over more, but that happens when kids grow up and start their own families. That's just how life is.

I locked up the house and nudged Howard awake so that he could get to bed. Albert was waiting for me, in his infernal silence, upstairs in the dark of our room. I knew it as if I could see up through the darkness and down the hall and through the doorway. Howard went to the kitchen for a last cup of milk. I heard him moving around on the linoleum as I climbed the stairs.

My mind kept mourning for my Shellye. My heart seemed to beat harder and faster than usual. I guessed that the day had been harder on me than I'd expected. But my thoughts flew back to Shellye, and I saw the bruise again, like a snapshot in front of my face. It stopped me three steps from the landing. That purple stain had the shape of someone's fingers.

Pearle's Dinner Rolls

¾ cup warm water
1 package dry yeast
1 teaspoon sugar
3 to 5 cups flour
1 teaspoon salt
¼ cup fresh chives, chopped
¼ cup grated Parmesan cheese
1 egg
1 tablespoon olive oil
¼ cup melted butter
freshly ground black pepper

Mix the warm water, yeast, and sugar in a small bowl and set aside. After a few minutes, it should start to foam. If it doesn't, start over with a new package of yeast.

In a large mixing bowl, combine 2 cups flour with the salt, chives, and cheese.

Whisk together the egg and olive oil. Add them to the dry ingredients. Add the yeast mixture. Stir, adding flour a little at a time, until the dough holds together well.

Turn the dough onto a floured surface and knead for several minutes, adding flour until the dough is no longer sticky. When it has been kneaded enough, it should have a slightly silky texture.

Turn the dough into an oiled bowl and turn the dough once so that it has a thin covering of oil all over. This will prevent the dough from drying out as it rises. Cover the bowl with a clean towel and set it in a warm place. In about an hour, the dough should have risen to twice its size.

Put the melted butter in a bowl. Grind some pepper into the bowl, half a teaspoon or more.

Once the dough has doubled in size, put it back on a floured surface. Knead it enough to get rid of air bubbles. Divide the dough in half. Then divide each half into 12 equal pieces.

Get out a 12-muffin baking tin, but do not grease. Roll each piece of dough into a ball. Mix the butter and ground pepper well, then roll each dough ball in the mixture. Place 1 ball into each muffin cup. Flatten the ball into the bottom of the tin. Then put another ball on top of the first and mash it down too. You can also put the balls side-by-side in each tin. Cover and let rise until doubled, about 45 minutes.

Bake at 350° for 15 to 20 minutes or until rolls are golden brown.

16

Pastor Thomas

But if the sentinel sees the sword coming and does not blow the trumpet, so that the people are not warned, and the sword comes and takes any of them, they are taken away in their iniquity, but their blood I will require at the sentinel's hand.

—EZEKIEL 33:6

After the holidays, Pastor Thomas became a person afflicted. He developed a cough that hung on for weeks. Toward the end of January, his lower back got real bad. He had to preach sitting down a couple of times, which, I must say, looks mighty strange in a Baptist church, the preacher sitting on a folding chair beside the pulpit. Then, wouldn't you know he developed an allergy. They never figured out what it was that made his face and arms and chest break out. The man was a mess, a person who seemed to be a target for trouble.

Although I work in the church a couple days a week and Pastor comes through and nods on his way to and from his office, the man's rarely had much to say to me. His wife, Clare, would always thank me for the fine job I did polishing all the woodwork and keeping the place clean, but Pastor tended not to be that generous. Maybe he figured that sometimes I listened in when he had meetings at the church (I only did that one time, when they were meeting about Shellye and Len) and when he brought deacons or other people to the café to talk. I confess that I hear snatches of everyone's conversations without trying. But I've learned to not really engage my mind unless I feel invited in. When people I know sit there and gossip or tell stories, they glance my direction or speak up, and I know the story's for me, too. And if they're including me, they won't mind if I share the story myself, with another customer, maybe.

For instance, one day a year ago, Lee Sharply, a woman who cleans houses for some of the elderly, was at Lottie Sweeps's place, way on the south end of town. Lottie had been senile for at least six years, but her neighbor, Tim Blant, almost her age, looked in on her every day, and for years the nuttiest thing she'd ever done was to sit out on her little porch and visit with people who'd been dead for decades. She was perfectly happy doing that, and she still cooked for herself—sometimes for her "visitors" too—and stayed reasonably clean. Tim made sure she took her medications. Lottie had no family left, and none of us deemed it necessary to call Social Services to have her taken to a home. She'd go shopping at Avery's and pay her utilities at City Hall just like a sane person. She'd owned her tiny one-bedroom house and its weedy patch of yard for as long as anyone could remember.

Well, this particular Thursday, Lee was at Lottie's cleaning, which she did every Thursday. Sometimes Lee would stick around to cook a meal for Lottie or load her in the car and take her shopping. The Social Rehabilitation Services paid Lee to do this at several places in the community. That day, Lee was scrubbing the bathroom, and she smelled smoke, like grass burning. She looked out and saw Lottie standing beside a little brush fire, watching it burn. It was August, and the grass was dry enough to catch, so Lee ran out with a bucket of water and doused the fire.

Lottie protested, claiming there was a strange little creature that had been looking in the window at her. She'd set him on fire so he wouldn't bother her anymore. Lee looked around and didn't see any creature or any burnt remains of one. She said, "You tell me if you see it again, but don't set a fire—it's too dry out here." Lottie seemed to agree, and Lee walked her up to the porch to sit in the shade, and then Lee went back in the house. Fifteen minutes later, she smelled smoke again. She went out to find not one, but four little fires at different spots all over the yard. Lottie was standing beside the fourth one, arms folded, cackling like a witch. "See if you look at me again!" she kept saying to the fire. Lee could see the first fire spreading, so she ran in for a bucket of water, threw it on that fire, then guided laughing Lottie back up to the porch. "There's lots of 'em—did you see? I set 'em all aflame!" Lee found the garden hose under the edge of the house, near the spigot; she hooked it up, but all it did was belch at her. The third fire was creeping down toward the road, and Lottie was creeping back toward the fire closest to the house. Lee decided it was time to call 911. Brennen and a couple of volunteer firemen came out with the truck, squirted out the fires, and did their best to contain Lottie, who was hopping mad at them for letting the creatures escape, and calm down Lee, who was covered with smoke and dust and sweat. She was in her late forties and hadn't done so much running since her children were toddlers.

Lottie had to go to a home after that. Lee visited her a few times, and it turned out that Lottie was pretty happy anywhere, since she was always residing in her imagination anyway. But the story of the little fires spread almost as fast as the fires themselves. And, Lord forgive us, none of us could repeat the story or listen to someone else repeat it without doubling over. The image of Lottie trotting from fire to fire, cackling at imaginary Peeping Creatures and Lee running herself ragged, throwing buckets of water everywhere, was just too funny not to laugh. We'd never laugh at Lottie for being senile. She was an old dear. But how could you not appreciate such a drama right in your own town? Even Lee couldn't tell about it without cracking up.

A story like Lottie's you have to tell. Another regular walks in, and before you've even taken his order, you're saying, "You hear about Lee's adventure out at Lottie's?" and then you're set for at least ten minutes of conversation and laughter and head shaking.

Maybe Pastor Thomas thought that I gossiped about him because I cleaned his church and chanced upon his conversations from time to time. Maybe he didn't understand that I'd never repeat a story I wasn't invited to repeat. Maybe Pastor just didn't like me at that time. For whatever reason, he didn't talk to me usually unless he had to.

He was always meeting with his deacons and doing other things with the men in the church. They'd have prayer breakfasts; they went fishing as a group a couple of times; they piled into Frank Delbert's minivan to go to conferences once or twice a year. Much of the time Clare stepped in, along with a couple of other women, and kept the women busy too. I suppose it's a better fit for women to lead women. But it always bothered me that Pastor called only on the men to pray.

And that he said so little to me when I spent so much time there in the church, making sure it was ready for this service or that, keeping it clean and organized.

I mentioned my dissatisfaction to Doris once. I said church should make everyone feel loved and welcomed. Even people who didn't have teaching or singing talents, even people who didn't talk much at all or who would never do important things. Even people like Howard, who, though he turned out not to have AIDS, should have been embraced even if he had.

Doris listened calmly while I complained, then asked, "Why don't you go to another church, Velma?"

For just a moment I considered that possibility. But, you know, in our little town, pastors come and go. But I'll always be around. If things go sour, why should I be the one to leave? That's what I told Doris, and she laughed at that. "You've got a point."

The last Sunday morning in January, Grady and Shellye walked in late. They'd missed Sunday school altogether and got in after the morning worship had started. They didn't take their usual seat in the third row back from the pulpit. They slid in beside me. Grady's face was pale, but not pale like Howard's face. He looked angry. But then he saw me looking at him, and he smiled. Shellye smiled too and whispered, "Hi, Velma."

We stood to sing a hymn, and Grady reached for a hymnal from the rack directly in front of Shellye. I saw Shellye jump a little when his arm darted in front of her. We stood, but Shellye didn't. We'd already begun to sing, but I could hear a snatch of Grady's sharp whisper, when he bent down toward Shellye:

"You get yourself out of that pew. Stop making a spectacle of us."

Hearing that, I couldn't help but stare at Grady. As his eyes caught mine, I looked straight ahead again. I couldn't believe what I was hearing. I felt trembles in my stomach. I wanted to know everything about Shellye and Grady; at the same time I didn't want to know any more.

During the next week, Pastor Thomas called me early in the afternoon. He never called unless he needed me to do something at the church. But this time he asked if we might have coffee together. I said sure, come on over, but then he invited me to his and Clare's house. That surprised me, but I went over there. Pastor showed me to their little sitting room, and soon Clare showed up with a tray of coffee and cookies. She served me and then her husband, then got some for herself and sat down with us.

We'd hardly taken two sips when Pastor said, "Velma, I'd like you to talk with Shellye."

I just looked at him.

"You know she and Grady are going through a rough patch lately. I'd . . . rather not bother Doris with it. She tends to get too upset."

"What do you want me to tell her?"

"Just, well, I don't think she understands that marriage is a spiritual partnership. It's more than cooking and taking care of the baby. It's prayer together, Bible study, being attentive to the other person's needs. Grady's pretty frustrated with her right now."

"The girl's only been a mother for two months. Anyone can see that she's worn out. What exactly is she not doing that she should be doing?"

"She's just not cooperating. It's important for Grady to be able to lead his family spiritually as well as in other ways. She's got to learn to be part of that."

"To let him lead?"

"In a way, yes. After all, Grady's been a Christian for fourteen years, a leader in this congregation for nearly five years. Shellye's not been a believer nearly that long. She's stumbled in the past in her relationships, and she needs to be a learner now."

I looked at Clare, whose eyes were wider than usual. Finally, she said, "I think it's just that she's young, Velma, and with her own family split up when she was little and no father in the picture all these years, she doesn't understand things sometimes."

"I'm still not sure what you're talking about. What is she not doing?"

Pastor shifted and leaned toward me just a little. "She's not allowing Grady to give spiritual leadership in the family. He's tried to do a number of things, such as family devotions, Bible study together. And when he tries to offer any guidance from Scripture about daily matters, Shellye tends to get angry or find excuses not to participate."

"Oh. Well, I'll try to bring it up with her. But I don't know what else she could fit into her day, to tell the truth. She takes care of the baby and her own house and until the baby was born worked for me. Are you sure Grady's not expecting too much?"

"It's not a matter of how much or how little. It's a matter of Shellye's attitude. This is what concerns me. What concerns both Clare and me."

I took a deep breath and could see in Clare's eyes that she really wanted my help. "I'll try to talk with her. Have you talked to her?" I looked at Pastor.

"I've tried a couple of times, but I don't feel that she's heard me. I know she listens to you."

"I'll do what I can."

"Thank you, Velma." Clare put a hand on my arm. "And we'll talk to Grady a bit more, about his expectations. Most young men don't understand just how much a wife and mother does on a daily basis. They're both young and in a period of adjustment."

Actually, the pastor asking this of me provided the opportunity to ask Shellye more about her marriage. I'd not felt comfortable with that, even knowing that things weren't going well. I called. Grady answered. I explained that I wanted Shellye to come over for coffee, that Pastor had asked me to talk with her about some things. Grady seemed to understand when I mentioned Pastor, what I was doing. Without even asking Shellye, he told me she'd be over.

"You want to talk about something?" Shellye stood on my back step, looking confused.

"Come on in, honey." I touched her shoulder as she walked past me. "There's a pot of tea in the dining room. Have a seat at the table."

I heard Shellye make a happy sound. I'd put out some carrot cake beside the tea. "Something wrong, Velma?" she asked, while she settled on a chair and I poured the tea.

"Oh, I don't know if anything's wrong. Just wondering how you've been."

"All right. Do I look sick or something?"

"No. But . . . Pastor thought maybe you were struggling. With a new marriage and a new baby—"

Shellye had stopped watching me pour and looked straight into my eyes. "What did Pastor say, exactly?"

"I don't remember exactly. The gist of it is, he thinks you and Grady haven't got things sorted out yet."

"What things?"

I sat down, wondering why I'd agreed to this. I didn't understand that well myself what Pastor had been driving at. "It sounded to me as if Grady's trying to be a spiritual leader and he doesn't think you're cooperating. I think that's what Pastor was getting at."

"Oh." Shellye's eyes shifted from me to something behind me.

"I don't know that much about the spiritual leadership part. Back when I got married, we just went to church and otherwise we figured out how to get along as man and wife." I smiled, trying to get Shellye to look at me again. "I guess things are more complicated these days."

"Grady has a lot of ideas about what I—we—should do. Sometimes I don't agree with everything. That's probably what he's frustrated about."

"Doesn't sound like anything you can't work out with a little time."

"I know I should listen better, but . . ."

"But what?"

There went that stare again. Then she seemed to snap out of it, and she looked at me again. "Nothing. I'll try harder, Velma, if that's what you think I should do."

"Marriage takes work, and compromise sometimes."

She nodded and did her best to smile. I felt that something was amiss. Then I heard myself charge ahead.

"He's good to you, isn't he, Shellye?"

"Of course he is!" Her eyes widened. "He's a wonderful man, and he loves me in spite of my past, and he loves Lisa Layne. There's nothing wrong. I'll try harder—I really will."

"Because if he's not good to you, that's a different story."

"How would he not be good to me?"

I can't remember that question and my answer without feeling a sharp pain slice through my soul. When Shellye asked the question, there was something in her eyes that begged the chance to speak. I saw it, I know I did. But it scared me, and I might as well not have seen it at all. *How would he not be good to me?* she asked. It was the perfect opportunity to say, "For one thing, if he's leaving bruises on your arm, that's not being good to you." I could have made those words come out of my mouth. But they didn't come out. Instead, I shrugged.

"If he's being disrespectful in any way. He shouldn't be disrespectful no matter how frustrated he gets."

"He's always respectful. Don't worry. It's just taking me longer than I thought to get used to marriage. I think that's all it is."

"Well, honey, you're not the first nor the last new bride to go through that."

Shellye gave me a kiss on the cheek, and then she walked out of my house, and I felt that it had been a good talk. I hoped that we'd gotten on a good foot again, that maybe she'd come visit me or drop into the café more often.

But I saw Shellye even less after that. January and February slogged their way through Leeway like a huge glacier that took its time moving the cold and mud through and keeping spring trapped behind it.

In the middle of February, old Zeke shuffled in the door. He was walking slower than he had the other three or four times he'd come in. In fact, he seemed to be limping. Some other customers were in the booth he usually sat in, and he stood in the middle of the room for a few seconds, looking mad. I walked over to him but didn't get too close.

"You want to sit over here? There's a table near the counter."

He gave a little snort and limped to the place I was pointing to.

"Did you hurt your leg?"

"What's it to you? People get hurt."

So much for Christian charity.

"You got anything around here besides toast and potatoes and bacon?"

I didn't hide my sigh. "What do you have in mind?"

"I like soup. Potato soup."

"Tuesdays I've got split-pea soup."

He made a face. "No thanks."

I waited.

"You got fried chicken? All restaurants fix that, you know."

"I can fry some up pretty quick. It's five and a quarter for the dinner, three seventy-five for the snack."

"What's the snack?" Zeke picked up the salt shaker and seemed to examine it for dirt or some other imperfection.

"Four chicken tenders with gravy and a biscuit."

"Does it come with some of that old coffee?"

I felt my neck get hot. "You think you might pay today?"

With that, Zeke put the salt shaker down. He was breathing hard, almost snorting. "I can pay you a dollar."

"I'll bring out the dinner."

"Make sure the gravy's hot an not all glumpy like it's been scraped out of the bottom of the pot."

Sheri watched me fume as I lowered pieces of chicken into the fryer.

"Maybe he can do something in exchange," she said.

"Heavens no. Can you imagine trying to give directions to that old stinker? Besides, he's limping. Wouldn't want him to fall and hurt himself. He'd probably sue me."

Howard kept working at the library in the afternoons. There in the dead of winter, his leukemia decided to take a break. His blood count improved for a while, and about mid-February, he started making plans to help me redecorate the café. In his mind, VELMA'S LITTLE GERMANY was a foregone conclusion. The doctors had told him that leukemia, just like any cancer, can go into remission on its own, or it can get worse suddenly. So we were grateful for his season of feeling better. He still bruised if you looked at him too hard. The rash that had caused such a stir had disappeared as suddenly as it had appeared. I no longer heard talk around town about him having AIDS, but Howard never was as free as before when it came to visiting at the church or socializing much at all. He always claimed he was too tired, but I knew he was hurt from the misunderstanding.

Then, the third week of February, Howard went into the hospital. His heart was beating irregularly, and he was having trouble breathing. Dr. Henderson chased me out of Howard's room about midnight. He was sleeping, with oxygen. Had an IV in his arm with antibiotics. It was an infection of some sort. Doc said that Howard's immune system wasn't what it should be. When I heard that, my hopes for Howard all but died. But Doc told me he'd have the hospital call if Howard got worse through the night. For now, we were in a holding pattern. I went home exhausted but of course couldn't sleep.

Bad things always come in bunches. The next evening Howard was still in the hospital but a little stronger. I finished at the café, drove over to see him, then came home to find Shellye sitting in my kitchen. Lisa Layne was squalling in her carrier, which was on the table in front of Shellye. I put down my purse and picked up the baby. Then I saw the red mark on Shellye's left cheek.

"I'm sorry, Velma, to come over here like this." Shellye's voice sounded so small and weary. "Grady's . . . going through a really hard time right now. He's doing a correspondence course from the Bible college, and he's trying to prepare a new Sunday evening series for church. All of that's about to do him in."

I just looked at her, and the anger started in my stomach and rose to my eyes.

"What is that on your face?"

"I overstepped, that's all. He told me to stop arguing, and I wasn't really trying to argue, but I should have stopped." A tear trickled out of her eye and down the red patch. "It was a reflex. He slapped me and then knew he shouldn't have. He's real sorry."

I sat down close to her and lifted her face up so I could see the mark better. "Oh, sweetie, he should never have done a thing like this." Then I thought of the bruise I'd seen at Christmas. "Has he hurt you other times?"

Shellye didn't answer because she was crying. Lisa Layne was finally quieting down. I rocked the baby while Shellye went to the bathroom to wash her face. She came back and sat down.

"I never know what I do that makes him so mad."

"Nothing should make a man that mad. If you throw his supper out the back door, the worst he should do is walk out of the room."

"He says that I make him crazy."

"Hon, if he's crazy, he came that way."

"But he loves us, Velma, I know he loves us so much."

I decided to hold my peace. I understood what she meant, but I couldn't bring myself to admit that such a boorish man could have love in him—no matter how full he was of Scripture and sanctity.

I was glad Howard was still in the hospital. I think seeing Shellye like that would have finished him. I wanted to call Doris over, but Shellye begged me not to. Then I remembered that Doris had been coming in the hospital doors as I walked out. To see Howard. I didn't know if Howard would appreciate it or not. He seemed to run hot and cold where Doris was concerned. Just a few days before, he'd gone over to her place in the afternoon to have coffee. He'd stayed a long time. I'd managed not to think about that much.

In half an hour, Pastor and Grady were at my door. Grady looked like a whipped puppy. He went over to Shellye and hugged her as if they'd been apart for months. "I'm so sorry, I'm so sorry," he kept murmuring. The three of them sat in the living room. I didn't offer anything to eat or drink. I sat with the baby in the chair nearest the dining room, in the room with them but not with them. Shellye was crying, and Grady was begging her to forgive him, and Pastor wasn't saying much at all.

Several times I almost motioned Pastor over so that I could ask, "Has this happened before? I have reason to think he's hurt her before." But then the three of them were talking, and they seemed to be calming down and making progress, and I decided that this was Pastor's field, not mine.

I did tell the three of them that Shellye and Lisa Layne were welcome to stay with me any time she and Grady needed to cool off. But a look of fear crossed Grady's face, and Pastor just smiled and said, "Velma, you're a generous soul, but marriage problems need to be worked out right in the marriage."

"We're learning how to forgive each other, Velma," Grady broke in.

"Yeah, it's all right." Shellye smiled as she lifted Lisa Layne from my lap. "Thanks, Velma. Sorry we disturbed you."

The next day, I brought Howard home from the hospital. Doris had offered, but it was Thursday, and I didn't have to be at the café until late morning.

Howard looked a lot better. He walked out of the hospital under his own power and chatted on the way home. When he paused, I cut in.

"Shellye and Grady had a fight yesterday. She and Lisa Layne came over to our house."

"A fight? What do you mean?"

"They argued, and he slapped her face. He and Pastor came over and they made up. But I told her to come stay with us if she needed to."

"That . . ." Howard didn't finish describing what he was thinking of Grady. "But she didn't stay? She's back with him?"

"Yes. Probably just a spat."

"That's no excuse for him to slap her. Does Doris know?"

I just looked at him, and he nodded, his lips tight. "I guess Doris isn't much of a comfort at times like this," he said.

"She's been a comfort to you at least." My words hung between us. My emotions were doing fistfights inside me. I wanted to understand how it was with him and Doris.

"Well, Doris has been a good friend."

"I think she sees herself as more than that."

"Sometimes she seems to be more than that, I'll admit. But who am I kidding? I nearly saw heaven a couple days ago. I can't plan a future." He no longer sounded sad and weepy, just resigned.

"I know about Deborah, Howard. Don't ask me how, but I found out a while back."

He didn't say anything for a long time. I drove, and he watched the tan fields of winter stubble slip by. I heard him take a deep breath and let it out. "Did Pearle tell you?"

"No. Don't ask how I know."

"You probably think I'm worse than Grady, walking out on her."

"I don't know what to think. It's clear as can be that the woman loves you—"

"You've seen her then?"

"—and she's willing to be with you now of all times. But you never said a word about her. Why was that? And now you're carrying on with Doris, who, I can tell you, won't weather a breakup or a death very well."

"We're not carrying on. We've . . . a couple times we've spent time together."

"I really don't want to know. But I'm not happy with you, Howard. I shouldn't be so hard on a dying man, but you've done a bad thing here, taking off from a relationship and never saying a word."

"I know. You're absolutely right. But you have to understand, Deborah's lost so much already. Her parents died within a year of each other. The last thing she needed was to lose a husband, or even a fiancé."

"She thinks you just decided you didn't love her."

"That's what I led her to think."

"Why on earth for?" I took my eyes off the road and glared at him. "Any woman would rather a man leave out of consideration for her than because he doesn't love her anymore."

"If I'd told her the truth, she would have insisted on staying with me. She would have promised that she was strong enough."

We both fell silent. We were almost home. It was a typical, miserably cold and damp February day. The wind could cut diamonds. I was afraid it would blow Howard over when he got out of the car.

The next week, I got home late from the café, and Shellye was sitting with Howard in the living room. The television was on, and Lisa Layne was on a little blue blanket on the floor. I said hello and sat down. Then I saw the suitcase beside the couch.

Shellye saw me notice it. "I need to stay here, Velma."

"Another fight?"

Shellye didn't answer. She kept watching the news. But Howard looked up at me, his lips white. "He threw her against the wall. And look at her hand."

"Oh, Shellye, what is that?" Her hand was wrapped in gauze.

"Just a scald. It's not too bad." She wouldn't let me touch it, and she wouldn't tear her eyes from the television.

"Water from the teakettle," Howard said. "He poured it on her hand."

As I stared at Shellye's hand, the room got fuzzy. For a moment I thought I would pass out. I couldn't say a word. Shellye was still watching television.

The phone rang. I was closest, so I picked it up.

"Velma, I know Shellye's over there. And I know she's already told you lies about me—"

"A burnt hand doesn't lie." The words could hardly get out of my throat, which suddenly felt frozen.

"That water spilled out of a saucepan. Shellye knocked into the handle, and it went everywhere."

"I don't want to talk to you, Grady."

"Shellye's not been herself lately. I've kept this quiet, not wanting to embarrass her. Pastor's the only one who knows, but she's not been doing well for several weeks now. I think it's postpartum depression or something. Please, I'm going to come over and bring her home. We'll have a counseling session with Pastor tomorrow. I've already called him. He knows what's going on. Please, Velma. It's not the way it looks."

"It won't hurt anybody for her and the baby to stay over here. If she's not herself and not feeling well, maybe she shouldn't be there with you. It might be more upsetting. Good night." I hung up on Grady while he was still protesting.

"What's this 'not herself' business?" Howard wanted to know.

"Grady says she knocked over a saucepan of boiling water and that she's lying."

"Maybe I am. I don't know. I don't know anymore. Maybe I'm going crazy." Shellye spoke so quietly and with such a monotone, she could have been talking in her sleep.

"Don't you say another word, Shellye!" Howard leaned toward her. "Don't ever say that you're crazy. We know better."

"Maybe I'm just like Mom, not tuned into reality all the time."

"Stop it!"

"Maybe I didn't really confess with my whole heart my sin with Len, and maybe I was confused about that too. Grady says that girls who grow up without a daddy often become promiscuous. That's why it's so important for Lisa Layne to have a father who loves God, so she won't make mistakes like that."

Shellye stared at the television while tears ran down her cheeks. "I should be grateful that Grady's willing to take me in the way he has. I mean, who else would have wanted me? Pregnant and no husband, no job, a crazy mother—"

"Your mother is not crazy." I sat next to Shellye and did my best to dab at her tears with the tissue in my apron pocket. "She's had a lot of grief, but she's never been crazy. And you're *not crazy,* and any man should thank God for allowing him to have you in his life." Now I was crying too.

Howard's voice was very calm, but very dark. "You're not going back over there, and you're not going to any session with Grady and Thomas. Grady's got him convinced that you're lying about all this, so the guy won't be any good at all. You're not going anywhere. And they're not coming here." He got up and picked up Shellye's suitcase. He carried it up the stairs, while Shellye and I sat on the couch and sniffled and Lisa Layne played with the fringe of her blanket.

The next morning, Pastor Thomas came to the door. I did a strange thing: I didn't invite him in. He stood on one side of the storm door, and I stood on the other. He asked to see Shellye, and I said she was resting and that when she was ready to talk to him, we'd give him a call. He walked back to his car in frustration. A little while later he called me.

"Velma, I don't think you understand what's going on."

"I understand it very well."

"Shellye staying with you isn't going to help keep this marriage together."

"I'm not so certain the marriage needs to be kept. Not with what's been happening lately."

"You don't really know what's been happening, do you?"

"I know that this girl has never told me a lie her entire life."

"How would you know? And how would you know what goes on between a husband and his wife? Have you lived with them? Have you seen any of the things Shellye claims have happened?"

"Have *you* lived with them? How do you know Grady isn't lying?"

"Grady has a history with me and with this church. I have full confidence in him."

"Well, I don't."

I heard an exasperated sigh at the other end of the line. "This can't go on forever. When Shellye's feeling better, have her call me. But she can't wait too long. This is putting a strain on everybody—Grady and his mother, Doris, the whole church. We'd like to settle this privately. But if Shellye's living somewhere else, eventually people will want to know more than they need to know. I'm just trying to maintain some control here, before we've got these kids in divorce court and the church in turmoil."

Howard had already called Doris, and Doris was sitting in my living room when Pastor told me what a strain this was on her. But, maybe because of Howard's presence, Doris was upset about Shellye being hurt, but she was steady, too, especially about Shellye not going back right now.

For the next several days, Shellye and Lisa Layne stayed in the west bedroom. The phone rang off the wall. Grady kept calling, said he had to talk to his wife. After a day of that, Howard told Shellye not to answer the phone. So Howard would answer. We'd hear his side of the conversation, which usually went like this:

"Grady, she's not willing to talk to you right now. . . . I think you should honor her wishes. . . . When you call up and you're saying these kinds of things, I know for sure I don't want you talking to her. . . . There's no need to insult me or Velma. . . . Nobody's trying to break up your marriage, Grady, we just want Shellye and Lisa Layne to be safe. . . . We all know what the Bible says about that, but that's not what we're talking about here. . . . I'm going to hang up now, Grady, and don't you call back. Give Shellye some time to clear her head. Give yourself time to not be so angry."

Sometimes the conversation was much shorter and not as polite. Howard, thin and gray and always exhausted, was ready to rise up and fight Grady physically if it came to that.

But on the last day of February, Shellye went to the church office. Doris went with her. Grady was there with Pastor Thomas and Clare. They talked a long time, and at the end of it, Shellye went home with Grady. He'd confessed to pushing her a couple of times and that he'd slapped her that once. He still claimed that the burn on her hand had been an accident. When Doris told me about it later, she said that after a while Shellye didn't talk much, that Doris had asked her there in front of everybody if there were other times Grady had hurt her, but she'd said no. They prayed, and Pastor helped Grady and Shellye set some goals for their prayer time and for memorizing verses of Scripture to help them through the temptation to argue. Grady asked Shellye's forgiveness for losing his temper, and Shellye asked his forgiveness for pushing him when she knew she shouldn't. So that was that. I could tell from the way Doris gave us the report that she wasn't satisfied. Howard was too frail that day to say much, but anger snapped in his eyes.

Thinking about the men I've known—father and in-laws, uncles, husbands of my friends—it's occurred to me that most men in this world carry wounds. Wounds that change the way they walk and talk for the rest of their lives. Gashes in their souls so deep that generally some steady woman is called upon to climb down inside and drag them out. Except that some women end up living in the wound rather than healing it. It's a dilemma. A person should find healing and comfort, but you hate to see another human being used up, wasted even, trying to help.

Shellye kept trying to help Grady, and he kept using her up. She stayed with him two weeks, then landed at Doris's one evening while he finished raging at home. Then a day or so later, she went back. This happened several times. She'd leave Grady, stay to herself and get strong again, clear her mind, and dry her tears. Then dive back into Grady's darkness. All through the month of March, she kept clothes and photo albums in my west bedroom. She had a key to my house.

During one of these spells when Shellye was at Doris's, Grady walked into the café. I knew it would be a bad afternoon. I just didn't know how bad.

I had a crowd in for a late lunch, and only one person helping. But that didn't stop Grady from hammering me with questions.

"Why doesn't Shellye talk to her husband when he calls?"

"Is Shellye spending a lot of time with Howard, with just the two of them in your house? Or does he stay over at Doris's with them?"

"Who decided to break up my marriage? You all must have been working on this for a while."

"Is that Len Connor coming around? I don't trust him."

It just went on. He sat on the counter stool nearest the kitchen, drank coffee, ate pie, and grumbled these questions at me as I went about trying to keep everybody fed. The first cycle or two of questions I tried to answer, but he just kept asking them, so I stopped talking to him altogether. Finally, thank the Lord, Brennen stopped in for a cherry Coke.

As far as I knew, Brennen didn't know anything about Grady and Shellye, although if anyone outside our small circle had known, it would be Brennen, who seemed to have developed pretty good radar over the years. Grady seemed to understand that Brennen would take exception to his badgering me while I worked. And as paranoid as Grady was those days, he probably thought Brennen knew everything about him. So when Brennen sat down two stools away from Grady, Grady shut up. Brennen stayed to talk a few minutes, and Grady got up and left. Then Brennen went on his way, flapping angel wings behind him.

That evening I called Pastor Thomas. "You've got to put some limits on Grady. He came to the café today and harassed me half the afternoon. He wasn't even making sense part of the time."

"The man's terrified that his marriage is breaking up. I think I can understand how desperate he feels. Shellye just keeps bouncing back and forth. That would drive any man to distraction."

"You don't understand. The man just babbles on about things that aren't in the least bit true. He thinks everybody's trying to steal his wife. I never heard such nonsense. Tell him to stay away from me. It actually scared me today, the way he went on."

"I'll talk to him, but nothing is going to settle down until Shellye makes a commitment and sticks with it."

The second week of March, Pastor Thomas had a heart attack. It happened on a mild Sunday morning as he was getting ready for church. Clare walked into the bedroom to see why it was taking him so long to get ready and found him on the floor near the dresser. She called 911 and John Mason. By the time Sunday school should have started, the bunch of us were standing in the foyer and sanctuary in nervous knots of four and five. We had prayer, and another deacon, Dan Mallory, came up with a short devotional talk. We sang a couple of hymns and went home.

It turned out not to be a major heart attack, and Pastor Thomas was home within a day or two. But he was put on a strict schedule for rest and relaxation. He and Clare decided to use part of their vacation time and visit their daughter in Orlando.

We gave them our blessing and then wondered if we'd see Pastor Thomas again. I wondered who would deal with Grady in his absence. Other churches in the three-county area helped us find an interim pastor, and that was fine. But an interim doesn't know the little ins and outs of a church body. He's generally from another town, and so he's not available during the week.

The interim didn't know about Grady's troubles. Grady sidled up to him right away, after the first morning worship service, and I could see that Grady was trying to get on the new man's good side. At that time, Shellye was back with him—it was just too hard to live outside her own house, especially taking care of a baby. By now I was asking Shellye point-blank, all the time, "Is he being mean? Are you all right?" and she assured me that since she'd moved back the last time, he'd behaved himself.

It was a dreary March that year. Even on days the sun made it out and the air began to take on hints of thawed-out earth and little sprouts shooting up, we members of Jerusalem Baptist huddled in the sanctuary and Sunday school rooms and in a home or two, praying for our pastor and feeling left alone to fight our individual battles. I felt that, once more, Pastor Thomas had let Shellye down during a horrendous time in her life, but he'd spent a lot of time doing what he thought he should do for her and Grady, and he was responsible for any progress Grady had made with his temper. Although I'd hardly called Pastor Thomas for help a half dozen times in as many years, I did feel his absence.

Welcome to VELMA'S PLACE

Pastor's Pecan Pie

3 eggs
$\frac{1}{3}$ cup sugar
$\frac{1}{2}$ teaspoon salt
$\frac{1}{4}$ cup butter, melted
$\frac{2}{3}$ cup corn syrup
$\frac{1}{3}$ cup peach preserves
$\frac{1}{2}$ teaspoon cinnamon
$\frac{1}{2}$ teaspoon nutmeg
$\frac{1}{2}$ teaspoon ground ginger
1 tablespoon cornstarch
1 cup pecan halves

Prepare a standard pie crust, or buy one ready-made.

Heat oven to 375°. With a mixer, combine eggs, sugar, salt, cinnamon, ginger, nutmeg, corn starch, butter, corn syrup, and peach preserves. Stir in pecans. Pour into the pie crust.

Bake until set, 40 to 50 minutes. Let it cool at least half an hour before serving.

17

Lost Gifts

On my holy mountain, the mountain height of Israel, says the Lord God, there all the house of Israel, all of them, shall serve me in the land; there I will accept them, and there I will require your contributions and the choicest of your gifts, with all your sacred things.

—Ezekiel 20:40

In the spring of '97, not long before Easter, I lost my love for cooking. It happened without so much as a day's warning, as though a thief had entered my house while I slept and snatched away part of my personality. I woke up one morning and knew that something was different and very wrong.

I lost not only my love for cooking but my ability to do it. I couldn't even put together a decent pot of soup. I'd oversalt or forget a main ingredient or the thickening would go wrong. I cut myself chopping vegetables. The bread dough worked up as if the yeast had expired.

All of a sudden, I didn't enjoy my work. All of a sudden, it stopped feeling natural. After years of feeding the townspeople of Leeway, I had no heart for it whatsoever. All those hundreds of early mornings Avery would let me into the grocery before he opened, while he was putting out the fresh produce. And I'd look over lettuce and cabbage and carrots and peppers and potatoes and herbs and tomatoes and squash—taking in their colors and firmness and feel. I'd wander up and down the aisle four or five times, fill a cart, and plan the day's menu. It was my morning routine and felt as satisfying as a good cup of coffee. But now it was a chore, and the textures and colors had no meaning. When always before I'd hold a cucumber or new potato in my hand and start imagining what I could do to make it delicious and beautiful, imagine the faces of my customers when I set it prepared and arranged on a plate in front of them, now all I could think of was throwing all the vegetables in a pot of boiling water and letting them fend for themselves.

"Time I retired," I said to Albert and to myself on a Monday morning, sitting on the bed half-dressed, looking down Pickins Street toward the café that had been my life for so many years.

I didn't know who was responsible for my gift and love disappearing—the Lord or the devil. Every morning I dragged down to the café. It was hard, heavy walking. And when I opened the door, the tables and chairs and counters and coolers didn't seem like a second home, waiting for me. I had a sudden distaste for the knives and the napkin holders, the smoothness of green peppers and the smell of pie baking.

I told the Lord that it was time for me to retire, but as usual, when I really needed some kind of immediate response, there was nothing. My husband didn't have much to say, but Albert never was one to philosophize about major life events. Maybe he didn't see this as a major event, just a glitch in my ordinary life. With Albert, it was sometimes hard to tell what he was thinking.

After a few days, I was miserable but a little wiser. It had come to me that, no matter how crisp and colorful my salad was, cousin Howard would keep dying, day by day in my house, in front of my eyes. And regardless of how perfect the round steak with herbs turned out, Grady would continue to make Shellye's life a misery. The people I loved most were in horrible situations that showed no promise of change, and I could cook until the Lord came back, but what good would it do? We would still have piles of dirty dishes at the end of the day. Our feet would still ache. And, well, after every feast, we would just get hungry again.

About a week after I lost my gift, I went up into Gran Lenny's attic bedroom. I decided that I would lie on her old, creaky bed until I died. Until I starved and thirsted to death or until God got mad enough to smack me on into eternity. I didn't care.

I went up there on a Tuesday, fretted and slept the day away, the CLOSED sign hanging in the café window. I came down late in the evening and nodded to Howard, said only that I wasn't feeling well. He inquired a bit but seemed to know that I wasn't in a talking mood. Wednesday I did the same, cuddled up in that dark bedroom at the top of the house and waited to find my final rest, but came down in time for bed. Everybody was quiet that night. Thursday, I went to Gran Lenny's bedroom but couldn't sleep or rest. It was a rainy, gusty day, tree branches bouncing up and down just outside the north window. It was so dark and quiet up there, and still so full of Gran Lenny, dead more than thirty years now, that my memories—old, old ones—started stirring in my mind.

One day long ago, Gran Lenny had looked particularly tired, and as she wrote in her books, she dabbed at her eyes and cheeks with a pale yellow hankie.

"What's wrong?" I asked.

"This poem makes me cry."

"Then stop writing it."

I was only ten at the time. Gran Lenny looked at me.

"You think I write because I *feel* like it?"

"Why write if it feels so awful? That seems silly."

"I write because I must." Gran Lenny tapped the journal in front of her. "Of me it is required."

"Who requires it?"

She didn't answer me, just sighed, the lines in her face looking deeper than usual. I had the feeling she was talking about God, but God requiring someone to sit at the kitchen table twice a day, writing German poems that would probably never be read by anybody else, didn't match anything I'd ever heard preached on Sunday morning.

"These words course through me like blood, Vellie. That's what a gift does. It mixes with everything else that gives you life. This gift is all I have. And God requires *everything*." The distant look of her eyes made me think that Gran Lenny knew what God required because she'd argued with him about it for a long time.

All these years later, lying there quietly in the dimness, I felt heat gather around me, and I floated into a fever dream. I saw Gran Lenny's journals—the way they had lined up on the low bookcase under the east window that was now piled with back issues of National Geographic. I could see the skinny spines of Gran Lenny's journals plain as day. Suddenly I saw how painful a thing it had been some days for her to make the words go on the paper and then rearrange them and love them and offer them to God—even though God had taken her family and home during the war and had left her with a lingering sadness.

Then I drifted and was inside my café. I saw the pots and cups and saucers and grill. They were mine, and my gift of feeding people was the only gift I was sure belonged to me. I'd done it as naturally as walking for thirteen years. And my customers trusted me. They knew what day of the week I served their favorite soup. They knew that if no tomatoes showed up on their salads or burgers that it was because I couldn't find decent fresh tomatoes that day. And if things were a tad spicier than usual, they figured I had a cold and my taster was off. Leeway's citizens forgave me and shared their family news and praised my menu year in and year out. And I served them—on my feet ten, twelve hours a day, year in and year out. The food I gave them was mainly from recipes in my head, and no matter how many times I made a certain dish, it always felt like a new creation. And that gave me a deep-down happiness.

Until now. Now it suddenly hurt me to do it. It hurt me for whatever reason. But I could see that it didn't matter. There was such a thing as being faithful to your own gift. I'd have to climb out of the attic and walk down the street and cook just because. Because it was my gift, my best gift, maybe my only one.

"You feeling better, Vellie?" Howard asked, as we walked down to open up the next morning.

"No, I feel terrible."

Surprise flashed across Howard's face.

"I feel worse than ever, Howard, but I've got responsibilities."

"Everybody's missed you these three days," he said softly, his voice tripping through the green-gold air that smelled of coolness and fresh sun. "Bailey was at the hardware store yesterday, swearing that his intestines were acting up because they'd missed your split-pea soup on Tuesday."

"Don't these people ever cook for themselves?"

"Oh, they can cook," Howard said with a little smile. "But when you do it, they feel loved."

So I cooked out of obedience only from then on. I gritted my teeth every day and loved my customers and helped Howard make plans for the redecorating. It gave him so much energy, this turning VELMA'S into a German restaurant, that I couldn't deny him that much. I figured we'd never make it to the new restaurant. Sissy's troops had stepped up their refurbishing, pouring a new sidewalk just last week. They still hadn't replaced my sign, even though I asked one or two of them about it. Said they knew it was somewhere and that it would turn up soon. I went home every night and told God I was tired. God wouldn't say a word.

A week after I'd decided to cook in spite of everything, Zeke showed up. His eyes were full of fire, and his limp was worse. He went to his booth and made a loud grunt when he sat down. The way he was tapping his fingers on the table, I could tell he'd be anything but sun-shiny today. Sheri took a deep breath and started in his direction, but I stopped her.

"Would you look after these burgers?" She fairly skipped back to the grill, and I headed for that corner booth.

When I got to Zeke, I had to stop for a second. All of a sudden I could see a sadness in his face and in the droop of his shoulders. He looked completely worn out. I wondered how hard the winter had been for him. Brennen told me back in January that some guys from the county had ousted Zeke from the old farmhouse and took him to a shelter in Helmsly. Maybe he'd stayed warm and had gotten fed at least. But he looked more unhappy than ever. I heard myself chirping in a voice that tried hard to be happy for him:

"What'll it be today, Zeke? We've got roast and vegetables and brown gravy. Also chicken noodle soup."

Zeke didn't answer. His head hung from his shoulders like a sun-flower drooping from its stalk at the end of summer.

"Coffee's excellent, as always," I added.

"Just coffee."

"That all? On a cold day like this? The roast is better than usual." I could say that because I hadn't cooked the roast. I was considering letting Sheri just take over the place, since my own cooking had gone sour.

"Just coffee!" Zeke snapped. "I don't have money for any roast and soup."

His eyes didn't look up far enough for me to see that ornery glint. I noticed then that his hands shook just a little.

The hands did something to me. Zeke had probably come into VELMA'S ten times in the last few months, and he always looked a mess and always had some comment to make. But at the moment, I wanted to cry for him. I sat down across from him.

"I know that," I said, lowering my voice so other customers wouldn't hear. "There'll always be a hot meal for you here, money or no money."

Zeke didn't say anything or look at me. I got up.

"I'll bring you coffee. Then you can tell me what you're hungry for."

I wasn't three steps from him when his voice rumbled out from under the beard.

"You're a mean old woman."

I turned around. "What?"

"I said you're a mean old woman."

"How am I mean?" I walked back to him, feeling the heat rise in me the way it did nearly every time Zeke and I had a discussion.

"You're stingy and selfish. Just mean and selfish."

"Now you hold on. I've given you free food every single time you've walked in here, no matter how rude you've been. I don't appreciate you harping at me, old man."

Zeke looked straight into my eyes then. His eyes suddenly looked deep and ancient. Then he leaned forward and aimed his chin at me.

"You could have told me that the first time."

I didn't know what he meant, so I didn't have an answer. He kept glaring at me.

"You could have told me the very first time I walked in here that there would always be a hot meal for me. But instead you've always made me ask. Every time I come in here you know I can't pay, but you make me ask. You could have said that very first day, 'Zeke, I know you're down on your luck and you can't pay, but don't you worry, there will always be a hot meal for you.' But you couldn't say that much. I have to ask how much is this and can I have that too. That's why you're a stingy, mean old woman."

There are some moments in your life when you're flooded with awful realization. One second everything's as usual and the next you understand that you've done a terrible thing. I looked at Zeke and could feel my face drain of its color and my heart pound in my chest. I couldn't say a word. Three or four arguments squeaked in the back of my mind, such as, "Why should I make an offer to you and not everybody else?" or "You've not made it easy, yourself, what with your grumpiness." But I didn't dare say any of that. Zeke still had me locked into that awful gaze.

"Well," I finally managed. "I suppose that's true. I never considered saying that until today. I didn't mean any harm."

"Most people never *mean* any harm."

"I'm sorry."

Zeke leaned back in his booth, not seeming quite so mad.

"So, from now on, you just come in and eat."

"Thank you." He looked straight ahead. "You say the roast is good? Not tough?"

"You could have said that a long time ago, too."

Zeke swung a glance at me. "Said what?"

"'Thank you.' You could have said that a long time ago."

He grunted, as if that were a ridiculous idea. "You like to fight, don't you? You're an argumentative woman."

"Never mind. I'll bring your roast."

"Good cook, but an argumentative woman."

That's the warmest that things ever got between Zeke and me. But he came by more often after that, and I always made recommendations, and he always had to be sure that things were fresh, not overcooked, not too salty.

And that conversation haunted me often, I must say. I'd always thought of myself as a generous person, especially when it came to feeding people. But I suppose I was generous only to the people I chose. And the more I considered Jesus' words about such things— I even read Matthew chapters five through seven again for myself— I didn't see Jesus putting any qualifications on who we were to be kind or generous to. In fact, he talked about giving things to people who could never pay you back. There was Zeke, sitting right on the page of Scripture. You'd think that a lifetime of reading the Bible and listening to sermons would help a person get down the basics at least. But now, this far into my life, it seemed that I had failed a very simple spiritual test.

And, of course, on a day when I was sure that every customer was going to walk out on me because no dish turned out the way I'd planned, Sissy Fenders Scott walked in. She glowed more than any woman should at that age. I had the hot tea on the counter before she could ask for it.

"Don't you think the front of the building looks better now, with the new shingled awnings and the sidewalk?"

I looked at her long enough to be polite. "Yes, Sissy. It looks fine."

"I heard that you may be introducing some new menu items." She lowered her head to look at me coyly over her glasses. "That maybe I could get German potato salad if I wanted."

"We're just thinking about it." I felt like saying, *The way my cooking's going, you'll be lucky to get a boiled sausage in this place.*

"What a wonderful idea," she said.

"Do you really think so?" I stopped rearranging salad plates in the refrigerated shelves and looked at her. I actually put a hand on my hip, which Mama always said was rude. "You think we'll make enough profit as a German restaurant?"

Sissy noticed that the tone in my voice had changed. She stared at me, her teacup halfway between the counter and her mouth. Then she put it down and said, "What do you mean?"

"You know exactly what I mean. You're just waiting for us to fold up so you can move some trendy restaurant in here. One of your high-class business friends from Tulsa, no doubt."

For the first time in history as I knew it, Sissy had nothing to say. She gasped for a few seconds like a cat that's been in a hot room too long. Then she leaned forward on the stool.

"Whatever are you talking about, Velma Brendle?"

"Your plans for this building, for the whole town as far as I know."

"Why, you're out of your mind, Velma, out of your mind!" Her voice had shifted up and gotten sharp the way it used to when she'd call across the street, "Albert Brendle, wherever did you get that suave jacket? You look too handsome for words!" I looked around, but the only customers at the moment were three teenage girls sharing life secrets in the far north booth.

"Am I out of my mind?"

"Why, yes you are! I've got no plans for this place—other than you staying here until they have to wheel you out of the kitchen. Why, half of Leeway at least would run riot if VELMA'S closed."

Well, there's nothing like being completely wrong to take the wind out of a person. It was my turn to gasp. "It just looked like to me, with your buying the building and doing all this remodeling, and—well, the shingle men didn't even put my sign back up when they were finished. What happened to my sign?"

"Oh, it's probably in Avery's storage area, to keep it out of harm's way until they finished. Velma," her voice was softer now, "I mean no harm to you at all."

I didn't know how to respond to such a statement coming from this woman. Sissy looked at me hard and took a deep breath.

"I know we've had our troubles, years ago. But I'm not the same person I was then." Sissy looked away from me and seemed thoughtful. "When I married Leland, I felt that I'd finally proven to the world that I was worth something. Heavens, I was so selfish. I went after him for his money, his prestige in Tulsa. And I caught him fair and square. He was so in love with me."

Her eyes clouded up, and I waited while she blinked a few times.

"But we'd only been married four years, and I lost almost a quarter of his savings. Got involved in the stock market. I was in this woman's club, and most of what we did was play the market. You know, I read up on everything, got hooked up on the Internet, was checking my stocks two or three times a day. And I was making money at it. At the top of the world. And then I made some bad decisions, and, oh, Velma, I can't even bring myself to say how much I lost.

"Leland came in from work that evening, and I hadn't cooked dinner or anything, I was so upset. I just knew this would be the end of us. He'd worked very hard his whole life to build up his estate, to have plenty to leave to his children and grandchildren. I told him what had happened, and then I rushed to tell him all my plans for making up the loss. He stopped me before I finished and just hugged me so hard, and he said, 'Everything I own is yours, Sissy. And none of it matters to me but your love. I hope my love is enough, even without the money.' His eyes were full of nothing but kindness."

Sissy was fingering the teacup, seeming shy for once. "Something inside me changed that day. I didn't need the money or the good standing in our community. I walked around in a daze for a week or more, trying to put my mind and heart around Leland's love. I don't know, Velma. Somehow, I could stop working so hard to be worth something."

She looked at me, teary eyed. "I didn't dream that you thought I wanted to close you down. I'd never do a thing like that. I don't need to be hateful anymore. All I want is to be here where I grew up and try to help build the town in some way. And what you're about to do with VELMA'S PLACE is wonderful. It will attract visitors, help all of us be a little prouder of our town. You just need to tell me what to do to help. In fact, I'd like to pay for any remodeling inside you'd like to do. It will add value to the whole building, anyway, and I know you're not making a lot of extra to spend on such things right now."

I felt like an old fool as I walked home that night. I was glad that it was still dark fairly early, so no one could see the permanent blush of embarrassment. Howard was at the kitchen table with all sorts of plans for the redecoration. When I told him what Sissy had said, he hardly skipped a beat, just said, "Now, see, you worry for nothing" and went on telling me his plans. He jabbered away, and I felt silly as a small child who was so sure that Santa Claus didn't exist after all but then found a whole pile of presents under the tree anyway.

After that afternoon, Sissy's visits to VELMA'S felt different. I began to look forward to having her tea ready at about three in the afternoon. Before I knew it, we were chattering away. We still couldn't talk about old times; Sissy seemed as hesitant as I was to remember days when we'd been enemies. But there were new things to talk about. Her grandchildren. Lisa Layne's growth. Howard's ups and downs. And the work we needed to do to turn VELMA'S into VELMA'S LITTLE GERMANY. There are so many things to talk about in this world, even in a place like Leeway, that it seems a shame to search for subjects of contention.

Sissy's Ginger Squash Bake

3 cups butternut squash, peeled and sliced
¼ cup butter
1 or 2 tablespoons grated fresh ginger
1 teaspoon cinnamon
¼ cup apple or orange juice
1 teaspoon salt
½ teaspoon pepper
1 tablespoon fresh, minced sage
1 egg

Butter a 2-quart casserole dish. Layer sliced squash in the dish.

Heat butter in small saucepan. Add grated ginger and saute a minute. Add cinnamon and juice and stir an additional 3 minutes.

Pour mixture over squash. Cover the casserole dish and bake for 20 minutes, or until squash is tender enough to mash with a fork or potato masher.

Allow squash to cool a few minutes. Add the fresh sage, salt, and pepper and mash the squash. Slightly beat the egg (if you want a lighter, puffier dish, make that two eggs), add it to the squash (with a bit more juice if you like) and blend all with a mixer on medium speed. Cover the casserole again and bake for another 20 minutes.* Serve warm. This dish also goes well fresh from the refrigerator, as a cold relish with beef or pork.

*To make the dish even sweeter, sprinkle with brown sugar and uncover the last ten minutes of baking.

18

Easter Lilies

Like the bow in a cloud on a rainy day, such was the appearance of the splendor all around. This was the appearance of the likeness of the glory of the Lord. When I saw it, I fell on my face, and I heard the voice of someone speaking.

—EZEKIEL 1:28

Easter Sunday, the next to the last day of March, was stormy. I actually drove to the church, because by the time I was ready to walk out the door, rain was coming down in sheets. Normally in the spring, I get to the church early and open up windows for a while at least, to get that fresh air feeling in the sanctuary. But this morning the rain was blowing so hard I didn't dare crack a single window. The room was dark, not the way Easter should be.

This was the first Sunday Pastor and Clare were back from Orlando. They looked rested but troubled. Because it was Easter Sunday, we had a bigger crowd than usual, but, thanks to the contrary weather, the sanctuary was only half full for the opening Sunday school service. Most of the women wore their Easter dresses and suits even though the weather called for something heavier and more practical.

Whether it's fashion sense or piety, who can say? They came running in the door drippy and droopy in their pretty pastels.

Len Connor and his dad stood at the door to help the older folks get in—Len even walked out to a car now and then to grab an elderly arm. By the fifth trip, he was soaking wet, even with an umbrella. But that fifth car had a special meaning. Grady and Shellye pulled up, and I guess Grady was going to let Shellye and the baby out at the door before he parked the car over in the side lot. And, as usual, Shellye had both arms full and was wanting another, with Lisa Layne trying to pro-pel herself in eight directions at once. There was the baby bag and Shellye's and Grady's Bibles and Sunday-school materials. So Len opened the back door and got Lisa Layne out of the car seat while Shellye got herself and all their things gathered up. Len held Lisa Layne and the umbrella too, for Shellye to get under. When they came into the foyer together, they were laughing, just like most people were once they came in and then saw one another dripping all over the carpet.

No one thought anything about it—Len helping Shellye and the baby. But when Grady came in, he was fit to be tied, although that wouldn't have been obvious to anyone who didn't know him well or who wasn't looking carefully. He cornered Len back near the coat rack. He managed to keep his voice low, so it just looked like two young men in intense discussion. Neither one of them looked well when Grady let up and walked toward the sanctuary. I could see Len take a breath to calm himself down, but he took a seat, too, where he normally did, with his dad. Tim Connor had returned to church dur-ing the past couple of months, although right after Melanie walked out he'd kept to himself for a while. But Tim's parents were still there, and Len came when he was in town, which, since he'd started college in January, was the major holidays and an occasional weekend. I'd learned from Doris that Len had started college a semester late because his dad made him forfeit part of the college fund to cover medical expenses for Shellye and the baby. This seemed only fair, and I couldn't help but think that Len would turn out all right after all, with a dad who would make him tow the line like that. But it irritated me even more to see Grady being so spiteful. Grady had to know about the money. Maybe he resented even the Connors' help.

Shelly and Lisa Layne were in my pew, as usual, at the back where they could leave quickly if Lisa Layne needed tending. The baby grinned at me and put out her arms, so I grabbed her and sat her on my lap.

I felt the pew shake and knew that Grady had just sat down beside Shellye. His arm came around her shoulder, but not in that affectionate way so many husbands gather their wives close to them during church. I could have sworn I heard a clink and a key turn when Grady's arm came down on the back of the pew. But when I caught sight of Grady's face, he was smiling at Shellye as if she were the pride and joy of his life. Then she smiled back at him, and all I could do was be puzzled. So in love and yet so much trouble between them sometimes. Maybe Pastor had been right, though, about working out the problems between the two of them.

We finished the opening exercises and went to Sunday school class. When we gathered forty minutes later for church, the rain had stopped and shots of sun were opening the swollen clouds out beyond us. A bit of relief and happiness swept through me.

I was saying hello to Martha Bell when Deborah Beckers walked through the church parlor door. Just walked in wearing a pale forest green dress that draped down her tall frame in a striking way. That, and the fact that she was a stranger, caused people to make little starts and look a second time. She found a pew to sit in, sat down, and looked around at the sanctuary, the windows with their Easter dressing, and the dozens of potted Easter lilies Sue Baines and I had arranged on the front platform. Then she opened the order of service and read quietly while the room settled down. She looked up periodically, looking for Howard, I guessed. I thought about going up to say hello, but by the time I found my voice and feet, we were into the first verse of the opening hymn.

Howard arrived at the usual time and in his usual way, talking with half a dozen people at once and taking his place in the seventh row from the front, north side, ten seconds before the first hymn began. Deborah was situated in the fifth row from the front, south side. Needless to say, I was having trouble concentrating on the hymn. I wasn't about to miss the moment when Howard and Deborah saw each other. That happened soon enough, after we finished the hymn and opening prayer, and as we were sitting down. Deborah's eyes swept over toward Howard, and his swept over toward her, as if there was a magnetic field that involved only them. Their eyes met, and they lingered just a moment.

I've never stared at the back of someone's head so intently. Deborah's hair was a light auburn brown, full of satiny, natural highlights. She had a bit on each side pulled up in a small comb, looking smooth and perfect.

Even from behind her I could see that she was paying close attention to every person and every sound. She sat completely still, and there was an invisible current vibrating between her and Howard, who sat clear across the room. They looked at each other only that one time, never again, not through the rest of the service, but they felt each other's every breath. I know, because *I* could feel every breath.

I could feel Doris's breath, too. Doris had been sitting in the pew behind Howard the past few Sundays, behind and to the side by three or four people, not wanting to look obvious. When Howard and Deborah locked gazes, Doris followed Howard's gaze and saw Deborah at the end of it. There were now three people sitting terribly still, hardly breathing, and I doubt hearing a word of the sermon, which was a shame, because Pastor does a particularly smart job with Easter sermons.

I thought that service would never end. And, once it did, after our final chorus of "Christ the Lord Is Risen Today," all I could do was stand still and watch Howard and Deborah. They made their way toward each other slowly, taking their time to say hello to other people as all of us moved out of the sanctuary.

"Velma, would you tell Shellye I'm not feeling well and I'm going home?" Doris's eyes were crackling with pain. Shellye and Lisa Layne were in the women's rest room for a diaper change. "I was supposed to go home with her and Grady, but I'll go over there later in the afternoon." I could tell that it took all of Doris's strength to stand there long enough to say that little bit to me.

Howard hadn't given Doris a lot of hope, ever, but it hadn't taken much hope for Doris to start up with little dreams of love. I'd seen it happening, but what could I do? They were grown people. Right now, Doris looked more like a little girl, lost and trying hard not to cry.

I took her by the arm. "Let me give you a lift home, Doris. It's awfully soggy out there." The sun and clouds were still shifting in and out of each other. I turned my back on the Howard-Deborah drama. It wasn't my place to be nosing in anyway.

We were nearly out to my car, when I saw Shellye and Grady and Lisa Layne. They were standing near their car, talking with the Harreltons. Shellye looked fine, and I could hear Grady say, clear across the lot, "We're planning to get a group together to go hear Jars of Clay when they're in Kansas City. Just talk to Shellye or leave a message. We'll make it a party!" He was beaming and holding Lisa Layne in one arm and had the other draped affectionately over Shellye's shoulder.

"That Lisa Layne is looking more like Shellye every day," I said.

"Thank goodness she doesn't look much like Len," Doris said. She looked about to drop and dissolve into the rain puddle in front of us. We got into my car. It smelled musty from being shut up during the rain. I looked over at Doris, and she was staring out the windshield. "I think that's why he always answers the phone," she said. "Just has to be sure Len's not calling her."

"I wish he'd settle down about that. But they seem to be calmer, most of the time." I didn't know if Doris had been aware of Grady's little scene with Len that morning or not.

I wanted to say something comforting to Doris about her and Howard, but there wasn't anything at all I could say. It was a silent few blocks home, the car making swishing sounds through the wet streets.

I sat at home and stewed until Howard came in. Deborah wasn't with him.

"I thought you might have company," I said.

"We talked for a few minutes. She had to get back."

Howard had lived with us almost a year, and I could tell he was lying. Not with his words, but with the feeling he was trying to convey, that everything was fine.

"It was nice of her to come see you."

"She shouldn't have come. I didn't ask her to come."

Howard went upstairs and took a nap while I worked on Easter dinner for us. I had Bailey join us, and we ate and then visited until about three in the afternoon. When Bailey left, I went back up to the church. I'd forgotten to bring home an Easter lily. It's always been a tradition at Jerusalem Baptist that we have special donations for Easter lilies, and then whoever wants to take one home after the services is welcome to them. We take them to the shut-ins first. There were still several pots on the platform. I picked up two.

I took the best of the two lilies to Doris. I knocked on the door, and it took her a few moments to answer. She had that haunted look she'd get when she'd been walking the streets all night. A cigarette in her hand.

"Brought you a lily."

"Oh, thanks." She opened the door and I walked in. She directed me to a little table near the sitting room window, one of the windows that faces my house.

"Thanks, Velma."

"Easter lilies remind me of the Resurrection."

"I'm not sure what the Resurrection is supposed to mean, Velma." Doris tapped ash off her cigarette. I remembered back when she had quit smoking for a time, a year or two ago. That was when she bent Pastor Thomas's ear over everything that happened to her. She'd given him progress reports about making it through the day on just one smoke or two, some days none at all. Doris hardly talked with Pastor these days. She didn't seek out anyone. But I guessed she was smoking at least a pack a day now.

"To me the Resurrection means that we'll see Jesus someday," I said, "and when we die, we'll not really die but live better than before."

Doris made a sarcastic sound in her throat. "Jesus being raised from the dead doesn't make any real difference to me. All it means is that when I die with all my disappointments, I'll have a heaven to live in. That's all Easter means to me."

"I'm so sorry, Doris. Wish I could think of the right thing to say."

She made a little no-problem gesture. "Thanks for bringing the lily," she said, letting me out.

I watched Doris's lily die, along with her hopes, through the first weeks of April. At first it made me mad that she'd neglect a nice plant like that. But then I took the withered blooms as reminders to pray for Doris. Every time I'd look out my kitchen window and see the lily, I'd pray for God to give Doris a life she could love. Not a man's necessarily. Her own life.

I think that Doris could have a little hope as long as there was no competition for Howard. But it had always been her tendency to fade back when a room got crowded. She'd been that way when her husband was around, but nobody noticed, because she'd fade into him, and to the rest of us it had just looked like love. The day Deborah appeared in church and sat alone and glanced meaningfully at Howard and Howard glanced meaningfully back, Doris started her retreat.

Gran Lenny said once that it takes some folks longer to get mad at God than it does others. But everybody does get there, sooner or later. That sounded awful to me at the time, when I was a young girl. It happened, though, that the first time I got really angry with God was when Gran Lenny died. And it was such a fierce, mean anger that it might have done me real harm, except that Gran Lenny herself had warned me about it.

I can't say that I throw a lot of tantrums, but seeing Doris in such pain, and thinking about how life had treated her in general, made real anger rise in my spirit. It wasn't anger that could be directed at a person, because Doris's problems were much bigger than the effects of an act of sin here or there. For those wider, less specific troubles, I had to turn to God and say, "Too much. Too much. We need more help than what we're getting."

I live in a small town in the middle of nothing but fields, and the people I know have run through most of their hope by the time the first grandchild arrives. By then they understand their limitations in the world, and they're sad from it. But the world and the devil keep laying on more and more of the same. And I can't care about my neighbors truthfully unless, from time to time, I say to God, "Enough of this."

I hardly ever speak my anger out loud, and it's not something I'd ever discuss in church. The people there might think that I'm angrier than I actually am. And church time is probably best spent discussing doctrine or Bible stories that are fairly easy to understand. The simpler lessons aren't as rich sometimes as the harder ones, but they're better for nailing down beliefs.

But nailing down hope is another thing entirely. Sometimes I think that only poetry—those words and phrases that can mean several things at once—could express such an impossible, complicated thing as hope. I prayed that the Lord would give us some beautiful words. Words for Howard and Deborah, for Shellye and Grady. Words for Doris especially. Bright, deep words that would speak to her disappointments, her lost dreams, to her very soul.

Resurrection Coffeecake

2 cups flour
¾ cup sugar
3 teaspoons baking powder
I teaspoon salt
I teaspoon cinnamon
½ teaspoon cloves
½ teaspoon nutmeg
I teaspoon grated orange rind
I teaspoon grated lemon rind
I egg
I ½ cups milk
¼ cup oil
I teaspoon vanilla extract
½ teaspoon almond extract
I cup blueberries, fresh or frozen, but thaw and drain if frozen
I cup canned peaches, drained and chopped
¼ cup cream cheese, in little pieces

Topping:

½ cup pecans, coarsely chopped
¼ cup brown sugar
⅓ cup flour
2 tablespoons melted butter

Mix together flour, sugar, baking powder, salt, spices, orange and lemon rind. Add egg, milk, oil, and extracts.

Pour one-third of the batter into a greased and floured 9 x 9-inch round cake pan.

Make sure peaches and blueberries are well drained. Distribute peaches evenly over the batter. Distribute all the cream cheese pieces with the peaches.

Pour the next third of batter over the peaches. Distribute blueberries over that layer. Pour remaining batter over the blueberries.

Mix together topping ingredients and spread over the last layer of batter. Bake at 350° for 45 minutes or until toothpick inserted in center comes out clean.

19

The Deacons and Their Wives

When they come there, they will remove from it [the land] all its
detestable things and all its abominations. I will give them one heart,
and put a new spirit within them; I will remove the heart of stone from
their flesh and give them a heart of flesh, so that they may follow my
statutes . . . Then they shall be my people, and I will be their God.
—EZEKIEL 11:18–20

In mid-May, deacons Charlie Resnick and Dan Mallory and their
wives Therese and Anne went to a marriage enrichment seminar in
Joplin, Missouri. It was sponsored by some group that wasn't any
denomination but was well-respected by a number of churches in our
area. Pastor Thomas brought it up but didn't push it, since he didn't
have any experience with the seminar himself. Charlie and Therese
made a couple of calls and got more interested in it. Their tenth
anniversary was coming up, and they thought it could be a nice way to
spend it. They did a lot of things with the Mallorys outside of church,
so the four of them went together for a weekend. They came back that

Sunday morning looking pretty happy, so Pastor invited them to say a few words about the seminar before he started the sermon.

Charlie's always been outspoken, and he and Therese stood up to talk about the experience. Charlie began, and we were all surprised when he started to cry before he'd hardly got out two sentences. Therese smiled and grasped her husband's arm. She leaned shyly toward the pulpit microphone.

"Charlie and I thought we had a pretty good marriage, and we do, but there were some things in our life that hadn't been right in a long time. We were able to talk about past experiences and disagreements. And once we'd got them out in the open, we learned how much healing we needed. I learned so much about forgiveness this weekend. It was possibly the most important time I've ever spent on my marriage. Charlie and I recommend this seminar to any couple, whether you're engaged or newlyweds or even married for a long time." I could see the Mallorys nodding in agreement.

Pastor thanked them and encouraged others to get information from Charlie and Dan. Then he preached as usual, and we all visited for a few minutes before going to our homes and Sunday dinner.

The oddest thing can stir up trouble in a church. You would think that two couples making their marriages stronger would be good for the community. But not two weeks later, Charlie and Ed Harrelton got into a heated discussion during business meeting. It was the most amazing and horrible thing. Everything one of them said got misunderstood by the other. Ed is church treasurer, and one minute he was concerned about the budget for the building maintenance, and the next he was accusing Charlie and Dan of taking over church business and allocating funds that hadn't been approved. Evidently, they'd been given a small scholarship from the education fund to help pay for their marriage weekend. But Pastor and the board of deacons had approved it, with Ed sitting there.

"I'm not talking about fifty dollars for a marriage weekend. I wouldn't be that petty. I'm talking about an attitude, Charlie. About decisions getting made by one or two people and then railroading through things that should be discussed."

Charlie raised his arms in complete exasperation. "Ed, I don't know what you're talking about. We didn't do an end run around anybody here." Some murmurs of agreement went across the room.

"All right, all right." Now Ed raised his arms, as if he were the one trying to break up an argument. "Whatever you say. I just—I just don't feel right about things lately. I think you know what I'm talking about. But let's not discuss it here."

Pastor moved the discussion to which Vacation Bible School materials to use this summer. He looked as confused as the rest of us.

"My, I don't know what got into Ed this morning," I told Howard when I got home. Howard never stayed for business meeting. He had leftover roasted chicken ready to reheat for our lunch.

"I bet I know what's got into him," Howard said. "Ed's wife is bothering him to take her to that marriage seminar."

"For heaven's sakes—are you sure?"

Howard nodded. "Therese and Ann have quite a few of the women buzzing. They're passing around a sign-up sheet for the same seminar that's going to be held in Wichita two months from now." He turned around to look at me with surprise. "How come I know that and you don't?"

"Oh." I sat down at the table, feeling that I was halfway through a workweek already. "I do well to carry myself up there and cook these days. Not as tuned in, I guess. So you think Ed's afraid of being dragged away and forced to talk about his marriage?"

"Not just Ed. I see a couple of other guys resisting the idea too."

"It's a wonder we haven't heard Grady go on about it," I muttered. "He's always for going on trips to this workshop and that."

"Grady doesn't like the idea, either. I heard Dan mention something about Grady and Shellye going, and Grady just said they had plenty going on already, that they were working through some materials and reading two books together now. He turned Dan down cold."

We both fell silent. I was thinking about how Grady probably needed a marriage seminar more than anybody. Things had been fairly calm with him and Shellye lately, as far as we knew. Shellye stayed at home most of the time, and whenever we saw her, it was with Grady along or Grady and his sister and mother. But he and Shellye were more affectionate than they used to be, so maybe their "program" was working.

But Ed and Charlie just got along worse and worse. One week it was the education budget; the next it was choosing the Sunday school summer outing. Some summers we went to the Passion play in Eureka Springs; sometimes a Christian concert in Kansas City or Joplin or Tulsa. It was a big deal, but this year some of us were wanting to drop the summer outing altogether. Ed and Charlie didn't argue outright as much as get in little digs here and there. There would always be some perfectly reasonable objection one of them had to the other's idea. They didn't raise their voices or get nasty, not enough that someone could call them down for it. It was more like an atmosphere that arrived when the two of them were in the same room.

Ordinarily, Pastor would be right on top of any trouble among the church leaders. But his back pain had him going to this doctor and that. He shut his office door most days when he was at the church. Clare came and went, but even she stopped visiting with me—didn't seem to have the time or the interest.

Then, toward the end of May, Pastor and Clare's daughter, Lilian, showed up with her two boys, ages ten and seven. They filed into church one Sunday, and Pastor introduced them and said they were here from Orlando for a visit. No one mentioned Lilian's husband, although he'd accompanied them on previous visits.

Anne Mallory walked in the café later that week, with Ed's wife, Darlene. They sat in the far corner and put their heads together. I walked over to pour coffee, and Anne looked up at me and said in a low voice, "What have *you* heard about the Thomases' daughter?"

"Me? Not a thing. Why?" I felt that I was losing my grip completely on this community of mine. It really was time to retire.

"Dan heard that she's separated from her husband."

"I think she's already divorced," Darlene said. "They're just not breaking the news yet."

I shook my head and said something sympathetic, then walked back to the kitchen. My head hurt. I looked with disgust at the pork chops I'd just dredged through flour and seasonings, ready to fry up for the next order. How I wanted to be out of this place, my church, this town. I'd never wanted to be out of Leeway before.

Then, when I was at the register taking a check, I noticed a note on the pad by the telephone: *Henry Carpenter called. He asked if you would please call him.* I wadded up the paper. That's all I needed, a bad bit of past intruding on my already lousy afternoon. I couldn't deal with Henry unless I also dealt with Albert. Sometimes life requires too much on a given day.

News of Lilian's family trouble was all over the church, of course, by the next Sunday. Clare sat in her pew as usual, Lilian and the boys beside her, and both women appeared not to hear or see anything the entire service. Clare hugged the boys, one on either side of her.

The subject of Lilian's family trouble turned out not to be the main trouble that week. After the sermon, Pastor Thomas announced that he was calling a special meeting of the deacons. It was a closed meeting, which of course piqued everyone's interest. After the closing hymn, Shellye came up to Doris and me as Grady followed Pastor and our four deacons back to the pastor's study. She looked scared. "Do you mind waiting with me?"

The three of us sat in the parlor and played with Lisa Layne. For a long time, we didn't ask Shellye why Grady was being included in a deacons' meeting. And we didn't ask why she looked so worried. Finally, I asked, "Do you have any idea what this is all about?"

"Some people are wanting to nominate Grady to be a deacon. He'd start in the fall, because Frank Delbert's term is up then."

Doris looked at Shellye in surprise.

"They might make him deacon? Isn't that good?"

Shellye's face was a mixture of dread and anticipation. "It's what he's always wanted, I think. But Charlie already told Pastor Thomas that he doesn't think it's a good idea, as long as Grady and I are having trouble."

"Well, it probably isn't," I said. "Deacons have a lot of responsibility. You don't want to be leading other people while there's a lot of stress at home."

"But Grady would be so disappointed." The dread on Shellye's face overshadowed her other emotions. She didn't say anything else, but I was sure that what she wasn't saying was big enough to cancel out any other thoughts that were buzzing between the three of us.

When Grady came out of the hallway, forty-five minutes later, I couldn't tell anything from his face. He came up and immediately put a hand on Shellye's shoulder. She looked up at him, her face full of questions.

"Well, I guess it's not the Lord's will that I be deacon just yet."

"Oh no," Shellye murmured. She seemed to hug Lisa Layne tighter.

"And—" Grady cleared his throat. "The deacons feel that I probably should step down from teaching, for the time being. They think that, with doing the correspondence courses and working full-time, teaching just adds pressure I don't need."

"Oh, but this will ruin everything," Shellye said, putting a hand to her lips. "We're fine, we're just fine. Did you tell them we're fine? Teaching is your gift!"

Grady squeezed her shoulder. "It's OK. Let's go."

Doris and I followed them out. We could hear the others coming out into the sanctuary. Dan and Frank were discussing basketball.

Someone else laughed. It was the oddest feeling, to have Grady and Shellye comforting each other ahead of us and the deacons and our pastor acting like everything would just get better if Utah grabbed the championship this year.

That afternoon, I found myself alone on the screened-in porch. I tried to puzzle out how people in the very same room could be in such a different place. It was a gorgeous afternoon, full of soft, spring light and fragrances from all over town. But the weather hardly touched me at all. I could only sit and look at the sun patches on the floor of the porch and wonder what was happening in my church.

That's how I felt all that week, after Grady got demoted in church and Shellye cried all the way to their car. It kept feeling that way the next Sunday and the next. Ed and Dan managed not to talk to each other at all, and only two or three of the women kept talking about the next marriage seminar and planning for it. Howard heard from John Mason that Charlie was the one who had suggested Grady be relieved of his teaching responsibilities. Evidently, Charlie's zeal for everyone else's marriage was beginning to rub a number of people the wrong way. I didn't know who besides Pastor knew about Grady's temper; evidently at least one of the deacons knew. But the strange thing was, when the deacons voted on whether Grady should be nominated to be a deacon, the vote had been split right down the middle. Which meant only one thing; Pastor Thomas had cast the deciding vote. I couldn't imagine him siding against Grady, after the way he'd defended him when he was at his meanest.

Pastor's daughter, Lilian, brought her children to Sunday school, but she didn't always stay for church, and one Sunday Clare went home with Lilian and the boys before Pastor had stood up to preach. By then, people had stopped asking Clare or Pastor about it, because it was clear they weren't talking. It was a strange thing to see Clare, so open and talkative about every subject imaginable, clam up and shut us out.

I sat on my porch when I could during those days, and I brought all their faces to my mind and asked God to do something. Everything was splitting in two with hardly a sound. I didn't even pray in the sanctuary anymore while I cleaned on Wednesdays and Saturdays. It felt unpeaceful in there.

Late one night, Pastor Thomas called. Howard answered and passed the phone along to me, but he stayed close by.

"Velma, how are things with Shellye and Grady these days—do you hear anything?"

"No. Everything's been pretty quiet."

"Shellye seems all right?"

"I never see her except at church, and when she and Grady come up for dinner on Thursdays. She's not said anything to me."

There was a long silence.

"Do you know of anything?" I asked.

"No. I just . . . I just want to be sure Shellye doesn't get hurt. Her or the baby." He didn't say, "Like when Len hurt her and we didn't believe her," or "like when Grady hurt her before, and we didn't believe her," but those words were flapping on the phone wire between us like dingy laundry.

"I'll call you if I know of anything," I said.

"Take care, Velma," Pastor said. When I heard the phone click, I felt that I'd just talked to someone else, not the pastor I'd known all these years.

Best Church Casserole

3 cups noodles, cooked
½ cup chicken stock
½ cup milk
4 slices of bacon
2 cups mushrooms, sliced
½ cup red onion, minced
1 cup frozen peas
1 ½ cup sour cream
1 cup cooked chicken, cubed
1 to 2 teaspoons tarragon
Salt and pepper to taste

Cook the noodles until they're almost tender. Fry and crumble the bacon.

Pour out most of the bacon grease, then saute the mushrooms and onions in the remaining grease.

Mix together noodles, mushrooms, onions, peas (still frozen), crumbled bacon, sour cream, stock, milk, and chicken in a greased, 2-quart baking dish. Cover and bake at 350° for 20 minutes. Uncover and bake an additional 10 minutes.

20

The Opening

See, the day! See, it comes!
Your doom has gone out.
The rod has blossomed, pride has budded.

—EZEKIEL 7:10

Then he said to me, "Prophesy to these bones, and say to them: O dry
bones, hear the word of the Lord. Thus says the Lord God to these
bones: I will cause breath to enter you, and you shall live. I will lay
sinews on you, and will cause flesh to come upon you, and cover you
with skin, and put breath in you, and you shall live; and you shall
know that I am the Lord.

—EZEKIEL 37:4–6

Four days before the opening of VELMA'S LITTLE GERMANY, I took to
bed with a fever. People said I'd been pushing myself too hard, but
I knew better. Important things were happening. Cousin Howard
seemed more weary than ever. Doris was night wandering again. And,
after another bad spell with Grady and living with Doris a few days,
Shellye had moved back home. She'd actually done this against Pastor
Thomas's counsel. He thought it was too soon. But Shellye was determined to make her marriage work. "He needs my support now," she'd

said, Lisa Layne in one arm and a basket of fresh laundry in the other. She'd packed both into the Cavalier and headed down the street, so determined that she didn't look back to wave at Doris and me.

Thanks to Howard and Sissy, the redecorating of the café had been finished in record time. They'd had the walls painted and printed borders put around the ceiling and baseboard. They packed away all those tablecloths the church women had made years ago, bought new seat cushions and matching tablecloths that were a type of plastic but looked like cloth. I just imagine Sissy thought that clear plastic covers over real cloth looked cheap. I just watched her work and decided that cooking would keep me busy enough. Sissy found the nicest little vases to put on each table, and she bought silk flowers that actually did look real. I suppose that since I've never been too finicky about decorating, it's only fitting that I make friends like Betty Webb and Sissy Fenders Scott.

But here I was in bed, dizzy, even sick to my stomach, which was rare with one of my fevers. Everybody else had to do things for me. I'd open my eyes, floating back to the bed from wherever I'd been, and there would be Howard or Shellye, with Albert's sweet voice always in the background.

One afternoon—Wednesday, I think, I lay there with the shades open. The sky was a pale, pale gray behind the green flutters of the oak tree. I thought suddenly, *This is the answer to all my prayers.* I'd done all I could do. I couldn't bear to see Shellye suffer under Grady any more. I couldn't bear to watch Howard die; after all this time I was attached to him as though he were a brother or a son. So the Lord was taking me home. I could feel him close. I could feel Gran Lenny, smell the lavender in her silk scarf. I saw Albert in the doorway, looking at me hard.

The very day before the grand opening, my dizziness left, and my fever broke. I sat up in bed, soaked with sweat, and I didn't have to vomit. Howard knocked on the doorjamb, looking like Father Time.

"I need to sleep awhile, Vellie. But everything's ready for tomorrow. Several of the women from church will be there to help you cook. So if you're still feeling puny, all you'll have to do is sit and give directions."

"Everything's ready?"

"All but the cooking. Shellye and I took the list you'd made and bought all the groceries. We can go to Avery's tomorrow morning if you need more."

"Go rest, Albert."

"Did you call me Albert?" His tired eyes opened a little more. "Do you know who I am?"

"'Course I do—Howard. My brain just flickered."

He disappeared from the doorway, and I heard his weary steps on the stairs, soft squeaks under the carpeting—as if the old wood stairs weren't even under there anymore. Just like Howard's frame wasn't under him anymore. Life had lost its bones.

I felt Albert close by me. He rested his hand on my forehead and said, "I think it's been good for you to have Howard around. He can do for you in ways I can't, you know."

"Not a lot of comfort to me now, seeing him die."

"But you've given him a good place to die."

Albert usually wasn't so talkative. But I always liked that about my husband. Never talked unless it truly counted. I enjoyed his warmth a few more seconds, then got myself out of bed.

As important as opening night for Velma's Little Germany was, as much as I'd come to look forward to it and recognize what a good thing it could be, I went around in a daze. The day took on the feeling of my fever dreams, all sorts of people walking in and out of it. The place was in a bustle nonstop all day. At five o'clock, Shellye (who'd decided to help me opening night) and the other waitresses went home to change. Of course, Sissy had found colorful skirts and blouses for the girls to wear. They actually looked more Swiss than German, but who in Leeway, Kansas, would know the difference? The girls tried to get me into an outfit, but I wouldn't go for that. What I did do was dig into Mama's buffet and pull out an embroidered apron that Aunt LaVonne had made and sent for Christmas years ago. I pressed and starched it and wore it over my most comfortable slacks and shirt. It looked good enough.

Somehow, with me down during the last few days, just giving what instructions I could, every dish I'd planned was ready for whoever walked in the door at 6:30. Howard had marinated the sauerbraten as if he did it all the time. The potato salad was ready, the red cabbage, the rye bread, creamed spinach, fresh vegetables ready to braise, the meats and salads. I'd created a soup just for Velma's—sage and carrots, barley, and rabbit sausage. An old butcher who owned a grocery three towns over still made whole batches of the sausage himself.

It's a good thing we planned big, because we were full of customers by eight o'clock. People from Leeway of course, but also from towns all over two counties. This was Sissy's doing, because she'd advertised on a local radio station and in several area newspapers.

There hadn't been but a couple of German families in Leeway for years now. But a few others popped up from around the area. One middle-aged woman came up to me and said, "Mrs. Brendle, you don't know how I've longed for a restaurant like this. Mother used to cook these dishes at home when I was a little girl. This is my daughter, Louisa. She's been so excited ever since I told her about this place."

I shook Louisa's hand. She couldn't have been more than twenty. "I've been trying to learn more about my heritage," she said, her smile young and pretty. "This is wonderful! Thank you!"

I thanked them and then stood back to watch the party. Howard and Bailey were pouring bottles of champagne into little juice glasses for people. I guessed that George McCallum had donated those. We didn't have a liquor license, of course. But Sheriff Brennen was sitting in the midst of the party and didn't seem to be bothered. I've never drunk anything alcoholic, except a taste or two of the hard cider Papa used to make. But I was surprised at how tasty the champagne was. Howard laughed at me and told me not to have more than one glass.

Nearly all of my regulars came. And they came all dressed up, as if for church or a holiday dinner. They sat at tables and grinned and ordered more than they normally would and tasted items from one another's plates. I went around and identified foods and went on about how nice everybody looked. Shellye and Sheri and the other waitresses were giddy too. Sissy, of all people, seemed to gear down and spent most of the evening sitting at one end of the counter and visiting quietly with the folks around her. She could have razzled and dazzled, sweeping from one table to the next. But she didn't. At eight-thirty, she called me out of the kitchen, and I walked into a room of applause. I'd just been introduced. As I recall, I stumbled through some thank-you's. But they wouldn't let me back into the kitchen—just perched me at the counter to enjoy the rest of the evening.

The party went on forever, but then it was over so quickly. What I mean is that much of the time everything passed before me in slow motion, and I felt that I could stop it at any point and replay it. But before we knew it, it was nearly nine o'clock and the crowd had slowed down.

I sat for awhile at Bailey's table. I scooted close and squeezed his arm. "Betty would have loved this wouldn't she?" I said. Bailey grinned, and his eyes misted over. "Oh, she would have been right in the middle of it."

"She and Sissy would have fought over the decorating." I giggled, and then wondered if I should have had an entire glass of champagne. I was pretty sure Bailey was on his second.

Just then I heard a strange sound. I knew before I looked that it was Howard. There he was, standing up in the center of the room, right under that old chandelier. He had a juice glass raised in one hand, and he wore the stupidest grin I ever saw. And he was laughing, deep laughs from his belly or his soul. That was the sound. And it hit me then how wonderful he looked. How good his color was and how healthy-thick his arms were. His hair was bushy and brown, and he moved as if he felt no pain at all.

I kept studying him, knowing that I must be seeing things. "Bailey, how does Howard look to you?"

"Great. His new treatments must be working."

"He's not had any treatments for a long time—that I know of."

"Oh. Well, he looks healthy as a horse. Probably your cooking." He turned then, because someone else was talking to him. I just stared at Howard and felt my soul fly around the room. We were eating and drinking and talking together and getting to know out-of-town people, and here was a miracle among us. I knew it wasn't the time to say anything. I just watched Howard the rest of the evening, and he kept looking and acting like a new man.

In the midst of Shelly's misery and my own grumbling and worry, I'd failed to see it. The Lord had actually answered our prayers and healed Cousin Howard. It occurred to me then that Howard had been tired lately, more than usual, but then he'd also been putting in hours and hours a day at the café, helping me get ready. He'd been working longer and harder than any of us. So of course he'd be tired. But there'd been no episodes with his heart, no infections or trips to the emergency room. The Lord had healed Howard in the midst of the work. It had happened under the surface of everything else. And none of us had even noticed.

Along about ten, when the last of the partyers had left, Howard and I gathered some leftovers to take by Shellye and Grady's. They'd left around nine, because the baby needed to go to bed. I promised

Shellye I'd bring some of the leftover pork chops Grady had especially liked.

"You sure we should go by, Vellie?" Howard asked, once we were in the car. All I could do was stare at his profile as he maneuvered around potholes. "Howard," I said, "you look like a miracle."

Howard's grin was unmanageable. I thought his teeth would pop right out of that smile. "Velma, I *feel* like a miracle." He looked as if he would say more, but the words seemed to escape him. He just kept grinning and shook his head. "If I died right now, it wouldn't matter at all."

I stared at him, hearing that same sentence, only in my memory of just a few months ago, back when Howard had grieved his own death and was empty of all hope. Now the very same words meant the opposite of what they'd meant then. It made me think that maybe everything has an opposite side to its character, that we may see something as good or bad but that it is always full of other possibilities.

We pulled into the drive and saw the kitchen light still on, but the rest of the house was dark. We decided that if no one answered our knock at the kitchen door, we'd just slip inside (unlocked doors are pretty common in Leeway), put the leftovers in the fridge, and not wake anyone. No one answered, so we opened the screen door and entered the kitchen quietly.

It's odd how a person's body will react sometimes before her mind does. As I walked over to the refrigerator, I noticed my stomach turning, and then my nose kicked in. I set the leftovers on the kitchen table and looked at Howard, who was still smiling, only a bit calmer now. I knew he was disappointed that Lisa Layne and Shellye weren't up. Howard had become one of Lisa Layne's favorite people, and he picked her up every chance he got.

"Do you smell anything, Howard?"

He sniffed. "No. Do you?"

I've spent so many years cutting up red meat, my nose picks up blood even if it's a few drops on butcher's paper in the garbage can. "I smell blood."

The rest of Howard's smile melted away. "You do? What—what do you mean?"

We saw, at the same time, the stream of blood running on the floor toward the refrigerator. We gasped at the same time. We followed the blood around the kitchen table, where there was a larger pool of it.

"Dear Jesus, what's happened?" Howard whispered. He'd already headed through the door and into the family room. "Shellye!" His voice hit the floors and beams of the house. "Shellye?"

We found nothing in the family room. Howard turned on the hall-way light, and we saw a bloody smudge on the floor. The bathroom door was ajar. Howard reached inside for the light switch, and two legs, in long pants, appeared on the floor just inside the door.

"No, no, no! Oh please no." Howard knelt in front of me, his back blocking my view. Our hard breathing filled the small room. "What's happened, Howard?" I said into his shirt, trying to get closer. He lifted the body, and I saw that it was Doris. One side of her head was covered with blood. It had saturated her clothes. Her eyes were open, but they didn't see us.

"Call 911."

I didn't move, and Howard turned and saw that I was frozen, so he got up. "You stay with her, and I'll call." I scooted up to Doris and did my best to hold her. I grabbed a towel that was on the floor beside her. It looked as if someone had already tried to clean her up. I tried to wipe blood, but there was so much. I tried to see if she was breathing.

"Howard? Howard? Should I try to give her mouth-to-mouth?"

He didn't answer. The house was so quiet. Then I thought that Grady could still be in this house. Then I thought of Shellye and the baby.

"Howard! We've got to find Shellye." I wanted to run and look for her, but I couldn't bear to leave Doris there on the bathroom floor. I was feeling weak from looking at all the blood. The smell of it filled my mouth.

I could hear Howard, then, wandering through every room of the house, turning on lights, calling Shellye's name. He came back to where I was with Doris. He bent down and held her wrist. I saw his face tremble and the tears stream from his eyes.

"Doris, what happened?" He held on to her wrist. Her hand didn't even twitch.

"Is someone coming?" I asked, trying not to vomit all the blood that was filling me up. It was everywhere. Doris and Howard and I were spinning quietly in the middle of redness.

"Brennen's coming. And he's called others." We heard the siren that very instant.

I remember being lifted up from behind by Brennen. He and Howard and someone else were talking to me, saying something, but the words reached me garbled. When the late night air hit me, my mind cleared.

"We've got to find Shellye and the baby!"

"We're looking, Velma," Brennen said, his voice close by. "Several of the men are looking around the neighborhood. They must be on foot—the car is here."

Where would Grady have taken our girls? Where on earth? Not his mother's—everyone would look there first. I asked myself suddenly how I knew it was Grady who had done this. I must confess that it never occurred to me to think of anyone else. I never thought of some outsider coming through in the dark of night and doing this thing. Brennen seemed to know it too. He called Pastor Thomas and told him Doris was dead. He asked if the Thomases had heard from Grady or seen him, but they hadn't. Brennen received calls on his car radio from police in Helmsly, who were on their way. He called the highway patrol, just in case Grady had taken off down the road. He told them to be careful, because he might have a woman and child with him.

I remember all this in little pieces, words and gestures and sounds and long, painful pauses while people tried to think of what to do.

They sat me in Brennen's car. I heard Howard's voice and John Mason's voice. I heard the Hinleys stirring from two doors down. The Thompsons, who lived next door, were on vacation, and their house was dark. I heard Brennen knocking on doors and asking people if they'd seen or heard anything. He asked them to turn on their porch and yard lights. Small yellow lights and larger floodlights came on, looking like sore spots on the soft night, gleaming over gardens and front steps and garages. I heard the ambulance whine around the corner, exploding the crickets and bullfrogs and breezes. I watched them take the gurney in the house and then come out a few moments later with Doris on it, one foot bouncing out from under the sheet. They'd covered the bloodied head. I couldn't look at it directly, but felt the scene slide across the bottom of my vision, making shadows in the bright lights that had now appeared all around us.

As the paramedics went by with Doris between them, I saw someone standing in the sharp shadows of the big maple on the east side of Grady's house.

"Who's that?" I couldn't make my voice loud enough for anyone around me to hear. I saw then that it was Shellye, walking as if in a trance, the baby in her left arm. Her right arm hung oddly at her side.

"Shellye?" Surely she was a ghost, walking toward us so calmly and without a word.

Mrs. Hinley saw her and shouted at the others. I saw several people run toward Shellye and then slow down when they were close enough to touch her. Brennen reached out and took Lisa Layne carefully in his arms. The baby was awake but not making a sound.

"Where's Grady?" Brennen asked.

Shellye just looked at him. One of the paramedics approached her and led her to the porch steps, helped her sit down. He looked carefully into her eyes, then turned his attention to the arm.

"He was chasing us. I don't know where he is," came a small, scared voice. "Mom? Where's my mom?"

The paramedics had surrounded her now. She just kept calling for Doris.

I sat in Brennen's car while the conversations flew around me. In all the confusion, Howard's voice rang out.

"You should check the church. He might hide there." I followed the sound and saw that Howard was standing just a few feet from me. His eyes were glistening the way they had the night he'd had the bad drug reaction, as if he had more energy in his body than it could handle and it was seething and snapping, about to explode inside him.

I'll always feel bad that I couldn't move or talk. I needed to go over to Shellye and be with her, even though she didn't seem to be aware of much around her. But all I could do was sit in Brennen's car. Then Howard was scooting in next to me, and we were headed down the street, toward the church.

The church lights were out, even the east hallway light that I always left on. Brennen told Howard and me to stay in the car. I couldn't seem to move anyway, but Howard stationed himself at the hedgerow that divided the churchyard from Pastor's home.

Several of the Thomases' lights were on. I could see Clare's silhouette in the window of the front door.

"Clare!" I called. She moved toward me immediately.

"It can't be true!" she said, coming up to the car. "Tell me they made a mistake."

"Howard and I found Doris. Shellye came wandering out of the dark with the baby." My voice was out there somewhere, talking to all of us.

"We have Shellye and the baby? Oh thank God." Clare had been crying, and she reached out to hold my hand and cried some more.

Maybe I sobbed, too, but I don't recall. I could sense the police cars easing into the driveway and parking in front of the church. We watched as two officers circled around Clare's garden to get to the back church doors.

Another car, highway patrol I think, was making its slow way around town. I remember seeing a police car from Helmsly. Brennen wouldn't let anyone get close to the church, but eight or ten of us stood together in the dark, just beyond the church lawn.

Brennen talked at the church through a megaphone, just like they do in the movies. He talked and talked to Grady, who he hoped was in the building somewhere. From where I stood, I could hear that Brennen's voice behind the megaphone was gentle, but of course it came out the other end harsh and demanding. He pleaded with Grady to do the smart thing, so no one else would get hurt tonight. That everyone understood how a person's temper could flare, that nobody judged him, that nobody would hurt him. Brennen just kept talking, and officers crept here and there. It seemed as though hours went by, but when I looked at my watch, it was only an hour since we'd found Doris.

We saw lights go on in the church foyer, behind the small high windows in the front double doors. There was a sound then, slight and sharp, of the front doors being unlocked. One of them cracked open, and someone called out, "We have him. We're coming out."

Clare and I were out on her front walk by then, looking hard across the side yard at two officers coming clumsily but quickly down the church steps. Between them, held tightly by each arm, was Grady's lanky form. His head was bobbing up and down, his feet slapping the sidewalk. He was sobbing loudly. He didn't try to talk, just looked down and sobbed.

We heard Brennen reading him his rights. In all the years Brennen had been sheriff in Leeway, I'd never heard him speak those words.

We saw lights then, coming on all through the church. The sanctuary lit up and looked odd and yellow, bright but with no singing or movement inside. Somebody said they were looking for the weapon, since none had been found in the house. Clare and I slipped together to the side entrance of the church, the door to the kitchen. We turned on lights and walked down the hallway toward the sanctuary. I don't know why we did that. I'm sure the police didn't want anyone wandering around in there. Maybe Clare and I just felt protective of the place that was so sacred to us. Or maybe we were looking for something.

Two men in uniform were wandering through the sanctuary. We could hear one or two others on the creaking floors of the hallway, the pastor's study, the classrooms.

I stood and looked at the sanctuary that I'd made sparkle so many times. My heart's throb was sick and sad at once, seeing strangers with guns striding irreverently down the aisles.

"Let's leave, Velma," Clare said, her voice trembling. I nodded, and we kept holding onto each other as we walked back out the side door and toward her house. As we came close to the front porch, the scent of her pink geraniums tickled my throat.

Howard and I followed the ambulance to the emergency room, the same one we'd visited two or three times before in recent months. We knew that Doris was dead, that she was dead before we found her, but they were treating Shellye and checking the baby. Shellye was in shock, and a ligament in her elbow was torn. For a long time we were in the waiting room, and then they allowed us to go to her room. She was sleeping, an IV in place and her arm wrapped. Howard and I stood on either side of the bed. We stroked the young face and the honey hair, and cried.

After a while the nurse tried to chase us out, but I told her they'd have to remove me by force, that someone Shellye knew needed to be there when she woke up. Finally, the head nurse said I could stay and sleep in the chair, but only if I agreed to take a mild sedative to help me rest. I agreed, since I was sure nothing could knock me out anyway. I was more awake than I'd been in my entire life. But I sat down in the chair, and when I woke up, the sun was bright in the room.

Shellye woke up once or twice that morning, but they kept her sedated, because she would start asking about Doris and then begin to cry. During the day, a number of people stopped by. Pastor and Clare of course. Others from church. Doris's Aunt Sal arrived around noon, having jumped in the car when Pastor called her early that morning. At four o'clock, Clare Thomas came back, I think to be there with me as much as with Shellye. Sal had left shortly after noon. She had to go to Doris's house, go to the mortuary, make those awful arrangements.

A police officer, one of them who had been with us the night before, came in mid-morning, but Shellye was too groggy to answer any of his questions. His name was Linman. After talking with the doctor, he told Sal and me that he'd come back in the evening to see if

Shellye could talk then. We hoped he'd get busy or forget. But around seven o'clock he appeared at the door.

Shellye was awake. She'd not spoken much to Clare or me, but she seemed to know what was going on. She had asked about Lisa Layne, and we told her that the Masons had taken her home with them and that she was fine. She asked about Grady's mother, Thelma, and we told her that she was home, that they were trying to get in touch with her daughter, Nora, who had gone to a conference in Manhattan related to her job at the bank. Shellye didn't ask about Grady, and we didn't say anything about him. But officer Linman was about to bring up Grady and more.

"Mrs. Lewis, as difficult as it is, I need for you to tell what happened last night."

Shellye didn't look at him. Her hair was flat and her skin looked dull. She fingered the wrapping on her arm.

Officer Linman stepped a bit closer. His voice was completely gentle. "Shellye, I understand how hard it is to talk about what happened between Grady and your mother, but it's important for you to tell as much as you can, while you can remember the details."

Shellye's eyes moved toward Officer Linman in slow motion, as if she were trying to translate what he'd just said into a language she knew. "I don't expect that I'll ever forget a single detail, as long as I live," she said in a voice that hardly moved up or down.

"Would you tell me what happened?" The officer glanced at Clare and me. Clare very gently touched the sleeve of Shellye's hospital gown.

"Would you like Velma and me to leave, or would you feel better with us here?"

Shelly turned toward Clare, her eyes wide. "Oh, I want you to stay." She took a deep breath and sort of relaxed back against her pillows. She stared at the lump in the blanket that was her right knee.

"Grady and I dropped Mom off at her house, after the party at the restaurant."

"What time was that?"

"I think about nine-thirty. Maybe a little earlier. We dropped Mom at her house. She seemed worried when she kissed Lisa Layne goodnight."

"She seemed worried? Do you know what she was worried about?"

"I think she could tell Grady was upset."

"Grady was upset?"

Shellye made a small movement, more with her eyes than her head, that meant yes. "He felt slighted because Pastor Thomas had sat at the same table as Len Connor and his dad. I could tell then it would be trouble."

"You thought Grady would start a fight with your pastor or with one of the Connors?"

"No, he would never do that."

"How could you tell Grady was upset?"

Shellye's shrug was as slight as her nod had been. "I just know. Little things set him off sometimes. But I can see in his eyes." She paused and seemed to be someplace else for a moment. "And when we got in the car, he said something to me about how I'd worn the short skirt to waitress in. It wasn't that short. It just fit me better than the below-the-knees skirt. And I wanted to be comfortable. And then he grumbled something about, 'I don't know what to do to make you pay attention.' He said it low, but I think Mom heard him."

"Did she say anything to him, or you?"

"No. But she looked at me extra long when she got out of the car."

"Had Grady made any threat to your mother directly?"

"Oh no. He wouldn't do that."

The room was quiet. I feared that, even though Shellye was speaking in low tones, the whole hospital might be hearing this nightmare. A nurse walked by the room and peeked in for a second, then went on.

"We got home, and he started in. He'll pace, sort of, and talk to himself, but loud enough to be sure I hear. And if I go to another room, he'll follow me. But I usually don't go to another room, because that just makes him madder."

"What was he saying?"

"Things like, 'I try and try and try with you. I pray and pray and pray. There's some hardness in your heart, and it's ruining us.' Then he starts pointing out things he's unhappy with, like, I left a dirty dish on the kitchen table, or Lisa Layne's toys are underfoot again, or . . ." Shelly's voice shook, and she had to stop. "Or, just, how if I would get right with the Lord, you know, God would bless us. And me leaving him sometimes to stay with Mom or with Velma, that's hurt him with Pastor and everybody else, it's why he can't be a deacon, and I've lied about him all over town." Shellye bent her head, but I couldn't see tears.

I remembered in a flash how it had upset Shellye so when the deacons had asked Grady to step down from teaching for a while. Shellye had been more upset than Grady that he couldn't be appointed to deacon. I felt as if a stone was in my stomach. She'd known that he would blame her. How could we have missed that?

"You've been leaving him, to stay with other people?" Linman asked. He was writing her responses in a small notebook.

"Just with Mom or with Velma. Usually just for day or two."

"Why do you do that?"

I wanted to step in, but it seemed that Shellye needed to say whatever would be said.

"Grady's got a temper, and sometimes it's not safe to be with him."

"Has he taken his temper out on you?"

Shellye nodded, staring down at the sheets.

"Have you ever filed a complaint?"

Shellye shook her head. "I'd just leave when I thought it wasn't safe."

"Grady and Shellye belong to our church," Clare broke in, "and my husband will tell you that he's been violent, and that we've encouraged Shellye to leave the house sometimes."

The officer looked at Clare. "But no one has ever filed charges?"

"No."

I saw a muscle work in the officer's jaw. He kept writing, then looked up at Shellye again. "So you felt that Grady might get violent last night, after you returned home from the party?"

"Yes. I was so tired and wanting to go to bed. Lisa Layne was asleep on the couch in her clothes, and I wanted to go in there and undress her enough to put her in the crib, but when Grady paces and talks like that, I have to stay right there and hear it, or he gets so mad. And I was so tired and wished he'd just—" She let out a sob. "—just beat me and get it over with."

"Why didn't you go to your mother's if you thought he would beat you?"

Shellye's head was perfectly still. She didn't answer.

Officer Linmen covered a sigh. "Why don't you tell me what happened after you got to your house."

"We'd been home about a half hour when Mom called." Shellye's eyes left us for a few moments. I thought I could sense a rumbling way down in her soul, a gathering of courage to go to the next part of the story.

"What time did she call—do you remember?"

"It was near ten. It surprised me, because she never calls that late. She called, and Grady picked up the phone, and he told her I was already in bed and couldn't come to the phone. But I guess she insisted, because he shoved the phone at me and said I had thirty seconds. I said hi, and Mom asked me if I was all right and did I want to stay with her that night. And I said that everything was fine, because Grady was right there, I couldn't tell the truth, and Mom said that if there was trouble for me to clear my throat. And—" Shellye was rocking now, back and forth, as if in pain. "I shouldn't have, but I cleared my throat and then said goodnight, because Grady was reaching for the phone."

"What happened then?" Officer Linman's voice was very gentle, but he was taking notes methodically and quickly.

"Grady put down the phone and grabbed my wrist. He just squeezed, not saying anything. Then he sort of pulled me around the room, talking mean, the way he talks when he's getting ready to . . . he pulled me around the room for awhile. And I tried to pull away, and he jerked me harder, and that's when I hurt my arm. I cried out, but he didn't seem to hear." She couldn't go on. She was trembling all over. I moved close enough to pull the blanket up around her shoulders.

"What happened then, Shellye?" Officer Linman asked.

"He pushed me, and I fell on the floor against the kitchen cabinet." Her voice had gone back to that flatness, no tears or anything. "He started slapping me, not very hard, just enough to sting, to scare me. That's where I was when Mom came in. She started yelling at Grady to stop. She was so mad. She was saying, 'You take your hands off her' and she's saying to me, 'Get the baby and get in the car.' Then Grady starts screaming at her to stay out of our business and get out of his house, and Mom keeps telling me to get Lisa Layne and run. And I managed to get up. I ran into the living room and picked Lisa Layne up from the couch, with my other arm. Mom and Grady are yelling at each other in the kitchen, and the baby wakes up and starts to cry. And I should have gone out the front door and not through the kitchen, but he keeps the front door padlocked, and I don't have a key, and so I ran back through the kitchen. And I felt him grab my hair, and I almost fell down he jerked so hard, and then Mom grabbed him from behind. She did something that hurt him, because he yelled out and let go of me. And she screamed at me to run, and the baby was screaming by then, because she was scared, all the screaming and jerking and fighting."

Shellye's voice faded while a few tears escaped. She wiped them away. "And I looked back when I got to the door. I looked back and saw Grady knock Mom down. And he was kicking her. And I ran next door to call the police, because I couldn't do much. Grady's so strong, and I had to get Lisa Layne away from there. I thought I could call the police, that they'd get there soon. But I was knocking at the neighbors' door when Grady came out of our house and ran straight for me. So then I just ran and ran. I still don't know how he didn't catch me. I ran through Bentons' garden and down the alley. Mr. Hinley has all those little sheds on his back lot, and he never has a light on at night. I ran into one of them and just waited. I got Lisa Layne to stop crying. We stayed there a long time."

"How long do you think you were in the shed?"

"I don't know. Maybe it wasn't so long. We didn't come out until I heard Howard calling for me. And I peeked outside and saw the lights from police cars. Mr. Hinley turned on his yard light then. All I remember is walking toward the light."

Shellye stopped, in the way a person stops when every word has been said for all time. None of us said anything. Shellye was staring at the wall. Officer Linman was still writing, his pen making the only sound in the room. When he stopped writing, he looked at Shellye a long time.

"How long has Grady been hurting you?"

"Since about Christmas."

"How long have you been married?"

"Since September."

Linman put his notepad away.

"I tried not to make him so mad. Our pastor tried to help us, but it didn't go too well. I guess I should have done something?" Shellye's eyes looked so filled with pain as she gazed up at Officer Linman, needing some kind of answer from somewhere.

"These situations are always hard," he said. "But you couldn't have kept him from hurting your mom. You did the right thing by getting out of the house." He reached over carefully to rest a hand on Shellye's shoulder.

"He thought I was in love with someone else, but I never was." Her features changed then, trembling and looking horrified. "If I'd done the right thing, my Mom would be alive. I want my Mom! I want my Mom!" She was crying hysterically. Clare and I tried to hold her, but she didn't want anyone near her. A nurse came in and called another, and they shot something into her IV. Officer Linman ventured close enough to speak to Shellye.

"Mrs. Lewis, I'm sorry you had to relive all that. Thanks for telling us the truth. You take care now."

He left, and Shellye settled down. Clare and I stood on either side of the bed, as close to Shellye as we could get without climbing in with her. Scripture says that the Holy Spirit can turn even our groans into real prayers. I have to believe that some of the strongest prayers must be the silences that follow our tears.

21

Pastor Thomas's Daughter

Moan therefore, mortal; moan with breaking heart and bitter grief
before their eyes. And when they say to you, "Why do you moan?"
you shall say, "Because of the news that has come. Every heart will
melt and all hands will be feeble, every spirit will faint and all knees
will turn to water. See, it comes and it will be fulfilled," says the Lord
God.

—EZEKIEL 21:6–7

Istayed with Shellye the three days she was in the hospital. I didn't
think about VELMA'S LITTLE GERMANY a single time; only later did I
find out that Sheri, Howard, and Sissy opened it for the evening hours
the two days it was supposed to be open, since it was the first week
under its new identity. They didn't call me about anything, just looked
at my lists and menus and recipes. Bailey enjoyed telling me (*much*
later) about the dumplings that flopped but Sissy, in desperation,
served them anyway and told people that my family had always fixed
dumplings that way.

On the third day of Shellye's hospital stay, Lilian Lorenson, Pastor
and Clare's daughter, stopped by. Pastor walked in with her, but then
left after saying hello to us. Lilian came up to the bedside, smiling at

Shellye as if they were already friends. She looked to be about ten years older than Shellye. Her blond hair was cut short and stylish, and she wore jeans, although motherhood had given her fuller hips and she was clearly a woman and not a girl. (After all this time, I still thought of Shellye as a girl.) Lilian stood just a foot from the bed, her arms relaxed and at her sides. Shellye didn't seem to know what to expect. She knew who Lilian was, of course, but they had no relationship to speak of.

"I saw Lisa Layne this morning," Lilian said, and smiled. "She's doing fine. The Masons are spoiling her though—I should warn you."

A small, shy light glittered in Shellye's eyes.

"I'm so sorry for what's happened to you and your family."

Shellye looked down at her hands on top of the sheets. "Thank you."

"How are you, Velma?" Lilian's head turned to me slightly.

"Doing all right. Nice of you to stop by."

Lilian leaned a bit against Shellye's bed. When she spoke, her voice was like a whisper. "Dad and your great-aunt have taken care of all the funeral arrangements. The service will be tomorrow afternoon."

"I know. Aunt Sal told me. Do you want to talk to her? She just went down to the cafeteria for coffee."

"No. I came to talk to you."

Shellye's eyes held hope, fear, and confusion.

"I know how you feel," Lilian said, and her hands came together in a tight clasp at her waist. That was the only sign that she was nervous. "I had to get away from my husband because he was destroying our family."

Shellye gave a start, but her eyes locked onto Lilian as they hadn't before now.

"He didn't hurt us physically, the way Grady hurt you. But the mental and emotional cruelty . . ." She shook her head. "Some people still won't believe the kinds of things he said and did. They don't believe it because he was a perfect gentleman around everyone else. He was a totally different person in private with us."

Shellye nodded, eyes wide. "That's how it was," she said, barely loud enough for us to hear.

"I always thought it was me, or the kids. He blamed us for his temper and the nasty things he would say. He'd be harsh with the boys and say it was for their own good. But last year Joey stopped eating. I took him to the pediatrician. She did some tests and then sent us to a child psychologist. And—" Lilian's voice caught. "he told me that my son— this eight-year-old child who'd never been a day of trouble—was severely depressed. He started asking about how things were at home. And I fell apart right in his office. That's when I decided that something had to change. I had to save my children from this constant emotional battering. Part of me still loved Hal, but he resisted getting help because he didn't see anything as his problem. And when he did see a counselor with me, he would say what he had to to get through a session, but he never lived up to those words."

Possibly because tears had become common in Lilian's life, they ran down her face now, down smooth cheeks that didn't contort. The tears were just gentle slips of water tracing her skin, no apparent emotion behind them. But Shellye was just now crying tears that seemed to torture her very self, even though she was making almost no sound. The two young women now lightly held hands.

"I never really believed I was good enough for him," Shellye said. She wiped her cheeks. She wouldn't look at Lilian or me. "After we were married, I found out he didn't believe it either. He said there was something wrong with me, in my spirit, something I hadn't confessed or that I held back from God. He thought he could teach me, then he'd just lose patience." She shuddered suddenly. "He said he hated that he couldn't be more patient with me."

"That's a lie from hell, Shellye. There's so much wrong with those ideas, I don't know where to begin. Whatever you needed, he wasn't giving it to you by beating you."

Shellye didn't seem to hear completely. She stared out the window and kept talking. "And it was so clear that God had brought us together, right when I needed a husband. Everything seemed perfect. I just figured that I was the one ruining everything."

At this point, Aunt Sal came in with two cups of coffee. She saw Lilian and Shellye and looked at me. I put a finger to my lips as she handed me my coffee.

Shellye pulled back from Lilian and eased into her pillows, wiping at tears with her hand. Lilian found the box of tissues on the bed stand.

"It would be wrong to divorce, wouldn't it?" Shellye asked no one in particular. "But I can't live with the man who killed—" She shuddered again rather than finish the sentence.

"You can so get a divorce," Sal broke in angrily. Lilian looked up at us for the first time since she and Shellye had begun to talk.

"That's something you don't have to decide now," she said, turning back to Shellye. "That's another issue altogether. What you must do now is make a safe place for you and your daughter. That's the one important thing for you to do now. Everything else can wait."

"I just want to know God's will. That's all. That was always important to Grady and me."

"God's will is not for you and your child to be hurt. It's not for Grady's temper and whatever problems he has to control your lives. Shellye—" She made sure their eyes met. "God loved you before Grady married you. He loves you all on your own."

I could see from the look on Shellye's face that this idea was hard for her to get hold of.

"God loves you no matter how your husband treats you. It took me a long time to separate those two things." Lilian studied Shellye a moment before continuing. "Mom and Dad told me all about you. And you need to understand that God loved you when Len Connor did what he did. He . . ." Lilian seemed to consider her next words carefully. "He loved you when your dad left."

Shellye was rocking now, head bent. She made a low, moaning sound. She cried so hard that the bed shook. Sal and I gathered around her and Lilian. We wept together for some time. I heard the soft squeak of a nurse's shoes behind us, then the sound of the door being pulled shut against the noises and business of the hallway outside.

The patterns that revealed themselves in Leeway after Doris's death were not new lessons. They were older than the town, older than church, maybe older than Scripture. And, once we saw them, they were so obvious that we were ashamed to admit how blind we'd been.

So much of your life you go through on a daily basis, with everything seeming good enough. A bad thing happens here and there, but overall life is fine, and you get into a certain frame of mind about good and evil. You see things in a kind light, figuring that you're doing the best you can.

Then some big, terrible thing happens, and it blows to pieces all the sense you had before, about how life works and how well things are going and how decent a person you've managed to be. Suddenly, all the day-to-day goodness and trying hard just get cancelled out completely.

Well, that's how it seemed to me with the events in Shellye's life, especially the one that ended the life of her mother and my friend. Before that night, we all thought life would correct itself as long as we stumbled on the best we could. In the next minute Doris was dead and Grady Lewis was in custody. And all the thoughts we'd formed about life and our town and ourselves turned out not to be true. When something that awful happens, you look back and see your whole life differently. Instead of noticing all the little things you've managed to maintain and do right by, all you see are those big faults in your character and the endless laziness in your soul. Right then, a new truth takes the place of the older, easier one. And you feel more than ever that all the bad things that happen, happen just because you're such an evil and forgetful person.

My grandmother, my German Gran Lenny, was never happy to come to America. She loved her homeland, her colleagues, her studies, her husband. But her real bitterness set in, not after the first World War, but the second. The only Gran Lenny I ever knew was the one that existed after World War II. My father, who was not German, returned from that war when I was two. I didn't know anything of the turmoil in our family at that time. I didn't know until years later, when my mother was old and weary of carrying secrets, that Gran Lenny had given Papa another mission when he was sent overseas. He was on his way to join Allied troops in Germany, and she asked him to look for the Grettingers. They'd stayed in Munich after the first war, and for a long time they'd kept in touch by letters. But during the last few years, she'd heard nothing. She feared for them. They were up in years by now, as she was, leaders in their community and of their church. My father James was to find out anything he could.

When Papa walked in the door in 1945, Gran Lenny and Mama both knew that he'd found the Grettingers. He said he hadn't, but Papa—as Mama was always delighted to point out—could never lie successfully to her. And no one could lie to Gran Lenny. But Papa insisted that he'd turned up no information. Gran Lenny badgered him for weeks, filling the house with contention. She was afraid he was protecting her from bad news. Her friends had always been people of strong opinions, and she feared that they might have suffered for that.

Finally one day, Papa's reserve gave way. He rose from the dinner table and told Gran Lenny everything. The Grettingers were not dead. They were doing quite well the last anyone had heard. They had risen in stature as Hitler's party had risen. They had believed him, put their faith in his dreams for a new Germany. They and others—whom Gran Lenny had studied with and worshiped with—had put all of their resources to the Führer's service. They had given names and uncovered those who were trying to hide Jews and other unfortunates. They had stood by as neighbors were taken to the camp at Dachau. Although I was still a baby, sometimes I think I remember the silence that overtook our family meal that evening. The last anyone had seen of Herman and Anna Grettinger, Papa said, was that they were fleeing the country as the Allied Forces moved in.

I'd always thought that Gran Lenny didn't like church because God had allowed her husband to die long before his time, that God had watched her home torn apart by war. But after Mama told me this story—a story in my family that had been too hurtful for anyone to repeat after that evening at dinner—I understood that Gran Lenny had lost her confidence in humanity itself. By the time Papa told her the truth about the closest friends she'd ever had, news of the concentration camps had stunned the world. My parents couldn't speak of it during all my years at home. It was never mentioned in my family. We still cooked the same traditional meals, and Mama would sometimes sing songs in that other language. They were happy that I had learned to read and write in German. But we lost something of how we thought of ourselves when Germany's sins came to light. We'd been Americans for two generations, but the memories that made our family who it was had always included memories in that other home and earlier time.

In a similar way, now that I was close to the age Gran Lenny had been back then, I was watching Shellye's tragedies split all of us open and crack apart the way we saw ourselves. Hardly a year after her belly began to grow, we watched her life ripped open by murder and our church thrown into shock. We saw every weakness of character we'd ever had. We saw how stupid we were. We saw that, not only was the Lord interested in our little lives, he took every part of them seriously. Everything stands for something. Sin has consequences, large or small.

Two weeks after the funeral, I was listening in on Sandra Meeson and Angie Bernardi. They were making their leisurely way through the roasted chicken special.

"I always knew Grady Lewis was strung too tight," Sandra said. She waved her iced tea in Angie's direction. "He couldn't have a normal conversation. Everything was 'the Bible says this' and 'the Bible says that.'"

Angie said something about how you know a person by his actions, not his words, but I was too irritated at Sandra's remark to pay attention. I wanted to say to Sandra, "Well, if you knew he was strung tight, why didn't you say something?" But I could have asked myself and everybody else the same question. We should have seen that Grady's devotion had a dangerous edge to it. In fact, it was becoming more and more clear that his devotion had simply covered up who Grady really was.

I guess when you live with somebody, and when that person is (or appears to be) spiritually gifted, you make allowances you wouldn't make for other people. Which is backwards, now that I consider it. Grady carried such authority with the young men, and we should have been harder on him.

I can't bring myself to speak of Doris's funeral, of all the conversations and arguments that rose and fell like angry waves for weeks afterward. All of it hurts too much. I tried to concentrate on the restaurant and on getting my house ready for Shellye and Lisa Layne to live there. Right after the funeral, they went to Springfield to stay with Aunt Sal for awhile, until things settled down. There was the matter of charges against Grady and all the legal mess that went along with them. Pastor and a couple of the men visited Grady every day at the county jail. In the beginning, someone would stay overnight, too, to be sure Grady didn't hurt himself, because after a day or two in jail, he began to feel the effects and possibly see his life clearly for the first time. Pastor or John or Charlie would show up at Sunday and Wednesday services looking more beaten and sad than I'd ever seen them.

In addition to dealing with Grady, his sister, and his mother, Pastor Thomas and others had to think of the four young men Grady had been discipling. After word got out about Grady killing Doris, one of the young men never came back again. He'd been driving in from Bender Springs all these months to be discipled by Grady and to worship with us. The other three boys were local; two were church members. John and Charlie knew all three well enough to step in and pick up the pieces. I don't think anyone at Jerusalem Baptist got a decent night's sleep for a month or more after Doris's death.

The world seemed deathly quiet with Doris gone. Quiet so deep that it made every minute of the day seem like a drop-off into darkness. I grieved her as though she'd been my closest friend, and I realized in the midst of my grieving what a good friend she'd been. I found myself listening for her steps on the back walk. I expected to see her through the window, Lisa Layne balanced on one hip, or I looked out into the moonlight in the middle of the night, expecting to see the lit end of her cigarette wandering up and down Pickins Street. Once or twice a day I'd whisper her name, as if to bring her close one more time or to remember her more clearly.

I remembered a day back in March when I'd said something to Doris about not having any recent pictures of Shellye. All I had was a wedding picture, which was fine, but not as natural as I liked (plus it had Grady in it). One picture Shellye had given me of the baby had part of Shelly's chin and one arm in it.

The very next day, Doris came over with a large envelope. She dumped it out on my kitchen table, and we sat there for an hour or more, going through pictures from Shellye's life. Doris told me the stories that went with the pictures, the way I'd told stories about the pictures on my buffet when she and Shellye were getting acquainted with Howard. Doris and I chose two good pictures, one of Shellye when she was four and the other her high school senior picture. Doris put those two in a smaller envelope and took them to a photo place; a few days later she brought my copies. She'd bought a double frame and put them in it—gave them to me like that. They're on Mama's buffet in the dining room now. The day Doris came over with the pictures was a good day.

When Shellye returned to Leeway from Springfield, it was a good day only for a little while. She came with her cousin Gena, a few years older than her. They had Lisa Layne and Gena's daughter Alison with them. They came up to the restaurant, then met me at the house later.

"I've got your room all ready," I said, putting a pot of tea in front of them. I saw Shellye glance at Gena.

"Velma, I'm not staying in Leeway. At least not for a while. I'm going to live in Springfield. I've got family there. Lisa Layne has little cousins to grow up with. Gena and her husband just moved back there a few months ago."

I looked at the two of them and then at Alison, age ten, who was holding Lisa Layne, like some little mama in training. Of course Shellye was right. This was a good thing. My heart was breaking, but I acted happy and said, "I think it's good for you to be away from here, after all that's happened. But when you come to visit, your room's ready."

I knew she would be back, because Grady was still in custody, awaiting trial. He'd spent a week in the psychiatric unit because he'd stopped eating and was threatening violence to himself. Deep down, I hoped they would find Grady mentally ill. With all the emotions I had toward the man, I couldn't imagine prison making him any better, and we all needed some sort of explanation for what he'd done. It was more than a bad temper, surely. It was something wrong in his soul. They needed to have experts examine him to determine his mental condition. Once that was done, they'd have to reconsider what charges should be brought to trial. And there was a list of us who would have to tell our part of the story. In real life, all of these legal matters take a lot longer than they do on television shows.

And while all of that was going on, Jerusalem Baptist was battling within itself, people struggling not to take sides or place blame for what had happened. There were Grady's mother and sister, who had stopped coming to church, and some people thought this was just as well, but others said that this of all times was when they should all be in church together. Pastor and the deacons agonized over how they had allowed Grady to get so far afield. They second-guessed themselves almost to their graves. And of course, everything leaked into conversations at VELMA'S. Leeway was the last place Shellye needed to be.

"Where's Howard?" Shellye asked.

"He's at Pearle's. She tripped over her garden hose and broke her ankle. He's staying with her a week or so, until she's steadier."

"Is he still . . . OK?" None of us knew how to talk about Howard anymore. After Doris's funeral, he'd gone to Dr. Henderson, who'd been overseeing him all these months. He'd also put Howard on a new chemo treatment, a last hope. Of course Howard hadn't told me, didn't want to raise my hopes. But Henderson had confirmed that Howard's blood was perfectly normal now, that the leukemia seemed to have disappeared.

"He's still right as rain. Doctor said that it could be a remission—that happens sometimes. There's always the possibility that Howard'll get sick again, just as mysteriously as he got well. But there's no reason he shouldn't go about life in the normal way." I didn't mention that, after Dr. Henderson had warned Howard not to assume too much, he'd mentioned that his grandfather had been a doctor over near Chetopa, Kansas, back before chemotherapy and other such treatments. Old Doc Henderson would make house calls to terminal patients and do nothing but pray for their pain to be eased. That original Dr. Henderson had seen a few miracles himself, and the present Dr. Henderson wasn't offended at all by the possibility that the Lord had stepped in and done what medical science couldn't.

When Shellye and Gena and the little girls left, I walked through my empty house. Howard was in Parsons with Pearle, which was good. I could imagine how happy she was to see him healthy and having him there to help out the way any son would. Shellye was likely to stay in Springfield, once all this with Grady was over. She had taken Lilian's advice and was putting off thinking about divorce or no divorce. There was enough to worry about for now.

That evening, I was resting by myself on the sunporch. I could see Doris's empty house from the corner of my eye. I could feel my empty house hunched up against my back and shoulders, its rooms and hallways quiet. I leaned back and tried to appreciate how nice the pale sky looked, so clean and calm. I closed my eyes . . . and fell into a fever dream.

I floated down the street and into a high, back window in the church kitchen. No one was there. I floated past the cabinets and through the fellowship hall and entered the quiet sanctuary. Just a few people were there. I drifted above them, in thick, warm silence, and looked down on their heads and shoulders and laps. They were so deathly quiet, as though their voices and expressions had been taken away. The pulpit was empty. Lonnie Myers wasn't at the piano. My ears rang with the silence. I aimed my soul down closer, to see faces, to try to talk with someone, but I could go only so far. Finally, an arm reached up to pull me down. I sat in the pew and turned to see Gran Lenny. Her eyes were large and full of love, but sad and deep and wise. I tried to talk to her, but she guided me with her eyes to look at the other people in the church. There was Grady, by himself, staring straight ahead. There was Melanie Connor, a pew over, her head bent. There was Pastor Thomas, a hand in front of his face. There was Len Connor, looking at me hopefully. I smiled at him, and he disappeared. I looked and looked for Doris, but she wasn't anywhere. Someone touched my shoulder, and I looked into the face of Sissy Fenders Scott. At her touch, I started floating again. I floated through the window and out the door, around the ash tree near the front walk, then out the back gate. My feet dipped and grazed the tops of gravestones. Names and dates of birth and death buzzed around my head. Dear Lord, I felt so hot, so full of misery. I begged the Lord to take me away from this place. And, to my surprise and relief, I felt cool arms lift me and carry me home.

I was still feverish the next morning. Early, when it was barely light, I got out of bed and put on my clothes and walked to the graveyard behind the church. Jerusalem Baptist has been around so long that it actually has its own graveyard, although it filled up a generation ago and no one gets buried there now. I stopped in front of graves whose names meant nothing to me. I pulled a few weeds. Then I heard a voice. It wasn't a voice in time, but from a conversation Doris and I had had barely two weeks before her death. It was a conversation I had driven from my mind. Maybe that's why it had to come back to me in a fever.

Doris had come up behind me while I was weeding in this very spot in the graveyard. "Hello, Velma, don't you ever rest?"

I turned to look at Doris and noticed that her toenails were painted a metallic, light green. Since Doris had taken a shine to Howard, she'd been inspired to go out on a limb in some ways, mostly harmless, such as odd shades of toenail polish and earrings that dangled nearly to her shoulders. And though Howard's attention had been short-lived and the month after Easter had been woeful as could be, it looked now as if Doris's womanly self had received just enough of a spring shower that wild little shoots had sprung up in her life. It had to mean something that, while her heart still grieved its losses, her toes and earlobes were flashing around in the sun.

She looked worried and unhappy. "Velma, what can we do about Shellye?"

I searched for a response, and Doris kept talking. "I know she's unhappy. Grady has done it to her."

"They might just work through it."

"This is all my fault."

I turned around to read her face. She had Lisa Layne, bright awake, on one hip, looking so pleased to be outdoors.

"How could it be your fault?"

"I made her think that if her dad hadn't left everything would have been fine. I believed that myself. I made her think that the most important thing was to have a husband. If I hadn't made her feel so desperate, maybe she wouldn't be with Grady now."

As much as I wanted to tell Doris she was wrong, her words had the ring of truth to them. It amazed me how much Doris had changed during all her daughter's trials. But these same words could land on me too. I'd never liked Grady as much as some people had, but I'd encouraged Shellye. I had seen bruises before anyone else, but I'd never said a word. It had seemed to be a private thing, and I'd been afraid to get in the middle of it.

"There could be some truth to that," I said, tossing weeds toward the small pile nearby, "but Shellye's always been a smart girl, and when she said yes to Grady, she looked as in love as anyone I've seen."

Lisa Layne was kicking to get down, so Doris put her at our feet. She sat on the nearest gravestone and talked to the wildflowers bobbing at its edge.

"Why are our mistakes always too big for us to handle?" Doris wasn't asking me really. "Why do we figure them out too late?"

Lisa Layne had taken out on hands and knees, so Doris grabbed her arms and helped her step across the dewy grass and back toward home. My, but she'd for sure be walking by her ninth month. I followed them out the gate. Suddenly, Doris turned to face me—I nearly ran into her.

"Velma, now I understand what difference the Resurrection makes." With the breeze and fresh light of morning hitting her face, Doris looked like a person born again. "Easter really does make a difference, doesn't it? It means the wrong things will finally be right. It means our mistakes will stop hurting us, once and for all." Her voice was steady, but there was a bright sheen in her eyes.

"Oh yes, Doris. The Resurrection is all we have."

"Except one another. We have that, as long as we're here."

I remembered that conversation so clearly now. I played it over a few times as I walked back home. By evening, my fever was gone. I wandered around the house, trying to contain all the emotions that had been stirred up. In that flight through the church, in my dream, Gran Lenny had said something with her eyes, but I couldn't make out what it was. I sat in my grandmother's room, trying to smell the lavender of decades past. How awful it is, to feel your very memories of loved ones slipping away.

The next afternoon, I had beets cooking for Gran Lenny's favorite salad. And the red cabbage was simmering in a sweet sauce. I thought absently of the day Mama had taught me to make the sauce. I'd been contrary all afternoon. I was fourteen, and those were contrary days, sometimes for no reason. I'd argued with Mama over something to do with the laundry. I'd spoken out of line. Worst of all, I'd thrown a dish across the room. Somehow, Mama and I had ended up in the kitchen, working on dinner together. Mama said not a word about the broken dish; she seemed intent on teaching me this sauce recipe.

I felt so awful by then, about what I'd done. I tried to talk about it. I stirred and stirred that sauce, working up the nerve to bring up the broken dish.

"I'm sorry about the dish."

"Don't speak of it, Velma."

"But I'm sorry, and I want you not to be mad."

"I'm not mad. Don't speak of it. It does no good to bring up such things."

"But I want to explain—"

"Velma." Her eyes held me in that power that was always Mama's. "What's past is past. Explanations mean nothing. The dish is gone. I'm not mad. Don't ever speak of it again." She turned back to trimming radishes and celery for dinner. Her face was like iron.

Now I stirred the sauce without seeing or smelling it. I remembered how much I'd wanted to confess and be forgiven, and how Mama wouldn't allow it. She couldn't have understood how much I needed it. But our family had ways of not speaking of things. Whether they were large sins or little ones, we had learned to pack them away. We wrote them in journals no one would ever read. Or we simply never spoke of them again.

Suddenly I had to sit down. I put my face in a tea towel and felt the tears exploding through my whole body. I asked God to forgive me for not speaking up when it had been in my power. I asked him to forgive not only my silence but my mother's and my grandmother's. No wonder the very floors and walls of our house had developed voices of their own, and for years I had felt so haunted.

Clare's Brussels Sprout and Artichoke Salad

1 small package frozen Brussels sprouts, cooked until tender,
   then drained and halved
1 can artichoke hearts, drained and quartered
1/3 cup crumbled blue cheese

Dressing:

1/8 to 1/4 cup olive oil
1/8 to 1/4 cup cider vinegar
1 teaspoon oregano
1 teaspoon sugar
Salt and pepper to taste

Combine brussels sprouts, artichoke hearts, and blue cheese.

Combine dressing ingredients in a small jar and shake, then pour over vegetables. Mix well and refrigerate for at least 2 hours before serving.

22

My Albert

Wherever the river goes, every living creature that swarms will live . . .
On the banks, on both sides of the river, there will grow all kinds of trees
for food. Their leaves will not wither nor their fruit fail, but they will
bear fresh fruit every month, because the water for them flows from the
sanctuary. Their fruit will be for food, and their leaves for healing.
—EZEKIEL 47:9, 12

In August, when all of us were sweltering and tomatoes were taking
over gardens, and when Howard had come back from Pearle's, Bailey was on his usual perch at my counter. Thayer Murdock was on the
stool next to him, and they were discussing weather patterns. Those
guys can turn low pressure cells into daily drama. As it happened, it
had stormed earlier in the morning, a real thundershower that had
come up quickly and drenched everyone, since no one had expected it.

"Rained cats and dogs this morning," Thayer said.

I looked out the window. The sun was trying to get through, and
the rain had lessened to sprinkles. "Now it's just raining puppies," I
said.

"That's just the kind of comment Albert would make." Bailey
laughed.

I felt a grin crack my face. After all this time, I still had to smile like a schoolgirl when anybody mentioned Albert's name.

Then Thayer asked, "Velma, did he die in '95 or '96?"

I looked straight at him, wanting suddenly to hurt him.

"Ninety-five," said Bailey, "three weeks before Christmas."

"I knew it was winter, but couldn't remember which part of it. I sure miss that guy," Thayer said, but his voice was light, as if he were talking about dessert, not death.

The café was quiet after Bailey and Thayer slapped on their caps and walked out. They told me to take care, but this time their words were heavier with meaning. *Take care not to scald yourself with hot soup. Take care not to slip on the mopped floor. Take care not to walk in front of a truck coming through town later this evening, when it begins to get dim. Take care, Velma.*

I realized that the café was quiet because I was. My humming had been silenced by sadness. Something about hearing "die" and "Albert" in the same sentence had pulled a shade somewhere. An ugly feeling came to rest on me.

That feeling had weighed so hard the first few months after the accident that I thought I would never take in a full, easy breath again. I'd wake up and the first light on my face and the first air in my lungs would shoot me full of that heavy pain. I'd fall back into bed and just try not to be. But I kept being. No dark, rumbling truck came for me, as it had my Albert.

The next day, Thursday, I closed the café. Put up a sign that said it would reopen on Monday. I didn't say why. Didn't need to. I'd been there for thirteen years, and the town would still be there next week.

Howard saw the sign on his way home from the library.

"Velma—you sick?" he called when he came into the house.

"Yes. About to die."

"What?" He appeared in my bedroom doorway. I was sitting on the bed, feet up, leaning back against the pillows.

"What do you mean? Oh." He noticed what was all over the bed. The guest book from Albert's funeral. The newspaper notices. A little prayer book: *For Days of Grief and Healing.*

Howard sat down on the bed, careful not to mash anything. "You've never really talked about him, Vellie. I've always felt that you should talk about it, but I didn't know how to ask."

"Nothin' to say. There still aren't words for it." Any moment I think of it is almost as bad as the moment I saw Albert landing on the pavement, and then the moment his breathing stopped. Then when Brennen bent over him and shook his head and picked me up to take me to Bailey's house. Every moment just got worse—more pain, less hope, more darkness.

"Do . . . do you still talk with Albert?" Howard peered carefully into my face, almost as if I were a child.

"Oh." I shrugged. "I don't try to anymore, not really. Things got quiet along about Thanksgiving. Howard—" I touched his arm. "I'm not as crazy as I sound."

"You're not crazy at all. You're the sanest person I know. Can I get you some tea or anything? Something to eat?"

"No. There are leftovers in the refrigerator, if you get hungry."

Howard had that gift of knowing when to leave a room. I looked through the funeral guest book another time, bringing to memory the face of every name written there. The faces at the funeral had been so much different from the faces of those same people who came in to eat, week after week. We were in such shock that we looked like strangers to each other, kept walking up to one another to touch a shoulder or grasp a hand, making sure we recognized the person standing there. In a few weeks, the rest of them changed back into their old selves. But I kept groping for something familiar. Then that spring the trouble with Shellye started, and there were other things to think about. I had to be content to snatch some moments with Albert as I could.

For a long time after Albert passed, I could carry on discussions with him. Oh they weren't actual discussions, of course, but they were talks I imagined between us. Those talks were especially clear out in the yard at evening, I suppose because we spent practically every evening of our life together with our hands in the dirt, talking over every little part of life. But then his voice faded out there. I could stand near the rosebushes or kneel among my snapdragons and hear nothing at all that sounded or felt like my Albert. I didn't even put out a garden that spring—haven't since, actually. But I could nearly always hear him in the house. But then the rooms of our house—even our bedroom, where we had so many peaceful discussions—stopped whispering my husband's voice.

Bailey and all the rest tried to talk to me about Albert, but I suppose I told them in one way or the other that I didn't want to speak of him or the accident. My good friends picked up on my feelings, and they protected me from the good intentions of people who didn't know me as well. I'm sure Bailey and John had filled Howard in when they drove him and his suitcases from Parsons to my house, that first day. But I don't think anyone but Howard ever knew how much I talked to Albert. And I feel certain that Howard never told a soul about it.

Now, since that evening in the café, when Thayer put death back into spoken words, I don't hear much from Albert at all. His voice has soaked into the walls and trees and breezes and silences. He's absent even in the places that used to be so filled with him.

I do hear Jesus now. More often and more clearly. His voice is different from Albert's, but I like the voice of Jesus, after not hearing it for all those months. I'm thinking that maybe Albert was drowning Jesus out—that I could hear Albert because he was so present with me. Dying of a sudden, my husband and close companion one day and the next day just air beside me, he couldn't really be gone, not in a way my mind could grasp. Like when you stare so long at something bright that when you look away the image is still hanging there, flat against the air and sharp at its edges. Albert's absence was sharp to the point of hurting me. And when he spoke, I wasn't hearing things as a crazy person would. That was just his voice roaming in my head, lots of echoes of all the real things he'd said to me during our life together. I knew him so well that I could even imagine what new things he would say. There's nothing crazy about that.

I'm grateful that Howard was so patient all the time he was here at the house. He let me get away with talking about Albert in the present tense. Sometimes I think Howard was really an angel, he was so wise about things.

So now Albert's fading, and I'm tuning in to Jesus again. It's good to find that he waited for me to ease back into his vicinity. If I've learned anything, it's that God is never in a panic the way people are. And it takes a very long time for him to lose patience or to jump to another plan if one doesn't work. He knew that, sooner or later, I'd be able to bear the thought of Albert being gone, that I wouldn't need to talk with him or imagine his voice or his face or the way he'd hold me at the end of the day. But God knew that a person can't just give up such miracles in a few days.

Like Gran Lenny once said, the soul is eternal, so it can see farther than the mind. My mind was just so full of that man I'd spent most of my life with that I couldn't bear to imagine him away from me, even in heaven, and I couldn't bear to see myself alone. Now I can turn these things over to my soul, which the good Lord was holding gently all along.

Albert's Favorite Trout

1 whole trout for each person, cleaned and beheaded
2 tablespoons butter
1 cup corn, cut fresh from the cob
1/4 cup slivered red onion
1/4 cup dill pickles, chopped
1/4 cup fresh parsley, chopped
2 tablespoons olive oil
1 tablespoon fresh lemon juice
salt and freshly ground black pepper to taste

Cook the corn and onions in the butter for five minutes. Add the parsley and dill pickle.

Lightly oil or butter a 9 x 12 baking dish.

On a plate, lay open each trout, one at a time. Put about 3 tablespoons of the corn mixture inside each fish and close it up. Then carefully lay the trout in the baking dish.

Whisk together the olive oil, lemon, salt and pepper. Brush the mixture over the fish.

Bake at 350° for 20 to 30 minutes, until fish is flaky.

23

Writing the Love

I will make a covenant of peace with them; it shall be an everlasting covenant with them; and I will bless them and multiply them, and will set my sanctuary among them forevermore.

—EZEKIEL 37:26

I feel almost done in, now that I look back on our story. It's a relief to have told it, if only in my notebooks. I think all these pages would please Gran Lenny; in fact, she's probably sitting in Heaven, nodding her head with approval. In writing all these hard things, I've used words the way Gran Lenny used them, to talk with God, to get through bad memories, to find some solace or some sense peeking out.

These months have required so much from us. It seems that I spent all my time brushing myself off or throwing out my arms before I hit the ground. It's been a time when my prayers, and my fears, multiplied. A time of groping for words or even thoughts. There are no human thoughts that can contain or describe such suffering as we've had. Maybe in Heaven Gran Lenny has a whole new vocabulary that can make such things understandable. But we only get little whispers of Heaven's language here. I suppose that's why the Holy Spirit has to pray for us, especially during the times when we have no words.

In August, Howard went through the house and gathered his things. After a lazy breakfast one Sunday before we headed to church, he put his coffee cup in the sink, stretched there at the cabinet, the window light shining across his face, and took the little praying hands magnet off the refrigerator. He just took it off and put it in his pocket. I expected him to say something, but he walked into the dining room and lifted up the picture of Albert and Albert's dad and uncle, Howard's dad. I'd told Howard he could have that picture. He held it with both hands and stared into those young faces. Then he carried it up the stairs.

I'd followed him as far as the dining room. Then I stood at the bottom of the stairs and didn't know what to do. I did know what it meant, that Howard had taken the praying hands and the picture. He was going home. Meaning that my house wasn't his home anymore.

There was no reason for me to think that a man not even forty years old would need or want to live with a sixty-ish cousin by marriage for the rest of his days. When he thought his days were numbered, our old house was a good, comforting place. It's been a comforting place to die for a number of people, and I suppose I'll die in it myself. But Howard . . . where would he go now? For just a few seconds, I stood there at the stairs and felt so angry and cheated. I'd lost Albert, then Doris—really, Shellye too—and now Howard was leaving. The echoes in my home were getting louder as the rooms got emptier. I looked up those stairs and just couldn't bear it. A person gets weary of losses, she really does.

We needed to leave for church in a few minutes. I climbed the stairs and stepped into Howard's room. He was sitting on the bed, looking out at the leafy branches of the catalpa tree just outside his window.

"Where will you go now?" I asked.

"Back to Wichita."

"For your old job?"

"For Deborah. If she'll take me." I could hear him swallow.

"I think that's a good decision. I'm surprised. I thought you two were really finished."

"I was. She wasn't. At least not then. Who knows? After all that's happened, I can't take anything for granted. But I need to be with her enough to either finish or begin." He looked at me, those hazel eyes clear and calm.

"What made you change your mind?" I sat on the bed beside him and looked out the window too. The storm window was open, and there was a thread of air that smelled like Doris's marigolds growing at the boundary line. I've never cared for that strong smell, but right then I loved it because it was part of my life, my old familiar life that bloomed the same flowers year after year, flowers I was sure of at least, even if I didn't like them that much.

Howard started two or three times to give an answer. Finally, he said, "It always amazed me how Shellye could keep loving people." His voice was soft, maybe so that the mention of her name wouldn't hurt me so much. "The girl took every opportunity to love. She stayed with the church, after all that mess with Len. She even forgave Len. She stuck it out with ol' Grady, the pig. I'm sorry, Vellie, but I can't extend much Christian charity to him yet. But I'm sure Shellye will forgive him, too, with time. The girl knows how to love through all kinds of hell. It's like she looks for the least opportunity."

The way Howard was talking, you'd have thought he'd been in love with Shellye. Tears stood in his eyes.

"You're right about that," I said.

"I never did much to invite people's love. I looked after myself, and I was too busy planning my future to get interrupted. But I fell for Deborah, and finally I was willing to give some time to another person. Then a specialist told me to put my affairs in order. I'd finally made some time for something as important as love, only to have all my time stolen.

"When she showed up at Easter, I felt that God had given me what I needed most right then. I knew that when Deborah got a good look at me and saw that I was practically dead, it would be easy for her to walk away. We'd be finished in the right way, in agreement about the situation."

"But she was ready to be with you again."

"I know! She wouldn't walk away. So, like an idiot, I turned her around and gave her a push. Vellie, I can barely admit this, but I would rather the church see her reject me than know that I'd left her. What's made me so selfish?"

"Oh, Howard, that old sin in us makes us that way. We're all like that."

"No, not all of us. Some people are actually the way people are supposed to be, so the rest of us have no excuse. Like when Jesus lived as a human being and proved it could be done right. There have always been a few people around to prove that it's possible."

"Are you talking about Shellye?"

He nodded, then looked down at his hands. They looked much fuller and stronger now, the way a man's hands are supposed to look.

"Ever since Doris was killed, I've thought what a waste it was, for her to be so ready to love but be left all alone, and then to die before she could see her granddaughter grow up. But then, here I am, talking about waste . . ."

I grasped Howard's hand. Mine looked so old next to it. Hands hardly ever lie about a person. I could look down and see every dish I'd ever washed and every time I'd held a paring knife or gripped a wooden spoon. My life was written on my hands. Howard's were still fairly smooth and able to bear a lot more of his life story.

"Have you called Deborah?"

"Actually, I did, or I have, called her a few times since Easter. First it was to apologize for being so harsh. But then, when Doris got killed and Shellye was hurt, I felt this need to tell her. She remembered Shellye from Easter Sunday, her and Lisa Layne. She didn't know that Doris had been interested in me, but she remembered her. She cried when I told her. Then we kept talking. Then she called awhile later to see how I was doing."

"Did you tell her you were healed?"

He shook his head. "I was still afraid to call it a healing. And I didn't want to get her hopes up. But now it doesn't matter. Whether I live or not, Deborah and I have this time. Last month I wrote to her, told her about all of it. Didn't hear from her for a long time, but she'd been out of town, on vacation. The day she got back she called me."

"So, you two are moving ahead a little."

"I've hurt her an awful lot. All I can do is move back and get a job and start from scratch, but I think she's willing to try." He checked his watch. "Oh boy, we need to get to church."

We walked through the muggy air past brown yards and quiet houses. I asked God's blessing on each one as we passed it. It's a habit I'd started back when I had that spell of not being able to cook. The morning walk up to the café was such a torture then. I blessed houses to keep from stewing and spitting at the Lord.

Pastor Thomas and Clare were not there that Sunday. That nice Jacob Morgan from Bender Springs was filling in; he had a seminary student practicing his preaching back at Bender Springs Baptist. Pastor Thomas and Clare had announced last Wednesday night that they had family business to attend to and would be gone several days. They didn't say, but we all figured it had to do with Lilian and her husband. She and the boys left too.

A few minutes before the worship service started, Sissy walked in looking frazzled and sat in front of me. Her hair no longer had that magazine look, but the more average person look of Lana's Salon. And Sissy's clothes weren't all that distinguishable from anyone else's. Oh, she didn't look frumpy, not at all. And she carried herself much the way she always had, only calmer and with less need to make an entrance.

She bent back enough to whisper to me, "Would you believe that the grocery representative came out this morning at nine? Left a message on my answering machine that I didn't get until late last night, so what could I do? On a Sunday, can you imagine? I showed him Avery's space, but kept the business short. I told him as politely as I could that business meetings on Sunday is just not the way we do things around here."

"Does he like the space?"

"Oh yes. He talked as if they'd move in next month. A nice man, overall. Moved back here from Springfield, because he likes small towns."

It was Sissy who, over the past few weeks, had managed to get Thelma and Nora Lewis back in church again. They sat on the side opposite Len and Tim Connor. I looked from one side of the church to the other and was in awe that these two families were snug in their pews after all that had happened. The Lewises had generally considered themselves somewhere near the top of the social ladder, which, in Leeway, is not that far from the ground. But Grady's crime had undone them. They hardly ever left the house. Pastor and Clare had tried to talk with them, as had a couple of other women who'd been friends with Thelma. But Sissy seemed to figure out what wavelength they were on. Given Sissy's status in the community, Thelma and her daughter respected her.

Late in August, Deborah showed up in her Toyota. She and Howard packed his things into her back seat. They did this while I was at the restaurant. I only knew what was going on because they stopped by on their way out of town. They walked in together and I gave Deborah a big hug and told her how glad I was to see her. I kept chatting with Deborah—about her work at the college, about foolish things like the weather—because I knew what was coming. Finally, Howard sidled up to me and put his arm—a strong, warm arm—around my shoulders.

"We need to hit the road."

"I know, I know." So far, I'd managed not to cry. But I glanced past Deborah and saw Lois Simms and Jess Franklin, two of my senior regulars, getting teary eyed. Howard had always made a point to visit with them and help them with their coats, walk them out to the car in slippery weather whenever he happened to be around. Seeing Lois swipe her napkin under one eye made it harder than ever for me to keep my composure.

"Will you miss me, Vellie?" Howard smiled big.

That did it. My tears started. "You know I will. Don't you make me cry now."

"Are you sure you'll be OK?"

"We'll be fine. Thanks to you, my restaurant will save me from retirement for another twenty years."

He hugged me then, a long time, and I felt a sob or two vibrate between us. Deborah gave me a long hug too.

"Vellie," Howard said, after he'd wiped his nose, "we'll be here in a couple of months, or even sooner, depending on how things go. I'll call you late on Wednesday nights, after church, OK?"

"Oh yes, that would be so good, to talk with you and keep up on how things are going."

"We'll be back, for sure." Deborah said. "Somebody's got to teach me to cook, now that you've spoiled him."

They looked good together, walking out the door. I had the feeling that they'd find their way to forgiveness. Holding the door for them was Bailey. He walked in and headed for his perch.

"Oh Velma," Sheri called from behind the counter, "that Carpenter guy called again, wanting to talk to you."

My high mood shifted down. I sensed Bailey's head turn from the pastry case and saw him looking at me sharply.

"What's *he* want?"

"Oh, I'm not sure. Probably some little thing."

"He's got no business calling here."

"It's all right. Ready for your soup?"

Bailey decided to let it drop. "That's why I'm sittin' here."

I served him his soup. He put a hand over the coffee cup I'd set in front of him. "Cuttin' back."

"Again?"

"Haven't had a real night's sleep in four days. I'll see if this helps."

I would have asked him what the doctor said, but Bailey prided himself on not going to the doctor unless an organ was about to rupture or a limb was dangling. You learn when to save your breath. I left him alone and starting clearing the west booths. It was right after lunch.

"You should go talk to that guy."

That was Zeke's voice. I looked over at him and saw him slurping his vegetable soup. "Zeke—I didn't even see you."

"You should talk to him," he repeated.

"Who?"

"Mr. Carpenter."

"Zeke, you don't know a thing about it."

"Yes I do." Another slurp. "I know lots of things."

"You know who he is?"

"Yep."

I turned back to the table I was wiping. "Still doesn't mean you know anything about it."

"Oh well," Zeke said, then gave a little cough. "Follow your conscience. It's always worked before."

I went back to the counter, took a pie from the cooling rack, and sliced it into eighths. Staring down into juicy cooked apples and cinnamon and crust that would melt in the mouth, it occurred to me that God had decided that I needed one more regular irritation in my life. I wondered why Zeke couldn't be just another homeless guy who took gifts gratefully and never said a word. But he had to be a philosopher and food critic and an extra little conscience put here just for me. First, to tell me I'm selfish. Now, to remind me that you can't ignore insistent people forever.

That evening, late, my feet soaking, I picked up the phone and called Henry Carpenter. My hand shook a little, and I could hardly breathe. I decided I would let it ring only three times. But the line at the other end opened up right after ring number two.

"Hello?"

"This Henry Carpenter?"

"Yes."

"I'm Velma."

He breathed into the phone. "I'd given up on you calling."

"What do you want?"

"I want to see you."

"There's no reason for that."

"For me there is. Please. We don't have to meet in Leeway."

It was a gentle, if tired, voice.

"Where did you have in mind?"

"There's a Denny's right off Highway 169, about ten miles north of Leeway. My route takes me by there all the time."

"What time?"

"Whatever's good for you."

I nearly said, "Nothing's good for me," but decided to carry this through. "Wednesday, sometime during the afternoon?"

"That would be fine. Let's say two o'clock?"

"All right. If you think this is really necessary."

I hung up and knew I'd made a mistake. Wednesday was tomorrow. I didn't sleep but wouldn't allow myself to think, either, so I kept the television on all night long, the way Howard had when he was afraid that falling asleep would lead to death.

When I got in the car at 1:45 the next day, it felt as if I was saying good-bye forever. To what, I didn't know. To Leeway? But I was coming back, would probably be home by 3:00 or 3:30. To something else. But every time I came close to knowing what it was, I shut down my thoughts. I'd said good-bye so many times lately that I felt this one would finish me off.

Henry was there when I walked in. I saw him in the corner right away, isolated from the few people who lingered over lunch or coffee. As I walked up to the man, he looked grayer than he'd been when I last saw him, nearly two years ago. The face was softer, though, much softer, as if life had worn it away and uncovered its better qualities.

He rose and put out his hand. I shook it quickly; he didn't squeeze too hard.

"Thanks for coming, Velma."

"I still don't understand why this is necessary. I told you before that there are no hard feelings."

"I think there are. I don't blame you, but I think you won't talk to me because there are hard feelings."

"We can't change our feelings. We feel what we feel."

"I understand that. But I've wanted to help you out. Since you're alone now, I wanted to come over and help you."

"Help with what? I have friends."

"Anything. Repairs around the house. Help with the café. I just wanted to help. That's why I called."

"If that's really why you called, you would have stopped calling after the first or second time and left me alone. You want something else from me."

Henry couldn't have been much over forty. He was graying early, and the lines in his face told me he'd lived a full life already—full of things both bad and good. If he'd been any other person sitting there, I could have liked him a lot. But he was who he was.

Both his hands were flat on the table, as if to show he had nothing to hide, nothing up his sleeve. But he sighed, and his hands made a sighing gesture.

"Yes, you're right. There is something I want."

We locked eyes, briefly.

"I want to know you've forgiven me."

My throat was dry, and I took a drink of water the waitress had just poured. "I told you at the funeral there were no hard feelings."

"Forgiveness is different—"

"—everyone agreed it was an accident. The light was bad. Albert could have looked where he was going. He'd just crossed that street at dusk so many times—"

"But I was tired, too tired, from doubling the route that day, making up for a guy who called in sick. I was too tired to be driving. I should have seen him."

"So why—why do we have to talk about this one more time?"

We stopped, both of us shocked by how angry my voice had become.

Henry looked away, out the window at the parking lot. "You're right. There's no purpose to this. It was selfish of me. I—I can't get past this, no matter how things were or weren't. I just need to feel forgiven, Mrs. Brendle. By somebody."

I swallowed. "We go to God for forgiveness."

"We go to people too."

"People can't always do what they need to do. That's why we've got the Lord."

"But sometimes the Lord forgives us through each other, doesn't he?" Henry's eyes were watering. I saw that and didn't feel anything. This man *had* been driving a mile or two over the speed limit, and he *was* too tired to be at the wheel. He turned one corner and just like that, the man who was everything to me was gone. I looked at Henry Carpenter and saw with my mind that he was a decent man, but in my soul, that didn't register.

The soul can bear things the mind can't bear. Forever the soul lives, and so further it sees. I could feel my grandmother sitting close by, all the pain from her life on earth gone, and her mind and soul together at last. She had told me that in her mind she'd stayed angry all those years. But all at once I knew that she was wrong about that. It's the soul that stays angry, the soul that shuts out the people we love, the soul that makes old men into beggars and calls it generosity. I sat there while Henry wiped his eyes, and I saw how angry I'd been all this time. Angry at the Lord for taking my husband, angry at this man for being part of it. It wasn't my mind holding me back from saying the words Henry Carpenter needed so much to hear. It was my soul, my very self.

I asked God for a fever, for cancer, for another word from Gran Lenny. But there was nothing to save me from this moment at this table. It seemed to me then that Gran Lenny and Doris and a lot of other people were waiting for something to happen. The Lord was waiting too.

I reached over and placed my hands over Henry's hands.

"I forgive you, Henry. I really do. That doesn't mean my feelings don't torture me sometimes, but know that you're forgiven."

Henry lowered his head. Our hands together made a warmth that moved up through my arms and into my chest, up into my head and down my spine. As the sensation moved through me, my mind and soul both came clear, and I finally figured out that the Lord wasn't sitting there at all. He wasn't part of some unseen audience, waiting to see if I'd pass the test. The Lord Jesus was in the very words I'd just spoken. I'd just brought him into this place on this day. And Henry and I both felt the effect.

I convinced Henry that I really didn't need him to help me with anything, since I had neighbors and friends and a church family. But I said it would mean a lot to me if he'd come over for dinner some evening. I quoted him the best menu items. He smiled and said he'd only had German food a couple of times, and he'd like to come and bring his wife and daughter.

The farmland was ablaze with late summer sun as I drove back to Leeway. I watched cows and ponds and hedgerows and fences and wildflower fringes move by in slow motion, their colors dancing in the air like angel dust. I saw all this even though I was crying hard, like a little girl who's finally confessed her misdeed and gets gathered into Papa's arms.

Good-bye, Albert. Good-bye, Gran Lenny, Mama, Doris, Shellye and Lisa Layne. Good-bye Howard. Good-bye old sorrowful soul. Good-bye hard feelings and hurtful thoughts.

L ast Sunday, just three days ago, Pastor Thomas and Clare, Lilian, and the boys returned from Orlando. I was surprised at how happy I was to see Jack Thomas. But, just as his opinions had been changed by recent events, my opinion of him had been changed by seeing him change. I convinced the whole family to come to my house for Sunday dinner. On the way out the door, we grabbed Sissy, and in the parking lot we picked up Len and Tim Connor.

I had enough odds and ends from the café to put out a decent, if odd, buffet. There was a time when I couldn't put on a Sunday dinner unless everything was just so. The chef in me, the part of me that Gran Lenny named years ago, still gets anxious when something looks messy on the plate or doesn't reheat well. But sometimes you eat just to sit down with people; you don't sit down together in order to comment on how wonderful the feast is.

Afterwards, we lolled on the screened-in porch, nursing cups of coffee and waiting for enough to settle in our stomachs to make room for dessert. Out of the blue, Clare said, "We found out this morning that there will be a discussion over whether or not Jack and I should stay on here."

We stopped sipping coffee and stared at her. We looked at Jack, who shrugged. "Something was bound to give, with all that's happened this year. We're not that surprised."

"I would think that this year has proved that you're perfect for us and this church," I said. We all knew that Jack blamed himself more than anyone for what happened with Grady. But we'd all seen him working with people day in and day out for months. When we hit bottom, he was right there with us, when many a pastor would have suddenly "felt the call" to minister at a new church in another part of the country.

"Absolutely," said Sissy, her concern scooting her to the edge of her seat. "What a foolish proposition. No one I've talked to recently has expressed such an opinion."

"Well," Jack said. "It may come to nothing. But this could be a long autumn."

We sat together quietly and considered that. What could we say? Maybe we were all just a bit too weary to think or talk anymore today. No one mentioned that Grady's trial date was coming up in a week. We didn't talk about the depositions a number of us had been put through since that awful night. We sat and let the warm breeze brush past us to the backyard, and on to Doris's empty house.

"All right. Name your dessert." I hoisted myself up. "Len, you want to heat up folks's coffee?" I took dessert orders, and Len and I rattled in the kitchen together. He started hot water for doing dishes.

"Leave it. Time for that later," I said. He ignored me. I was about to repeat myself when the phone rang. I picked it up.

"Mom?"

"Jimmy?"

"Yeah—you ready for some company?"

"When have I not been ready? What continent are you calling from?"

"The one called Colorado."

"You're actually home?"

"Yes, and we'd like to camp out with you for a week—starting next Thursday?"

"Everything's ready. I just hope I recognize you."

There was a silence, and I realized how bad my boy felt for being away so long.

"I think you will," he said. "How've you been?"

I paused. "Fine." Jimmy didn't know of much that had happened around here. He didn't know Leeway people very well anymore, and I'd decided not to burden him. I'd told him about Howard, since he was family.

"I hear it's not been fine at all. I ran into Jill Mason when they came through on vacation last week."

"Oh." Jill was John Mason's daughter and an old classmate of Jimmy's. "Well, we've had some troubles, but things have settled down."

"Why didn't you call?"

I realized that I had no real answer for him. "I don't know. Just too caught up in things."

"You can tell us all about it next week."

I hung up and wondered how communication had gotten so complicated this late in my life. I spent the next few days daydreaming about having my boy and his wife home. And I wondered what I'd given him from my life. From my own mother and grandmother I'd received so many good things. But they'd passed on their inability to talk about their troubles, and here I had stopped talking to my own son. Would I give him bad things along with the good? Would he repeat my failures and think they were good just because they came from home?

If Gran Lenny's presence is strongest in the attic room, then I suppose Shellye's and Doris's touch me most in my own kitchen. Sometimes I turn around too quickly and catch a memory of one of them sitting there. Shellye would be chatting about her day, and Doris would be having a smoke and dipping into conversation when she was able. Such flashes of the past give me as much pleasure as they do pain. Much the same as memories of Albert both hurt and heal me.

Folks in Leeway speak of Doris's death as "that tragedy," and I think that's an accurate description. A time or two someone has wondered how everything fits with God's will over the world, but nobody tries to find an answer for that. I don't believe it was God's plan for Grady to refuse God's own wisdom or correction. If Grady had been the man of God he pretended to be—or convinced himself he was—Doris would be alive, I do believe. Some days I still catch myself wishing it were Grady who was buried and that my neighbor was still living in the house beyond the marigolds or appearing at my back door at strange hours.

I do take great comfort, though, in knowing that when Doris died she was walking toward Jesus. In the end, she was indeed the perfect mother, the kind of mother who gives up her life for her child. I suppose that when her heart stopped beating, Doris's spirit just kept on its journey. And her journey is looped into mine and into Grady's and Lisa Layne's and Len's and Shellye's, and even Howard's and Jack Thomas's. All of us are who we are, partly for Doris having been who she was. That becomes more clear to me all the time.

As for me, well, Velma still cooks in Leeway. The restaurant is doing fine (Sissy keeps up the advertising, always coming by to see what my specials are—now she's talking about an Octoberfest for Leeway, of all things). I don't have the energy I used to have, but I've come back around to loving my own gifts. I still feed people and listen to their stories. I still pray over them while I refill their coffee cups.

I've had to cut back some on my own work hours lately—the doctor said I'll ruin my feet for good if I don't get off of them more—but I'm not hurting for help. Clare and a couple other people manage to find girls who need not only a job but a healthy place to be. I've got one with a baby on the way, another who's living with a family in town because her parents were abusive. Both girls catch on quickly, and both of them are hungry for love. Isn't that just like God's turning the tables—Velma, who never had a daughter, now has more girls than she can keep up with. Life's a wonder—a grief and a mystery. But somehow the good Lord's love slips in wherever it can. And, as we all make our journey together, we'll end up in the place he's prepared for us.

Welcome to VELMA'S PLACE

Velma's Soul Soup

1 pound breakfast sausage, rabbit sausage if you can find it
1 cup leeks, chopped, the white part only
2 cups carrots, sliced
6 cloves garlic, minced
1 cup pearl onions
½ cup uncooked barley
1 tablespoon dried sage or 1 teaspoon ground sage
6 to 7 cups chicken or vegetable stock
Salt and pepper to taste

Brown the sausage in a large skillet, breaking it up as it cooks. Remove sausage from skillet and drain most of the grease. Saute leeks and carrots for a few minutes, then add the garlic and cook a minute more; remove all from the skillet.

Place all ingredients and 6 cups of the stock in a large saucepan. Bring to a boil, then turn down and simmer for 2 hours, adding another cup of liquid as needed.

Die Anziehungskraft des Lichts

Naturgesetze weiss ich keine,
das Wesen des Lichts zu erklären;
seine Anziehungskraft.

Und doch: der funkelnde Himmel sickert
durch die Poren
der wogenden Luft
im feurigen Atem.
Davon gibt es kein Gesetz
und keine Worte
dafür.

—Lenora Hamden

Translation:

Light's Gravity

I have never known physical laws
to explain the burden of light—
a gravity.

Still, the candled sky
seeps through the slits
of the scrolling atmosphere,
with fire—
there is no law,
and there are no words
for this.